THE CURSE MANDATE

THE DARK CHOIR - BOOK 3

J.P. SLOAN

CURIOSITY
QUILLS PRESS
A Division of **Whampa, LLC**
P.O. Box 2160
Reston, VA 20195
Tel/Fax: 800-998-2509
http://curiosityquills.com

Cover Art by Eugene Teplitsky
http://eugeneteplitsky.deviantart.com

ISBN 978-1-62007-201-1 (ebook)
ISBN 978-1-62007-205-9 (paperback)

For Courtney, whose dedication and patience allow these fever-dreams to find their words.

CHAPTER ONE

In my experience, I've found "fairness" as a Cosmic principle to be a load of horseshit. Why should it be fair for one man to be born into privilege while another struggles to escape a life of squalor? Most sweeping forces for change appear to be utterly arbitrary. An odd assertion, I recognize, from a man who deals in karma manipulation. Still, the observation holds. A freak tornado, the right lottery number, a sudden onset of cancer... these are things Man cannot control. Such fortunes, either enjoyed or suffered, are not of our own making.

Other fortunes, on the other hand, we bring upon our own heads. Take losing your soul, for example.

Most times, when a person loses his soul, he is rendered into a husk of a human. Worse, really. There are those who become little more than marionettes for the Dark Choir. That space, once occupied by something permanent and worthy, becomes a receptacle for those ancient forces that prey upon Humankind.

Well, I wasn't there quite yet. So that was something.

Often it didn't seem fair to me how I had come to this position. How did I manage to detach and immediately after, misplace my own soul? The short answer: I got fucked. The more circumspect answer: I assumed I was a bigger deal than I was, and if I didn't correct this metaphysical conundrum, I would pay for that arrogance.

Perhaps it was my karma that, despite all the knowledge I'd crammed into my skull over the past decade-and-change, I still had zero clue how to reunite myself with my own soul. It was my karma to be tasked with the tutelage of a dabbler in the hermetic arts, lest we both end up the target of particularly frightening Netherworkers.

And most certainly my karma that, immediately after I just claimed I didn't need to ask directions into Gettysburg, I'd miss my turn.

"That was the exit," Ches grumbled from the passenger seat, her face illuminated by the glow of the map on her phone as we drove through the night.

"No, it wasn't."

"That... that was it, Dorian. I'm looking at it on my phone."

"I never trust those phone apps."

She cocked an eyebrow at me. "You still use a flip phone. What do you know about apps?"

"I know that York Avenue is quicker."

"It isn't," she chimed with an amused shake of her head.

"It totally is."

I double-checked the next exit sign. It totally wasn't.

I managed my way off the highway and through perhaps more of Gettysburg than we needed to see, before my headlights found a tiny stone-faced building, a daycare tucked behind a row of street-front restaurants and shops. A thin, gray-haired woman stood waving next to a Prius parked by the front.

"Is that her?" Ches asked.

"That's Deirdre."

"Deirdre the Dowser. Think she puts that on her business cards?"

I put the car in park and grinned. "She goes with Geomantic Consultant, I think. Feng shui had its moment a decade or so ago, but she's staying alive despite passing out of fashion."

Ches put a hand on my arm as I went to open my door. "So, why did she call you? Feng Shui isn't really your thing."

"No, it isn't," I replied, keeping my eyes on Deirdre, who had wrapped her arms in front of her as she eyed the front of the modest, bordering on decrepit, childcare facility. "Which means something's up. Come on. She looks like she's about to crawl out of her skin."

We stepped out into the foggy night air. I approached Deirdre with a tense smile. Deirdre was more of a "black book" contact, less an actual acquaintance. I knew she was a dowser, one of the few left that managed to earn a living in that particular craft. Her specialty was geomancy, spatial affinities and sacred geometries that often form the foundation for what nose-lifting snobs like myself would refer to as "higher magics." She had given me a call two days ago to help with a problem client. I wasn't sure if it was the client or Deirdre who was the actual problem, but I knew she was desperate when she agreed to the first number I threw at her for my fee. So, a two-hour drive to Gettysburg wasn't too much of a gamble. Plus it gave me a rare opportunity for a little on-the-job instruction for Ches.

"Welcome," Deirdre chirped as she extended her hand.

I shook her hand and discreetly cleared my own with a salt-filled sachet in my pocket... a habit I'd formed as of late, thanks to my dealings with Osterhaus, Carmody, and a host of other practitioners who seemed intent on bending me over a barrel.

"Thanks." I gestured to Ches. "Deirdre, this is my assistant, Francesca Baker." I stifled a smirk as Ches's shoulders tightened over the word "assistant."

"Hi," Ches replied as she gave Deirdre a nod.

Deirdre turned to the brick building in front of us. "So, this is it. Eager Minds Daycare. The owners are a lovely Korean couple. I've basically remodeled the entire building for them. At least, as far as I can. This building's old as Hell."

I asked, "What's the problem with the client?"

"Nothing," Deirdre answered with a quick huff from her bottom lip that danced a tendril of gray hair from in front of her eyes. "It's the building."

"The building?"

"Something... something's in there," Deirdre added with a squint. "Causing trouble. I've done everything I can think of to dissipate it, but things are just breaking."

I glanced over to Ches, who was taking it all in. Good. I might need her input on this one.

"Define 'breaking' for me, Deirdre," I said.

"Toys falling apart. Literally disintegrating in children's hands. Window panes falling out. Plumbing. Electrical. It's putting these poor people into debt. And, I mean, there's kids here. They hired me to make this place safe. Now it's worse than it was before."

I nodded and surveyed the building itself. Short and squat. Old brickwork wrapping around the side. Wood windows set at odd angles. Old construction. "Does this place have a history of unexplained phenomena?"

Deirdre replied, "Used to be the old Wickham Inn. The current owners bought it for a song, and turned it into a daycare. The building's changed hands, like, fifteen times in the last century. Locals call it 'haunted,' but I'm assuming that, like me, you don't subscribe to that particular belief system."

With a slow shake of my head, I answered, "You might be surprised." I finished a slow pace along the front of the building, then stepped in front of Deirdre. "So, I had two questions drilling a hole through my brain as I drove up here. The first, I think, I've figured out on my own."

She asked with a wrinkled brow, "What's that?"

"Why we had to come at night. I'm guessing your clients have no idea you've called me in, and that's fine. But it's the second question I want to iron out with you before we proceed here."

"Shoot."

"Why me? There have to be a dozen practitioners in Pennsylvania. Maybe even someone with experience in Geomancy. Definitely someone who would have been easier on your checkbook."

Her lips pulled tight, and her eyes slipped to Ches.

"Your reputation," she muttered.

Sweet Jesus, here it was.

"My reputation?"

"You're not the type to go blabbing your business to the Presidium. In fact, it's said the Presidium gives you a little space, which would be preferable for me."

Ches asked, "You're a Netherworker?"

Deirdre shook her head with vigor. "No. Absolutely not. But, you don't have to be a Netherworker to wind up on the Presidium's shit list."

I added, "And you're not wrong. The Presidium grants me some latitude."

"I just don't want to stand out. Something like this," she declared with a gesture to the building, "earns you notice."

"Understood. Shall we?"

Ches stepped around me and gave me a slow blink with a confused twist between her eyes as Deirdre unlocked the freshly painted door.

She ushered us inside. I checked the threshold as I stepped through the door, finding nothing particularly notable about the building's wardings. Most defense-minded practitioners built permanent energetic shields, or wardings, into place on their threshold. But this was a place of business, and maintaining a solid line of intent on a warding would be difficult… especially with children pinballing around the place all hours.

I pawed at the light switch to give it a flip. Nothing.

"No power," Deirdre called from outside the door. "Electrician's been out twice this week."

I turned to find Deirdre handing over a couple penlights.

"Thought you might need these," she added with a cautious eye toward the interior.

"What's the diagnosis from the electrician?" I asked, stepping onto a particularly squeaky toy left in the middle of the room.

"He said the breaker box is fine. The problem's somewhere between the box and the fixtures, but he can't isolate it."

"So, what do you want me to do here, Deirdre?"

She took a step away from the door. "I just need a second opinion. What's going on? I'll figure out how to fix it, but I… I just need to know what it is."

I gave her a wink. "We'll get to work. Why don't you wait in your car?"

Deirdre gave me a brisk nod and rushed back to her Prius.

Ches closed the door behind us, twisting her penlight to life. "Christ, she looked terrified."

"That, she did."

My stomach burned at that thought. This simple consultation was getting worryingly complicated, and Deirdre's anxious posture was infectious.

"So, is this where you warn me about crossing the streams, or—?"

"Well, I can tell you with a degree of certainty that we're not dealing with ghosts."

"Old building. History of poltergeist-like activity. Why not ghosts?"

I turn a circle with my penlight, sweeping more toys aside with my foot. "Because there's no such thing as ghosts."

"Wait, you've gone toe-to-toe with a self-aware thoughtform, but ghosts are your hard limit?"

"Not in the way you mean it. The human soul doesn't persist outside of a specific construct. Requires a very particular vessel to contain it."

Ches shined her light on the toys scattered on the floor. "I happen to know a thing or two about soul magic, Dorian. I'm mostly just busting your chops... are those toys in a spiral?"

"You noticed that too?"

I took a step back, adding my light to hers. The toys littered across the floor were not, in fact, simply tossed around. They fell in a rough spiral across the center of the room. A widdershins spiral, at that.

I lifted my light to a shelf and illuminated the face of a stuffed dog with an eye missing.

"Well, the bright side? This isn't the absolute creepiest place this could have gone down."

"That so?"

"Sure. Could have been a doll factory or a clown school or something."

"Fair warning. You say the word 'clown' to me in the dark again, and I'll sneak into your house at night and kill you in your sleep."

I smirked. "Sorry."

"Not joking. You'll never hear me coming."

I flipped her the bird with my free hand as I stepped around the spiral toward a cased opening.

"All right," I declared. "Seems like a good time for a teachable moment. Let's do some palpation."

She slipped her penlight between her teeth and mumbled "sounds kinky" around it.

"Ground and center," I added as her personal energy tightened around her mainline, and balanced along her chakras, "Now give it a feel."

"What, this doorway?"

I nodded, and she lifted her open palms.

The swirling pane of energy in front of me twisted, tugged and stabbed in unnatural, random tides. This was no simple exercise for Ches.

"How does it feel?" I asked.

"Prickly."

"Yep. Anything else?"

"Temperature's weird. Kind of hot and cold, on and off."

"Bingo," I chirped. "What does that tell you?"

"That the energy in this place is in flux. Not really Earth-shattering, though."

"It's not *that* the energy is in flux," I replied as I stepped through the doorway. "It's *how*."

We proceeded into a hallway lined with several doors. I spotted an octagonal mirror at the far end. That would have been Deirdre's touch. It created a means for energy to flow out of the hallway without bunching up like an old wet sock in the toe of a boot.

"What do you mean, *how*?" Ches whispered over my shoulder.

"No pattern. It lacks a pulse or any sense of Cosmic language. This is a random fluctuation."

Ches reached around and gripped my arm. "You think this is a jinx?"

"That's my theory."

"Oh, great." She released me and turned a tight circle in the hallway. "Wait, what about that spiral on the floor? That's a pattern."

"No, it's an exit wound. The original pulse drained back into the Earth from there. Wouldn't be surprised if they keep picking up the toys and they just keep falling on the floor in that pattern. What we're dealing with here are echoes."

"Who the crap would jinx a daycare?"

I shrugged as I reached for my pendulum. "A good question, assuming it was intentional."

The next room contained two rows of double-decker cribs. Infant's room, most likely. The thought of babies trying to sleep in the fallout of a jinx made my toes itch. A jinx is a forced concentration of chaos, unpredictable natural forces that undo orderly systems like bank accounts, the structure of a building, or even a toddler's circulatory system. I had to assume this particular jinx was a spectacular accident, perhaps some meltdown from a dabbler. It made no sense to jinx a daycare like this. If curses are bullets, then jinxes are hand grenades. A jinx isn't a practitioner's tool; it's an act of war.

I hooked my pendulum chain around my middle finger and let the tiny copper-caged nugget of quartz dangle. My breathing and heartbeat put a natural spin to the stone. Here I was, dowsing for a professional Dowser. I imagined Deirdre had already tried this, but for whatever reason she couldn't sort this mess out.

To be honest, I wasn't sure I had the answer myself. Good news was, I didn't have to give her an answer. Just a diagnosis.

Ches leaned in to watch the pendulum. "You're going to show me how to make one of those, right?"

"Sure. You're buying the copper, though. Shit's skyrocketed these days. Gillette never taught you people dowsing?"

"If it wasn't lethal, we didn't bother."

"Charming woman, that Gillette."

Ches leaned in. "It doesn't bother you that the best dowser on the East Coast is hiding in her car while we do the dowsing?"

I looked over to Ches. "It's scaring the hell out of me."

"So, why are we still here?" she asked. "Instead of, you know, fleeing?"

"Because we're getting paid. Sometimes you gotta—"

The spin of the pendulum halted abruptly with a tiny figure eight and reversed direction. Classic shift of energy. What wasn't so classic, however, was that it reversed again almost immediately.

"Yep. I'm about ninety-percent sure we're dealing with chaos magic," I grumbled.

"So... fleeing?"

"I don't hate that plan."

"I notice we're not leaving."

I cast a glance back to the baby bunks inside the nursery. "Someone jinxed children, Ches. The Fleeing Center of my brain is being overridden by a strong desire to find whoever did this and shove a hex up his ass sideways."

Ches chucked my shoulder. "There you go, giving a shit again."

"I know. Bad habit."

I continued down the hallway as my pendulum did gymnastics at the bottom of its chain, which teased on and off with heat and cold. Just when I thought I could make some sense of the shifting, I reminded myself this was chaos. The more sense it made, the less likely I had found the source.

When I approached the last door on the left, the chain went stiff. I held up my free hand and Ches froze behind me. We watched as the quartz lifted just a bit to my left, as if drawn by a magnet.

"That's a result," Ches whispered.

I followed the chain to the door and tried the knob. As the door swung open, Ches shone her penlight inside to reveal a toilet.

"The bathroom?" she grunted.

"Remember. This is chaos. Any positive hit is probably a false positive."

"I don't know. A toilet seems pretty random to me."

The chain pulled tighter against my finger. I stepped inside. The pressure eased a little, but the quartz tipped slightly toward the porcelain fixture.

I waved my free hand in a circle around the toilet, palpating the ambient energy. Nothing specific... just the usual insanity filling this entire building.

Ches whispered, "You know, in any other context, this would look really stupid."

"Well, you know what they say about context. It's always the—"

A loud *SNAP* jarred me as my hand trembled. Something pelted the side of my face.

Ches gasped and stumbled backward, taking her penlight with her.

The chain dropped limp against my palm. I fished out my penlight to inspect the pendulum, or what was left of it. The quartz had completely shattered. More accurately, it had exploded.

Damn it.

That was my pendulum! I made that thing ten years ago, and had used it ever since. I'd developed a solid working relationship with that little hunk of rock, and the wild-ass energy in this joint just blew it the fuck up. Not good. Not good at all.

I turned back to the hallway to find Ches cradling the side of her face.

"You okay?" I asked, jumping to my feet.

"Something in my eye."

"Come on, let's get you to the car. We are so done here."

I guided Ches back through the front room, stepping gingerly over the toy spiral which had corrected itself from our earlier intrusions.

Outside, Deirdre spotted us from inside her car. She rushed out as I eased Ches against my hood and aimed my penlight into her face.

"What happened?" Deirdre asked. "Are you hurt?"

I inspected Ches's eye as it teared up. It was bloodshot, and I found a few crimson drops welling up along her cheekbone.

"We need to get you to urgent care," I whispered.

"Bad?" Ches gasped.

"Doesn't look bad, but I'm not a doctor."

I helped Ches around to the passenger seat, and closed the door before turning to Deirdre.

"Well, I think we both know what we're dealing with in there," I grumbled.

Her eyes dropped, and she half shrugged. "I was hoping it was something else."

"Was it you, Deirdre? Did you screw something up, uncork a little pocket of chaos by accident?"

"No," she spat. "None of my practices would have caused this."

"Any enemies who might want to embarrass you?"

She squinted a single eye at me. "I'm a Geomantic consultant, Mister Lake. I don't make enemies."

"Look, I have to go. But I think it's time you put some thought into that statement." I pointed at the building. "And this daycare remains closed!"

She huddled up her arms and nodded.

I navigated back to the highway, taking the more direct route, as Ches kept checking her eye in the sun visor's mirror, swearing under her breath.

"You okay?" I asked.

"Just stings."

"For what it's worth, I think you'd rock an eyepatch."

Her lips lifted into a faint grin.

I prodded, "Well, all said, how was my first field trip as your official mentor?"

She slapped the sun visor back up and leaned back. "Painful." We continued in silence a while before she added, "Does this mean I'll get to start crafting soon?"

I gritted my teeth. "Not yet."

"I'm not a novice, Dorian."

"No, but you're still dangerous."

"I've practiced the Arts for years."

"And how did that turn out?"

She glowered in silence for most of the way back to Maryland. I knew she had trained under one of the most organized yet vicious cabals in North America. She had chops, and she had plenty of background knowledge. This allowed me to skip a good deal of the basic education I'd slogged through under Emil Desiderio. However, quickly into our tidy little shotgun-marriage tutelage, I'd discovered enormous holes in her instruction. Quinn Gillette had armed her people with just enough information to wage war. Safety wasn't exactly a priority, it seemed. As capable a practitioner as Gillette was,

I had serious doubts her heart was into the pedagogic side of the mentor-disciple relationship.

I could say the same for me, if I wanted to be brutally honest about it.

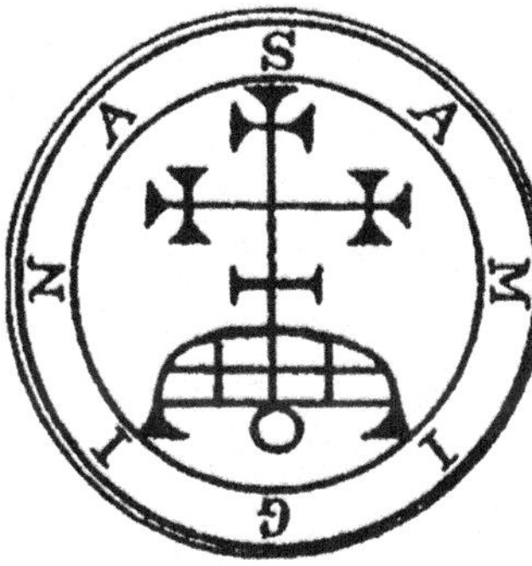

CHAPTER TWO

I meant to wake up extra early the following day to put in some much-needed face time at the Light Street Tavern. My alarm hand, however, had other plans, and I ended up hammering the snooze button a couple dozen times. I was going to catch hell from Julian, for certain. He'd poured a staggering amount of his own cash money and credit into our little joint venture. I'd done my best to chime in with opinions, mostly to have them countermanded by Big Ben, our bartender. When it came to bar management, Ben was the seasoned veteran. My experience with taverns and clubs was strictly from the stool side of the equal sign.

In my defense, I'd been distracted. Getting a grip on my new relationship with Ches had turned out to be somewhat more ball-breaking than I'd counted on. I had no idea how to teach someone the hermetic arts. Plus, I still had my soul to locate. That's a few too many plates to spin, and if I had to make a choice, I was going to save my soul first and sort the rest out when I had the opportunity.

But I didn't have my weekly rap session with Father Mark until Monday morning, and Ches was taking a day off to have her eye looked at by her regular doctor, so there really was no excuse not to put in some work hours at the tavern. Besides, Julian was holding one of his side-room meetings, and knowing the people he invited to these little court sessions, I figured it would be fun to bust his chops if given the opportunity.

I parked around the back of the building, squeezing into a terrifyingly tight space between the dumpster and the new brick-and-glass hotel next to us. I'd learned the hard way never to park next to the dumpster on Wednesdays. Trash trucks, it seemed, weren't instruments of exacting precision. I almost felt a sense of mirth as I locked my car and moved for the rear entrance. This was typically the moment when I'd spot some shadow slipping out of view in the corner of my eye, reminding me that the Dark Choir was hungry for my soul, wherever the damned thing was. But on this morning, shadows didn't catch my attention. Instead, it was three men in suits stepping from around the dumpster to cut me off.

Fantastic.

I froze by the car and sized up my options. These guys were big. I'd probably get my ass handed to me if I tried anything physical. They were well-dressed, including the center goon who wore a sports coat over a turtleneck and jeans. This wasn't the Presidium's style, necessarily, or I'd never have seen them coming. And as they weren't rushing at me with pipes in hand, I figured this wasn't a mugging.

No, this smelled more like a shakedown.

They came to a halt at a comfortable distance, and turtleneck man cracked a broad, tobacco-stained smile.

"You Dorian Lake?"

"Occasionally."

"Yeah, I heard you was a smart mouth."

"How can I help you gentlemen?"

Turtleneck gave his partners a *get a load of this guy* smirk before answering, "I'm Nick Polo. Maybe you figured I was coming already?"

I shook my head slowly, though I had this Nick Polo fellow figured out well enough, already. After McHenry's embarrassing failure to purchase City Hall and his subsequent departure from the public eye... thanks in no small amount to a sum of undeclared capital gains my new accountant kept in several computer hard drives... the power vacuum left in his wake had flushed out a slurry of would-be gangsters. Seemed I chose one hell of an atmosphere to open a bar.

Polo nodded at me thoughtfully.

"This your bar, here?"

"It is, in part."

"Nice location."

"I like to think so."

Polo took a step around to my side to survey the surrounding buildings… the hotel, the two-story office beside me, and the back of a public parking garage beyond our lot's fence. "Not a lot of lighting, though. Could cause a problem for you, what with crime in the city the way it is."

"Let me just take a quick stab, here," I offered with an outstretched hand. "You're in the security business?"

Polo's eyes eased as his smile broadened. "Yeah, that's right. Security. I got men on this block who can keep an eye on things for you. Keep things from turning ugly. We want to keep our new neighbors safe and sound, you know?"

I gave all three a good, measured look before nodding. "I think I understand you, Mister Polo."

"Call me Nicky."

"So, the last thing I want is trouble on my property. What are your rates?"

"Tell you what. Since you're new, and you could probably use a helping hand getting started and all… I'll cut you a break for your first year. Two thousand. That's monthly."

I stifled a sneer. "Very generous of you, Nicky."

"I thought so."

"Don't suppose you take checks?"

He lifted a brow and guffawed with considerable volume.

"Right," I grumbled, moving around him. "Well, the safe's inside. Follow me."

Polo snapped a finger to one of his goons and said "stay here" to the second.

I led him through the kitchen entrance, side-stepping around two plastic-wrapped fryers Ben had ordered last month but had never made it out of its wrapping. I pushed through the kitchen door into the space between Julian's office and the restrooms. I didn't keep an office here. Even my ego didn't permit quite that much hypocrisy.

Rounding the corner past the restroom, we stepped out into the seating area. We usually didn't get customers until early evening, what with us not having a working menu quite yet. So there was no one but Big Ben Setleigh to watch the embarrassing turn of events about to transpire. Ben gave me a nod and a two-finger salute. His face was leaner than I'd seen it in years, with a good color. Either the change in profession since he ditched the Druid Hill Club to work for me had agreed with him, or he was starving to death under my employ. Ben wasn't the type to suffer in silence, so I just assumed he was happier here at Light Street.

"You okay, son?" Ben called out as he spotted Polo and his goon following tight behind me.

I waved him off casually. "Great. Had a good night last night, feeling ready to put in some hours."

"Good," he chuckled, eyes still planted hard on Polo. "I got some inventory for you to tackle."

I gave Polo a smirk. "The glamorous life of a bar owner, am I right?"

Polo grinned awkwardly, but he was locked onto getting his grift and moving on.

I gestured toward the oak door that fit almost seamlessly into the wall paneling just beyond the four-tops. "I keep the safe in my event room. Follow me, and I'll get you taken care of."

"It's good to do business with a smart man," Polo sniggered.

I paused at the paneled door and gave Ben one more look, and a wink. When I opened the door, I practically brushed Polo and his thug in with my arm, closing the door behind us.

Inside the room, a group of about ten people sat with papers and tablets spread across several tables. Their conversations immediately ceased, and in unison they raised their faces to us. Julian seemed particularly alarmed at my sudden appearance. He was flanked by several faces I'd recognized from his "private court sessions" he held in the event room most Thursdays. Of these faces, most notably, was Police Commissioner Bettis.

I side-stepped with as much intentional clumsiness as I could muster, slipping past the closest of Julian's political companions.

"I'm sorry about this, folks. I won't be just a minute. Mister Polo, that was two-thousand, you said? Per month?"

I finally stole a glance at Polo, who stood rigid, his face stony but his eyes wide.

"For protection, I believe was the concept you vaguely outlined in the parking lot?"

He cleared his throat. "Well..."

"I want to be sure we're solid, Mister Polo. Sorry, I mean Nicky." I added with deliberate gravity, "Like I said, I don't want trouble on my property."

I gave him a smile. In that moment, he realized he was done, and I was the one who did him in.

A sneer crept into the corner of his mouth, and he turned for the door.

Chief Bettis stood slowly and growled, "Have a seat, Nicky."

Polo froze, then turned painfully slow and dropped into a nearby chair. He urged his goon to do the same with a thrust of his finger.

I turned to the others in the room with a smirk. "Again, I apologize for this. Please continue. I'll get out of your hair."

Julian flashed me a grin brimming with amusement as I climbed back around his guests to take my exit. Polo didn't make eye contact with me. Good call. I wasn't feeling particularly charitable at that moment, and it would have been simple to snatch a hair on my way back into the bar. Oh, what I could do with just a single hair or a drop of blood!

Ben had rounded the end of the bar, his hand tucked behind the rail, probably clutching his baseball bat.

I waved him down. "We're good, Ben."

"Who was that?"

"Some jerkoff trying to air out a protection racket."

Ben snickered. "Picked the wrong goddamn day to shake us down."

"With luck, word will spread that we're a cop bar, and things'll quiet down."

"About that," Ben added as his smile dropped. "We really have to get that kitchen up and running, you know."

"We will."

He fished a handful of paper from the side of the bar and waved them at me. "This is Maryland, Dorian. We have rules about percentages of sales. We're nowhere close to selling the amount of food we are required by law to sell."

"I thought you were hiring a kitchen manager?"

"We hired two."

"What happened to them?"

"One quit after two days. The other I caught shooting up in the back."

I shook my head. "All right, I'll post another ad."

He dropped the paperwork in front of me. "Inventory's here."

"And I do... what, now?"

His face settled into something professional yet sadistic. "Count and measure, son. Count and measure."

I spent the next hour eyeballing levels in bottles and counting glassware. Mostly. As my mind drifted into a zen state, I found myself fidgeting with the bar tools. Ben snapped me back to task once or twice, but my thoughts were elsewhere. I toyed with the inventory as I considered last night's scene. A jinx, of all things. Over ten years of private practice in hexes and charms, and I hadn't once run into a chaos magician.

I had a tiny ziggurat of toothpick boxes constructed on the front bar by the time Julian's meeting let out. I curtailed my plans to reenact tiny pimento sacrifices with the martini olives. Commissioner Bettis marched Polo and his goon out the back door with the aid of who I assumed were a pair of plainclothes cops.

Julian lingered by the event room, deep in conversation with a dark-skinned woman in a snappy business suit. They exchanged several notes on their tablets and finally concluded their business with some whispered confidence from the woman, and Julian's lending her a literal hand on her shoulder. She took her leave, exiting through the front, as Julian noticed me dismantling the toothpick boxes.

"Quite a show you put on, Dorian," Julian announced.

"Guy pissed me off. What can I tell you?"

Julian chucked my arm and moved for his office. "Ben's got you thumb-nailing bottles again?"

"I don't know what that means, but it sounds horrible."

I followed Julian into his office, alarmingly tidy with stacks of folders in those tiny wire racks only manically organized super genius types use. He dropped his tablet onto his desk and ran hands over his face. Unlike Ben, the last couple of months have taken an enormous toll on Julian.

"Here," he mumbled as he tossed a hand at the corner of his desk. "This came for you."

I spotted a tall brown paper-wrapped package jutting from between a stack of what I really hoped weren't bills, and one of his wire racks of folders. I lifted it, checking my fingers against its surprising weight.

"What is it?"

Julian shrugged as he dropped into his chair. He'd certainly carved a tiny nest in this office already. This was his turf, to be sure.

"Booze, I'm assuming."

"So, good meeting?"

"It had a better closing act than anything," he quipped.

"These meetings have you tapped out every Thursday. Getting lots of calls from that woman, too. I mean, I'm just noticing."

Julian scowled. "You're using your preachy tone again, Dorian. I don't like Preachy Dorian."

"You look tired, is all."

"I'm okay."

"You need to unplug and unwind." I snapped my fingers. "Hey, why don't you bring whats-his-name over one night? I'll make cassoulet."

"His name is Cleve. Think I'll pass."

"Come on. You and him are a thing, right? I'm not crazy."

His eyes narrowed ever so briefly. "Well, we're nothing at the moment."

"Oh, crap. What happened?"

Julian waved his hands frantically between us. "I'm not discussing my love life with my business partner. And your cassoulet is straight poison. Sorry, but it is."

"Oh, hell. I liked him. He was funny."

"It's nothing. I'm too busy, anyway."

"Julian?"

He took a breath. "Yes, Dorian?"

"You quit City Hall."

He stared at his hands folded in front of him on his desk. "I know."

"You're here, now. Listen, I'm going to make an effort to be here more often. After what that turtle-necked palooka pulled on us just now, I'm kind of interested in taking over this town."

Julian snickered. "Did you really just say 'palooka'?"

"I'm expanding my vocabulary."

Julian dropped a flat hand on the nearest stack of notes on his desk. "Well, you can stop belly-aching about me surrounding myself with the Old Main. I've made an arrangement for the Tavern that'll probably drum up some nice exposure."

"Do tell."

"You heard of Jerome Durning, of course?"

I shook my head.

"Seventh District? He's your Representative, for Chrissakes."

I snapped my fingers. "Right. What about him?"

"Monday morning, he's announcing his bid for re-elect in two years."

"Not exactly a crack of thunder across the sky, is it?"

Julian leaned forward, pointing toward the front of the tavern. "He's announcing it from just outside those windows. Sullivan will be there. A couple from the city council. TV cameras, print. You're following me, right?"

I reached over and lay a hand on Julian's shoulder. "I take back everything. You're a genius, and I love you."

He snickered and tapped my hand. "Just tell me you'll be here."

"On my life, I'll be here."

As I moved for the hall, the package cradled in my arm, he added, "And for God's sake, bring Francesca."

I carried my package back out to the front bar. Ben gave me a stern look and pointed at the back bar bottles. I ignored him and settled onto a bar stool to open the package. It had no name on the return address, which was in New York City.

As I tore off the paper and opened the innocuous black cardboard box within, I found a shiny new bottle of Gideon Reserva sherry within. My fingertips chilled. I knew this sherry. I'd seen it several times in my past, but not for a good decade-and-change.

Not since Emil died.

This was his preferred spirit. Hell, it was all he drank, nursing it out of his cloudy little glass all hours of the night as he pored over some new acquisition for his Library. Holding that bottle in my hand, I could practically smell the nutty aroma, mingled with the rancid cigarette smoke that clung to his clothes. The musty bouquet of old manuscripts and moldy pages in age-cracked leather bindings. The hints of curry from the restaurant down the lane and the ever-effusive head of ale from the tavern below us.

This package was a message.

I inspected the inside of the wrapping and discovered a tiny white card with inked calligraphy.

A GIFT TO CELEBRATE OUR TEACHER. I GREATLY DESIRE TO MEET YOU. LE REYNARDIN, SATURDAY, 1PM. I'LL SAVE A TABLE. ~JEAN CLEMENT

I set the bottle of sherry gently on the bar and stared at the card.

Our teacher?

Ben called from the other end of the bar, "Taking a break from scotch?"

I shook my head slowly.

I was familiar with Le Reynardin. My father used to make business lunches at that restaurant. It was one of Manhattan's top destinations for French cuisine, and a notorious den for soused businessmen and lawyers killing time between acts of ill conscience.

And now I was invited to one such "business" lunch, though I had zero clue what sort of business another student of Emil Desiderio would have with me. Before I came along, Emil was a world-renown Netherworker. Which meant, by force of reason, this Jean Clement studied under Emil during his less savory years.

My naked curiosity prodded me to make this sudden appointment on Saturday, though my recently cultivated sense of self-preservation screamed for me to give this individual as wide a berth as was physically possible.

Well, shit. When had I ever passed up a chance to completely screw myself?

CHAPTER THREE

As my cab wound up Seventh Avenue, I took in the ever-changing streets of New York. It was late Spring, and the weather had warmed enough for folk to shed their coats. Le Reynardin looked busy for a Saturday. This would be a very public meeting, and that suited me just fine.

I poked my head inside the bronze and glass door, and was greeted almost immediately by a girl in a black necktie and vest.

"Mister Lake? Dorian Lake?"

I paused and looked around at the other customers hovering around the hostess station. Eyes swiveled to me, then quickly away. I barely rated notice here. Again, that suited me.

I gave the hostess a nod, and she snapped her arms to her side with a rifle-shot of a grin.

"Mr. Clement is expecting you, if you'll follow me?" She actually pronounced it "monsieur," which meant this hostess was either incredibly pedantic, or Monsieur Clement was a regular here. My money was on the latter. She led me around tables and bustling wait staff until we reached a row of booths set within brick arches.

A gray-suited man with a mop of salt-and-pepper hair combed directly back over his high brows stood up with a genial grin. The hostess paused a half-second before turning back for the front of the restaurant, leaving me alone with whom I assumed was Jean Clement. He was remarkably tall, not strictly in a physical sense but also in an odd manner of spine-straightened gravitas that towered over me. His skin was a shade toward olive, his features well-manicured. Dapper son of a bitch.

"Dorian Lake," he declared with a smile full of bleached-white teeth. "I am so happy to make your acquaintance, at last."

His voice was generously seasoned with the cracked peppercorns of a French accent, but not so much that his words didn't come off without a fine spit-polish. He extended his hand, and as I shook it he gestured quickly to his booth. As we sat, he reached immediately for the salt shaker on the table, tossed half a dash into his palm, and rubbed it into his hands briefly.

"Jean Clement, I presume," I finally replied.

He lingered as he swept the fallen salt from the table. "I would apologize for this impolite gesture, but I believe that people such as we are beyond facile ploys for pleasantry."

I offered a nod and pulled my sachet of salt out of my pocket, wiggling it in the air just beside my ear.

Clement laughed and snatched a glass of water to take a long sip as his eyes took me in.

I cleared my hands, pocketed my sachet, and leaned forward. "I got the sherry, obviously."

"The old man reeked of that swill."

"It is dreadful, isn't it? So, you knew Emil during his Netherworking days?"

Clement folded his fingers. "Most people did. You appear to be the sole exception." Before I could respond, he added, "Emil's associates, at least those still alive, are all familiar with his Magnum Opus."

I sneered. "His Magnum Opus, huh? Crap. Guess I belly-flopped that one."

"In what way, if you don't mind my asking?"

"Well, I don't know. I'm not exactly a world-famous practitioner, some Great High Most Superlative or anything. I figure I'm probably as far from Emil's standards as he could have imagined."

Clement's smile drifted. "I can't agree with that. You were meant to be his compass. His chance for redemption. A legacy of something beyond Netherwork. The reason he turned his back on the rest of us who had devoted our lives to his tutelage. You were his soul, Mister Lake."

"Now I feel like a total jackass."

"You shouldn't. It was Emil's choice."

We sat in awkward silence for a moment.

I finally asked, "What's your practice?"

"I'm largely retired, at this point. I made a living through international brokerage during the nineties, but I found myself... conflicted."

"International brokerage? I assume we're not talking about light sweet crude or pork bellies, here."

With a smirk, he replied, "I am intermittently involved with a consortium of practitioners who refer to themselves as the Free Market. We've found our means to trade with the Old World in recent years. Despite their best efforts, the Presidium hasn't completely sealed our ports, Mister Lake. The old cabals still hunger for access. In my years I've amassed a gallery of items unique and relevant to the Craft. I fill my hours tending to them."

"You're a Collector?"

"More of an avocation. I find it suits my appetite for calm."

"So, toward sending a wrecking ball through these facile pleasantries," I offered, "Why have you summoned me here?"

This brought what sounded like a genuine chuckle out of Clement, and he unfolded his fingers.

"I appreciate that. Fine, let us deal directly then. Emil bequeathed to you a compendium of his rare texts. I would like to purchase them from you."

I smiled and leaned back in my chair. "Emil's Library. That's what this is about?"

"Several of these texts have significant sentimental value to me."

"Twenty-two."

He blinked and eased forward. "Thousand?"

"No, you're number twenty-two. The twenty-second person to try and buy the Library off me. And for the record, it's way more valuable than twenty-two thousand dollars."

"Agreed, which is why I'm prepared to add a zero to the end of that figure."

I hung my head and laughed.

"Four hundred, then," he prodded.

"Why do you want Emil's Library?"

"As I said, I've spent hours upon hours with these books. They have particular value for me."

I waved a hand. "I thought we were cutting the crap, here?"

"So be it. That Library represents the single most valuable collection of rare texts not in the possession of an affiliated organization or cabal. 'Rare' being something of an understatement."

"Agreed."

"They deserve to be used, not stored away under lock and key."

I sneered. "I beg to differ. The knowledge in those books is unmitigated evil. Nothing good comes from that Library."

"Good, Mister Lake? That's something of an artificial dictum, don't you think? How would you define 'good,' beyond that which you find benefits the self?"

"Well, that's a whole other conversation I think... but the answer remains no."

Clement leaned back in his chair, a smirk lifting onto his face.

"I can tell I can't tempt you with a higher dollar figure. And you seem reluctant to discuss the true, intangible value of these texts. Then perhaps we should discuss Emil?"

I reached for the water. "Okay, then. How did he find you?"

"To the contrary," Clement replied while waving for the server. "I found him. He was legendary. Many dreamed of being accepted as his pupil."

The server arrived, and Clement ordered wine for the table.

I said, "He was a different man then, I suppose. The Emil I knew was basically a hermit. An irritable, unlikable hermit."

"In more circumspect hermetic circles, such character traits can actually add to one's *gravitas*."

"Oh, Emil had *gravitas* coming out of his ass."

The server returned with a bottle held out for Clement's inspection. He nodded and the server poured him a taste.

"You drink wine, Mister Lake?"

"Occasionally, but I'm getting the sense this is going to be a short lunch."

Clement frowned. "Why is that? No time to reminisce?"

I grinned. "If that was the point of this visit, then I'd be happy to. But that's not why I'm here. Inevitably, we'll circle around to my selling you Emil's books, and we'd both feel frustrated. And when wine lubricates my sass, bad things happen to me. So, what say we call it a wash?"

"I feel, perhaps, you're being a bit uncharitable."

"Well, I'm sorry about that. But the fact is… I don't know you, Monsieur Clement. We lack context."

His brows shot up. "Context?" With a snicker, he nodded. "Very well. Perhaps one day we shall finally share context?"

"Perhaps."

He stood, and I followed suit.

"And then," he added, "we may discuss the old man's obsession with Ann-Margret?"

"What's to discuss? She was the original bombshell." I fished my business card holder from my pocket, and pulled a card to hand it over. "And because I'm not a total ass, here's my number."

He took my card with a nod, then asked, "One more try?"

"Answer's still no, Jean."

He held up his hands in surrender. "Then, until next time. I'll have my driver take you to the station."

"Oh, that's okay," I muttered. "I'll grab a cab."

"Nonsense. I insist."

He took his seat and pulled a long sip of wine, focusing on the tablecloth, the silverware, anything but me.

And with that, I was dismissed. I stepped back through the restaurant and onto the street. A silver sedan pulled up to greet me. Clement's driver stepped out and trotted around to open my door. I shoved my hands into my pocket and gave the driver a tired nod.

And I froze.

As did the driver.

The two of us stood in silence for a painful moment, neither able to muster a reasonable greeting. Finally, after a line of cars began to form behind the sedan, Reed Malosi waved me into the back seat as he grunted, "Really hoped I'd never see you again."

CHAPTER FOUR

"**So, Penn State... how's tricks?"**

Malosi gave me a stern brow in his rearview mirror as he wove us through three lanes of traffic toward the train station.

Wilting under the tension, I added, "Kind of circling the mountain career-wise, aren't you?"

"Yeah, well, I'm doing all right." He steered us another block before adding, "My resume is kind of specific, you know."

"I do, actually. How did you end up working for Clement?"

"One of Osterhaus's contacts in New York. I worked a security desk job on Second for about a month before I started getting, I don't know... the itch."

I tried to stifle a grin, without much success. Part of the allure of the Life was the secret knowledge, that parallel existence we seemed to possess. After working for a practitioner, even one as miserable as Osterhaus, it must have been mind-crushingly dull sitting at a desk with a badge and a Tazer. He needed the Life. Somehow, that made me feel happy.

"Is Clement teaching you?"

"A little," he answered, pulling us right in front of the Penn Station plaza, slipping us into a line of cars.

"Does he let you practice?"

Reed turned in his seat and gave me a stony lift of his brow. "A little."

"Well," I declared as I extended my hand. "I'm actually happy to see you, Reed. Seems you're in good hands."

"Where are you going?" he asked, staring at my hand.

"I'll just hop out."

"Can't. I have to let you out."

I leaned back and smiled, then fished my hand to the door handle. Nope. Locked.

"Like I said," he grumbled, turning forward. "I'll cut you loose when we get up to the station."

"Just trying to save us some awkwardness."

"He's afraid," Reed said just loud enough for me to hear.

"Hmm?"

"He's scared, Dorian. I think he wants someone to talk to, but he's too proud."

I leaned forward. "What makes you think that?"

"He's not like Osterhaus. He's a hell of a lot like you, actually. Only, more polish, less asshole."

"Thanks."

"So, if he's asking you for something small? It's probably something bigger. All I'm saying."

"I don't know, Reed. He's not exactly asking to borrow a cup of sugar, here."

Malosi advanced us two more car lengths before pulling to the curb. I noted as he hopped out to open my door that there was very little need to have insisted I exit at this particular spot. As I stepped onto the walk in front of Penn Station, Malosi closed the door and straightened his jacket.

"He has my number," I told him. "If he feels like some real-talk, he can call. But you can tell him I said Emil's Library is staying where it is."

I turned to make my dramatic exit.

"Stay safe, Dorian," he called.

I looked back to Malosi. He paused halfway into the car and looked into my face, eyes firm. He got into the car, closed the door, and cut off a cab swerving back into the street.

My train ride back to Baltimore was a blur. I spent the trip inside my own head. Jean Clement, a former student of Emil's, appears out of nowhere and offers quite urgently to buy the Library from me. This wasn't anything new, apart from the fact that this was the first person who could be said to have a legitimate claim on some of these books. But I'd held the line when it came to selling those books. Hell, even Edgar had learned not to badger me too hard about that Library. Of the whole encounter with Clement, I could say it was interesting to have met the man, but he didn't make much of an impression on me.

Reed Malosi, on the other hand, put a hook right in the center of my brain. What did Malosi know about Clement's intentions? Was this truly some cry for comfort from a Netherworker too well-polished to ask outright? Or was there something specific going on in Clement's little world? Maybe Clement was staring down the barrel of his own brutal demise at the hands of the shadows?

How long would it be until I was staring down the same barrel?

When I finally returned to my red brick two-story on Amity, there were still a couple hours left of daylight, a moment's peace to gather my thoughts. I paused at my doorway to check my wards. With Ches coming and going as my full-time student, I had to make certain arrangements, one of which being that she now had a key to my house. Another accommodation was to alter the wardings on my threshold.

Wardings are a specific kind of charm, a tiny pinch in the natural ebb and flow of Cosmic energies. They're defensive charms specifically anchored to a geographic area or an individual. Portable wardings, usually called talismans, are nowhere near as powerful as a fixed house warding. There was a reason Deirdre the Dowser managed to pay the bills each month. Geomancy is a very real, if underestimated, branch of esoteric thought.

I ran a hand along the jamb just beside the doorbell. My warding rolled beneath my palm in its usual hills and valleys, except for that tiny thread of vivid, thrilling energy sweeping back and forth between my fingers.

Ches was here.

I unlocked my door and tried not to think too much about her energy, still buzzing in my palm. After I dropped my valise next to my roll top desk and checked a stack of hand-scribbled phone messages she had apparently taken in the last few hours, I strode for the hallway and the reinforced steel door leading to my basement work space.

Sleater-Kinney strummed from a portable speaker down the stairs, and as I cleared the last step and poked my head into the cedar-lined walls of my work space, I found Ches hunkered over her desk, head bobbing to the music. I'd hired Tatapoulis to expand the basement after discovering most of the cellar beneath my building had gone unfinished. I now sported a hermeticist's bunker of sorts, complete with a larger sigil-scribed workbench, three times my previous reagent storage space and bookshelves, and the dark-stained cabinet presiding over the entire scene.

Emil's Library.

I eased around the workbench, trying not to disturb Ches.

"Where were you?" she asked, announcing my utter failure at stealth.

"New York."

She spun quickly in her chair, brows twisted into a knot. "You went to New York without me?"

"And here I am without so much as a souvenir."

"Visiting your aunt?" she asked, turning back to her notebook.

"No." I stepped toward the Library, adding in a lower tone, "Business meeting."

The cabinet loomed, still somehow sucking in the light around it. I'd embraced its presence in my life as of late. For years, I'd kept it literally caged, sequestered in a mini-storage in Catonsville. It had been a frightening reminder of the fate of Netherworkers. But after recent events, I'd accepted my charge to keep the books closer. Safer.

I reached into my pocket, fingertips touching the tiny brass key to the cabinet. Ches may have had a key to my house, and to the steel door that kept my work space secure from outsiders. But I was the only one who could open this damned cabinet. On my soul, wherever the fucking thing was, I was going to keep it that way.

Ches leaned back with a huff, stretching her neck.

"Issues?" I asked.

"I hate Linear B. It's like someone threw up the Greek language and decided to finger paint with it."

"You'll get used to it. It's kind of like jazz. Makes no sense until it gets inside your head. Once it gels, you'll thank me for torturing you with it."

"How long did it take to gel in your head?"

I looked up to the ceiling. "About eight years."

"Oh, joy." She stood up and turned down the music. "Why can't we just use French or Spanish or some language that isn't older than Jesus?"

"Kind of a good question, actually." I leaned against my workbench and folded my arms. "These are the languages of the esoteric pioneers, the first human minds to ferret out the secret knowledge. We maintain the language partially because we don't want to re-invent the wheel, magically speaking, but also because there's a degree of resonance that's built up over the thousands of years these practices have been honed."

"So, why isn't there any new magic?"

"Probably has to do with the state of the human mind. As a species, we've been on an arc from animism to spiritualism, then from theism to rationalism. Maybe it's social pressure, maybe it's evolution. Don't know. But the human mind is slowly losing its ability to access the Arts. In another thousand years, we practitioners may be extinct." I reached down and knocked on my bench. "Okay, pop quiz time."

Ches rolled her eyes and slumped back down into her chair. "Ready."

"Name the four spheres of magic."

"Affinity, Ego, Nature, and as that little romp to Gettysburg has just seared into my memory, Chaos."

I followed with, "Name three practices of Affinity Magic."

"Geomancy... thank you again, Deirdre. Religion. And charms."

I nodded, unfolding my arms to pace around the bench. "What is Padraig's Dogma?"

"There is no Magic but Ego Magic."

"And what does that mean?"

She twirled in her chair a moment, her way of searching for an answer. She'd nearly made me motion sick when we'd drilled the Tarot last month.

"It means, I guess, that James Padraig wasn't a believer." After a lengthy stare from myself, she added, "It means that anything that appears to be magic is just a figment of one's imagination."

"You're being a little hard on Padraig. He was a believer, in a strict sense. The idea of Padraig's Dogma is that any worthwhile magic should be easily dismissed as illusion. The most powerful forms of hermetic tradition slide just beneath the notice of the average person. It works in tandem with natural law. If it looks obvious, then something has gone wrong, and it has necessarily lost some of its effectiveness."

Ches stretched a grin across her teeth. "So, no fireballs then?"

"Moving on. Nature magic."

She snapped her fingers. "This is where you lose me. I keep asking what's the difference between witches and us, and you keep saying 'Nature Magic.'"

"Which syllable do you not understand?"

"Okay, so, you make hexes and charms. I get those. Affinity magic. Twists of Cosmic laws tying one thing that can or should happen to another that might or mustn't. "

"I should get some of those little gold star stickers to put in your notebook one of these days—"

"Shut up. So, what about witches? Aren't they doing the same thing when they light a candle or burn some incense?"

I stepped to my shelves of reagents, pulling out the jar of myrrh, clearly marked with enormous letters in Sharpie. "These are components to us, ingredients for a recipe that allows us to alter reality. Sometimes we nudge it, sometimes we bend it over our knee and spank it hard. But to us, that's all this is." I gave the jar a jingle and set it back on the shelf. "Crap, we're running low. Remind me to get some more myrrh when the Swains get back."

"Where are they?"

"They had a date with a giant mouse in Orlando."

"They'd better bring me a souvenir, or I'm going to think you guys just don't care about me."

"Anyway... Nature magic. To a witch, the ingredients aren't just ingredients. They're the spell. Witches stitch themselves into Nature—capital N—as if it were a deity in itself."

"Is it?"

"More like a parallel structure, a separate set of rules they identify as Nature. But to us, it's just another sphere of practice their forerunners stumbled across. It's the oldest magic, but also the most limited. They surrender control of their effects to the mental confines of what they call Nature. It becomes a power source, but also dictates what they can do and when."

"It's unpredictable?"

"Not entirely. They obey the cycles and flows of the natural world. You get sun and moon worshipers, or witches that flavor their workings according to the four seasons. If I could come up with some analogy... with hermetic theory, we spend years researching metallurgy and chemistry in order to craft the perfect cannon to fire our spells. Witches? They'll smack a bear on its ass and make sure they run faster than the person they want to get eaten."

Ches scowled. "So, how is that different than Chaos magic?"

I folded my arms again, and lowered my voice, as if to avoid the mention of Chaos being misconstrued as an invitation.

"When you piss off a bear, you basically know what's going to happen. With Chaos magic, well... you don't know if the bear's going to eat you or slap on a tutu and dance Swan Lake, or if the grass will suddenly eat your feet or turn into lemon candies, or if you're even real or just some mad god's temporary sense of wish fulfillment. Chaos magic is a sphere of magic, but it isn't a practice. No one practices Chaos. It just doesn't make sense for anyone, and it can blow up in your face as quick as it'll help you. It's the practice of lunacy."

With half a squint, she asked, "So, where does soul magic fit into all this?"

My stomach tightened just a touch. "It doesn't. That's Netherwork."

"Netherwork doesn't fit into your system?"

"It doesn't fit into any decent school of practice. Netherwork has nothing to do with Man. It's entirely powered by—"

"The Dark Choir, yes. I'm just wondering why you still dance around it? Like it's some kind of land mine?"

"Ches, you have to realize, all organized systems of hermetic practice seek to add to the human experience, either by mastery of secret knowledge or the achievement of gnosis. It's a humanist pursuit. The Dark Choir are creatures of ancient evil, and to them we're not noble beings. We're not masters of any kind of knowledge. We're basically lunch."

Ches's eyes drifted slowly down to her lap.

I continued, "So, if you're looking for someone to round out the holes in your esoteric education and give you a firm foundation in honest hermetic pursuit, shit, I'm your man. But if you want to continue in the pursuit of Netherwork, then you're going to have to take your chances back west with Gillette, because I'm having none of it."

She held up her hands. "Message received, Captain White Light."

I took in a solid breath, and clapped my hands. "Besides, you're doing very well," I announced. "Honest practice suits you. I am to be congratulated."

Ches stood up and smirked at me. "Congratulations. Now go make some coffee. I'm going to fall the fuck asleep down here."

"The Kenyan blend or the cinnamon hazelnut?"

"Kenya."

I turned back to the stairs. "Oh, there's a thing Monday morning."

"What kind of thing? You really need to learn how to be more specific. It's like playing Mad Libs, talking to you. 'Ches, there's a noun tomorrow. You should verb adverbially.'"

"The Tavern. Julian has an event planned. Some legislator is going to announce a run for reelection."

She gave me a thumbs-up along with as unimpressed a smile as one could conjure.

I continued, "I'd like you to come along."

"What's the angle?"

"No angle. Just... you haven't been to the bar, yet."

"I have classes."

I sighed. "Not a problem. It was just a thought."

My palms still buzzed with her energy as I climbed the stairs back to the "real" world. I pieced together my coffee pot, a weird knot forming in my chest.

No, I wasn't disappointed. It wasn't rejection. She just didn't want to waste time with a bunch of politicians. And there was nothing to learn from the whole thing. Light Street Tavern wasn't her business. It was mine.

Still, though.

She wasn't wasting time with my business at all, anymore. It annoyed me that this observation made me feel uneasy.

"Nothing to see here, Dorian," I mumbled to myself as I made coffee. "Move on."

CHAPTER FIVE

Father Mark drummed his fingertips against his chin as he watched me from across his desk.

"I'm not entirely sure a soul can be destroyed," he said. "It is an eternal essence, rendered by the hand of God, Himself. Any notion of an eternal afterlife is hinged on the assertion that the human soul is eternal. It may find itself disposed one way or another, but what could actually destroy it?"

I answered, "Ancient-ass monsters."

"Well, most mature belief systems have rejected the notion of personified evil, Dorian. Evil now being more the sum of human cruelty than the Devil and demons."

I leaned back in my chair, taking in Mark's office. Several diplomas hung in tidy frames along the stile-and-rail oak paneling that gave the room a whiff of academia.

"I'm not as worried about the afterlife as I am this life."

Mark smiled and finally stopped drumming his chin. "You're afraid you'll become something cruel if you don't have a soul?"

"Well, yeah. I feel like I've made progress, somehow. Ever since Osterhaus, I feel like I've become a better person. Which is really screwed up when you think about it."

"Why is that screwed up? Isn't that what you want to happen?"

I glanced down to my lap. "Because that's what happened to Emil. At the end, he was trying to make things right. Trying to train me not to be a Netherworker. He was trying to save his soul, and he failed. It wasn't righteousness. It was fear."

"And you feel afraid, too?"

I sneered. "You think?"

Father Mark stood up and strolled to the tall, thin window in his office. He looked out over the street behind St. Aloysius. He was doing his best with me, and I was grateful. But he was still calling his plays from a very limited view of the larger esoteric reality. From our weekly meetings, however, I felt his horizons had expanded.

As had mine.

He tapped the glass with his knuckle. "But there's a difference, from what you told me. Your old teacher didn't lose his soul, right? He had stained it. Tarnished it. He had committed to evil practices, and then regretted it." Mark turned back to face me. "That's not you, Dorian. You believe your soul is disembodied, not damned. From an outsider's perspective, who's to say you're evil?"

"I have committed evil practices. I cursed a man, and he died. That's murder, isn't it? Doesn't get more evil than that."

"But was it?" he chided, returning to his desk. "Murder? You told me that he had your soul in his clutches. Not just your soul. He had a hundred souls, and if you hadn't intervened he would have consigned them all to... well, nothing good."

"You're saying it was an act of magical self-defense?"

Mark smiled and dropped into his chair. "More than that, Dorian. It was an act of heroism. You put your soul on the line to save the others. Self-sacrifice? Not evil."

"Well, you're being awful charitable, Padre." I added with a squint, "And you don't actually believe I cursed him, to begin with."

He shrugged. "Look at it from my point of view. The welds were fatigued from a cut-rate contractor. It was a spectacular accident, and you were inches from dying alongside your enemy. You must have needed to see a purpose in it."

"Coincidence?"

He nodded.

With a sigh, I said, "That only means it was effective. Don't get me wrong. I'd love to delude myself into thinking it was self-defense. If the Cosmos wants to toss me that kind of mulligan, I'd feel a lot better about things."

"But you don't think it will?"

I thought about the Presidium. They still seemed to be on the fence regarding my actions. Maybe the Cosmos was, as well.

I checked my watch. Just a couple hours until Durning's press conference at the Tavern.

"Gotta cut this short. I have a thing."

Mark stood up with me and shook my hand over his desk. "Next Monday?"

"I'll bring doughnuts."

I hopped out onto the sidewalk to make the long walk to the Tavern. One unexpected benefit of taking my weekly soul-searching with Father Mark was that St. Aloysius was only about fifteen minutes on foot from Light Street. The late spring sunlight cut the chill out of the harbor air enough to make the stroll tolerable. Almost pleasant. I crossed into the shadow of one of the tall buildings on Monument Street when the hairs on my neck started doing The Wave.

The air wasn't that cold in the shade, and it was nearly noon.

I shivered and paused to take a look up the street. This wasn't physical. This was energetic.

I stood still on the sidewalk as only a couple pedestrians wound around me. I had to center and open up my senses. Christ, this was exactly what I was drilling Ches on all week. Energy palpation. Something was pinging me hard from nearby, and if I couldn't tell the difference between my own energy and theirs, I could end up with a nifty little hex hanging around my neck. Once I had my chakras nice and tight, I turned a nonchalant circle, feeling the push and pull of the ambient energy on the block.

The push was most certainly more of a pull, and it was tugging from directly across the street. I gave the far sidewalk a sly glance, trying not to look the part of a hermetic tourist. Something caught my attention, but I couldn't see it. More accurately, someone.

I knew who it was instantly. It was the one who had been watching me for roughly half a year, now. This "shadow man" had robed himself in such an exquisitely executed glammer, I still hadn't caught a solid look at him. Hell, he could have been a "shadow woman," so thorough was this charm. And as glammers work best when they slip beneath notice, or hover in the corners of eyes, this audacious display of direct light-bending affinity magic was as much a declaration of ability as it was an invitation to look.

And look I did.

The form of a man sketched itself into my subconscious, but for the life of me I couldn't make out his features with any more distinction than the lines of mortar on the bricks across the street. There was no overt shielding, nothing to announce "Hello, world... I'm violating natural law." Just an impossible-to-remember face.

And with the speed of a thought, the entire glammer fell. I saw him. I finally saw the shadow man.

I'd caught my first real glimpse of him last November. It was the night of the election. He was camping out across the street from my home, just watching me. He'd offered me a gesture, a literal tip of his hat. It was as confusing as it was frustrating. This man had gone to great and subtle lengths to make me feel like a magical infant, and by this point I was beginning to buy into it.

He was older. Not just older, elderly. His crystal blue eyes perched in tiny wrinkled pouches of ruddy skin. A neatly trimmed pelt of white swashed across his narrow chin. The hunch in the top of his spine brought his head low in a hermit's crouch, but nothing about his dress or his condescendingly cordial smile made him look humble.

I feared this man.

He possessed the unassuming command of an apex predator. And in any intelligent hermetic circle, age was widely embraced not as a sign of weakness, but of terrible strength.

Shadow Man moved along the street toward a corner deli and stepped inside. Was this an invitation? Of course it was. He'd never bother to drop his glammer if he didn't expect me to confront him. I willed my feet to the nearest corner and crossed the street. When I reached the deli, he had reappeared with two cups in his hands, clattering as his fingers shook, and sat down at one of the cheap plastic tables the deli owner probably considered "patio dining."

I stood by, watching blandly as he emptied a packet of sugar into his cup. Finally, he gestured to one of the two chairs huddled with the table, and without looking up, said, "Sit."

And by all that is holy, I sat my ass down.

He nudged the nearer cup toward me, still yet to grace me with eye contact.

The aroma of coffee filled my nostrils, the earthy bouquet quieting down my nerves a couple degrees. Or was it him? I couldn't tell. Any sense of centeredness was flushed right down the crapper the second I decided to confront this man.

He took a long pull from his coffee and leaned back in his chair.

"I've been watching you, as you well know."

I nodded and took a sip of the coffee. It was dreadful.

His eyes lifted and latched onto mine, freezing me in a moment of panic and humility.

"I decided it was time we spoke."

If his frame seemed feeble, his voice still possessed a hearty basso-profundo instead of the wavering lilts of an eighty-something-year-old.

"What do you want from me?" I asked.

"Your soul."

I set my cup down very, very slowly. "You don't say."

"Mister Lake... oh, I do apologize." He held out a hand, bent at an arthritic angle. "Felix Parrish. It's time you made my acquaintance."

I shook his hand with the barest tips of my fingers.

He gathered his cup again and continued, "You're feeling well?"

"Peachy."

"Flippant and arrogant, as expected."

I leaned back in my chair, balling my toes in my shoes. "I do that when I feel threatened."

"Let's discuss your contract."

"The one Osterhaus burned? Sure. Let's talk about that."

His eye landed on me, shrinking my spine a good inch. It was a polite means of letting me know I was pushing too hard.

"The physical document was destroyed. And as Osterhaus chose a particularly crude method of binding souls to the literal parchment, your soul in particular was set loose."

"And the contract was broken."

The corner of his mouth flickered into the faintest of grins. "Hardly broken, Mister Lake."

"Come again? The damn thing was burned to ashes. No parchment, no spell, no contract."

He fumbled with his coat for a moment as he replied, "Indulge me, Mister Lake. What is the first law of affinity magic?"

This was sounding sickeningly familiar.

"As above, so below; as within, so without. Basic stuff."

He pulled a tiny black cylinder from his coat. It looked like a cartoonishly oversized cigar tube in black lacquer. Parrish twisted off the top, allowing it to dangle by a tiny silver chain before sliding out a tightly-wound document.

"As you should well know," he mumbled as he spread the document out on the table top, "any magical working exists on multiple levels of what we call reality."

I surveyed the document, and sucked in a breath. I nearly knocked over my chair as I stood up, putting space between myself and what appeared to be a perfect copy of Osterhaus's contract.

My soul contract.

"How—how did you get that?"

"I won't bother with the specifics, Mister Lake. Suffice to say, you've brokered an agreement with beings that consider physical parchment to be clumsy but necessary tools in dealing with our course flesh."

I rasped, "What are you?"

"I'll explain, if you sit down."

I took in several breaths, looked up and down the street, and gathered enough poise to take my seat again. The contract looked identical to the one Osterhaus had scribed. Tiny, sloppy Greek calligraphy in what appeared to be dried blood.

"This is a copy, then?" I asked.

"In the sense that this is not the same physical document you signed with Neil Osterhaus. But don't mistake this for a mere forgery. This is as equally binding as the original."

"That's not how it works."

"Isn't it? Perhaps that is for your benefactor to decide?"

My stomach clenched. "My benefactor?"

"You wish to know what I am?"

I nodded slowly.

"I am a representative of interested parties, tasked with the re-acquisition of your contract."

"You're an agent... an agent of the Dark Choir."

I'd heard of them. Hollow humans whose bodies were co-opted by infernal beings to act as their eyes, ears, and hands in the affairs of humanity. Tales of such agents were something of a campfire tale among Emil's circles in London. Emil treated the subject with a degree of amusement and dismissal. He certainly never professed to actually believing in them.

Hell, this was what I'd feared when Carmen had pulled the paternal wool over my eyes. A baby born without a soul? A perfect vessel for the Dark Choir to foster such an agent. Turned out, she was lying the entire time, but the sentiment was real enough to coerce me into signing that fucking contract in the first place.

And now a real, honest-to-whatever-passes-for-God agent of the Dark Choir was giving me one staggering glare as I tried not to vomit.

"If you will," he muttered.

"My soul... it's not here. In the contract, I mean. Is it?"

He shook his head. "Your soul remains itinerate. My employer finds this circumstance to be, shall we say, untidy? He wants it resident in the contract once again."

"Who is he, exactly? What... is he?"

"You elected to receive Consideration for your contract, Mister Lake. Such an arrangement isn't open-ended. A specific source of power remained in waiting until the contract was fulfilled. And you did receive your Consideration, albeit short-lived."

"Blood magic."

"Blood magic," he parroted. "A particular specialty of your benefactor."

"Does he have a name?"

"Names aren't necessary for such beings as my employer."

"I know a Goetic on Charles Street who would disagree, Parrish. Names are everything to the Dark Choir."

He chuckled, a dusty noise resembling the scraping of a door over a warped wooden floor.

"Mister Lake, I do believe you've confused the foot soldiers for the generals. Goetia is the sport of hedge magicians, throwing gossamer chains over imps and chamber-slags. It provides a degree of amusement to those of consequence on the other side, as well. Suffering is quite the universal diversion, it seems."

I glared at Parrish for an awkward moment.

At length, he sighed and continued, "He is known. For thousands of years, he's treated with the likes of Osterhaus. From the modern day to the first stirrings of the Golden Dawn, into the dark ages with its gallows swinging with over-anxious dabblers. Rome, the days of Iskandar, the blood rites of the Philistines and the Assyrians. The brilliant days of each of the Kemet Dynasties. The Akkadians. Eridu. Even the first practitioners of the Khambat Empire, such as it was, had benefit of his offers."

Less than half of that made sense to me, but as he rolled out the archaeological roll call like it was vacation slides, I began to realize how thoroughly screwed I really was.

Parrish sipped his coffee for a moment, affording me a beat to gather my thoughts.

I took a sip of coffee and cleared my throat to give my voice a touch more clarity. "If he's so hungry for my soul," I whispered, "then why bother coming to me? I can't be that important. Seems like a lot of trouble."

"Less trouble, honestly, than trying to find your soul on our own."

"What, this benefactor can't be bothered?"

"Indeed. There is a hierarchy at play, here. The fewer who are involved, the less damage it will cause. Hence my coming to you." He tapped the contract. "You have Consideration that remains unclaimed, Mister Lake. It's been interrupted, but it can be easily restored."

"You want to give me back the Blood Magic?"

"It would make the requirements for your profession considerably simpler."

I scowled. "I don't work in curses."

"Evidence to the contrary."

"That was one time."

Parrish waved a dismissive hand. "Nonetheless, an agreement was reached. Your benefactor has no interest in one-sided predation. It's a waste of energy. Much simpler to work cooperatively. And as such, should you re-engage in a mutually constructive relationship, the resulting affinity will make the task of locating your soul that much simpler."

He was finally making sense. Two sources of intention working in concert created a total greater than the sum of its parts. This additional resonance was what he wanted. It was the foundation of all group workings... the more brains that focus on the goal, the easier it is to achieve that goal.

I just wasn't convinced I wanted to cooperate.

"I'm just going to put this out there, Parrish. I re-sign this contract. You find my soul and trap it back in the parchment. What's to keep me from executing my escape clause immediately?"

He crossed his legs in his chair, swiveling to the side.

"Have you read it?" he replied, tapping the contract with his finger.

I leaned in to give the text a thorough examination. The script was relatively easy to follow, thanks to my having just drilled several dialects of Greek with Ches over the past couple months. By the time I reached the end of the text, I realized his point.

"You've... redacted the out-clause?"

"As you said, we've gone to great lengths already. More, perhaps, than you merit. We must recoup our investment."

"Then why in God's Green Hell would I ever cooperate with you, or your boss? Seems like a no-win situation for me."

Parrish finished his coffee and set down the cup hard.

"You have two outcomes. The first: you sign the contract and receive a considerable amount of power as your Consideration to enjoy for the remainder of your life in this world. The second: we find your soul without you, inconveniencing your benefactor in the process, and we come to collect without Consideration... or discretion. These are your options, Lake."

He fished a curious instrument from his pocket. Thin and silver, resembling a pen. At one end was the nib of a fountain pen. His thumb triggered a tiny lever along the side of the pen, and a vicious, serrated blade sprung from the opposite end. A handy tool for blood scribing.

"Decide now," he grumbled, setting the pen on top of the parchment.

And thus it was presented to me. My choice. Repeat the mistake that had cost me my soul, an act that would grant me the same blood attraction I had used to manipulate Osterhaus, and would allow me to curse anyone, anywhere, without the need to collect a piece of their body. Or, I could flip the table, walk away, and begin a race in earnest to find my soul before the Dark Choir could.

I stared at the contract for a long moment. Parrish, to his credit, didn't prod me. He was a man of patience. Well, limited patience, it seemed. I could tell he despised dealing with me. And that thought was what made up my mind.

"I think I'll take my chances," I answered, standing and running a hand over my shirt. "But I thank you for your offer."

He stared at me, eyes calm and level. "One more chance, Mister Lake." He brandished his pen.

I shook my head and shoved my hands in my pockets.

With a long breath, he rolled up the contract and slipped it into his black lacquer canister, triggered the blade back into the pen.

Parrish stood and turned away, taking his leave without another word.

I called out, "I'm not as helpless as you think."

He stopped and swiveled on one heel.

"In the coming days, you may reconsider that statement."

My brain fuzzed, and he vanished in a small crowd of pedestrians. I searched the street, but his glammer was back, and I was alone.

Well, that was it. The starter pistol had fired, and I was already a step behind my dark benefactor.

I checked my watch. I could deal with this after the press conference. Eternal debts could wait... keeping the lights on and the water running had to take precedence for the moment.

CHAPTER SIX

Julian's face melted with relief when he spotted me weaving through a couple press vans.

"Dorian!" he shouted over a throng of overcoated men and women bearing serious expressions. "You're very nearly late."

"Sorry. Had to see a man about a horse."

"Where's Francesca?"

"She couldn't make it."

"Durning's inside. Did you want to meet him? We probably have, maybe, twenty seconds."

I nodded, and we stepped through two lines of very tall men with bulges under their blazers and earpieces slithering from beneath their collars and into their ears. The inside of the Tavern was as crowded as I had ever seen it, though Ben was standing stiff behind the bar, arms crossed, probably bored as hell. It was just a little early in the day for the day-drinkers to start tipping pints, and most of this press circus would likely dissipate immediately after this announcement, leaving us our usual ghost town. It's the coverage, Julian would argue. We get free advertising, even if no one buys a beer.

Julian nudged me toward the front of the event room where the portly, dark-skinned Jerome Durning stood staring forward with echoes of his speech ricocheting inside his smooth, bald dome.

Julian tapped his arm, jerking him from his thoughts, and gestured toward me.

"Congressman? I'd like you to meet my partner, Dorian Lake."

Durning's face snapped into a well-practiced mask of telegenic charisma. "Oh, pleasure. Pleasure to meet you."

"Likewise," I answered with my own well-practiced charisma. "Thanks for having your to-do at our humble little hole-in-the-wall. Means a lot to us."

Julian muttered, "Not so humble."

"I was going for demure and grateful."

"No need to scrape," Julian chided.

Durning grinned. "Oh, it's no accident that I chose to announce here."

"That so?"

"Ms. Claye speaks so highly of you two."

Julian beamed, as I stood still.

Durning continued, "Gentlemen, you must excuse me, my assistant is either having a heart attack, or I'm on."

He shook my hand again and slipped around us to the front door.

I leaned into Julian. "Think he realizes we're 'business' partners?"

"After that display, I'm sure he's thoroughly confused on the matter."

"So," I asked, "who's this Ms. Claye?"

Julian smiled and stepped over to the front door, waving in the woman with whom he had been engaging his private court sessions in our event room.

She was polished, her makeup reserved but expertly planned. Her hair slung over her face, flat-ironed to create an oval frame. Her eyes were sharp, and her posture straight, a real bucks-and-business air about her.

Julian turned to his colleague with a smile. "Dorian, I'd like to introduce you to Deputy Mayor Ronetta Claye."

"Deputy Mayor?" I blabbed as she held out a hand.

"I've heard a lot about you, Mister Lake," she chimed as I shook her hand.

I mumbled, "Oh Christ."

"Thank you for your patience these past few weeks," she added with a nod to the event room. "It's been a sprint trying to reach the standards Julian set, but we're getting there."

"Ah," I said. "You're the new Julian?"

She half-shrugged with a grin. "Filling in more than my fair half while Sullivan finishes his search."

Julian interjected, "She's been in City Hall as long as I have. Whereas I'd been wrestling with governmental affairs, Ronetta's headed up public safety. Now David has her shoring up my old duties until they promote someone else."

"There's more than one deputy mayor?" I asked.

"Five, in fact," Julian replied.

Claye corrected him, "Four."

"Right." Julian's eyes drooped slightly.

"Well, thank you again, Mister Lake." Claye pointed a finger at Julian as she back toward the circus on the street. "Expect a call later, you."

Julian smiled and waved her off. When she was out of sight, his shoulders wilted.

"She's doing just fine," he muttered.

"Is that a statement or a question?"

"A hope."

We stepped outside and fell in behind a clutch of onlookers, mostly aids and security, as the Congressman moved toward the podium nestled conveniently beside the Light Street Tavern window signage. I spotted Mayor Sullivan as he emerged from his car amid a police escort, intentionally dialed a degree toward the casual in his navy suit. He waved to the press corps as his wife stepped out, dwarfed beside her tall husband, but no less visually commanding in her light blue suit. He held her hand as she stepped to the sidewalk, reaching out to smooth a bit of her hair from beneath her pillbox hat.

Julian turned to me. "Madelyn's here? She never makes these events."

"Sullivan's wife?"

"Yeah. She hates the public eye. The election last year drove her nuts. Interesting."

We hugged the last available space on the narrow walk, roughly twenty yards away from the podium. The press corps had already hushed, their various recording devices forward, as Sullivan stepped up to the podium.

"Thank you all for coming," he bellowed in his hearty country-gravy voice. "Jack," he added with a thrust of his index finger to one of the radio people, "nice tie."

He flipped his own tie out of his jacket, identical to the reporter's, and a few nearby reporters chuckled.

"Everyone here knows Jerome Durning." Heads nodded. "The Congressman is a personal friend of mine. We were both Lambda Oh at UMD. We spent years together in Knights of Columbus, Habitat for Humanity. Had him over for Thanksgiving... he ate more than his share of crab cakes, I'll tell you."

Chuckles from the crowd.

"Then he goes and gets elected to the Hill. And he gets elected again." Sullivan turned to Durning. "I guess they like you, Jerry."

More laughs.

"So, it came as no surprise when he gave me a call and said, 'David, I'm going again.' Of course he was. He's done more for Maryland Seventh in the past three terms than any predecessor. Federal funds for schools and highways, advocating to keep our military bases intact and people safe in their jobs. So, here we are in front of the Light Street Tavern in the heart of downtown Baltimore to take another swing at the ball."

A spattering of applause rippled around the crowd as I gave Julian's shoulder a nudge with my own.

Sullivan reached into his pocket and produced a baseball. He tossed it in a lazy arc to Durning, who caught it with a slight bobble. Sullivan then produced a tiny hand broom from inside his jacket and bent over to literally sweep the sidewalk in front of the podium.

"You're up to the plate, Jerry!"

The crowd clapped as Sullivan stepped aside to grant Durning his stage, though he had more than stolen the show by this point.

As Durning gathered himself at the podium and thanked Sullivan, I whispered to Julian, "That was quite the show."

"You noticed that, too?"

"Didn't Sullivan just get re-elected?"

Julian squinted. "Well, governor's race is in two years, but I can't imagine he'd be ramping up..." He balled a fist as his spine straightened.

I peered at him. "Julian?"

He turned back toward the tavern with a huff. "Son of a bitch."

"What?"

"Ronetta made this comment the other day. Something about Barclay and McClaren."

I gathered him closer to the door as Durning began his speech.

"I'm supposed to know who Barclay and McWhatshisnuts is?"

Julian ran a hand over his forehead. "Maryland Democratic committee. Compliance and political directors. That explains why Madelyn is here. My God, he's running for governor!"

I smiled. The thought of Sullivan running for yet another office struck me with a degree of fatigue, but I liked him. He was honest, straightforward, and managed to pull off that folksy charm without having to engineer it.

"This is a good thing, right?"

"Maybe."

Julian stared over the crowd, which seemed especially riveted to Durning's words.

As was Sullivan and his wife, who was gripping her husband's arm.

Julian pulled me aside. "What did he just say?"

Durning shuffled papers on his podium as microphones and recorders inched closer.

"I have a list of names here. Lobbyists, directors and executive officers of corporations in and around the Beltway, and more alarming... members of the Senate and House of Representatives."

I stepped forward. What was he doing?

"I'll remind you, most of these people have never been elected to public office. Yet they control significant power within the capital. I dare say they influence decisions within the White House, itself."

Murmurings spread throughout the crowd as the sole cameraman jockeyed for a tighter angle.

"These men and women belong to a secret society with very strong occult connections. Their private observances, clearly un-Christian and contrary to all common decency, may include acts of bloodletting, devil worship, and may even be sexual in nature."

The murmurings bubbled to a flurry of questions.

Sullivan turned to his wife and began to ease her away from the podium.

I turned to Julian, whose face was awash in confusion.

Durning held up his hands until questions subsided. "This group of individuals who call themselves The Presidium represent a core disease within our American democracy, and they should be held accountable." With a deep breath, he added, "I shall now read the list of names."

My knees buckled, but I managed to grab hold of Julian's arm to steady myself.

"Bob Alonza, Senior Partner of Alonza Duggins and Reznik. Senator Ron Blankenship. Alderman Clifford Brinks."

Julian pulled me inside as the list of names continued, swallowed by barks and shouts from the press corps.

Ben straightened up as we crashed into the tavern. "What's going on?"

I dropped onto a bar stool.

Jesus.

Durning was outing the Presidium on live television!

And he was doing it in front of my bar.

Julian took the stool beside me and said, "The Congressman's committing political suicide, is what's going on."

"Huh."

"Remarkable. He must have had a nervous breakdown, or something. It's unbelievable."

Ben shrugged. "Still, can't be bad news for us, though. Right? Any press is good press."

Julian replied with a look to the window, "It's bad news for David."

"Who, Sullivan?" Ben asked.

"If he's planning a run for Annapolis in two years, this won't help him. My God, this is embarrassing for everyone."

The Mayor's car slid out of view and up the street. Only about four blocks from City Hall, but it would be a long four blocks.

Julian turned to me. "I'm sorry, Dorian. This was supposed to... this isn't helping."

He had no idea.

Of all the damned places for Durning to pull this stunt, it had to be in front of my bar. The Presidium was going to be pissed. Not just normal pissed. Mounting heads on pikes levels of pissed. And my status with the Presidium could have been charitably described as "dubious" to begin with.

Julian put a hand on my shoulder and turned me toward him.

"Dorian? You have that look, again." He pulled his hand away. "This wasn't random, was it? You know what he's talking about?"

I didn't answer.

"Dorian? This Presidium crap. Please tell me it's crap."

"Durning said this wasn't an accident," I muttered.

"What is the Presidium, Dorian?"

I stood up. "I very much doubt there are any blood orgies involved, but yes. They *do* control basically everything."

Ben snickered. "This ain't some Illuminati thing, is it?"

"This isn't a joke, Ben," I snapped. "Durning just painted a giant bulls-eye right on each of our asses. Mine, in particular."

Julian waved his hands as he winced. "No, this isn't going anywhere. No one's going to believe this is bonafide. It'll be written off as the ravings of a man in need of retirement, and possibly lithium. No one will care."

"They'll care, Julian. The Presidium will most certainly care." I paced a slow circle. "We have to get ready for the blowback."

"What blowback?" Julian shouted.

"We'll need wardings. Lots of wardings. And get your accounts overseas, if you can."

Ben huffed. "You mean my first million? Sure. I'll get right on that."

"These people are vicious and unforgiving, Ben. The only real defense is to not be important enough to merit their attention. It's possible they'll overlook the fact this happened outside the tavern, but I doubt it."

"Have you merited their notice?" Julian grumbled.

"More than once. It's never ended well."

The crowd outside swelled into a roar of questions as Durning tucked his head, pocketed his pages, and slipped into his cadre of security to be whisked away. The press corps remained outside the tavern, taking notes and frothing in general. The water had just been chummed.

"I have to warn Ches," I announced, turning for the back door. "Try not to talk to anyone with a microphone."

Julian lifted a brow. "This isn't my first scandal, you know. I'll be fine. You, on the other hand, really need to take a breath."

"I should probably reach out to them. Make sure they know I had nothing to do with this."

"Think that'll help?"

"At this point," I called out as I wound around the back hallway, "I'm as lost as you are."

CHAPTER SEVEN

I sat in my car, parked in the alley between my two-story red brick row house on Amity and the high-rise bank building next door. That building went up quick, and ever since McHenry broke ground on Carrollton Estates the entire neighborhood seemed to have become a non-stop work zone. I gripped my steering wheel as reflections in the bank's windows skittered in and around the roof of my house. This was a bad sign. The shadows always grew anxious when my life was threatened.

I finally stepped out of the car and rushed for my door, like I was ducking in from a rain shower. I keyed my lock, but the bolt was already open. I froze for a moment, spying up and down the street.

I knew I had locked this door before I left that morning.

In the silence, I heard voices inside. One of them was Ches; I could tell from the warding on my threshold. The other? No clue.

With an easy nudge, I opened the door and stepped inside. There was no one in the front room, but as I closed the door behind me, I spotted Ches hopping up into the kitchen doorway.

"Dorian!" she bumbled with her arms stiff at her sides.

I watched her for a second, then strode toward the kitchen.

"You alone?" I asked, knowing full well she wasn't.

She occupied as much of the doorway as she could, but without fully blocking my way she couldn't stop me from spotting a middle-aged woman sitting at my kitchen table. Two glasses of water sat on the table alongside a notebook with Ches's handwriting filling the pages.

The woman looked up to me, bloodshot eyes and a line-worried brow watching with anticipation.

"Uh, hi," I blurted.

She nodded, straightening in her seat a bit.

Ches turned to the side and lifted a hand to me.

"Mrs. Garcia, this is Dorian."

The woman's eyes eased, and a smile finally stole into her mouth as she muttered, "Hello."

Ches cleared her throat and lay a hand on the side of her forehead. "Mrs. Garcia and I were just having a consultation. I, er, your thing's over already?"

I glanced over to her notes, and recognized a series of logograms I've used in charm-crafting before.

I brushed past Ches just enough to extend a hand to Mrs. Garcia. She took it with her fingertips, clenching them away quickly to hide the tremors. Her shoulders hunched and she looked quickly down to the table.

I squeezed the salt packet in my pocket to clear her nervous energy. "I apologize for interrupting. May I borrow Miss Baker for just a quick moment?" I asked with as cordial a tone as I could muster.

Mrs. Garcia nodded, and I swept back around Ches, ushering her into the front room.

"This is... what?" I whispered.

"Don't freak."

"I'm not freaking."

"She's part of a project for class. I'm interviewing subjects for a class on addiction psychology."

I crossed my arms.

Ches looked over to the window.

"Right, okay, it's not just for class."

"You're making charms for addicts?"

Ches huffed and stretched her neck. "I know you told me I'm not allowed to practice, but I was already interviewing them—"

"How many?"

"She's the third."

"You made charms for all of them?"

Ches shook her head. "I haven't made any... just one. The first, so far. Mrs. Garcia was going to be my second."

I turned away, bracing against the foyer archway. Fantastic timing.

"Go wrap up," I grumbled. "Then come downstairs."

"Dorian—"

I turned on my heel and took a step into her, whispering as low as I could, "Get her out of here."

With a squint, Ches turned back to the kitchen.

I descended into the work space, pacing several circles around my bench, reviewing every conversation Ches and I had specifically about her not practicing any kind of magic until I had given her my blessing. I was sure I wasn't even remotely unclear on the subject.

The front door closed overhead, and at length, Ches trotted down the stairs with her hands held up.

"Don't shoot. I'm unarmed."

"You're making charms?"

"Just the one."

"Two, if you count Mrs. Garcia, which we won't, because you're not making shit for Mrs. Garcia."

Ches rolled her eyes. "I get it, I know. I'm not allowed to practice."

"Damned right, you're not."

She crossed her arms. "Dorian, we really need to air something out. Okay?"

"Air what out?"

"I know you're supposed to be my teacher. And I've played ball as best I could. But let's neither of us pretend you have the first clue what you're doing."

I stepped back. "Excuse me?"

"You're just taking your experience with a man who, let's face it, was a fossil even in his own time... and you're using that as a template for whatever this is." She waved a finger between the two of us. "You're not, in fact, my mentor."

"Quinn Gillette might insist otherwise."

"Quinn was—is—a killer. She's a warlord. An alpha beast. She taught us exactly what she needed us to know, because we were all just soldiers in her army."

I rubbed my face. "And that's what you call mentorship?"

Ches took a step forward. "No. That's my point. She didn't make illusions that she was a teacher or a mentor, or babysitter. Whatever. I don't think you really understand that. She doesn't have any expectations of you, Dorian. She wasn't entrusting me to your care, or trying to do the right thing. She was dumping me off. I was dead weight, and it was cleaner for her to just stick you with the disposal of my remains, however long it would take you to figure it out."

"I'm not a babysitter."

"My point is, you're trying too hard. You're taking this too seriously, because you're afraid she's going to drop in one day for some kind of spot inspection."

"Not true," I grunted.

"Dorian, I'm going to start practicing. I was practicing in Portland, I'm going to start practicing here. You can bitch me out all you like, but you actually have no authority to stop me."

I sucked in a breath to rejoinder, but held my tongue.

Because she was absolutely correct.

I turned away and reached for the stool at my bench to take a seat.

"I'm not afraid of Gillette," I finally muttered.

"Shit, I am."

"I mean, I'm not doing this to protect myself."

Ches stepped up to the bench and leaned on her hands. "I don't need protecting, Dorian."

"You do, actually."

She looked up, then shrugged. "Yeah, maybe. But it's not your responsibility."

"I know that. I'm not doing it because anyone's forcing me to, Ches. I want to help you."

"And I'm not completely ungrateful. That—that really sounded lame when it came out."

I reached for one of her hands, but she pulled them off the table, stepping back and shoving them into her pockets.

"Listen," I said, trying to avoid the awkward moment, "if I feel you're not ready for something, it's only because your lack of knowledge makes you dangerous."

"I don't lack knowledge. I'm not some newbie practitioner that bought a book on Amazon and decided to go Full-Hogwarts." She took a breath and added, "I know what I'm doing. I know enough, anyway."

"Did you know enough when you made the servitor that almost killed a thirteen-year-old girl?"

Her face tightened.

"Ches, we all have filters. Sometimes it's hard to see our own failings."

She shook her head and threw her hands up into the air. "Jesus. James Padraig was absolutely right. There really is no magic without ego."

"Maybe there's a little ego going both ways, here?"

She scowled. "I'm good at this, Dorian. I feel like every practitioner I've met was good at one thing in particular. Gillette was a natural at soul magic. Judith was an accomplished sigilist. Carmody, as big a fraud as he came off, was actually decent at luck charms. There's this one thing that aligns with our personalities, and that's usually the thing that sucks us into the Life. Well, I think I found mine, and I want to explore it. Why do you think I stayed, Dorian? In Baltimore?"

"The fact that if you left, Gillette was probably going to have you killed?"

"Well, besides that. I was doing something in Portland. Something bigger than I guess what you'd call 'regular.' Now that I'm not beholden to Gillette, I feel like I can do better. I can actually do some good. I mean, if we can't do anything positive with this Life, then what's the damn point?"

I traced the spiral on my bench with my finger, thinking over what she'd said. Doing some good. That was the point. Wasn't it?

"Okay, you're right. I don't have any real authority over you. So, I can't forbid you to practice."

She exhaled and nodded. "Thank you."

"But, if I can't forbid you, then can I at least try to convince you to pump the brakes on this charm-making business? Something's happened. Something you need to know about."

She leaned against the far wall and tilted her chin. "What?"

"I... I want you to move in here."

She shook her head and leaned forward. "Say that again?"

"I want you to pack what you need for a few weeks, and move in here. I'll clean out a room upstairs. Not like I don't have space, now."

"Dorian?"

"Yeah?"

"Have you lost your mind? That's never going to happen. I don't know what you think this conversation was—"

"It's not like that. You're in danger. We're both in danger."

She eased back against the wall. "So what's new?"

"Jerome Durning."

"I'm supposed to know who that is?"

"Congressman. He had an announcement at the tavern today."

She nodded. "Oh, right. Your thing."

I hopped off my stool. "Well, it wasn't the thing I was expecting. It was another thing entirely, and now it's possible we're both completely screwed."

She held up a hand. "Start over."

"Durning outed the Presidium on live television."

Her face froze. "Try again."

"Durning. For some reason, he decided to announce the existence of the Presidium in front of a press corps. He even named names. A couple I recognized. His information was... accurate."

"What the hell would he do something like that, for? What, is he one of them?"

I thought that over. "Don't think so. Seems to me like someone got to him, maybe put him up to it. Point being, the Presidium's about to go on a tear. Last time that happened, we got the Red Scare. Before that, Manifest Destiny."

"Where do we stand?"

"Unknown. But I don't want to take chances. I've always been kind of on the cusp with the Presidium. So, if we can avoid aggravating them?"

Ches nodded. "That's all you had to say, Dorian. But, I don't think this merits moving my crap into your guest room."

"They work silent and quick, Ches. They grab you off the street and disappear you. I want to keep an eye on you whenever possible."

"I have classes."

"Which are basically three blocks away."

She searched the ceiling for another excuse before finally waving me off. "No, let's just see how things play out. Okay? This would be... it would get weird."

"Yeah. It would."

"We'll be Switzerland. Right? Neutral."

I nodded. "Switzerland."

She lingered a moment, then turned for the stairs.

Before she could disappear, I asked, "What's my thing?"

"Hmm?"

"You said everyone you met had that one magic they're good at. What am I good at?"

She grinned at me, then replied as she turned up the stairs, "I don't know, you're pretty good at getting your way."

"That's not magic," I called up the stairs.

Good at getting my way, huh? At the moment, my most regrettable quality was being "in the way." But Ches was probably right about the Presidium. Making a move too quickly would only make me look guilty. Best to sit tight and hope for this all to blow over. Switzerland.

But as I sat back down on the stool, I considered Durning. If he was strong-armed into this whole media attack against the Presidium, then whose arm was pushing him? The gears in my skull kept clicking despite all common sense screaming to leave this alone. Admittedly, solving the Presidium's problem for them might ingratiate me enough to keep from getting a gift-wrapped curse dropped on my head, but nosing into their business has never ended well for... well, anyone to date.

After Ches had gone home, and I had retired for the evening with a couple fingers of my Glenrothes in hand, I sat in front of the evening news without paying any real attention. The media was abuzz with what they were calling Durning's public meltdown. They had already declared Durning's political career over, and were just re-hashing the event over and over. At least Light Street Tavern was popping up on the video at least three times per hour.

I had an entire plan in place by the time I was done with my scotch. I would approach Durning, ingratiate myself... somehow... and step directly into this mess in order to save Ches.

And myself.

Well, both of us. It wasn't much of a plan, but the first step was clear. I had to get Durning alone. He needed to trust someone. And I was on the outside. Neutral party. I was pretty sure I could sell that.

I reached for my remote to turn off the TV and the Breaking News banner flashed across the bottom of the screen. My gut twisted. Somehow, I knew this wouldn't be good.

Sure enough, my plan shattered as a blanched news anchor announced that Congressman Jerome Durning's body had been found in his living room. He was survived by three grown sons and a wife who had been at a Black Caucus meeting in Michigan.

To the news, it meant Durning's story had ended in tragedy. A public meltdown ending in what everyone was speculating was a long-overdue heart attack.

To me, however, it meant the Presidium had begun its counter-attack.

CHAPTER EIGHT

Despite my assurances to Julian otherwise, I decided to keep my distance from the tavern for the next few days. If the Presidium was in a lather, I didn't want to present an easy target. Ches returned daily for her training, but continued home each night. My tension with the entire scenario eased over the space of a couple days. No one had gotten themselves black-bagged yet. My accounts were intact. And most of the media had moved on to another news cycle. My butt could only pucker so far, it seemed, and I needed to tend to business.

In the quiet hours of Thursday evening, after the buses on the MLK backed off of rush hour timing, I grabbed my phone and gave Deirdre the Dowser a call to follow up on her daycare conundrum.

She answered, "Hello?"

"It's Dorian Lake."

After a weighty sigh, she responded, "I've been debating calling you. How's your assistant?"

"She's okay. More to the point, how's the daycare?"

"I can't clear a jinx, Mister Lake. I'm not on that... level."

I sat at my roll top desk, looking out over Amity. "Few people are. Which begs the question, who the crap could or would do this?"

"I thought about what you said. About me having enemies?"

"Yeah?"

She cleared her throat. "I honestly can't say."

"But?"

"But... there's something else I didn't mention."

I knew it.

"Go on?"

"The couple who ran the daycare told me they'd found graffiti on the walls. They cleaned it up before I could see it."

"Did they describe this graffiti?"

"Not very well. It scared the Hell out of them, though. Said it looked like Satanism. Symbols."

I swiveled in my chair to jot down notes: *SIGILS ON WALL, INTENTIONAL.*

"Is this why you're so eager to duck the Presidium on this?"

After a long breath, she responded, "It's not what I do that heats the Presidium's hackles, Mister Lake. It's who I do it for. There's hardly any market for my skills anymore. The only way to make a living is to cater to immigrants. Believers. Sometimes they belong to formal groups."

"Foreign cabals. Yeah, that'd be a no-go for our little friends in D.C. What about the Korean couple who owns this place. Any known affiliations?"

"I don't ask."

"Well, I'm going to call that my Number One Theory, Deirdre. If you do some digging, you might find out these folk have family in one of the old cabals in Korea. This is probably collateral damage from some old blood feud. At any rate, you'd probably do best to dissociate yourself and stay out of the line of fire, if you know what I mean."

"This affair with Durning?" she asked.

"Just keep your head down, and stay in touch. Things are going to be tense for a while."

Deirdre harrumphed her agreement, then hung up.

Tense... that was an understatement.

I checked my burgeoning voice mail box, and decided to give the tavern a call.

Julian answered, "Dorian? Are you still alive?"

"Despite all evidence to the contrary. How's business?"

"Did you listen to any of my messages? I mean, I'll take just one. Just one message."

I sighed. "If I said yes, do you think I could fake my way through this conversation with any kind of satisfaction?"

"Business is up. That hullabaloo with Durning actually worked. Which is kind of the problem."

"I'm lost. More business is a problem?"

Julian called out to someone nearby, muffling the phone, before answering, "Sorry. Yeah. Too much business, too few employees. Not to mention Ronetta basically presides over the liquor board, and she's had a few too many notices she's kept in orbit until we get the kitchen running. I don't think she can keep it up, Dorian."

"I got it."

"You said you'd interview managers."

"I said I got it."

A knock on the door provided the perfect opportunity to duck the rest of this conversation. "I'll call you later, Julian. Got someone at the door."

I pocketed my phone and took my time walking to the door. My darquelle sat mounted to a plaque on the wall within easy reach of the front door. I hadn't had to use the blade since I brought down Ches's errant servitor last summer, but with the Great High Muckamucks in the Presidium on the hunt, I made sure any constructs or energy bonds that found its way as far as my threshold wouldn't make it much farther.

I peered through the peephole to find an unassuming blond man in a polo shirt hoisting a duffle bag over his shoulder. I didn't recognize him. Like, even a little. I was pretty sure he wasn't one of my former clients, and if he was, I hoped he hadn't lost a pet recently.

I eased the door open against the chain. "Hello?"

He tucked his chin and gave me a tidy wave. "Hi."

"Hi."

He shifted on his feet, looking up the street, before finally saying, "Um, is Ches here?"

"I'm afraid not."

"Oh."

We stood in awkward silence for a moment.

He cleared his throat, and asked, "But she comes here after school, right?"

"Not to be a dick, or anything, but how is that your business?"

His eyes widened and he took a step back. "Oh, I'm not some freak or anything. Holy crap, this looks really bad. Sorry."

He turned to walk off, but I called out to stop him.

"Wait, are you here for one of her interviews?"

The man froze and turned slowly back toward me. "What interview?"

"Her thing."

He blinked. "Thing?"

Jesus, I really did need to work on my pronouns.

"Sorry. Her addiction studies. I guess you're not here for an interview?"

"We're talking about Francesca Baker, right?" he asked. "You are Dorian Lake, aren't you?"

I eased the door closed and unchained it to step out onto my stoop.

"I am, but who are you?"

"Oh, I'm Ricky."

I shook my head. "Ricky?"

"Baker?"

"Ricky Baker."

He nodded. "I'm Ches's brother." His face wilted. "Shit. She didn't tell you."

A ball tightened in my gut, and I rubbed my temple. "What didn't she tell me, Ricky?"

He shook his head and held out his hand. "I'm sorry, boss. I'll go."

"Hold on," I blurted, trotting down my front steps. "Let's start this over." I held out my hand. "Ricky Baker? I'm Dorian Lake. Pleased to finally meet you."

Ricky considered my hand, then shook it with a vice grip. "Yeah, finally."

"So, you're Ches's brother, huh? What brings you to the East Coast?"

He tucked his head again. "Nothing. Just visiting Ches."

"That so?" I gestured for the door. "You need a coffee or something?"

"Coffee sounds just about perfect right now."

In the space of five minutes, we were both sitting in my kitchen with empty mugs as the coffee pot worked its magic behind me. I watched as he sat stiff in his chair, though his shoulders had begun to relax.

"Wish I knew you were coming," I chimed in to break the silence. "I would have made a bigger deal about it. Banners, a bowl of punch, or something."

"Yeah, wish you knew I was coming, too."

"Right. So, things have been a little crazy this week. Ches probably just forgot to mention it."

He lifted a brow. "That's probably it."

"So, how are things in Portland?"

His other brow lifted, and a sneer crept into his lip.

Well, this was going well.

"You said she comes here after class? When's that, usually?"

"Somewhere after lunch, depending on whether she grabs fast food or insists on hunting down the Taco Muchacho truck on her way in."

He laughed, full-on mouth open belly laugh. "Shit, Ches and her tacos."

"What, that's always been her thing?"

"Ever since she discovered tacos on that stupid trip to San Diego when she was six. Longest road trip ever. She gets bored, like, super-quick. Right? All the way back up I-5, she was whining to stop and find tacos somewhere. Mom put a ban on tacos at our house for basically a year, and that only made them more mysterious to Ches."

"So, she's always had an appetite for forbidden things?"

"If you only knew."

"No... if you only knew."

We shared a look, and I leaned back in my chair.

The lock clattered up front, and I stifled a grin as the door swung open.

"Ches?" I called out.

"What?"

"I'm in here."

She shuffled around up front, dropping off her backpack with a loud thump of what sounded like a handful of books before she stepped into the kitchen.

"Got lunch," she said, dropping a Taco Muchacho bag onto the table.

"Got enough for three?" I asked, nodding across the table.

She looked up and froze.

Ricky stood up slowly, shoulders stiff again.

Ches balled a fist a few times, then whispered, "You're here."

He wound around the table and threw his arms around her. She returned his embrace, pulling her head to the side, eyes latching onto mine.

"Hey, kiddo," he grunted.

She laid a hand alongside his face when he pulled away. "You okay?"

He shrugged.

"How long do you have?"

"I'm supposed to pick up the kids a week from Monday."

Ches nodded slowly and gave him another hug.

I raised my hand until I caught both of their attentions.

"Hi," I chirped. "Dorian Lake. I live here."

Ches sighed and guided her brother back to his seat. "You've met Ricky?"

"Briefly."

"So, Dorian, I need your help. We... need your help."

I folded my hands in front of me. "Let's start from the beginning so we don't miss anything important."

CHAPTER NINE

"**So, she's suddenly threatening to contest your visitation** privileges?" I asked as I poured some coffee for Ricky. I'd have offered some scotch, but having just learned that Ricky was a recovering heroin addict, I figured sticking to the coffee was a wise course.

"She's turning into some kind of vicious bitch. Ever since she kicked me out. It's like she just drank the Dr. Jekyll Haterade and has had it out for me ever since."

Ches put a hand on Ricky's arm to give it a squeeze.

I holstered the coffee pot and leaned against the countertop. "You're not far from the truth, Ricky. The change feels sudden for a reason."

He squinted. "Yeah. Ches tried to walk me through that, already."

I looked over to Ches, and she just shrugged.

"She's not crazy, Ricky," I said as I handed him the mug. "You're suffering from a slow-burn curse."

He pushed away from the table with the barest lift of a smirk. "Okay, here it comes. Ches told me you were into this voodoo stuff."

Ches gave him a quick shot to the ribs. "It's not voodoo, Ricky. This is important, so pay attention."

I took a long sip from my own mug to let Ricky recover.

"This isn't the worst possible news, you know," I added. "This means there's a chance the curse can be countermanded. This isn't something you did to yourself. This is something that was done to you, and as such it flows contrary to the natural order of things. Nature, frankly, hates having to deal with shenanigans of any sort, and tends to want to put things right. That means getting you off the heroin, and putting your family back together."

Ricky snarled. "What did I ever do to these... what are they called?"

Ches answered, "The Dead Dragons. A chapter from an old cabal from China. Spiteful little fuckers."

I pulled a chair from the table and took a seat. "It wasn't you they were targeting, Ricky."

Ches sighed. "It was me."

I lifted a hand and looked to Ches. "No, it wasn't you either. It was Gillette. She picked the fight with the Dragons, you happened to be in her group. It's a pernicious, dick-hole way of doing magic, but destroying the lives of loved ones is classic old school magical warfare. It's not your fault, Ricky." I turned to Ches and gave her a slow nod. "Or yours."

Ches's eyes softened, and she pulled her hand from Ricky's arm.

Ricky gave us both a look and smiled. "Oh, okay."

Ches straightened. "What's okay?"

"Nothing. Just, saying okay."

She slugged his arm. "Don't get like that. There isn't..." She made a back-and-forth gesture between me and her chin.

"I didn't say there was—" He repeated the gesture.

"I'm just saying, he's just my teacher."

"Okay."

"Stop it!"

"What, I can't say okay?"

I cleared my throat, and they both turned to face me.

"Focus, people."

Ches took a breath, and dove back in. "So, now Susanna—that's his wife—she's holding another court hearing over his head."

"She actually filed?" I asked.

Ricky shook his head. "It's just a threat. But, with the smack and all... I know she knows. That's where this is coming from."

"Tell me about the heroin."

He pulled his hands off the table and shrank a couple inches. "I don't know, really. I was at a bud's house. I'd just spent a week on someone's boyfriend's couch, and I was feeling kind of shitty in general. Someone came downstairs to shoot up, and then everyone had this stash they were pulling out. Pure stuff, they said. Didn't have to inject it, just had to snort it. I had maybe three vodka sours in me by then, so I just went with it. And, I don't know. For the first time since Suze kicked me to the curb, I actually felt good about myself. Crashed at his place for another week, sponging shit off of him when he felt charitable, then I decided I had to go find my own. They had the connections. All I had to do was..."

He stared at the table for a long moment.

Ches exhaled. "Dorian, it's important to know he didn't do this. I mean, it's the curse the Dragons put on him."

I gave Ches a cock of my head. "Huh?"

"It's not his fault he got hooked."

"That... doesn't matter, Ches." I pushed my mug away. "Look, I've worked with addicts for over ten years, now. I lost my righteousness over the subject a long time ago. It's a hell of a thing to happen to someone, and even if he did fall down the rabbit hole all on his own, I'd still want to help him."

She rocked back in her chair, eyes rimming red.

As did Ricky's.

"You're working on a charm for addiction?" I asked Ches.

She nodded.

"They were all a proof-of-concept for him, weren't they?"

A tear wandered down her cheek.

"Okay. I know a thing or two about addiction charms. Making them and breaking them. Here's the problem, though. This isn't normal addiction. It's a curse. I don't want you to stop what you're doing, Ches. Seriously. I think it could be your calling. But nothing you do for Ricky's addiction is going to lift the curse. We'll have to try and dismantle it energetically, or else some other damn thing will happen and he'll lose his kids anyway."

"I don't think Quinn will help," Ches mumbled.

"Agreed. So we'll have to do this the hard way." I turned to Ricky. "And we have ten days?"

"That's when I'm due to pick up the kids for my visitation day."

"Does she know you're out here?"

He shook his head.

"All right. I have some research to do. Happily, I don't have to go far. In the meantime, we really, really have to keep him out of sight."

Ricky's eyes shifted back and forth between me and Ches. "Why's that, exactly?"

Ches added, "Yeah, I was just going to put him up at my place."

"He's a pawn in Gillette's chess match with the Dead Dragons, is why. With the Presidium looking to scratch an itch, I really don't think it's smart to have him anywhere near an ATM or traffic camera, or anything else that'll paint a bullseye on him, or you, or me."

We sat in silence for a moment until I ran out of coffee. I stood up and set the mug in the sink.

"I'll put him in one of the bedrooms upstairs."

Ches let slip a dry snicker. "Which one? The room full of boxes or the other one full of boxes?"

"Ricky's choice. Whichever room he wants to stay in, he cleans out."

Ches's jaw stuck out, but Ricky tapped the table. "Sounds good, boss." He turned to Ches. "I think he's right. I don't want to give you any more stress."

"Ricky," she muttered, "I'm the reason you're in this to begin with."

"Still, you have school. A life. I'm going to be more problem than you need right now."

Before Ches could resist, I countered, "He's going to get worse."

They both looked up at me.

"I assume you're going to detox? You're not going to partake as long as you're here. That's just a given. We're all on the same page?"

They looked slowly one to another.

"You're about to pass through the gauntlet, Ricky. I can help with some charms, but it'll be Hell. I mean it, it'll be the Christian Hell. But

I'm here to tell you, from experience, there are worse fates to suffer. You get through this, you keep your strength and you survive this ordeal, and I'll do everything in my power to put your family back together."

Tears flowed as the siblings gripped one another in a tight hug. Once they composed themselves, they moved upstairs to start clearing out a guest bedroom.

And just like that, I had a roommate.

CHAPTER TEN

It didn't take long to move Ricky into the first hallway guest room. He didn't exactly pull up with a U-Haul full of furniture, after all. With Ches lending a hand, and Ricky doing most of the heavy lifting, we had him settled in an afternoon.

The trick wasn't the space he'd occupy. The trick was the withdrawal. Even though the heart of his addiction was a curse by the Dead Dragons, there was nothing I could do to allow him to avoid the body-churning turmoil he'd have to endure to get clean of the heroin. Nor was I an expert at that particular aspect of recovery.

Ches ran down a few volunteer organizations with support for addicts, one of which offered personal "coaches" for extreme cases. But Ricky wasn't exactly an extreme case, and it wasn't long before a couple thousand dollars secured Ricky an in-house facilitator to do some medical hand-holding.

That was the easy part.

My end of the equation was most certainly the bitch of the bundle. How would one dismantle a Chinese curse? Curse deconstruction was unfamiliar territory for me. This was a skill Emil had no problem skipping. I had to try and break this down on my own.

Curses are far more difficult to shake when you're the target. But if you're outside of the energy equation, the mechanics of a curse aren't so different from a hex. The major, crucial distinction being the power source. One can power a low-level hex with one's own personal energy... a bad idea, but still, possible. One could hitch a hex to a natural source such as a leyline or a lunar cycle. Or one could use my particular cheat... karma.

All Netherwork curses, however, require the Dark Choir to keep the gears running. As long as I kept clear of the power source, deconstructing a curse would simply be a matter of identifying which wire was red and which wire was black, and snipping the right wire.

I say "simply" largely because I'm an asshole. Truth is, the Dead Dragon curse was assembled from a Chinese context, and Asian magic was something Emil never had any real experience with.

Still, it was worth a few hours' study in my workspace. I took advantage of a late evening after Ches had gone home and Ricky had collapsed upstairs to descend into the basement and hit the books. I ran a quick finger over my standard texts along the expanded wing of my workspace, finding nothing remotely Chinese in content. This wasn't a problem I'd be able to run down in-house. I'd have to find a good source for Far Eastern Netherwork, and brave a face-to-face. Only one name from my recent dealings came to mind.

Lillian Hsu.

She was technically one of Edgar's contacts, keeping shop in downtown Pittsburgh. She made trips down to Frederick now and again to acquire certain materials her associates in Pittsburgh didn't need to know she was purchasing. I'd met her once on a reagent run, and she gave me her card if I ever wanted to "trade notes." At the time, I'd assumed that was some kind of pick-up line, but in retrospect one shouldn't assume that much about a career professional involved in Ancestor Enslavement.

I gave Lillian a call that evening, and reached voicemail immediately. Recognizing it was common practice for Practitioners to screen all calls, I left my name and number, and a brief reminder that I wasn't some random yahoo calling her business line. By the time I was halfway through whisking together an alfredo sauce for two, my phone rang.

"Mister Lake?" Lillian's voice buzzed into my ear.

"Yes, thank you for calling me back."

"I was not inconvenienced."

I whisked the skillet, searching for a pithy comeback.

"Awesome."

Shit.

Lillian prodded, "What can I do for you, Mister Lake?"

"Actually, I want to pick your brain. I have a new client whose problems are pulling me into unfamiliar territory. I think you can help me fill in some gaps."

"This is an active client?"

I pulled the skillet off the burner to keep the sauce from scorching. "Yes."

"Hmm, best not to converse over the phone." After a space, she continued, "I can't leave the city, but if you're able to drive in, I wouldn't mind being inconvenienced over a working lunch."

"I can do that. What day works for you?"

"Tomorrow, of course. Why wait?"

Why wait, indeed? Ricky was on a short clock, here.

I made arrangements with Lillian and hung up just as Ricky wandered back downstairs, hair a mess but otherwise chipper. Perhaps a bit too chipper.

"Hey," he chimed. "You look like you just won a lottery."

I shrugged. "Just not used to talking to a Netherworker who wasn't trying to make life more difficult."

Ricky leaned into the range to check out the dinner unfolding under my less-than-expert hands.

"Going all Food Network on me?"

"Don't get too excited, not until you taste it."

As we ate in awkward silence, I stole a glance or two. He was beaming with enthusiasm, head bobbing to music he was humming just under his breath. Every motion seemed to telegraph "I'm okay; everything is okay."

But it wasn't. He knew it. I knew it.

This was the manic brace before the anvil that would land on his head. Perhaps less an anvil, which hits with a sudden strike, but more a hurricane that batters the coast before it makes landfall. The winds were already blowing inside his body. Soon, the storm would come.

"So, tell me about this magic," he announced in between bites of fettuccini. "Is this, like, something that's going on worldwide or what?"

I nodded. "Since before humans figured out how to draw in the dirt with sticks."

"You'd think we'd make a bigger deal about it than we do. Us normal people, I mean." He winced and added, "Not that you're abnormal."

"You'd be surprised how much of my world you actually see every day, Ricky."

He paused mid-bite and lifted his brow.

I explained, "Coincidences. Those little nagging injustices you don't figure make any sense. Long spells of bad luck. The fortunate turns of the card that seem to give the same few people all the advantages."

"That's magic?"

"No, that's this shitty world we live in. Magic lies just underneath all of that, getting on with business."

He finished his bite and shook his head. "Figured you'd be rich, if you could make things happen."

"There's not that much I can do to improve my own situation. Magic is generally a zero sum game. If you take today, you'll pay tomorrow. I try to let the Cosmos decide what karma is available for cashing in."

"How did you get started with all of this?"

I pushed my plate away and leaned back in my chair. "My dad."

"He was a magic man, too?"

"The term I prefer is 'practitioner,' but no."

"I don't get it."

He obviously wasn't going to let this go, so I had to just dive right in and give him a double-barrel truth blast directly to the chest.

"I studied the hermetic arts to avenge my father's suicide."

Ricky blinked a few times, then slowly lowered his fork to his plate.

"How?"

"Hmm?"

He cleared his throat. "How do... how did you avenge a suicide?"

"Short answer, I didn't. There was nothing to avenge. He was an investment banker, and he made some poor decisions. Lots of them. He tried to shelter our family's money from the fallout, but when he discovered federal charges were on deck, he took a loaded Browning nine millimeter into his home office, put it under his chin, and shot himself."

"Damn."

I took a deep, cleansing breath. "Then it was just Mom and me. I was a senior in high school, already accepted at Yale. Everything was... impossibly horrible. But Mom and I had each other. Then her cab got t-boned by a truck at an intersection. Killed her instantly. Then it was just me."

Ricky ran his hand over the back of his head, eyes wide. "Holy crap!"

"They gave me my high school diploma, even though I never went back to school. Didn't make it to Yale, either. I spent half a year obsessing over it all. I mean, how the hell does a kid lose both parents in a week, right? There had to be something going on behind the scenes. I made a nuisance of myself with NYPD. They courteously requested that I stop contacting them. And by 'courteous' I mean 'we'll arrest you for offering a false instrument for filing.' Can you believe that's an actual misdemeanor?"

"That sucks, but what does it have to do with magic?"

I stood up and took my plate to the sink, dropping it unceremoniously with a clatter. "Thoughts get twisted inside a brain latched onto an obsession. Add grief and a healthy dose of entitlement, and you get a notion that you've become the victim of some kind of conspiracy." I turned to face Ricky. "I honestly can't tell you what drew me to esoteric alleys of inquiry. I think, yeah... it was some lame back page advertisement on one of those free papers you find sitting in the subway benches. Guy offering scrying services for money. I didn't really know what scrying was." I paused as Ricky's brow twisted in the middle. "It's the practice of following energy trails to distant locations. It's GPS for spooks."

"Gotcha."

I very nearly pulled out a lowball glass to pour myself a scotch, but caught myself. Okay, this roommate arrangement was going to be a problem.

Instead, I grabbed a tea from the fridge and continued, "It just got my wheels turning. I called this guy. Real asshole, I might add. But he gave me another name to contact. That one led me to another. So on, so forth. Spent a good year trying to find someone who could help me find out who was behind this... curse. I suppose that's what I thought it was. Some curse on my family. Funny how that sounds in retrospect." I took a swig of tea. "Then Emil found me and pulled me out of the fringe practitioner circuit before I got myself in real trouble."

"That was nice of him," Ricky offered with a helpless shrug. "Wasn't it?"

"Nicer than you realize. Emil... was not a good man. In fact, he was somewhat notorious around the world as being one of the preeminent Netherworkers. Had his heyday in the early seventies when the sheer insanity in the Middle East kept the old Levantine cabals busy."

Ricky stood up and brought his plate to the sink. "I understood maybe half of that."

"He was one of the bad guys."

"All right, that I understood."

"But he was scared, because... you know how I said magic is a zero sum game? Well, Emil had taken and taken in life. He knew his debt was going to get called up one day, and when it was, it wasn't going to be pretty. That's the price of Netherwork. You take tremendous, unbelievable power from a truly sinister source. The Dark Choir, he called it. And those ancient beings own you at that point on, into eternity, or whatever passes for eternity in their realm."

Ricky blanched. "You're talking about demons and crap?"

"Demons and crap. Heh. Well, they're a bit bigger than demons and crap, and a lot older."

"So that's why everyone isn't signing up to be a magic practitioner? It's evil?"

"Not always, but it's too easy to let evil in. Takes practice just to keep from getting people killed. And maybe that's why people don't get involved." I gestured with my tea bottle in broad circles. "It's not like you have to be some kind of Chosen One. That's what surprised me most when I began my training. I figured Emil chose me because I had some special quality. But that wasn't it. Anyone can learn this. It just takes years and years and years of mind-numbing study. You have to sacrifice your own life to the study. Nothing else can distract you, steal your focus. Not friends. Or love." I took another long swig of tea.

"Yeah, sounds like a real drag when you put it like that."

I gave Ricky a grin. "It has its moments."

A headache took Ricky before long, and he turned in early. The hurricane was approaching landfall. Once he was upstairs, and the floorboards overhead stopped squeaking with his movement back and forth, I finally pulled out the scotch.

Chapter Eleven

I wanted to get an early start for Pittsburgh to be sure I wasn't late for my lunch date with Lillian Hsu, seeing as to how cooperative she was being. However, I knew I had to wait for Ches to arrive and take her turn on Rickywatch. I wandered down the hallway after I'd gotten dressed. Before I could knock on his door, the sound of Ricky's sobbing flagged me off, so I left him be.

Ches arrived just after 7 a.m., looking like she had rolled directly out of bed and driven herself here.

"Good morning," I said as I held the door for her.

"Hey. How's Ricky?"

Nodding to the ceiling, I replied, "Sounds like he's hitting some emotions up there."

Ches nodded. "It's really unfair, what happened to him. They were so happy, Dorian." A tear welled up in her eye, and she rubbed it away on her sleeve with a centering grunt. "This is going to suck."

"When's the coach arriving?"

"Eleven. I'm skipping my noon class."

"Good," I said, moving for the kitchen. "Had breakfast?"

"Why good?"

"I'm taking a day trip."

She followed me into the kitchen, hands on her hips. "Wait, you're leaving? Today?"

"Before you get pissy about it, it's for Ricky." I grabbed some orange juice from the fridge and added, "I'm meeting someone who can walk me through Chinese curse crafting."

"Oh," Ches muttered. "Is there that big a difference?"

I shrugged. "Never studied Far Eastern hermeticism, so I have no idea."

She reached out and patted my arm. "Thanks, Dorian."

"Besides, I'm expecting you to take point with your brother. I'm more than happy to help, but I'm not holding his head when he yaks in the hall toilet." I poured a glass and lingered. "You might want to reconsider moving in."

I braced for an argument, but received nothing but a thoughtful nod.

I took a few sips of juice before venturing, "It would be easier for everyone."

"You're right. It would." She rolled her head, then closed her eyes and nodded once. "I'll grab some things this evening after you get back."

Footsteps bumped along the ceiling near the front of the house.

"He's up. You should probably go to him."

She nodded again and slipped out of the kitchen and up the stairs.

Well, then.

Another roommate.

Oddly, I felt more nervous about Ches moving in than Ricky.

The drive to Pittsburgh was uneventful. I'd almost have called it picturesque. Fruit trees had started blooming, and yellow buds of leaves were washing into vibrant greens along the Allegheny hills.

Then I hit Pittsburgh, and most of the green evaporated.

Lillian had arranged to meet me for lunch on Penn Avenue. I struggled a while for parking, but managed to make the bistro just before noon. I wandered inside, hands in my pockets, clutching a notepad under my arm. It was a casual place, but entirely populated with men and women in suits with briefcases stashed underneath their chairs. Something of a finance crowd, by the feel of it. I stepped through the space searching for Lillian, and it wasn't easy. I had met her exactly once, over five years ago. She had long hair, then. Which was why when the tall Chinese woman with a salt-and-pepper bob gave me an affably condescending beckoning gesture with her fingertips, it took me a moment to realize it was Lillian.

I approached her table and set my notepad down before offering a hand.

"Lillian?"

"Dorian Lake, good to see you again." She shook my hand before briefly returning her attention to a tablet in front of her on the table. She waggled a stylus between her fingers, tapping her tablet overhand with a series of quick stabs, much like a drummer hammering out a snare roll. Her tablet streamed with what looked like commodity prices. Perhaps stocks. It was hard to tell, as most of it was in Chinese.

She looked up and gestured at the opposite chair. "Oh, do sit."

"Thanks for meeting me," I replied as I took my seat. "I'm in a situation, kind of feeling my way through a dark room if you will."

She nodded as she stabbed her tablet some more. I didn't seem to have captured her full interest.

"...and I'm hoping you can turn a light on for me."

"Tell me about it."

I waited for her to give me her undivided attention, but as she leaned back in her seat with her eyes and hand still glued to her tablet, I decided it was best to simply trust her multi-tasking skills.

"I have a client who was cursed with a heroin addiction."

Lillian looked up for a brief second. "Are you sure the addiction was the curse?"

"Actually, no. It could have been more general, and the addiction is just how it manifested."

"Go on."

"That's basically it. His wife has already left him, and now she's threatening to challenge his parental rights. I'm trying to help him clean up before she takes him to court, and if I'm right... dismantling this curse will take the pressure off. Maybe even patch things up."

She lifted a finger and tapped out a quick message to someone.

"I do apologize," she offered with a sheepish smile. "I'm not usually this rude, but I have a shipping container of *shi* from Nanjing arriving in an hour from New York, and my network smoke-blower is having more trouble with the Feds than I'd like."

I gave her a cordial if baffled look.

She nodded with a smirk. "You'd know them as Fu Dogs."

"Ah. Statues? I'm assuming... they're statues, right?"

"Yes, they're statues. But no ordinary statues. They've presided over ancestral tombs for several hundred years. After eight weeks of transit on a freight liner, they're going to be... grumpy."

"Again, we're talking about statues?"

Lillian set down her stylus and cracked her knuckles. "I have over forty bound ancestral spirits loaned out across the Mid-Atlantic, and some of my customers are complaining of poor behavior. The *shi* are as much enforcers as they are guardians, and should bring my assets back into a cooperative posture. Granted," she added as she reached for some coffee, "the *shi* are bound to feel a degree of distress at being removed from their generational posts, but they are just animals."

As she said that last bit, her eyes adopted a razor sharp quality, and in a split-second I was reminded that Lillian was, in fact, one of the more successful Netherworkers in North America. She was a capable and dangerous woman, and it was a damned good thing I remembered this before I got too deep into my dealings with Lillian.

"I'll try to make this quick," I said, pulling out a pen. "I'm willing to do whatever it takes to dismantle the curse. I'd prefer to do so with a minimum of collateral damage, if you know what I mean?"

She straightened her sleeves and shifted her posture, leveling me with a casual stare. "First thing you should know is that, in the Chinese culture, the dividing line between dark magic and medicine isn't so clear. Get rid of your Aristotelian notions of elemental theory." Lillian returned her attention to her tablet, hammering out a quick message to her associate while muttering, "Dammit."

"So, what is the foundation of Chinese magic?"

Distracted by her tablet, she responded with a wave of her hand, "Traditional medicine." Lillian swept aside a text with her stylus and leaned back to rub the bridge of her nose. "When it comes to cursing an enemy, there are infinite possibilities. It would help if we could narrow down the one who crafted the curse to begin with. Their specific traditions, area of influence, elemental affinity—"

"I know who cast the curse."

She opened her eyes and tilted her head. "Oh?"

"Are you familiar with the Dead Dragons? A cabal in the Pacific Northwest?"

She stared stone-faced for a second before erupting into a fit of laughter. I looked around, giving onlookers a queasy wave of my hand to assure the bistro that we were not, in fact, lunatics.

"Oh, Mister Lake. Of course I'm familiar with the Dragons."

My heart picked up a few beats per second, and I leaned forward. "That's good. I mean, that is good, right? You have a finger on their pulse, then?"

She wiped a tear from her eyes as she continued chuckling. "I apologize, Mister Lake. If I had known, I wouldn't have had you drive all the way here."

"That doesn't sound terribly promising," I grumbled.

She wiggled a few fingers at me and returned her focus to her tablet. "Thank you, though. I really needed a laugh today."

"Well, I'm happy to help, but I get the feeling I'm somewhat fucked, here."

"Fucked may be a strong word." She finished another text, then continued, "I should be more clear. The Dead Dragons are mostly second generation immigrants, like myself. Their hermetic practice is as American in its mixture of traditions as is any cabal on this continent."

"Oh. So, you're saying I probably have as much chance of taking these guys on with my own knowledge as I do any other group of terrifying, death-dealing psychopaths?"

She simply nodded.

I sat staring at my notepad, and tucked my pencil back into my shirt pocket.

"Well, I'm very sorry to have inconvenienced you, Lillian."

She looked up at me with a quizzical lift of her brow. "I am not inconvenienced. I've enjoyed this."

"Out of curiosity," I asked as I pulled the notepad from the table and dropped it onto my lap, "if you don't mind me shooting straight with you... why are you helping me? I'm used to professionals in our line of work leveling me with some demand or trade for information."

"Would you like to offer me anything in return?"

I shrugged. "Um, I would. But I don't know what you'd want that wouldn't be karmically toxic for me."

She smirked. "I'm helping you, Mister Lake, because it suits me to do so."

"Well, then. I'm grateful. And a little weirded out. Still, though... I suppose I should leave you to your Fu Dogs."

She reached across the table and shook my hand with her fingertips before returning her attention to her tablet.

I stood up, slipping the notepad under my arm, then halted.

"Lillian?"

"Hmm?"

"How much soul magic do you run into in Chinese traditions?"

She looked up slowly from her tablet. "Soul magic?"

"Right. Say, a soul is separated from a physical body. Any precedent toward finding it again?"

She swiveled her head left and right slowly, then leaned forward. "So, the rumors are true?"

"Depends on the rumors."

"I heard you eliminated Neil Osterhaus."

I took my seat again, and nodded.

Lillian clapped twice. "I knew I liked you the first time I saw you!"

"I'm... glad?"

"Osterhaus was a weasel. I could never abide his amateurish condescension."

A smile spread across my face. "Well, he kind of pissed me off." My smile faded as I added, "Do the rumors say how I did it?"

"Rumors are you're quite the disciple of Emil Desiderio."

My chest warmed at that. Not sure why.

"Then, let's assume the rumors are true," I said. "If Lillian Hsu needed to locate her own soul in the Nether, where would she start looking?"

She reached across the table and laid a hand on mine. We sat there for a strange, but oddly comforting moment, before she pulled her hand back and tapped at her tablet.

"I would look for the one person on this continent who specializes in soul magic."

"And that would be?"

"A practitioner in Portland. Her name is Quinn Gillette."

My stomach soured. I rubbed the back of my neck and sighed.

Lillian lifted her eyes to me, and her mouth drew down into an O.

"I'm sorry, you've met Quinn?"

I nodded.

"I'll assume you are not on cooperative terms with her, then?"

I shook my head.

Lillian traced a slow circle on the table with her stylus. "You may have time. I can research the matter for you, if you like."

"I would very much like... but I don't think I have that much time."

"Why do you say that?"

I shifted in my seat and gave the room another glance for no specific reason before replying, "I've been visited by Felix Parrish."

Lillian blinked. Then she straightened in her seat as her face blanched.

"You..." she whispered.

"Yeah. Turns out, he's real."

Lillian leaned forward, sweeping her tablet out of the way. "You've seen Parrish?"

My blood cooled as her face drew into perplexed fascination.

"Yeah. We had a real peach of a conversation, the two of us."

"You'll pardon me if I seem dubious, but you would be the only person I've met who has seen Parrish and lived."

I lowered my chin. “Well, we’ll see about that ‘lived’ part.”

She reached for her tablet again, and swept her text windows aside, tapping away on a fresh, clear screen.

“I have people who have people. You know how this sort of thing goes.”

I nodded.

“Give me a few days, Mister Lake. I have contacts abroad that specialize in such specific practices.” She gave me a firm look. “I know we can solve this problem.”

I sat in stunned silence, which for me is something of an accomplishment. I finally stammered, “That—that would be amazing. I can’t thank you enough.”

Her smile lifted into an interesting curve.

“I don’t enjoy seeing the bastards win, Mister Lake. I prefer seeing our kind,” she added with a shake of her index finger between the two of us, “slither out from under their boot.”

My drive back to Baltimore was a dreamy wash of confusion and awe. I had, in the last year, assumed the worst about my fate without really accepting it. I found it hard, therefore, to really believe there was someone out there who could help me. And without expectation of compensation. True, Lillian could have been playing me in a particularly hard, perverse game of emotional rugby. But I’d come to develop a nose for practitioners. She didn’t give me the sense that she expected me to wallow in a state of obligation to her. She seemed earnest. There was some edge to her last words... “people like us.” I figured she’d been screwed over by some other Netherworker in her past, and felt like playing out some kind of vicarious justice through my personal drama.

I was okay with that.

I gave Ches a call on my way into Baltimore.

“Hello?”

“Ches, it’s Dorian.”

“Where are you?”

“Rounding Gettysburg. Should be there in a couple hours. Did the coach show?”

Ches sighed into her phone. "Yeah. She came and went."

"Everything okay?"

"No, Dorian. Everything is not okay."

I held my usual smart-ass response. That wasn't going to help, today.

"But she came?"

"Yes, she came. Walked me through the process. Dorian..."

"I know. It's going to be hard. Fill me in when I get there." I added as I changed lanes, "You're strong enough for this, Ches. You're a fighter. We're going to get him straightened out."

"You sound weirdly optimistic. You're not high, are you?"

"Let's just say I have a firmer grasp of how to solve all our problems."

"Our problems?" Ches prodded.

"Yeah. For once, I think we're going to win."

Chapter Twelve

Julian had left a couple voice mails on my phone, and I couldn't figure a good way to avoid returning his calls. Once I helped Ches carry two of her bags into the second, and last, of my spare bedrooms, I figured I'd have to touch base and see how much crow I'd need to fricassee in penance.

"Dorian?"

"Hey, Julian. I haven't forgotten. Kitchen manager. I'm on it."

"Please get on it quickly."

I paused to hold the phone against my shoulder as Ches brandished an empty toilet paper roll at me in the hallway. I gave her a "one second" finger and continued, "Tomorrow. Honest to God."

How did my life get so complicated in such a short span of time?

"Dorian?"

"Julian?"

"Is everything okay with you? I mean, with this Presidio thing?"

"It's 'Presidium,' and yes. I'm totally Switzerland. Why?"

Julian tapped something in the background, probably typing on his computer.

"So, you're getting a call from Ronetta."

"Who's that, again?"

"Ronetta Claye?"

Oh, right. The new Julian.

"What's up?" I asked.

"No clue. And that worries me. Like, really. I don't know what she's up to, but the second she starts end-running me, I start stressing."

"I'm sure it's nothing, Julian. Probably just wants to buy a charm or something. Or, you know... not."

"Yeah. Keep me posted. I'm not joking. Whatever she tells you, I need to know, Dorian."

"Roger."

Ches spent her first night in my house in Ricky's room. The jitters and itches took him solid, and by midnight the retching had started. As I lay in bed, listening to the sounds of a man being tortured by his own body, I was thoroughly thankful to have Ches there to guide him along. I like people... generally. But I was ill-prepared to hold Ricky's hand through this. Ches was my human half, the decent soul to walk him back to center.

I, on the other hand, could barely think of anything beyond beating Parrish at his horseshit game. If Lillian really had overseas contacts who could find my soul, then I might end up thumbing my nose at the entire Dark Choir. Emil would have been proud.

Ches holed up with Ricky during breakfast. I flipped up a couple dozen pancakes, in case they decided someone needed sustenance, and jumped out for the tavern.

My phone rang en route. Ronetta Claye, as forewarned.

"Mister Lake?"

"Ms. Claye. How are you this morning?"

"Very fine. How are you?"

"Elated. How can I help you, Ms. Claye?"

"I was wondering if you could meet my associate, Detective Grant Turner, in the next couple hours?"

I turned north onto the MLK, gritting my teeth. Here it came.

"What's this about?"

"I'm aware of certain skills you've offered Julian Bright in the past."

Ah hell. I was very sure this was news to Julian, which meant she had more oars in the water than he had given her credit for.

"If that's the case, Ms. Claye, then I'd recommend we forego a cell phone conversation on the matter."

After a pause, she responded, "Detective Turner will be at the Enoch Pratt library downtown in a half hour. If you're available, I can have him wait for you."

Enoch Pratt? What the hell was brewing with this woman?

"Let's say I'm available, if very nervous."

She coughed out a thin chuckle. "I'm sorry. I'm not used to this."

"No sweat," I declared in an up-swing timbre, "if you ever get used to this kind of conversation, I'm afraid I wouldn't trust you much more than I trust black helicopters."

I killed a couple hours at the tavern, rummaging around a couple job sites before heading back up Light Street for my meeting.

I pulled up Cathedral Street and found a street spot near the Basilica. I spotted a portly, red-faced fellow in a cheap suit lingering by the front steps of the Enoch Pratt Free Library, flanked by two uniformed cops.

I stepped up the front steps and cleared my throat.

Turner spun on his heel and gave me a low, furry eyebrow.

"You the psychic?"

I winced. "Uh, no. No, I'm not."

"Oh." He turned away.

"Detective Turner?" I nudged.

He looked over to his compatriots with a sigh. "Dorian Lake? That's you?"

"That's me. Not a psychic, though."

His face blossomed into a particularly pissed shade of red, and he looked over to the taller of his two uniformed escorts.

"Deputy Mayor Claye said you was here to assist on Enoch Pratt."

I shoved my hands into my pockets and shrugged. "Yes, well, Ms. Claye sent me to help with something, Grant."

"That's Detective Turner, asshole."

Oh, lovely.

"Well, Detective Turner… before I turn around and drive back home, maybe we should give her the benefit of the doubt and start over?"

"Huh?"

Jesus. This was going to be an agony, I could tell.

I extended my hand. "Dorian Lake."

He looked at my hand like it was a limp, dead mackerel.

"Detective Turner. Special investigations."

Oh, thanks so much, Ronetta.

"What happened at Enoch Pratt?"

"Some stupid hooliganism. Probably teens being smartasses, but they left behind some Satanic shit, so we have to treat it like an occult crime."

"Well, let's go check out your Satanic shit then, shall we?"

The uniformed police flanked us as we proceeded along the steps. Two police units were parked in front of the building in the drop-off zone, and more uniforms were guarding the doors to keep the public out. Turner trotted up the steps and nodded to the police as he ushered me through one of the double-doors leading to the library's lobby.

As we stepped into the wide, marble-floored space, and that pungent, thrilling smell of old books smacked me in the face, Turner pointed for one of the two wings.

"Claye said you was some kind of psychic."

"She's wrong."

"Then what are you?"

I gave him a deadpan and replied, "Some weird Satanist." I winked. "Don't worry. We take care of our own, Detective."

I left him in the lobby as I stepped past two more police. The scene before me was one of frozen bedlam. Books lay strewn on tables, desks, and the floor. Most of the shelves had been emptied, leaving blank, yawning spaces where the books had been. I turned a slow circle and traced a series of symbols painted on the walls with my eyes.

Turner called from the wing entrance, "Any of that make any sense to you?"

I took a moment, lifting a finger to keep Turner quiet as I racked my brain. Some of these symbols were familiar, but only in a vague sense.

My eyes lowered to the floor, and my toes tingled. I trotted for an open staircase leading to the second-floor stacks, bustling halfway up.

Turner trotted into the room. "What's going on?"

I lifted another finger, surveying the pattern of the felled books. A widdershins spiral.

"Exit point," I whispered.

"You know what this is?"

I sucked in a breath and started descending the steps. "I do, in fact. Looks like a jinx."

"A jinx, huh?" he harrumphed. "Doesn't sound so bad."

"Yeah, well, Fat Man and Little Boy sounded downright charming until we dropped them out of a couple airplanes."

I knew where the exit point was... but I had more information here than I did in Gettysburg. The sigils, for one. It could have been the jinx in the daycare was a test run for something bigger. But seeing as to how this hit was somewhat harmless, I wondered what this was a dry run for?

The spiral of tossed books began in four distinct points, each at the termination of what I assumed were incantations. I reached into my pocket for my pendulum, but realized it wasn't there. In fact, that pendulum was dust.

"Crap."

I'd have to replace that thing.

Turner shoved his hands into his pockets. "Well, Lake? What's the verdict?"

"Hmm?"

"Who did it?"

I gave Turner a nice, slow side-eye. "I have no clue."

"Then what good are you?"

"A fine question, Grant. Let's start with the fact that someone's thrown a substantial packet of chaos energy into a public library, and finish with the fact that there are maybe three people the city can call for this kind of thing, and the other two are as likely to raze the site to the ground as anything. So, maybe just give me some time to decipher these symbols. I might have more ground to stand on."

Turner shrugged. "Don't matter, no how. Just a couple teenagers being smartasses. Like I said. We'll get this cleaned up in an hour, and we'll forget about it."

"Right."

He lifted his chin at me. "What?"

"Good luck getting it cleaned up in an hour."

He swiveled with his arms stretched out. "It's just some spray paint, some books tossed around. No federal case here, Lake."

"All right, then." I pulled out my phone. "When it comes seven in the morning, and you've tried picking up these books for the twelfth time, then maybe you'll cut me some slack." I lifted the phone to photograph the walls. "Will this be a problem?"

He shook his head with a sneer.

I snapped a dozen photos of the symbology, and one more of the floor before moving for the lobby.

Turner trotted after me with a quick mutter to one of the uniforms.

I led the way out of the library, pocketing my phone.

"So, Lake, you get paid for this?"

"Generally speaking. Though I've yet to make an arrangement with Ms. Claye, but yes. I am a professional."

Turner snickered.

"What's so funny?" I asked, instantly regretting baiting him into further conversation.

"No, I knew you had something worked out with that gay, Bright. I didn't—"

"Excuse me?" I grunted.

He snapped his head up, then smirked. "Huh? I said—"

"What did you say just now?"

I took a step into Turner, and he backed away a half-step before checking himself.

"That guy. Julian Bright. I said you had something worked out, you know."

"You sure that's what you said?"

Turner's mouth pulled into a snarl.

My pulse pounded in my neck, and my hands balled into fists.

The uniforms nearby approached, and Turner let them.

I managed to stick a finger into Turner's chest and say, "You're going to watch what you say about Julian Bright, my friend."

One of the uniforms slipped between the two of us, with a, "Take it easy."

"Yeah," I snapped. "Thought so." I turned back up the street, adding over my shoulder, "Good luck with the books."

My stomach was still twisted in a knot by the time I reached my car. I wasn't prepared for the visceral reaction I had with Turner. Really, it took me by surprise as much as him. But the jab at Julian just boiled my piss to no end.

"I'd say good afternoon, Dorian, but you look like you're ready to punch something."

I shook my head and looked to my left to find Father Mark watching me across the street.

I un-balled my fists and took a breath before jogging across to meet him.

"Sorry. Just had someone chap my ass, is all."

"Hopefully he won't end up on the business end of your... well, your business."

I grinned. "Jury's out. Visiting the Basilica?"

He nodded. "I want to say you're looking better, Dorian. I really do."

"That's two of us, Padre."

"Walk and talk?"

I stepped alongside him as we headed up Cathedral Street. "I just think maybe I haven't been the best business partner in the world."

"Business partner? This is..." He snapped his fingers "Julian, right?"

"Yeah. He's busting his balls making this tavern what it is. I want to hold up my end, you know."

"Sounds admirable."

"I know there's people who think right and wrong are a matter of how hard you work," I said. "Not sure if that's too Calvinist for your particular tradition."

Father Mark snickered. "It's something I recognize, though it's not particularly grounded in sound Biblical doctrine. It is something of an American tradition, though."

I ventured, "What about homosexuals, Padre?"

"What… about homosexuals?"

"Does the Catholic Church have any space set aside at all for homosexuals? Or is that still kind of a deal breaker?"

Father Mark laughed and lifted a hand. "I'm going to speak for myself here, Dorian. There are no deal breakers. All are welcome. What we make of ourselves as people, as believers, that's our personal mission. And I mean 'personal,' because it's a matter of relationship between yourself and God."

"So, a man can be gay, and he can be a good Catholic?"

"I find the term 'good Catholic' to be a smoke screen, more often than not. What say we focus on what's important toward being a good person? Then we'll sort out to what extent we rely on doctrine."

I turned a circle, taking in the buildings surrounding us.

"Padre? You really think there's some higher power for good out there?"

"I do. Okay… next softball question?"

"I think that would be an incredible feeling."

Father Mark crossed his arms. "What would be? Believing in God?"

"No. Believing in good."

He opened and closed his mouth a few times, before nodding. "You have good inside you, Dorian. You care about the soul of your friend. That's an indication of faith, if ever I saw one."

I nodded, then turned back to my car.

"See you Monday, Padre."

I drove around the block and steered myself toward the tavern. Julian would be inside, probably hammering out the want ad I was supposed to be writing. I pulled the Audi into the rear parking lot, then sat staring at the back door. I knew that, if I set foot inside, I'd get sucked into hours of responsibility. On another day, I could do it. Another week, when I didn't have Ches's brother detoxing in my spare bedroom. When I didn't have a curse to dismantle, or a cadre of chaos magicians with a serious hate-on for public libraries to track down.

When I didn't have the Presidium breathing down my neck.

So, I drove home.

CHAPTER THIRTEEN

The next morning was a slow, desperate struggle to drag myself out of bed. I'd spirited one too many fingers of scotch behind Ches and Ricky's back the past evening. Through sheer force of will, and a reminder to my subconscious that I had a real lead on finding my soul again, I managed myself upright and dressed. As I ventured into the hallway, I froze at the sight of Ches meandering from the hall bath with a toothbrush in her mouth, wearing a t-shirt and underwear.

"I, uh... oh," I stammered.

She paused and gave me an indifferent blink before continuing brushing her teeth.

Ricky's door opened. He took a half-step into the hallway before he spotted me. He was pale, his entire face glistening with sweat.

He cleared his throat a couple times to get his voice going. "Morning."

"How're you holding up?" I asked over Ches's shoulder.

He shrugged. "Not very."

"Well, hang in there. Or, you know, insert helpful platitude here."

Ches hopped back into the bathroom to spit before returning to join the conversation.

"How'd your meeting go?"

"Good and not-so-good. It's overall positive, I think. In a nutshell, the Dead Dragons aren't exactly Chinese purists, so I'm back to the primer books."

Ches shook her head. "Okay, that's the not-so-good, but you said there was good?"

"Lillian might be able to help me out with my… condition."

Ricky asked, "Condition?"

"Soul. I might finally have a lead on finding my soul."

Ricky ran a hand over the back of his neck and screwed his brow into a question.

Ches held a hand out to him. "It's kind of a long story." She turned to me. "That's great news, Dorian."

"Thanks. We'll see."

She added, "But how does this help Ricky?"

I sucked in a breath, then held it. She looked at me with wide, earnest eyes. As my stomach tightened, I recognized she wasn't trying to sound like a callous malcontent. She was just focused on her problem.

I wove around her for the stairs and descended to get some coffee inside me. Almost made it to the kitchen, too, before the doorbell froze me in my tracks.

Hardly anyone visited me unexpectedly. Maybe only Edgar, but with the Swains vacationing in Orlando, that left salesmen and really bad news. Steeling myself, I approached the front door, keeping a free hand near the darquelle mounted on the wall nearby, and peeked out the sidelite.

And I found the last person I expected to be standing on my door stoop.

I opened the door with what must have been a staggeringly baffled face.

"Morning, Reed," I stated something like a question.

"Dorian," he responded.

"What brings you back to Charm City?"

"I have a message from Mister Clement." He reached into his coat and produced an envelope.

I wrinkled my nose and eased my grip on the door. "I'm not selling Emil's Library. I think I was pretty clear."

He brandished the envelope, and I finally took it. As I moved to open it, he reached out a hand.

"You might want to open that inside."

I gave Malosi a trepidatious sigh, then ushered him in.

He stopped at the threshold and gave both jambs and the lintel a good, long look.

"Yeah," he grumbled. "He said this would need work."

"What would? Who said? What?"

Reed stepped inside and closed the door behind him. "Getting ahead of myself. I'm supposed to help you batten down the hatches."

"Batten down the—who says that?" I gestured to the couch as I moved for my roll top desk, but Malosi just continued lumbering near the foyer.

"Okay," he enunciated with an edge of impatience, "Jean thinks you need to bolster your wards."

I snatched a letter opener from my drawer and dropped into my swivel chair. "That's your specialty, now?"

"Security has always been my specialty."

I grinned. "Yeah, suppose that's true." I slid the letter opener into the corner of the large brown envelope and sliced it open. "Though it doesn't exactly fill my chest with rainbows and sunshine to think he's sending you to help me with my own—"

I swallowed my words as I slipped the contents of the envelope onto the desk. Glossy photos. Gruesome photos.

I pushed away.

"Oh, shit," I whispered.

"You know who that is?" Malosi asked, more with a tone of genuine inquiry than foreboding.

I nodded.

"Jean said this would mean something, and that you'd understand why I'm here."

Clement was correct. Absolutely, dead correct.

Voices rose overhead as Ches seemed to be talking Ricky away from some emotional ledge. Their murmuring faded into the spiraling chaos inside my head.

Malosi looked up at the ceiling, then drew a heavy breath.

"Sorry," I mumbled. "I have a thing. I mean... I'm told I have to use my nouns better, so I guess you can call them unexpected guests."

"That will make it more difficult."

I shot Malosi an impatient eye. "You think?"

Footsteps bounded down the stairs, and I hoped that, if it was Ches, she'd have put on pants by now.

"Dorian, where's—oh. Uh, hi."

I swiveled in my chair to find Ches, with pants, eyeballing the broad, manicured Polynesian in his tailored suit with significant tension.

I waved a hand back and forth between them. "Reed Malosi, Francesca Baker. Ches, this is Reed."

Ches held her position, frozen in place.

Reed, however, removed his gloves and took graceful steps forward to offer his hand. "Good morning."

Ches shook his hand as she stared up at his face, then turned slowly to me. "Dorian?"

"We have problems," I said.

"As opposed to any other week?"

I stood up, tapping the photos of a woman lying face-down in a pool of her blood, with an entry wound in the back of her head.

"I need coffee," I grumbled, sweeping toward the kitchen.

Ches grunted near the desk as I rounded the doorway into the kitchen.

"Do we know this person?" she called out.

"It's Lillian Hsu."

"Who the hell is—"

"The person I met with yesterday. About Ricky."

Ches stepped into the kitchen with Malosi close behind.

"Oh," she breathed. "Oh. Shit."

"Yep."

She turned to Malosi. "You did this?"

He drew in a breath to answer, but I cut him off.

"Reed's on our side, Ches. He may be the harbinger of stupendously horrible news, but he's one of the good guys."

"Well, glad to hear someone's on our side," she groused. "What does this all mean?"

I shoveled a nice, stomach-melting dose of coffee grounds into the maker.

"The Presidium's on the warpath, is what it means."

"The Presidium?" Ches repeated. "Why do they care about this woman?"

"She's a Netherworker. Deals in ancestor trafficking."

"You're going to have to walk me through that."

I wrapped up with the coffee maker and turned, crossing my arms. "She leverages ancestral debts. It's... horrible stuff. I mean, she was one of the nicest Netherworkers I've met in, well... ever. But she definitely fell on the Black Bag list when it comes to the Presidium's sense of Thou Shalt Not Be Criminally Vile."

Ches stepped toward me. "But, isn't that what the Presidium does? Why's this making you turn white?"

"Besides being my one hope for finding my soul? Oh, nothing. Except, of course, that this means the Presidium has likely started a purge."

Malosi shifted in place near the doorway.

"Reed," I barked, "you're making my teeth itch. Please sit."

He stared at me for a moment before finally stepping into the kitchen, sliding out a chair, and easing his enormous frame into it.

"Thank you," I murmured before turning to Ches. "This happens every now and then. The Presidium gets sloppy over time, indulging their political skullduggery. They lose sight of their mandate, which is policing all hermetic practices on this continent. Well, you and I both know Netherwork is at an all-time high right now. People like Quinn and the Dead Dragons prosper on the West Coast because the Presidium has their collective heads so far up their collective asses, no one has the means to shut them down."

"So, now they're pulling their heads out of their asses, is what you're saying?"

"Well, after what happened with Congressman Durning, I knew there would be a response. I just didn't think they'd go Josef Stalin on us."

Ches paced a tight circle. "So, what do we do?"

"We hole up." I gave Reed a nod. "Batten down the proverbial hatches."

"You think they're going to come for you?" Ches asked.

"Not sure. I have a really weird relationship with the Presidium. They've tolerated me so far. Now that they've got all available panties in a wad, I don't feel like pushing my luck." I turned to Malosi. "I'm guessing we're starting with re-working the wards on my house?"

He nodded once.

"Should probably hit the tavern, too."

Malosi asked, "What tavern?"

"Oh, I bought a tavern downtown."

"Really?"

"Yeah. Wood paneling, leaded glass. Real old English pub feel."

"Nice."

Ches held up her hands. "What about Ricky?"

I took a breath and thought about it.

"This will be exactly the wrong environment to reach out to Netherworkers. The Presidium probably knows I spoke with Lillian the day they punched her card. Might put extra scrutiny on me. Plus, it's no secret the Presidium has me in a special category, and I'll bet good money every Netherworker out there is going to equate 'talking to Dorian Lake' with 'getting shot in the back of the head.' We're going to have to work Ricky's problem in-house."

"Can we do that?" she asked.

"It'll be more difficult."

Malosi offered, "There is one Netherworker I know who will speak to you."

I gave Malosi a sneer. "Right. And I suppose Clement's going to help purely out of a sense of fond nostalgia?"

Malosi stood up. "Nostalgia's not exactly why he sent me here."

"I know what Clement wants. And we both know I'm not selling. So, if it'll save us all an awkward moment, maybe you should just hop a train back to New York."

Ches stepped between us and put her hand on her hip. "Wait, what's all of this about?" She turned to Malosi. "Who's Clement?"

Malosi gestured at me with a graceful lift of his wide palm.

I huffed and grabbed a mug from the cabinet. "Jean Clement was a student of Emil Desiderio. Before my time. Back when Emil was still balls-deep in Netherwork."

"And this man can dismantle Ricky's curse?"

I lingered as I poured my coffee. Could he? It was possible. Indeed, Emil was notorious for his grounding in hermetic fundamentals. If he had given Clement a more thorough education in Netherwork and curse theory than he did me, then Clement might be the best source of information I could hope for.

But at what price?

"He wants the Library, Ches," I muttered before taking a long sip of bracing java.

"The Library. Okay."

I watched her over the rim of my mug. "He wants to buy it. The whole thing."

"So, you're saying you can fold Ricky's curse into the price tag, and we're golden?"

Her eyes darted back and forth between me and Malosi.

"Ches," I whispered. "That Library was bequeathed to me specifically to keep people like Clement from using it."

"Dorian, I say this with all the respect in the world... but I don't fucking care what Emil intended."

I squinted and held my tongue.

She continued, "This is my brother. It's my fault this happened to him."

"You need to stop saying that. It's not your fault. It's the Dead Dragons' fault."

"Dorian? Please. Talk to this guy. We only have eight days until he has to be in Portland." She paced a quick circle and added, "We're on one hell of a stopwatch, here."

I pulled in a long breath, then answered, "Let me make a couple calls. See what I can do."

She stared at me for a while, her eyes lifting at the bottoms, fighting off some kind of raw emotion I couldn't fathom, before she turned and trotted back upstairs.

I finished my coffee and dropped the mug in the sink before turning to Malosi.

"Don't know anything about curses, do you Reed?"

He shook his head. "That's really more your thing."

"So, what about these wardings? How long will this take you?"

"Depends on how hard you fight me on this."

I shoved my hands into my pockets. "Reed, after what we went through, I figure you've earned the benefit of the doubt."

He let slip a brief grin.

"Then it'll take a couple days. I intend to be thorough."

"Well, all right. A, that's good to hear, because I'm about done with dabblers. But, B, you're going to stay here overnight?"

"I can get a hotel. Clement's funding this little field trip."

I shook my head. "Not with the Presidium's ass nice and puckered, you don't." I did some mental math, then continued, "Ches can share a room with Ricky. Already cleared out the second bedroom. You'll stay here."

"Only if you admit you just feel safer with me in the house."

I stepped around Malosi toward the stairs. "Oh, I absolutely feel safer with you around. I actually got kidnapped last year, and things would have been a hell of a lot more comfortable for me if you were there."

I froze in the doorway.

Wexler.

She was the one who'd nabbed me and had me hand-delivered in a black hood. Lucky for me, she just wanted to talk.

So, now I was the one who wanted to talk. If the Presidium was calling down another purge, it might behoove me to solidify myself in their good graces. And Wexler seemed to be on "my side," whatever that meant. Seemed. It was impossible to know for sure.

Then again, sticking my head out of my foxhole might be just the perfect way to get it blown off. It was academic, at any rate. I didn't have any means to contact Wexler. I remained at her disposal, not the other way around. Switzerland. Remember Switzerland.

Malosi cleared his throat. "So..."

"What do you need? Reagent-wise?"

"I brought everything I need."

"Good, because my guy is out of state at the moment."

Good thing, too. If I had to deal with keeping the Swains safe in this nasty climate, I might have had an aneurysm.

Malosi got to work scrying out the leylines of my house while I bustled more of my bric-a-brac out of the back bedroom. It was loaded with dust and choked with boxes of old books and mementos which I frankly no longer remembered. I took a water break after the eighth trip down the stairs, and took a good survey of the situation.

Primary need was defense. I had to shore up in case the Presidium, or Parrish, decided to go on the offensive. But Malosi was seeing to that, and as I watched him smudge several air registers in the front room, I recognized he was about to get anal retentive, hermetically speaking. I took that worry off my shelf for the moment to concentrate on my next priority.

Which was Ricky.

We had eight days to dry him up. Less a day, accounting for travel. He seemed to be progressing well. The vomiting had subsided, and now he was in the jittery itch phase. I felt confident he could put a decent face forward when he picked up his kids in a week. The question remained, however, would he stay clean? Breaking the curse had more to do with how his ex-wife treated him. I was certain her affections had soured thanks to the curse. If I could patch his family back together, it would remain incumbent upon Ricky to keep them patched together. It wasn't fair, but it was his burden now.

And with all of that taken care of, I had to deal with Parrish. Which was to say, I had to find my soul before he did. I was absolutely certain he was more capable than I was at locating and ensnaring an itinerate soul. And from his tone, it seemed he felt this task was well beneath him. That could've played in my favor, if he intentionally dragged his feet. Or, it could've screwed me if he decided to knock it out quickly in order to move on to whatever infernal business he was attending to.

Ches was right. We were on one hell of a stopwatch.

So I decided to make a call.

Chapter Fourteen

Hello?"

"Zeno? It's Dorian Lake."

After a particularly annoyance-saddled sigh, he said, "I told you I didn't want you to call me. Or talk to me. Ever."

"I know, but I'm up against it."

Another sigh, with yet more annoyance.

"Lake? I'm busy."

"You always are, being about the only Netherworker I know who can operate under the Presidium's skirt the way you do."

"You're trying to flatter me, Dorian. I'm very sure it isn't working the way you thought it would."

"Zeno? I need your help. It's probably a very minor thing for you. Won't take long."

His voice muffled as he barked some chiding command to what I assumed was his latest Lodge recruit. Finally, he returned his attention to me. "Like I said, I'm busy. Also, not interested."

"Come on, Frater. You know I can pay you."

"And you know I don't need your money."

Shit. He was right. Last time I dealt with Frater Zeno, I had juicy information to pass his direction. What did I have these days?

Well, besides the fact that the Presidium might very well have painted a bullseye on the back of his argyle sweater.

"I have information for you."

A long pause, then, "Regarding?"

"Your safety."

An even longer pause.

"This had better not be a threat, Lake. I'm having a bad week, and I might grow discourteous if I thought you were threatening me."

"No, Frater, I'm not threatening you. But you are in danger, and I think you'd want to know from where, at the very least."

This sigh was heavier, more annoyed, and arguably more condescending than any sigh I've heard before.

"One p.m. No sooner, no later. I have exactly no time for this, so if you meet me at the steps to my Lodge, I'll listen to what you have to say on the way to my car. I recommend you practice your speech ahead of time."

I gripped my phone, and took a cleansing breath. "It's always good talking with you, Frater. I'll see you at one."

I set the phone down and drummed my fingers on the roll top desk. God, I hated that prissy little man.

When lunchtime rolled around, I hammered out some grilled cheese sandwiches and a couple cans of tomato soup. Malosi inhaled his lunch and continued with his work. I left a tray at Ricky's door for the Bakers, then descended to gather my things. I wanted to run by the tavern before I made my meeting with Frater Zeno. When I had my attaché put together and was about to head for the front door, both of the Bakers stepped into the front room. I paused and gave Ricky a tuck of my head.

"Hey, there. How are you feeling?"

His fingers trembled, and his face was still pallid, but he gave me a good, solid nod.

"Hang in there, brother," I offered. "We'll get you ship shape and Bristol fashion."

Ricky smiled, then looked down at Ches.

She pulled her hair up with a grimace. "It's not just you. He always talks like that." She stepped forward with a sharp eye on me. "So, where are you running off to?"

"I'm going to see if I can't solve Ricky's problem."

Without missing a beat, she answered, "Then I'm coming with you."

I opened my mouth, but nothing came out. Probably a good thing, because she quickly added, "Unless you were under the impression that I was going to sit here and let you solve all our problems?"

"No," I mumbled. "I didn't think that... I wasn't—"

"Good." Ches turned to Ricky. "Your coach will be here right at noon."

Malosi lifted his head and lifted his brow with a bemused smirk.

I waved him off. "Don't worry about her. She's not a permanent resident. Not yet, anyway."

The two of us hit the road. Ches sat glum in the passenger seat, staring forward through the windshield. She didn't make a comment until I turned up Light Street.

"Where are we going?"

"Need to stop by the tavern."

"For what?"

"Business."

She sniffled and shook her head.

"What?" I prodded.

"Nothing."

"That was a something."

She crossed her hands and gave me a rigid smile. "No, it was nothing. You're doing great. This tavern is such a great idea, and I respect you not only as a teacher, but as an entrepreneur."

I took advantage of a yellow light and brought the Audi to an early stop. With a half turn in my seat, I asked, "Do we have a problem?"

"Yeah, we do. You spend half a year as a complete absentee partner in this place, but now that we have a real, urgent problem you decide this is the right moment to get involved?"

I lifted a hand. "I've been involved, Ches. Maybe not as much as I should, but this isn't some stall tactic. Julian put me together with one of the other Deputy Mayors... or is it deputies mayor? Is it like Attorneys General, or—"

"It's Deputy Mayors."

"Anyway, I have some consultant work for the city, and it's basically exactly what we saw in Gettysburg."

She blinked, then turned toward me just in time for the green light. "Wait, what?"

"The jinx? Yeah. Someone lobbed one into the Enoch Pratt Free Library."

"Who would jinx a library?"

I shrugged. "Who would jinx a daycare?"

"I figured it was some private grudge with the owners."

"Maybe not. Maybe it was some kind of dry run?"

"For the library? Again, I have to ask what's the point in jinxing a library?"

I pulled us into the alley to the back of the tavern. "Maybe it's another practice hit? These chaos magicians may be working their way up to something big. Like, huge. Deirdre told me the daycare owners found sigils painted on the walls, but cleaned it up before she could see them. This time, we still had them intact at Enoch Pratt. I took photos of the sigil work, and plan on cross-referencing it to see if there's some kind of identifiable cabal at work."

I put the car in park and turned to Ches, who had one eye squinted at me.

"Let me have a crack at those sigils."

"You're... busy. With Ricky."

"To be honest, I could use the distraction. I love my brother, but this is kind of killing me."

I nodded. "I'll send you the photos."

We sat for a moment, staring at the back of the tavern. Finally I turned off the key and asked, "Sure it's not Deputies Mayor?"

I led Ches through the still-plastic-wrapped kitchen and through to Julian's office. We found Julian clicking furiously through a spreadsheet on his computer. He didn't notice us until I cleared my throat.

He looked up and smiled. "Dorian?"

"Hey, partner." I lifted a hand to Ches. "You remember Francesca Baker?"

He stood up and held out a crisp hand to shake. "Of course, Miss Baker. Always a pleasure."

She shook his hand and gave me a cock of her chin.

"See? Some people know how to treat me with respect."

Julian stabbed a finger at me. "You're disrespecting her?"

I held up hands in defense. "No! What? No."

Julian dropped back into his seat and laced his hands behind his head. "So, any luck filling the position?"

"Not yet," I answered.

He nudged, "Put out an ad?"

"Uh..."

Julian nodded. "Good thing I did."

"I'm sorry. It's been a hell of a week."

"Always is, Dorian."

I looked to Ches for backup, but she seemed disinclined to provide it.

I grumbled, "Hey, if you knew what I've been up against—"

"So, tell me," he countered, leaning forward with an expectant face.

I stood in silence, looking back and forth between the two.

"It's complicated," I muttered.

Julian's face melted into defeat. "Maybe, Dorian, just maybe... if you let me in on what's dividing your attention, I'd understand? Maybe even help?"

I shoved my hands in my pockets, searching for the correct response.

Ches said, "It's my fault, Julian."

"No, it's not," I blurted.

She held out a hand and nudged me aside. "My brother's in town, and he's not well. Dorian's trying to help me."

Julian leaned forward. "What's the matter?"

"Heroin," she replied before I could stop her. "He's trying to clean up, and Dorian's putting him up at his place."

Julian turned his eyes to me, his brow easing.

"See? That's exactly the kind of personal information that makes me want to keep filling in for you, Dorian." He turned back to Ches. "Is there anything I can do to help? I know several people. The lead on the State Heroin Taskforce. Wonderful man by the name of—"

"We're set," Ches answered with a cheerful nod. "Dorian's taking care of it."

Julian nodded. "Okay, but you let me know if there's anything at all I can do to help."

She smiled and nodded again.

Julian turned his attention back to me. "So, if you haven't hired us a kitchen manager yet, then what brings you to the tavern during business hours?"

I pulled out a chair and offered it to Ches. She turned her shoulder to me and went to lean in the corner. So I took the seat and crossed my legs.

"I got a call from Ronetta Claye," I said.

"Finally happened, huh?" Julian quipped. "She's been asking about your peculiar skills."

"They had an issue at Enoch Pratt," I added. "I met with this lovely gentleman named Turner."

Julian rolled his eyes. "Oh, Jesus."

"So, you've met?"

He sneered. "That caveman is hard to forget."

With a smirk, I said, "Well, anyway. I'm on the case, so to speak, but I don't know what you've told her about my consultancy fee."

"Nothing. That's between you and her. I'm out of the game now, Dorian."

"Okay," I said.

He stared at me, and I at him.

Julian shrugged, and asked, "So, anything else I can do for you?"

Ches interjected, "One might think he's killing time."

I gave her a look over my shoulder. "I am, actually. Zeno only has a narrow window to meet."

Ches popped forward. "Who's Zeno?"

Julian cradled his chin in his hands. "Yeah, Dorian? That's too interesting a name for this to be a tax accountant or something."

Jesus, when the sharks taste blood in the water… "He's a Goetic up on Charles."

Ches's smile faded. "Holy shit."

Julian nudged, "I think I've heard of that. Goetia? Isn't that demon conjuration, or something along those lines?"

"Something along those lines," I countered. "Nothing you want to play with."

Ches asked, "What's a Goetic have to do with Ricky?"

"Zeno's smart," I explained. "Smarter than me. And that's exactly what I need at the moment. More than anything, really, I can trust him."

Ches guffawed. "Trust a Goetic? Your being able to say that with a straight face is the most impressive thing I've seen in—"

I held up a hand. "I mean he's no friend of the Presidium, and he has some peculiar standing with them."

Julian muttered, "Like yourself?"

"Eh, he's pretty unabashedly dark side. But the Presidium leaves him alone. So, even though he basically hates my guts, and the feeling goes both ways, he's the safest person I can talk to with this purge on."

Julian straightened in his chair. "Purge? Over Durning's public meltdown?"

"We can talk about that later," I replied. With a quick look up at Ches, I added, "It's the fastest option. I'd rather be careful, but we don't have that luxury."

"So, we have some time to burn," Ches observed with a sigh. "Where's the bathroom?"

Julian answered, "Across the hall, that way." He gestured with his thumb.

She stepped out of the office and into the hall.

Julian stood up and wound around the desk, sitting on the corner directly in front of me.

"How are things with her?" he asked.

"She's a good student. I mean, I've inherited a lot from Gillette. She knows more than just the basics. It's the holes in that basic knowledge that—what?"

He shook his head with a weary grin. "That's not what I mean." He leaned in a little. "You were tied in a knot over her not too long ago. Are you still keeping the candle lit over her?"

"No. I mean... why? I'm her teacher. And she's not interested."

"You know that for sure?"

"Pretty sure," I grumbled, shifting my legs. "And that's probably for the best. Things turned out weird between us after the thing with Elle."

"Well, okay. So let's play a hypothetical. What if she were interested? Would that change how you felt?"

"Probably not."

He sighed. "You still blame her for what happened to the Swain girl?"

I leaned over and looked out the door, checking that she wasn't eavesdropping.

"Thing is, she actually was responsible for Elle," I whispered. "That was all her doing. It's why Gillette shackled her to my arm. If I let her practice, I'm putting my own balls on the chopping block." I leaned back in my chair. "So, yeah. That kind of puts one enormous crimp in my feelings for Ches."

Julian's eyes softened. "That's a shame. I thought you had a chance with her."

I sat silent for a moment, joining Julian in staring at the floor.

Footsteps interrupted our reverie, and Ches slipped into the doorway.

"Dorian? There's some guy up front, wants to see you."

My stomach knotted. I'd grown profoundly uncomfortable with unexpected meetings in my recent past.

I stepped into the main tavern, giving Ben a nod and a chuck on the arm, before spotting Detective Turner. He had his hands shoved into his pockets, leaning against the corner of the front bar.

"Detective?" I declared. "How's that business at the library treating you?"

He grimaced, then caught himself. With a clearing of his throat and an application of some manner of forced courtesy, possibly at the behest of Claye herself, he responded, "We can't clean it up."

"Sigils still on the walls?"

"No," he grunted. "That cleaned up all right. Had to use lots of bleach. Shit was written in blood, if you can believe it."

"I can."

His eyes widened a touch, then eased back into its usual practiced contempt couched in professional comportment. "It's the books."

"The widdershins spiral."

"Yeah, that."

"Let me guess," I said as I stepped closer, "the librarians pick up the books, place them on the shelves, and the second someone turns their back, a couple more have fallen. And it repeats over and over?"

"That's about it." He ran a finger under his nose, then pointed it at me. "You said this was gonna happen."

"I did, didn't I? Holy crap, it's like I actually know what I'm talking about."

That professional comportment couldn't bury his sneer.

"I was asked to ask you... I mean, to approach you—"

Julian's voice spilled from the back of the bar, "Ronetta told you to apologize and get Mister Lake back on the case."

Turner angled his head to look behind me, and his face melted into a profound disquiet.

Julian stepped around my elbow. "That about the way this went down, Turner?"

He grumbled, and turned a half-circle.

Julian added, "Disrespecting us is not going to make your career any brighter."

The detective cracked his knuckles, took a heavy breath, then turned back to face us with more of that professional comportment than I figured he was capable of.

"Yes, former Deputy Mayor. That was the cut of it. And I would very much appreciate Mister Lake's continued assistance, and regret any perceived insult from me to his person."

I flashed Julian a smirk, then looked at Turner.

"No sweat, tiger. Already on it."

His shoulders wilted a touch.

"So..."

"I'm researching the sigils. I think that's our best chance at identifying the one who cast the jinx."

Turner nodded.

"I'll be in touch," I added.

He shuffled out the front door with a quick two-finger salute over his shoulder, leaving me and Julian soaking in our collective smugness.

"Thanks," I said, offering Julian a fist to bump.

He bumped it, and turned for the back. "Don't miss your meeting, Dorian." He paused at Ches and placed his hand on her arm for a quick second before retiring to his office.

Big Ben continued wiping goblet wine glasses with a towel, pretending he didn't hear absolutely everything.

Ches stepped forward and crossed her arms.

"Okay, now I really want to see those photos."

"Good, because I don't think I'm going to have time to devote to it."

"Hey, that actually does make me your assistant. Doesn't it?"

I cocked a brow at her. "Huh?"

"It's an upgrade from student, isn't it?"

"Ches," I muttered as I guided us back toward the kitchen, "you're way more than an assistant. I'm totally counting on you, and that makes you my cavalry."

Ches peered up at me over her shoulder, her lips painted with a demure grin. She looked away, her chestnut curls drifting back over her shoulder. These were the moments that made me feel less like an asshole teacher and more like, well... like I was more than just a teacher.

We returned to the car, and as I pulled us back onto Light Street, Ches gave me a long stare. It was enough to make me profoundly uncomfortable.

"Looking at me kind of hard, there," I mumbled.

"I wanted to apologize for being such a bitch, earlier. I'm just—"

"No need to apologize, Ches."

"I was going to say I'm just a little twisted up with this Ricky crap. But I do appreciate your help."

The tightness in my chest eased, and I gave her a quick smile. "If I've learned anything in the past couple years, it's that everyone needs help now and then. No matter how tight a grip you have on things, there's always someone better, smarter, or just straight meaner than you." I added as I turned onto Charles Street, "That's why we're talking to Frater Zeno instead of trying to clear Ricky's curse on our own."

"Even though we're supposed to be Switzerland?"

I shrugged. "This isn't the Presidium's business. Hell, clearing curses is supposed to be their thing."

"I appreciate you, y'know... letting me do some real practice. It makes me feel like you're not trying to stick me on a shelf, protect me, whatever."

The weight of the responsibility gathered in my gut. I had grown so tired of being the pedagogue. I wanted to hold onto that light feeling. That smile.

She continued, "It was getting kind of stifling, and I—"

"Julian thinks I'm still in love with you," I stated, not really knowing why I was saying it.

Honestly, that came out of nowhere.

Holy shit, why did I say that?

Ches snapped her head forward, staring out the front window for several blocks.

I gripped my steering wheel, flogging the communication center of my brain with intent and verve. So much for the light feeling. Now it was weird. Shit, I excelled at making things weird.

Finally, she asked, "What's with this kitchen manager thing?"

"What?"

"You and Julian were talking about a kitchen manager position."

I swallowed hard. She was ignoring my outburst, and I was happy to join her.

"Yeah. State law says we have to serve food. So much percentage of sales has to be food sales, and we're running out of time before even Julian can keep us from getting fined, or worse. Why?"

She bobbed her head with a crisp snap of attitude. "I might have someone in mind."

"Really? You don't think you're a little overloaded with school work and, I don't know, learning four dead languages and basic hermetic theory?"

Ches elbowed my arm. "Not me, numb nuts. Ricky."

"Oh. Oh?" I mulled the thought over for a moment. "I mean, isn't that premature?"

"Maybe."

"Does he have experience?"

"I think so. I think he worked at Applebees for a while. Moved him up to shift manager before he went back to school."

At the next light, I turned to Ches. "You're asking me to hire an addict, not knowing whether he's actually going to clean up. I mean, we're doing our best with Ricky, but there's no guarantee this will work."

"I know that," she snapped. "That's why I'm mentioning it."

"You don't think we'll break the curse, do you?"

Ches gave me a weary glance. "If the last couple years have taught *me* anything, it's that you have to plan for the worst-case scenario." She reached for my arm. "Dorian, there's a real solid chance this isn't going to work. We both know that."

"Why are you thinking this way?"

"Reality? If Ricky loses his kids, I might lose him. The odds are good. If he flies back to Portland, and things go bad with Susanna, I don't know where his head's going to be. I want him close, so I can watch him, try to keep him hanging on. That'll be easier if he has somewhere to be every day. Some income. Something to define his life again."

The car behind me gave me a courtesy horn, and I returned my attention to the green light.

"Okay, I get it. But do me a favor. Even though reality looks pretty fucking grim right now, try not to let that define the outcome. No self-fulfilling prophecies this week, deal?"

She nodded with a sigh. "Deal."

We continued a while before she added, "Are you?"

"Am I what?"

"Still in love with me?"

I didn't answer. I didn't have an answer.

"Okay," she mumbled.

CHAPTER FIFTEEN

Frater Zeno's lodge was a stately old masonry house facing an open green space on Charles Street, not far from the university. It was exactly the kind of pad you'd expect a sweater-clad Goetic to buy. It could have originally been an old professor's home, or even a provost. I wasn't sure where Zeno got his money, but he was clearly solvent enough to buy and maintain one cherry piece of property. What an asshole.

I parked in one of the extra spaces the Lodge had widened out of the driveway. They even had a handicapped space. It looked like a full-blown business.

Ches whistled as she took in the building. "Nice."

"Right? Pisses me off."

"Your house is nice."

"Well, it's nice-ish."

"It has character."

I rolled my eyes. "Thanks so much."

We got out of the car and stepped up the flagstone walkway to the steps leading up to the front portico.

"What did this Zeno guy do to get on your shit list?" she asked.

"You'll know when you meet him."

"You said he tried to exorcise my servitor last year?"

I paused by the front steps and gave Ches a side-eye. "Yeah. Didn't work."

She released a couple chuckles and stepped up into the portico.

"That's nothing to be proud about," I called.

"Yeah, yeah." She reached for the doorbell.

But she froze as the enormous oak door eased open, a bloodied hand sliding out to grip the jamb.

I caught Ches by the arm and guided her back from the door, wishing I'd brought my darquelle.

The door opened all the way, and out stepped a ragged Frater Zeno. Both of his hands were covered in blood, as was most of his sweater. His hair was tousled, and his face was pale. His spectacles were cracked in the middle, one of the lenses hanging at an angle over his cheek.

"Zeno?" I whispered. "The hell?"

He blinked rapidly, staring up into the space between us. Zeno staggered out onto the portico, sucking in deep breaths. As he stepped past us, I caught a strong whiff of sulfur.

"Zeno?" I repeated. "Are you hurt?"

He looked left and right, and finally his eyes seemed to focus on us.

"L—Lake?"

"Yeah. It's Dorian Lake, Frater."

He looked down at his hands, the gore seeming to register in his brain, and wiped them in broad strokes over his sweater.

"Apologies. I'm a bit untidy."

"What the fuck happened?" I rasped.

He inspected his fingertips. "I should wash my hands."

"Frater!" I grabbed his arm. "What happened to you?"

Ches gasped near the front door, nudging it open with her toe.

"He... that guy is very dead."

I released Zeno and moved for the door. Inside I could spot a body slumped over on the marble flooring, as if trying to sit up but somehow snapped in half. Blood pooled beneath the corpse's legs. I went to step inside, but the warding at the front of the threshold dizzied me.

Ches reached for my elbow, lifting a hand to her temple.

"You felt that, too?" she whispered.

"Yeah. Something's pouring energy into this place."

I reached into my pocket and palmed my sachet of salt, dumping the extra energy into it. When I'd cleared the threshold, the overload subsided. I handed the sachet to Ches to clear herself.

The anteroom was a mass of white marble, both on the floor and the wainscot. Grand, sweeping crown moulding led from the anteroom into a space beneath a circular stair. The only light in the building was sunlight streaming in from the tall windows, filtered through filmy drapes.

A sharp, acrid twang of rust and sulfur filled my nose, and I sniffled as I stepped around the pool of blood spreading across the marble.

Ches pointed over my shoulder at a trail of crimson-dappled footprints leading away from a tall pair of double-doors, nice wood inlay with enormous brass rings and a slide bolt. It looked like the classiest vault door in the Mid-Atlantic. One of the double-doors stood ajar, a barest flicker of light dancing inside. We inched closer and eased the door open.

We found a wide, roughly circular room with the remains of an intricate chalk-art summoning circle on what appeared to be a slate floor. The room was still illuminated by a series of six candelabras, each marking the points of a hexagram along the perimeter where the walls met the floor. The candles illuminated a series of bodies strewn around the perimeter of the room in various states of contortion and mutilation.

Ches sucked in a breath, and coughed.

"My God. Did... did this guy just murder these people?"

I shook my head and pointed to the center of the chalk art, where a large swath of the chalk had been swept in a line racing toward the perimeter, at the end of which lay a particularly crumpled body.

"These were his students," I whispered. "Something went horribly wrong, and I doubt it was Zeno."

I backed out of the room, grabbing Ches by the back of her shirt to urge her to follow.

When we returned to the anteroom, we found Zeno pacing a circle, his face flushed and his chest heaving. Seemed the shock had subsided and the panic had set in.

"Frater?" I said. "You with us?"

He shook his head, balling his fists. "It wasn't right. The key was perfect. It's always perfect."

"What key?" Ches asked.

I answered over my shoulder, "Key of Solomon. Summoning and binding sigils. The chalk on the floor."

She whispered, "Obviously, it wasn't perfect."

Zeno froze and gave her a skin-peeling glare.

"Every. One. Is. Perfect."

I held up my hands, hoping to keep him calm just in case I was wrong, and he did actually go slice-and-dice on his students.

"I believe you, Frater. But, still… something happened."

"It wasn't the key," he said, returning to his pacing. "It was the Aretic hedge. Had to be."

Ches gave me a look, but I could only shake my head in confusion.

Zeno paused as he stepped into the puddle of blood. He lifted his shoe slowly, inspecting the leather for "untidiness," before bustling to a side door in wet slips of red against the white marble floor.

Ches and I stood awkwardly as retching noises filled the silence of the building, followed finally by a flush of a toilet and a long rush from a sink. After several minutes, Zeno returned, much of his dignity seemingly restored. He had pulled off his sweater and balled it up under his arm. Now standing before us in shirt-sleeves, he removed his spectacles, and pocketed them. The odd transformation of his image was jarring. He almost looked normal.

"It was the hedge," he repeated with a steadier voice. "It was contaminated. The Arête was out of sync with the summoning circle."

"Ah," I muttered. I turned to Ches, and explained, "You know that surge of energy we felt walking through the door?"

She nodded.

"Someone's screwing with the Arête, or chi, or whatever you want to call the focused energy of this place. In Goetia, everything has to be perfect."

Zeno blurted, "It was."

I gave a so-so gesture with my hand. "Well, obviously not so much."

Ches lifted her hands and stepped between us.

"Boys. Seriously. Why are we not calling the police at this point?"

Zeno lifted a brow at Ches and scowled.

"Because, my dear girl, they would arrest me, and I simply can't have that."

She stiffened, then tossed a hand at the dead body in the room.

"You got dead guys. Dead guys need cops."

"They knew the risks," Zeno scoffed. "They all knew the risks."

Ches's voice wavered into a panicked pitch. "This guy right here. He's broken in half. In half! What did this? I mean, what the hell actually happened here, Frater?"

Zeno lifted a finger. "No. You don't get to call me 'Frater,' little girl."

Her jaw stiffened, and for a second I thought she was going to slug him across his smug face. More than half of me wanted to watch her do it.

Zeno turned to me and added, "Same goes with you, Lake. You are not members of this lodge and as such have no fraternal rights to address me."

Ches turned to me for one final reason not to take Zeno's head off his shoulders, so I gave her a calming lift of my palm.

"Zeno," I stated, "you don't have a lodge left, by the looks of it."

He cocked his head, and nodded. "That's true."

"Can we focus here, Zeno?"

He looked to the front door, then hopped over with renewed energy. "There's a tap in the energy. I can feel it."

"Yeah, I felt it when we stepped through the doorway."

He ran his hand along the door jamb, shaking it periodically. When he had concluded, Ches reached out and tossed him my salt sachet. Zeno rolled it in his palms and screwed his brows together.

"I'm more accustomed to siphons. Built protections against those. But this? Someone poured unreconciled energy into this entire property at just the right moment. This was quite intentional."

Ches and I exchanged looks, and Zeno spotted it.

"You know what this is?" he demanded.

I answered, "The Presidium is executing a purge, Zeno."

He shook his head slowly as his upper lip pulled into a sneer.

"This... was the Presidium?"

"They've taken out at least one other that I know of. Lillian Hsu, in Pittsburgh."

"What brought this on?"

"You don't watch the news, do you?" I quipped. After a space of baffled silence, I elaborated, "Congressman Durning. He outed a couple dozen members of the Presidium on live television just before his heart stopped in his own living room."

"What does a dead Congressman have to do with me?"

I rolled my eyes. "Clearly, it has plenty to do with you, and all of us whom the Presidium perceives as a threat." I took a breath and peered out the front window. "Ches is right, Zeno. The police will be here, and they're going to be all over you."

"Then I shan't tarry."

He swept around Ches and moved for the front door before he paused.

"What did you want?"

"Mostly for you to get the hell out of Dodge."

"No," he grumbled. "You wanted to ask me something. It's why you're here."

"Don't worry about it. I'll catch up with you later."

His brow lifted. "It's very unlikely you'll see me ever again, Lake, so ask your question."

I looked to Ches, who gave me an urging nod.

"I wanted input on a curse. How to dismantle it."

"You don't know how to dismantle your own curse?"

"Not mine. Someone else's. It's kind of urgent."

Zeno looked past my shoulder at Ches, then glanced back at me with an impatient twitch of his lip.

"Not really my expertise, Lake. That's really more your bailiwick, wouldn't say?"

"Not really."

Zeno shoved his hands into his pockets. "You're the Curse Merchant, Lake. Not me. You're the one with the enviable corpus of Netherwork tomes locked away. I grant you value my opinion, but I won't be of any help to you this time." He gave Ches a nod. "Best of luck to you both."

Before I could return the sentiment, he jerked the front door open and disappeared.

Ches sniffled behind me, and I turned to find her rubbing the bridge of her nose.

"Well, this was a complete abortion," she groaned. "What the hell killed these people anyway?"

"I think you know," I muttered.

"I'm not going to say the word 'demon' out loud, because I don't want to sound like a tourist."

"Then call it one of the Dark Choir's butt monkeys. Whatever you want to call it. Something dangerous and horrible and really pissed off." I reached for the door with my hand inside my sleeve, wiping the latch as I pulled it wider. "Speaking of pissed, if the cops arrive before we make a quick retreat, we're going to end up on the news."

Ches nodded and slipped out the door. As we pulled out onto Charles, she asked, "Are we really sure that Zeno dick didn't actually murder everyone?"

"He wouldn't. It would be... beneath him."

"Then why did he survive?"

I smirked. "When he took off his sweater, did you catch a glimpse at the shadow underneath his shirt?"

"Can't say I was paying that much attention."

"Fifth pentacle of Mars. Goetic protection rune tattooed directly onto his chest, probably by a capable sigilist practiced in blood scribing. He's basically bulletproof, Goetically speaking."

"You're going to have to teach that one to me," she said reaching over to me with a flat palm. "Give me your phone."

"Why?"

"Because you're driving."

"Why do you want my phone?"

With a sniff and shake of her head, she answered, "We're not just leaving dead guys lying there in their own blood and... stuff."

"Ches, the cops are going to ask us umpteen godzillian questions, and that's a lot of complications for—"

"—those boys have families, Dorian." She let a heavy silence hang in the car before adding, "We can't let them rot in that house."

I thought it over for a block, then fished Turner's card out of my pocket. "Here. Call this number, ask for Detective Turner."

"Isn't he that hard-ass from the tavern?" she asked.

"Tell him who you are. He'll remember you. He's probably won't make our lives much more difficult than he already has. And if he does, I can always call Claye."

Ches called Turner and described the situation, giving me hard looks when his voice bellowed from my phone off and on. By the time we returned to the house, Malosi was waiting for us at the doorway. Ches tossed me my phone and trotted up into the house as I paused by the door.

"What's up?"

"Your phone."

I held it up and evaluated it. "What about it?"

"No," Malosi grumbled. "Your land line."

"Again, what about it?"

"It's on the blink."

I shrugged. "Welcome to Baltimore, hon."

"There's an energy thread tugging at the entry into the house. I followed it as far as I could." He motioned for me to follow, which I did. He led me around the corner of the house where the cables rose to meet the pole on the side street. "Couldn't button down your wardings with this thing sending shit into the side of the house."

"Malevolent?"

"Possibly."

I nodded. "I'll call the phone company, and check to make sure." I turned to Malosi. "You're stuck here for the night, then?"

Malosi sighed, then shrugged.

"That's okay. Things are getting very specifically gruesome out there, and I don't mind a little muscle in my corner."

"I'm not your muscle."

"No, but you have more muscles than I do, so as if by magic you become the Muscle on Amity Lane. Congrats. I'll get you a shirt made."

I tapped Malosi twice on the arm before hustling back into the house with all alacrity.

Inside I found Ches and Ricky sitting across the table from Ricky's sobriety coach. She was a middle-aged woman with an impossibly warm face. She jotted notes as she gestured with her free hand at Ricky. His grins and nods led me to believe she was getting the job done. Money well spent.

Ches sat with her arm around his shoulder, her eyes set, dead serious on business. I watched the scene for a moment, feeling some weird call of nostalgia. My throat caught for a second as I remembered my homework sessions in my kitchen in New York. Long afternoons as Mom walked me through advanced algebra.

I turned away and nearly stepped directly into the wall of Reed Malosi. His brow was level and stern.

"You want me to be your muscle, you need to recognize two things."

I nodded.

"One," he spat with a lift of a single finger, "I work for Jean Clement. He pays my salary, and if you have any interest in securing my services toward short-term personal protection, you will have to come to an arrangement with him."

He was right, of course. Shifting Malosi into any kind of professional capacity would slip me into Clement's debt, as a matter of course. Malosi knew precisely what that meant. He was sharp, and I had to stop looking down on him when I got around to it.

"Two," he added with not the addition of a finger, but a substitution with a rather less polite finger, "I need full disclosure. Everything you encounter. Every cross-eye you catch from a stranger, every sound at night, every random phone call. I figure you had a moment today, out on your field trip."

"What makes you say that?"

He grinned. "Honest truth, you have a tell."

"What tell?"

He tapped his own chin. "You pucker."

"I pucker what?"

"Your bottom lip does this thing."

I crossed my arms. "I don't have a tell, and I'm not entirely comfortable with you paying inordinate attention to my lips."

Malosi slipped his hands into his pockets. "One tends not to preserve a long-term career in protection by missing physical cues."

"Jesus, Reed. I'm going to need to start apologizing for everything I've ever said about you."

He scowled. "What're you saying about me?"

"I'll call Clement tonight."

"You solid with that?"

"I better be. I need you. We"—I gestured to the kitchen—"need you."

He drew a long breath, then nodded. "Call the phone people, first. This is bugging me."

CHAPTER SIXTEEN

"This puts me in an awkward situation, Lake."

"I recognize that. But things have escalated here in Presidiumland, and Malosi is one of the very, very few people in this world whom I trust. So, as a student of Emil Desiderio, you should appreciate the gravity of that statement."

Clement snickered over the phone line. "I do, as a matter of fact. Fine. Reed is yours until the end of the month. Then I'll need him back in Manhattan."

"You're a peach, Jean."

"Have you reconsidered my offer, by any chance?"

I leaned back in my chair at my roll top desk, sneaking a glance through the windows at the utility guys climbing the pole by the side street. "I have not."

"When you speak of escalation, I grow nervous."

"So do I. But I'm not selling you the Library, Jean. Sorry, but that's going to be a non-starter with me." After a pause, I added, "Does this change your mind regarding Malosi?"

"Of course not."

"I don't mind saying, you are a very difficult man to get a bead on."

Clement released a throaty chuckle. "Good. Then my entire career in esoteric brokerage hasn't been an exercise in self-delusion."

"I'll be in touch," I concluded, ending the call and drifting to the window to watch the activities at the utility pole.

A hand landed on my shoulder, and I nearly pissed myself.

When I spun around, I found Ricky giving me what I'll charitably describe as an overly-amused grin.

"Didn't mean to scare you."

"How are you feeling?"

He nodded vigorously. "Really good. I think, for the first time, I have a grip on this."

"That's good," I replied with a chuck on his shoulder. "But I'm going to ask you this question again tomorrow, and the day after. And you're going to find it harder to say that."

His eyes wilted, and a twinge of guilt stabbed me in my pancreas. It was a dickish thing to say, but it was the truth. And in my humble opinion, Ricky was shy of good solid truth in his life as of late.

"Guess that's true. Anyways, I feel good now. That's okay, right?"

"It's one-hundred percent okay."

"Thank you, Dorian... by the way. For this. For everything you've done for me."

"I hate to break it to you, but I haven't exactly done much to lift your curse. And a week from today, you'll be back in Portland."

He shook his head. "But you're doing something, and you don't have a good reason to do any of it. I want you to know that I'm grateful. Even if this ends bad, I'm grateful."

"Well, you're gonna love this."

"Hmm?"

I turned a half-circle, trying my best not to look magnanimous and probably failing. "I hear you have experience in restaurant management?"

He backed away a step and held his hands behind his back. "Maybe? Why?"

"You know I'm part owner of a tavern downtown, right? We have this weird law in Maryland. A specific percentage of our sales have to fall in a category—"

"You have to serve food and not just booze."

"In a nutshell."

He rubbed the back of his head and released a dry snicker. "You want me to work for you?"

"For the week."

"And after I go back home?"

"I'll hire someone else."

"How does that work, exactly?"

I took a seat at my desk. "Let's just call this temp work. Help us unpack and set up this brand new kitchen. Pull off the plastic and get us running. Maybe set up a bone-crew staff so we can get food cooking this weekend?"

Ricky's smile thinned. "I appreciate your confidence, boss. But I don't think I'm ready—"

"You're ready, Ricky, when you decide you're ready."

"I don't know. I still get the shakes."

"You're almost out of the hard patch. Giving you a reason to get out of bed, out of this house, to do something with focus is going to help start up a forward momentum. Besides, I'm not shitting you. We really need some help, and I'm a little too busy to run a want ad."

He stared at the floor, and began to slowly nod.

"Well, if you're sure."

"I'll have Ches drop you off tomorrow around ten a.m."

He crossed his arms, holding himself as his brow creased.

I stood up and gave him a friendly nudge on the shoulder.

"And you'll be on a plane by Sunday. We're going to get you clean and free of curses, and back with your kids."

He surrendered a half-hearted smile and turned for the stairs, adding as he stepped out of the room, "Better ask Ches before you volunteer her to be a chaperone."

"What?"

He didn't respond, disappearing instead up the stairs.

Malosi stepped through the front door and gestured for me to join him.

"Are they finished?" I asked, hopping for the front door.

"Yeah. Guy wants to show you something."

I stepped out into the gray daylight. A young man in a white hard hat and a reflective vest gave me a two-finger salute as I approached.

"Are we good?" I asked.

"Yeah. Everything's kosher," he replied. "Did a line test. All's clear."

"Anything unusual?"

He cocked his head and snickered. "Yeah, now that you mention it." He reached into his pocket and brandished a highly-polished gold coin. "Found this just sitting in the box."

I leaned in and examined it as well as I could. It seemed to be an otherwise uninteresting Sacagawea dollar. Though I was very certain it was anything but uninteresting.

"Huh," I mumbled. "Haven't seen one of those since 2012."

The utility man curled his fingers defensively around it, and I had to think fast.

"Hey, I'm something of a numismatist. I'd love to round out my Sacagaweas. I'll buy that from you for a fiver?"

His brows lifted, and he rolled the coin around in his hand. I took solace in the observation that he was still wearing leather gloves. He wouldn't be scrubbing too much of the latent energy signature from the coin and depositing his own. I needed that coin to be as unspoiled as possible.

The young man nodded, and I fished a five note out of my wallet. He held out the coin, and I fished for a handkerchief or anything at all to catch the coin. Alas, nothing convenient was available, so with all the poise God gave a left-footed penguin, I held out my wallet for him to drop the coin into.

Malosi walked me back to the house after that awkward exchange with a chuckle.

"I would have used my shirt," he offered.

"Yeah, that would have been arguably less clumsy, but I don't really care at the moment. I got the coin."

"What do you think it is?"

I gave him a side-long glance as we stepped back into the house. "Pretty obviously a hex anchor."

"Sure it's a hex?"

My confident smirk lost a bit of its pluck as I led Malosi down into the basement. Ches was hunkered over her desk downstairs, running her fingers over three opened textbooks on dead languages.

"How's that going?" I chimed as I emptied my wallet onto my worktable.

Ches lifted a finger to put me on proverbial "hold" as she jotted down some notes.

"Maybe onto something," she grumbled as she paused to erase everything she'd just written.

I nodded without her actually seeing me, and returned my attention to the bright gold coin resting on my table. I didn't need a pendulum to palpate the energy slicing off this bastard. To answer Malosi's question in my own mind, I had to determine the power source of the particular hermetic twist that was pinched onto this coin.

"Hex vs. curse, is the question," I mumbled. "Hexes, I'm familiar with."

"They're your money-maker," Ches offered, still buried in her book.

I added, "Simple little packages of engineered karma. A decently crafted hex saddles a person with an artificial consequence to an otherwise karma-neutral action. It's a relatively low-energy working, and that'll be my barometer. Anchoring a hex to something small and neatly conductive like a gold coin wouldn't take much energy."

"Curses, though?" Malosi asked.

"Curses require something more substantial than the practitioner's personal energy to fire off. They require more preparation and engineering than a simple U.S. government-minted coin. I've crafted exactly one curse in my life. It required my own blood, a crap-load of substantially hateful intent, and approximately twenty square inches of human skin."

Malosi nodded. "Yeah, I remember that curse."

"I bet you do. Look, violating the laws of nature requires a squick factor several orders higher than this pathetic hex-coin."

This had to be a hex, but what were the terms? And who had placed it in the utility pole outside my house? I had my suspicions, and the more I dwelled on said suspicions, the more unsettled I felt about my state of affairs in the Presidium's backyard. And the terms seemed somewhat obvious.

Get involved; receive shit. Keep my nose out of this business; shit falls on someone else.

Shit certainly fell onto Zeno. A hex would have been insufficient to derail his Goetic summoning. I was vaguely aware of Zeno's reputation, and I knew anything short of a hermetic howitzer wouldn't have broken through his shields. This tiny hex the Presidium had saddled me with? Small peas compared to what they dropped on Zeno, which meant something.

I was on a different level in the eyes of the Presidium.

That meant everything. It was my indication, my compass for how to act.

"You going to do anything with that?" Ches mumbled.

I looked up from my table with a lift of my brow. "What?"

"You're just staring at it."

"And?"

"Well, you're the teacher. I'm the student. At least that's how this is supposed to work, right?"

I straightened up and wound my way around to her side of the table. "Yeah."

"So, what are you going to do next? How do you clear a hex?"

"You tell me. What would you do?"

She stood up from her chair and leaned in to inspect the coin. "Well, I'd sever the connection with its power source."

"And how would you sever the connection?"

She turned and looked my reagent shelf over, pacing along the back wall with a finger on her chin.

"You have yarrow. That could work if it's an emotional hex, particularly if it's in close proximity to the subject. There's myrrh... classic clearing agent. Best if it's a memory charm or hex that has to do with obsessions."

I took a step to the shelves, but she held up a finger.

"No, let me do this. We're thinking this is Presidium, right?"

With a lift of my hands, I replied, "That's my best guess."

"Fine. The Presidium deals in Enlightenment Era magic. Right? Franklin, Jefferson, real Founding Fathers New World deism stuff. So, I'm thinking it's a classic correspondence hex, likely of Rosicrucian or Paleo-Masonic construction."

"Not bad."

She flickered her fingers along the rows of mason jars until they landed on a particularly short, blacked-out glass.

"Gold," she whispered, then grabbed for another jar, "with quartz. A clearing, restructuring one-two punch. Should lay this out in a deosil spiral... the Golden Spiral probably, knowing their fetish for sacred geometry."

She brandished the two jars with a smirk.

"So, how'd I do?"

I smiled, leaned across her shoulder, and grabbed the large box of Morton's kosher salt at the end of the shelf. When she spotted the salt, her smirk melted, and she exhaled.

"Shit."

With a slow, steady pour I covered the coin in a generous pile of salt, and tipped the spout back into the box with a tiny creak.

"Problem with your theory is that the Presidium isn't a particular fan of the Rosicrucian system. Too much animism for their blood. Paleo-Masonic theory is... well, basically that. A theory. Borders on myth. The Masons borrowed symbology from the Egyptian Gnostics, but by and large they're a service organization only. And, not that I'm criticizing your scheme of gold and quartz laid out in what I'm sure would be a dazzling Fibonacci pattern, gold costs something like $1500 per ounce. Salt? Thirteen cents. And it doesn't require sacred geometry."

Ches's eyes narrowed, and she twisted away from me, slapping the jars back onto the shelf.

"Hey," I muttered. "Your thought process is solid. Don't feel bad. Or, mad, or whatever is going on, because Jesus I can't tell."

She lifted a hand and shook her head with a quick sigh. "I'm not mad, Dorian. Please stop being you for a second."

"What?"

"I'm allowed to feel discouraged. Okay? I get to feel this. Please stop trying to fix it."

I shut my mouth and crossed my arms.

I wasn't trying to fix her.

Really.

"Sorry," I mumbled. "It's hard to turn off the Me Machine, sometimes."

Ches ran a thumb over her eyebrow. "So, you cleared the hex. Now what?"

I nudged the coin out of its salt pile, and held it up to the light. I felt an urge. More of a yin, perhaps.

"This made sense," I declared. "A hex. Something simple. Something innocuous to keep me out of the Presidium's way. But throwing a wrench in Zeno's summoning? Doesn't that sound a bit disproportionate to you?"

Ches lifted her hands. "What's proportionate to the Presidium?"

"If this is a true purge, then why wouldn't they just black-bag the trouble makers? Why go through the trouble of side-slicing Zeno's hedge energies? It just seems a bit dramatic for the Presidium."

"Okay?"

"I think maybe I want to take a closer look at Zeno's property."

Ches grimaced. "What happened to Switzerland?"

I pocketed the coin and moved for the stairs. "It looks like the Presidium is giving me a little space, here. So, I'll just push it as far as I can until that space gets too narrow."

"At which point you're asking to get black-bagged, yourself."

"The smart thing to do. The right thing to do. Screw it. At the end of the day, I'm hitching my moral compass to the people who pissed me off the least." I added with a gesture at her desk, "You got this?"

"Oh, yeah. I'll be here actively not getting my ass kidnapped and shot in the head."

I brushed past Malosi and wound through the front room, snatching my keys from the front table as he followed.

"Got a free hour or two, Reed?"

He lifted his chin. "Why?"

"I need a pendulum. A good one. And I don't have time to make one."

CHAPTER SEVENTEEN

I'd parked several blocks down Carroll Street from Swain's Antiques and Oddities. Too many of Edgar's neighbors had come to recognize me and my car, and I wanted to keep the exposure down to a minimum. I slipped through the wood gate at the rear of the building and ushered Malosi through.

"He always keep his gate unlocked?" he asked as we hopped up to the steel door at the rear of Edgar's shop.

"Don't think there's a lot of crime around these parts."

I caught a glimpse of two of the tall church spires stabbing into the sky down the block. Frederick was littered with churches, an echo from its history as a center of religious tolerance in the colonial times.

Tolerance.

That's what this whole drama with the Presidium was about. How far would they tolerate unsanctioned magical activity? How did they define it? Who gave them the right to police it? All of this was something they had to revisit year after year. The answers would have to be as vague as the question itself. No one had given the Presidium the right. They just took the right upon themselves, and had done so since the old red-brick colonials surrounding me were first built.

I fished Edgar's key from my pocket. It was a spare he leant me for special occasions when he was on a trip, or his children were on fire, or whatever reason people give people keys. Malosi let me enter first, probably out of habit. He understood how affinity worked with wardings, and I was the one with affinity to the Swains.

Truth be known, Edgar wasn't that worried about security in general, which was bizarre to me, because he housed one of the most dangerous collections of cursed objects in the Mid-Atlantic. All of it sealed behind a hollow-core door with a length of "magic twine" wrapped around the knob.

It was yarn.

I was convinced it was just a bit of yarn someone sold him. I'd mused about it for years, wanting to reach out and just untwist it, hold it up to his face and say, "See? Yarn!"

Well, here was my opportunity, and my gut twisted with guilt. Sure, he'd given me the extra key. Sure, he wouldn't mind if I dropped by to grab some mugwort or dried scorpions or red amber dust. He had even made me an official offer for the object of my current quest.

The Gregori pendulum.

I'd used it once before to help find Edgar's daughter after a misguided servitor stole away with the girl's body. I used the cursed pendulum just that once. It was intense. I hadn't felt such clear, specific... vulgar magic before in my life. It took a hold of me, and I hadn't ever forgotten the power in that damned thing.

I meant "damned" very literally. It is said that cursed items doom the soul of any practitioner that uses it. My soul being displaced from my body, I rolled the dice.

And here I was, rolling the dice again, gambling that the Gregori pendulum wouldn't, in fact, seal my fate. Gambling that Edgar wouldn't end our friendship over this violation of his trust, or that Wren wouldn't kick the shit out of me for being here in the first place.

And most pertinent to the moment, gambling that piece of yarn wasn't, in fact, some kind of powerful magical lock.

This wasn't a complete burglary. Edgar had made an offer. Five large, and the pendulum was mine. This was significant, since he had effectively retired from active cursed item mercantilism. He had changed over the years. Perhaps afraid of the Presidium, perhaps given a new perspective once his two children had entered the equation. Maybe a bit of both. But he hadn't sold an honest-to-God item from his back closet in the past four years.

It was, perhaps, simply inconvenient kismet that the Swains would be in freaking Orlando the precise moment I required the Gregori pendulum. The envelope inside my pocket held a personal check for the five grand I'd owe him for the pendulum. I slipped it out of my jacket as Malosi and I wound our way through the storage room and into the dusty antique shop. I paused abruptly when I noticed that Edgar had sold the large, fuck-ugly green couch near the front of the store. He loved that couch. I was absolutely certain he was jacking up the price just to keep it handy for Drunk Canasta Nights.

Malosi cleared his throat, and I proceeded along to the very rear of the shop where a length of old wooden cubby drawers sat perpendicular to a glass case housing the more choice of Edgar's reagents.

And behind the glass case was the door to his special room. A closet, really. A walk-in. And inside that closet lay the most unheralded collection of distinctly rare and wicked cursed objects on the East Coast.

Malosi sidled up alongside me, tapping his fingers against the top of the glass case.

"So, here we are," he muttered.

"Yep." I nodded to the door. "That's Edgar's collection."

"Presidium know about this?"

"I figure they probably have to, though Edgar is really, really good at keeping off people's radar. How he manages it in those catastrophic Hawaiian print shirts really is one of the mysteries of our time."

I eased around the end of the case and crouched down by the doorknob, eyeballing that tiny, Hellish twist of gray yarn.

"So?" Malosi nudged. "You want to hang out until the cops decide to notice we're in here?"

"Give me a second."

"What kind of wardings does he have on that door, anyway?"

I shrugged. "This little bastard is basically it."

"What bastard?"

I gestured for Malosi to approach. He knelt down and stared at the knob.

"What is that?" he whispered.

"Edgar's magical yarn."

Malosi snorted, and I nearly jumped out of my skin.

"You're kidding me!" he guffawed.

"He's convinced it's some kind of ball-buster. Paid enough for it, that's for sure."

"Well, give it a try. See what happens."

I gave Malosi a side-eye. "You want to volunteer for this shit?"

He eased back.

"Yeah. Thought so." I returned my attention to the yarn. With a quick tickle of my fingers, I gave the doorknob an energy palpation. Nothing.

So, with a squint and a quick centering of my mainline chakras, I reached up and gave the yarn a twist.

It fell limply to the floor.

I gave Malosi a look. His amusement with the situation bordered on the obscene.

"Fuck you," I grunted as I stood up and opened the door.

The inside of the closet was about as exciting as any closet might be expected. Two parallel walls held bracketed shelves with rows of shoeboxes, spangled by the occasional brown paper-wrapped parcel. There was very little color. Mostly beige, brown, and white. Tiny strips of embossed plastic from one of those old school press label makers sat stuck onto the bottom right corner of each box. I skimmed along the first couple shelves, noting the labels. Herve Trement Oculus. Palimpsest Gruning Codex. Zauberstein Gavel. Crucifix Argentine. There were several of those Argentine crucifixes. Must have been a fire sale.

Malosi hovered by the door, watching the front windows with as low a profile as his massive frame could manage. He glanced over his shoulder with a sniffle.

"This going to take long?"

I shrugged. "Can't take that long. There's not that much stuff here." An odd-shaped package caught my attention. "Ooo, I think this is an actual Salem Doll!"

"Nice. We're trespassing, by the way. Might want to snap this up."

"Right."

I had seen the Gregori Pendulum's shoebox when Edgar had first offered it to me. I knew the basic size and shape, which should have helped. Turned out, not as much as I'd have thought. I managed to pull three shoeboxes of nearly identical size and color... probably all the same model of shoe. Where did Edgar get these damned things, anyway?

The first box opened to reveal a pendulum, but not the Gregori. This one was a fairly uninteresting piece of jewelry that was probably used by an important Netherworker at some point. The use of mundane items toward Netherwork is known to impart a kind of dark resonance onto the item. Not necessarily a curse in and of itself, but enough to affect the user.

The second box, however, was what I was looking for. There it lay in a wad of black tissue paper. Finely rendered gold chain culminating in a single-helix that caged an unpolished hunk of smoky quartz. The materials themselves weren't so noteworthy. The method of craftsmanship was.

I reached into the tissue and gripped the onyx knob at the palm-end of the pendulum, carefully lifting it from the box. It hung motionless from my hand. Not even a slight sway from my own pulse. It was an arrow pointing obstinately and unwaveringly toward Hell.

Malosi muttered, "What's so special about this particular pendulum?"

"You heard of Maximilian Gregori?"

He eased away from the pendulum.

"Yeah," he whispered.

"This was his."

"You sure?"

The energy from the gold crawled up the chain and around my hand like a swarm of fire ants.

"Pretty sure."

"He, uh… didn't he successfully curse a Pope to death?"

"That's the story. Benedict XI. Contributed to the schism in the Papacy." I eased the pendulum into the box and replaced the lid. "I didn't say I was a fan. Just that he made some impressive working tools."

I returned the other boxes, closed the closet, and set the yarn as well as I could on the doorknob. A part of my subconscious prodded that Edgar would spot that it had been disturbed the second he'd lay eyes on it. And that would be a real test of our friendship.

Reaching into my pocket, I laid the envelope with my check onto the glass case, then thought twice about it. Instead, I tucked it onto the frame of the locked sliding glass doors behind the case, out of sight.

"We're good?" Malosi nudged.

"No, we're horrible. But we're done here."

CHAPTER EIGHTEEN

The front door to Zeno's lodge mansion was crisscrossed with yellow crime scene tape. As I drove past the lodge, I wondered where Zeno had disappeared to.

Malosi pointed out a free street spot around a corner, and I parked us out of sight of the building.

"Sure you want to stick your nose up in the Presidium's business like this?" he asked.

"Nope. But it seems wrong just sitting on my ass, you know?"

"Not really."

I killed the engine and turned to Malosi. "Okay, I have an uneasy feeling about this. Instincts are popping off that this wasn't the Presidium."

He lifted a brow.

I continued, "Too violent. Too histrionic. The Presidium isn't into making grand, bloody gestures like this." I nodded to the corner. "They're more into black-bagging the problems and making them disappear quietly into the night."

"That was before they got outed on network television."

"Still, though. I don't see them making examples of people. This whole purge doesn't sit right."

Malosi nodded. "If not the Presidium, then who's mowing down these Netherworkers?"

I leaned back and thought of Lillian. That was a Presidium hit. It fit the profile, and she was pushing the Presidium's very specific buttons by importing hermetic contraband. But Zeno? This was more elaborate. Almost a punishment.

"That's what we're here to find out."

As we rounded the corner on foot, I reached into my pocket to feel the fire ant energy buzzing off the Gregori pendulum. It was a finely tuned piece of divination gear, and I was about to field-deploy it for the second time. We stopped across the street from the lodge, and I pulled out the pendulum.

"Okay, so let's see what—"

The pendulum levitated directly up and back toward the top of my thigh.

I sucked in a breath.

"You see that?" I whispered.

Malosi squinted, then shrugged. "See what, exactly?"

I took another look, only to find the pendulum hanging straight to the ground.

"You didn't see it rise on its own, just now?"

He shook his head with a dubious wrinkle between his brows.

Hell. This thing was tugging at my brain more than my hand. All that energy I was allowing to seep through my skin had already built resonance. This was the cost of dealing with cursed items. That, and damnation. But damnation was something of a fluid thing for me at that moment, so I just rolled with it.

I released my thoughts for a brief moment, and just felt the pendulum. It tugged upward, pointing again to my leg. I turned a slow circle, and images from the Gregori pendulum led my third eye to a green space just behind a row of upscale houses.

"There," I whispered.

I jogged up the sidewalk and found a wide patch of grass between two driveways. We slipped between two very expensive homes and climbed across a length of brush separating their garden-lawns from a careworn public park. Most of the grass surrounding the park had been walked over to the point of dusty topsoil. A couple benches sat opposite a towering piece of particularly ugly public art. It was a chimera of welded steel, glass, and what appeared to be sails of canvas. A line of orange netting remained strung between landscaping stakes surrounding the sculpture, and the smell of freshly-turned clay soil hung in the air.

Malosi rubbed his chin. "I like it."

"De gustibus non est disputandum."

"Hmm?"

"Taste can't be disputed."

"You don't like it?"

I held up the pendulum. It swung in a savage line back and forth between Zeno's lodge and the sculpture.

"You're seeing this, right?"

"Yeah," Malosi grumbled. "That, I'm seeing."

I walked a circle around the sculpture. It was newly erected, that much was obvious. But nothing about it seemed expressly esoteric. Just a series of geometric shapes and animal heads welded into a mass beneath what seemed to be some cubist realization of a schooner. I inspected the geometric shapes for convergences, sacred geometries, or any kind of glyphs I could recognize... and came up empty.

I gave Gregori another shot. Once again, it felt stiff and intense. Angry, even. Something about this damned piece of public art was pissing it off. So, in keeping with the new relationship I was forging with this tiny spiral of gold, I centered myself and did something I hadn't done since my training days with Emil.

I returned my focus to my third eye chakra, and released the guarded filter I had maintained to this point.

The pendulum poured images and insinuations, if not outright hallucinations, into my consciousness. If the faucet was at a drip, I wondered what would happen at a full flow.

Turned out, a full flow was fucking terrifying.

The third eye being the center of magical conceptualization, the input was largely visual. Individual images of places, people, and situations I didn't want dredged up out of the sewer of my subconscious. Moments of danger. Attacks, both physical and magical.

I saw my parents, both before and after their deaths. I saw Emil, vivisected and lying in his own bloodied bed in our London flat. I saw that dickhead from tenth grade who loved to sucker punch me in the stairwells when we were alone.

I saw Carmen.

Every pore of my being oozed alarm. This pendulum had tapped into my instincts for fear.

Danger.

And it pointed me directly to this structure of welded steel, glass and fabric.

I opened my eyes.

Malosi stared at me from several yards away, his eyes wide.

"Oh, you did not just do what I think you—"

"It's this statue, Reed. I know it."

"Looks clean to me."

"It's not. It very much is not." I paced around the front of the statue, then pulled the orange netting aside before pocketing the pendulum. "It's hot, Reed. Something inside this chunk of fugly art is cursed."

He shrugged and pushed the netting further apart.

I climbed up the six-inch concrete platform and gripped the top of what I assumed was a raven's head.

"Give me a boost, will you?" I called.

"Huh?"

"I need to look inside."

He stood behind me, then shoved his hands onto his hips. "I am not grabbing you around the waist, brother. Let's just get that sorted out right now."

"Oh, grow up."

He crouched down and made a cradle with his hands.

"Okay, good enough," I muttered as I stepped onto his enormous hands, guiding myself along the ridge of the steel animal shapes as Malosi hoisted me higher.

Over the top ridge of the raven's head I spotted a series of glass shapes completely occluded by the exterior of the statue. There was no point in having those blown-glass ornaments tucked so deep. No one would ever see it. Fishy as hell.

They encircled the central support pole which held the keel of the sort-of-schooner up at the top of the statue.

My forehead burned, and for a brief moment, the pole flickered.

It flickered.

Energy ants crawled up and down my side. The pendulum was itching to get back out of my pocket.

"Anything?" Malosi huffed.

"Hang on."

"Please hurry. Your bitch ass ain't as light as it looks."

"I'm wiry."

"The hell you say."

I centered myself again, and with a little effort focused those energy ants back up my back and over the top of my head... into my third eye. It felt like a very, very poor decision. I was opening myself up to random energy without proper precautions. This was precisely the kind of thing I'd have busted Ches on.

But it worked.

My eyes focused on the pole itself, which glowed with some kind of hateful light. It positively vibrated. And there, etched into the surface of the cold-rolled steel ran a line of runes.

"Fuck. There it is."

I reached into my pocket and grabbed my phone as Malosi complained below. Testing the limits of his steadying power, I snapped several photos before dropping to the concrete as he let me go.

I grabbed his shoulder and gave him a pat on the arm.

"Thanks, Reed."

"What did you find?"

I pulled the photos up on my phone, zooming in on the images. Runes. Definitely magical. This wasn't some random arthouse Viking homage. These runes ran in an intentional spiral up the pole.

"How's your Nordic?" I asked as I handed over my phone.

"Fair."

"Anything you recognize?"

He studied the photos, sliding them back and forth, continually adjusting the zoom. Finally, with a rub of his eyes, he handed the phone back to me.

"It's a niding pole. Looks like you were right."

I swore under my breath and pocketed my phone, turning back toward the statue that had taken a decidedly sinister caste.

Niding pole. That was serious next-level Netherwork. It was a stationary curse pole used by the Old World Asatruar. When a Viking took a wicked hair against his neighbor, he would scribe a niding pole with some notably hateful runes and pound it into the ground facing his neighbor's property. Then all he had to do was to sit back and wait for his neighbor's life to fall directly to shit. It was powerful, but unfocused, magic.

"This was planned," I whispered. "Well in advance."

"Hate to break it to you, Dorian, but niding poles aren't easy to break. I mean, we could take a bazooka to this statue, the curse will still be on the land."

I paced a circle, staring at the base of the statue. My brain sent alarm signals to my logic center, which unfortunately was still swimming with fight-or-flight hormones courtesy of the Gregori.

"Geomancy," I muttered.

It was starting to make sense. I lifted my phone and dialed Ches.

"You okay?" she asked immediately.

"Peaches and cream. How are you coming with the Enoch Pratt glyphs?"

"Um, okay I guess. I've been with Ricky since you left."

"Okay. Stay there with him, inside Reed's wards. We're going to check something out."

Ches seemed to move to another room, and whispered a response.

"Are you starting something I should know about?"

"No. Not really. I'm just seeing the bigger picture. If you identify the glyphs, call me immediately. It could be helpful."

I hung up and turned to an increasingly annoyed Malosi.

"Where are we going now?" he asked with a snarl.

"Harrisburg."

CHAPTER NINETEEN

I knew Deirdre's address from our first communication, should I have found occasion to invoice her. She lived in a tidy condo near the center of Harrisburg, Pennsylvania. Just an hour and a half drive north. I was willing to take the trip easy enough. Malosi, on the other hand, seemed about ready to drop me off on the side of I-83 and keep driving back to New York.

He gave me sidelong glances as we proceeded.

"This woman's a what, now?"

"Geomancer."

"Which matters why?"

"The niding pole is a geomantic apparatus in nature. Right? It requires a specific placement, a duration, a direction. I'm no Asatruar, but the fundamentals have to apply to all magical schools."

Malosi shook his head. "Still not shedding any light, brother."

"She's the only geomancer I know on the East Coast. Which basically means she's the only geomancer I know anywhere. And what little I know about geomancy tells me that these things are stupid easy to retro-engineer. If she can deconstruct the niding pole, we'll know a little more about the magical school that created it. Which helps us identify the people who rogered Zeno right and proper."

"You've committed to the fact that this isn't the Presidium, then?"

"Trust me, I'd rather it not be a giant question mark."

We pulled up behind Deirdre's condo. Malosi wouldn't let me go up the stairwell to her third-floor condo without checking the lay of the land first. He was a consummate professional, that much was certain. I hoped Clement was paying him adequately.

If I was right, and Deirdre could help identify the runes and by extension the craftsman of the niding pole, then maybe there was hope that I could deconstruct Ricky's curse. If I watched her do it, I might catch a clue as to how I'd approach the Dead Dragons' curse. Granted, the Dead Dragons probably didn't use geomancy on Ricky, but any insight was helpful.

Malosi nodded me up the stairs, and after six flights, I found myself in a blustery breezeway knocking on Deirdre's door.

No answer.

I checked my phone and dialed her number again. She hadn't answered, but that wasn't anything new.

"Sure she's home?" Malosi asked with an air of impatience.

"No."

His air ratcheted up a couple notches.

I gave the door another shot before pressing my ear against it, listening for a TV or anything.

And I heard something.

Mumbling. Distant, pained mumbling.

I gave Malosi a look, and he reached into his jacket.

"You best be right about this," he grumbled as he pulled a lock pick from his jacket. He had the lock open in less than a minute, after which I moved to open. I met with a meaty palm in the center of my chest, and to my admitted astonishment, Malosi pulled a handgun from a holster I never knew was tucked inside his jacket.

I swore softly, but his hand shoved me clear of the door without further protest.

Malosi disappeared inside the apartment for several seconds longer than I found comfortable. Finally, he reemerged, weapon stowed, ushering me inside.

The condo was extremely dark. My eyes took a moment to adjust before they caught up with the utter havoc spread out in front of us. Papers everywhere. Dishes. Clothes. It was complete chaos.

"Someone toss the joint?" I asked, before Malosi pointed to the back room.

I stepped carefully up the short corridor leading to the rear sleeping area. One door stood ajar, and I nudged it open with my foot. I found a bed inside. Small. Probably a twin. It was largely swallowed by the enormous *en suite* that contained it. And yet more improbably, the twin bed swallowed the tiny figured huddled in its center, holding her knees tight to her chest.

With a thin clearing of my throat, I called out, "Deirdre?"

She didn't look up at me. Her hair fell in ratty tangles over crossed arms, but I knew she heard me. Her rocking intensified.

"Deirdre," I repeated. "It's Dorian Lake. Are you hurt?"

She thrust a hand out, a trembling finger pointing at the wall opposite her face.

I reached into my pocket to grab my sachet of salt, but Malosi held out his hand before I could advance. With an upturned palm, he revealed a large oval of hematite.

"Good thinking," I whispered.

"Half of defensive magic is planning ahead," he replied.

I took the hematite, and trusting in its energy-absorbing capacity, stepped inside the room. My head spun instantly. The energy was swirling, flowing around me, cascading against the Gregori's particularly cranky bristle from my pocket. Nothing inside that room seemed correct, orthographically speaking. Up was down, left was right, and inside was outside. It was like a tiny vortex swam with every kind of reversal imaginable. How Deirdre was still alive inside this room frankly astonished me.

She waggled her finger again, squealing. I turned to follow her finger. The entire south-facing wall was covered in what appeared to be black marker ink. Seemingly random letters filling the entire wall in a kind of scribbled grid. Some letters backward, some upside down.

I shot Malosi a questioning glance, but he simply shook his head.

I crouched beside Deirdre on her bed.

"Hey, can you look at me?"

She clamped her arms tight around her face.

"Deirdre, it's Dorian. You can trust me. Listen, you're inside an energy vortex. A nasty one. It's cooking your noodle, so I'm not sure if you're even hearing the words I'm saying. But you have to try and trust me." I reached out for one of her hands, trying to pry her fingers away from her arms. "Come on. Let's get clear of this."

She squealed again, shaking her head. Deirdre could hear me. What's more, she could understand me. But she was sealed tight inside a cage of terror. Whatever was reverse-spinning the energy in her condo was turning her world into a living nightmare.

"Deirdre!" I shouted. "Come on."

Her breathing paused, then resumed with an intense renewal of panting.

"Reed?" I called out.

Malosi entered the room and helped me physically lift Deirdre off her bed. She nearly kept a tight ball posture as we hoisted her free of her comforter, her legs finally dropping to the ground by the time we reached the doorway.

Then the hallway.

And the front room.

But the spiraling energy followed us.

Malosi guided Deirdre to her couch before giving me a stern look.

"It's not her bedroom."

I nodded. "It's her."

Something had turned Deirdre into a vortex. What kind of cat-shaving lunatic magic was this?

"We can't move her. It would be... well, it won't work."

"Gotcha," I answered with several degrees of misery. I hunkered down on the couch beside Deirdre, trying to keep the maelstrom from my brain. "Hey. What's going on with you? Can you tell us anything?"

She snapped her fingers about a dozen times, before pointing down to the coffee table.

Which was completely empty.

"There's nothing there, Deirdre," I muttered.

She shook her head and squealed again. I finally caught sight of her eyes. White, wild, panicked. It sent chills up my arms.

"What? What about the table?"

I slipped off the couch and ran my hands over the table, though I couldn't tell much from the swirling energy all around us. However, I did spot a Sharpie lying on the floor beneath the table.

I crouched down to grab it, when I noticed some ink on the edge of the table's valance. A few more inches closer to the floor, and I spotted more words scribbled on the underside of the table. With a quick stretch of my back, I flipped the table upside down and revealed more of the random letters to Malosi.

Malosi squinted and leaned forward.

"You got me," he mumbled.

"You got both of us," I answered, giving Deirdre a sympathetic glance.

I took photos of the bottom of the table with my phone as she rocked back and forth, gasping for air.

"She's in Hell, Reed. There's no way we can just leave her here."

"You wanna bet?"

"How are we supposed to—"

"We'll leave a note with the neighbors. Call an ambulance. Anything that keeps her physically safe. But we are not going to move her with us. You understand that, right? I'm not asking you. I'm telling you."

I stiffened, but Malosi's posture was stiffer.

"Okay," I finally muttered. Turning to Deirdre, I added, "We're going to find help for you."

Her breathing eased, followed by a baleful weeping noise. She knew we were about to abandon her to this vortex. She knew she was doomed.

"I'm so sorry," I whispered as Malosi pulled me away. "We're going to help you."

He ushered me out through the front door, prying my fingers open as he closed it behind us. The hematite was impossibly hot. Red hot. It nearly burned my skin.

Malosi pocketed the hematite in his jacket, and gave me a brisk rub over the outsides of my arms. The surreality of the vortex inside that condo subsided, and I finally noticed where I was.

"Reed? What are you doing?"

"Grounding you."

"Thanks, but it's getting weird."

He stopped, and nodded for the stairs.

"I'm calling 911," I said as we began our descent.

"Negative. This isn't an emergency. Let me look for the city desk. Less likely to record it."

I waited by Malosi's car while he phoned in a non-specific complaint on Deirdre's condo, after which we made a discreet exit.

About fifteen minutes south of town, he finally asked, "Does this fall under your 'too histrionic for the Presidium' category?"

"Hell yes, it does."

"Where now?" he asked, pulling us onto I-83 heading back for Baltimore.

"The tavern."

I reached for my phone, and dialed home.

Ches answered, "That was quick."

"Unfortunately."

"Uh oh."

"Yeah. You busy?"

A shuffling of papers, and she replied, "I'm definitely onto something, but I can't be sure. It's still a hunch."

"Cool. Look, bring everything you got to the tavern."

She sniffled. "What's that mean?"

"Your research. Your books. Ricky. Everything."

"What's going on, Dorian? What's wrong?"

"Deirdre's been jinxed."

Ches responded with a healthy silence.

I acknowledged her silence with a simple, "Yeah."

"How?"

"Don't know, but you see where I'm going with this. Right?"

"They can target people. Not just places."

"It wasn't retribution. It was prevention."

"Okay. I'll be there. But why Ricky?"

"He has a job to do. Guy's gotta earn his paycheck, right?"

We drove back into Baltimore, and by the time we reached the tavern, Ches and Ricky were already there, lingering by the front bar. Big Ben was chatting them up, Ricky in particular… which was good to see, as I hadn't broken the news to Ben just yet that Ricky was the new kitchen manager.

Ches hopped off her stool, a clutch of papers and a large brown tickler file under her arm. "So, jinxing a person?"

I lifted a finger and whispered, "Bring everything into the event room. I'll be there in a second."

She glanced from me to Malosi, whose face must have brimmed with gravity, as she gathered her materials without complaint.

I turned to Ricky and extended my hand.

"How're you feeling today?"

With a smile, he responded, "Amazing. I think I might be over the hump."

"Good to hear!" I turned to Malosi and nodded for the event room.

He took the hint and moved to follow Ches as I turned to the bar.

"Hey, Ben," I called.

"Dorian," he replied with considerable weight.

"So, Ricky? You've met Ben Setleigh. He's my bar manager. And, well, he's about as close to a Dad as I've allowed myself. So, you know… be nice."

Ricky offered a hand to Ben with aplomb. Ben shook it, giving me a questioning lift of his brow.

"Ben, Ricky's our new kitchen manager."

Ben's face lifted into a broad, beaming grin, and he clamped onto Ricky's arm with his enormous paws vigorously.

"Well, Christ boys! Why didn't you tell me?"

A shuffling from the hallway behind me added to the wall of noise. I turned to find Julian poking his head from his office, a clipboard tucked under his arm.

"Dorian?" He looked us over and grinned. "The gang's all here."

"Yep." I grabbed Ricky and steered him around to face Julian. "I want you to meet Ricky Baker. He's Ches's brother."

"Pleasure." Julian shook his hand with ambivalence

I continued, "More importantly, he's our new kitchen manager."

Julian's eyes shot open. "I'll be damned. You actually did it." His grin broadened. "Welcome to the Light Street Tavern, Ricky. We're in dire need of your help."

Ricky shoved his hands in his pockets. "Thanks."

"Ben," I called over my shoulder. "Why don't you take him into the back. Show him what we got, and what needs unwrapping. Then he can sit down with Julian here and come up with a workforce plan."

Ben clapped his meaty hands and ushered Ricky toward the underutilized kitchen behind the bar.

Ricky gave Ches a look before disappearing into the back. Her shoulders were tight, practically hugging her ears.

"Ches? Reed? Why don't you spread out in the event room. I'll be with you in a second."

Reed shuffled off for the event room immediately. Ches lingered just a second, watching after Ricky, then giving me a genial nod.

When they were gone, Julian settled his clipboard onto the bar, then stepped directly in front of me.

"We're hiring him?" he asked.

"This is temporary. He's on the back side of a detox, and if everything goes well, he'll be home with his family by the beginning of next week."

Julian nodded thoughtfully. "And if it doesn't go well?"

"Then it might not be so temporary. At the very least, he'll get us working on a kitchen staff before he leaves."

"Okay." He pointed at the event room. "What's with the convention?"

"Working something big. Needed the space. Also, I wanted Ricky here sooner than later."

Julian gathered his clipboard and turned for his office. "I'll keep an eye on him. You two negotiate his pay yet?"

"Shit."

He waved me off. "I'll take care of it."

I stepped through the event room doors to find Ches unpacking her dossier while Reed pulled tables together.

Ches asked, "So, you're onto something?"

"Maybe," I replied. "You got your tablet?"

She pulled her tablet from her purse and handed it over, fingers locking on it as I gripped it. "You break this, I'll cut your thumbs off in your sleep."

"Sounds fair," I muttered.

"And don't get too exploratory," she jibed. "I have some particularly filthy porn on that thing."

Malosi lifted his head.

"Right," I grumbled as I looked for the maps app, pulling up the immediate area. I panned out until I could spot central Pennsylvania. "So, here we are. Baltimore, DC, most of Pennsylvania."

"Okay?" Ches said.

I tapped a pin onto Gettysburg. "Earlier this week, we ran into a jinx here, in Gettysburg."

Ches nodded. "Deirdre's thing."

I tapped the center of Baltimore. "And then, I was called in by Claye to investigate another jinx at the Enoch Pratt."

"Same people, we're assuming," Ches offered.

I said, "Probably. I was assuming these were trial runs, like they were ramping up for one big hit somewhere."

Ches cocked her head. "You're thinking not?"

"Not so convinced, anymore."

"So, what's your point?" she asked.

"Right here, on Monday, we had this giant drama with Durning outing the Presidium. In the space of, like, two days we start seeing

Netherworkers dropping off the map."

She nodded. "The purge."

"Again," I muttered, "not so convinced, anymore."

She wrinkled her nose. "I hate the way you say that."

"I was talking with Reed in the car," I added. "The Presidium doesn't do drama. Never has. They hate drama with nuclear burning. When they take out the trash, they do it quietly. Which is what happened to Lillian Hsu. You remember that Netherworker I visited Friday? She got busted importing contraband fu dogs. Long story, ends with a bullet in her head."

Ches ran a hand over her bangs. "So, that's the Presidium's work. What about Zeno? He had his hedge wardings delicately, elaborately pulled aside. Seems quiet, but the end result was that his own demon ended up tearing his students literally into pieces. That's more message, less punishment."

I replied, "I agree. It's something totally different." I pulled out my phone and brought up the photos I'd taken of the runes. "We found this inside a public art statue across the street from Zeno's lodge. Dreadful piece of crap, but you see this post on the interior?"

"Yeah?" she said.

I zoomed in on the picture. "See those runes?"

"Yes."

I held out a hand to Malosi, who offered, "It's a niding pole."

"What's a niding pole?" she asked, squinting at the photo.

He elaborated, "Viking curse pole."

"Boom," I punctuated.

Ches gave us an amused smirk. "You two are so bromantic."

"Don't tell Edgar that," I mumbled. "It's well established we only have bromance for one another."

Reed coughed. "For the record, I possess zero bromance for your ass."

"Thing about a niding pole," I continued, "is that it requires a specific distance from and orientation to the target. It's technically a curse on your neighbor's land, not your neighbor. Back in the day, that meant something. But it's not discreet. It's not particularly efficient. It takes a while for a niding pole to really get its transmission kicked into full 'Fuck You' gear. Why would the Presidium elect for that slow-burn, pants-you-in-public style of mischief?"

Ches shook her head slowly.

"I'll tell you why," I said. "Because it wasn't the Presidium. It was someone else."

She responded, "I'm following you, but this is totally different from the jinxes we've been dealing with."

"True. Which isn't to say they aren't connected. Still, though, something niding poles and jinxes have in common is geomancy."

Ches leaned back and frowned. "I didn't think jinxes were geomantic. You said they're chaos magic."

"Right. But who was the first target? The client of a notable geomancer. And then the second target? A public library."

"Point?" Ches asked.

"Wait for it... Third target."

"There's a third target?" she asked.

"That target being?" I pointed to Malosi.

He grumbled, "A geomancer."

"A fucking geomancer!" I shouted.

Ches frowned. "Deirdre."

I nodded. "Yes. It's following her, like she was the exit wound itself."

Ches frowned. "Where is she now?"

I answered, "In the tender mercies of County, I imagine. Whoever these people are, at first I was kind of game. You know? Giving the Presidium a nice and public black eye? But now they're just pissing me off, and the fact the Presidium seems to want me sidelined just makes me want to dig harder."

Malosi stepped around me and leaned in to look over Ches's notes. "Sounds like you, all right. These are the glyphs from the library?"

"Yeah," I replied.

Malosi studied them for a few seconds, then shook his head. "I got nothin'."

"Me neither," added Ches.

Malosi offered, "At least your geomancer friend was writing English."

I snapped my fingers. "Yeah, that." I pulled out my phone and swiped to the past few photos I took of her wall and underneath her coffee table, brandishing it for Ches to see. "That. Can't make sense of it."

"Random letters," she muttered. "Looks like gibberish."

"Agreed, but she was pointing to it, like it should have made sense."

Malosi cocked his head and tried the word a couple ways. "Maybe we need a chaos magician to decode it?"

I shrugged. "Sounds reasonable. Also, incredibly dangerous."

Ches took my phone and zoomed it in and out, flipping back and forth between photos. Finally she set the phone down on the table in front of her. "Guess I can dig into this, too. But are you really sure this is a jinx?"

"What are you thinking?" I asked.

"Well, it's too specific," she said. "You told me that jinxes are random. Hard to target any specific thing or person."

I nodded. "You're not wrong. But it felt like a jinx. I mean, just like that daycare, only fresher."

Malosi said, "Regardless, we're dealing with chaoticians."

"Right," I replied. "The ones who hit the daycare and the downtown library. They did something to Deirdre, whatever it was. And probably are the ones responsible for Durning. I think the Presidium is under attack from some spectacularly dangerous people."

"People who use niding poles," Malosi added.

"That's right. And that's our only solid lead, at the moment."

He lifted a single brow. "How do you figure?"

"It's public art," I said. "Planned art. There's a paper trail somewhere. And as fate would have it, we have an insider at City Hall."

Ches smirked. "Yeah, but Julian's out of the game. Isn't he?"

"Not Julian," I corrected. "Claye."

I stepped out of the event room. Ben and Ricky were huddled over a tablet at the bar, discussing something I hoped had to do with getting the kitchen up and running.

Julian spotted me from the hallway. I motioned him to join me.

"How's he sound?" I asked as Julian leaned against the wood-paneled wall beside me.

"Like he knows what he's doing. I'm not as pessimistic as I thought I'd be."

"That's great news. Look, I need a favor."

"What kind of favor?" he asked without a second's pause.

"I need you to call Ronetta Claye. Get me a meeting. Like, tomorrow morning if possible."

He turned to face me. "What are you doing in City Hall, Dorian?"

"I have a thing."

"Yes. I figured you'd have a thing. What kind of thing brings you into City Hall, is the question I'm asking."

"It's part of this Durning debacle. And Turner, too. It's all connected."

Julian glared at me for a long, hot moment.

"What?" I mumbled.

"Why don't you let me in on this?" he whispered, leaning in with a conspiratorial posture.

"This what?"

"This latest caper you're on. You want to talk to Ronetta? Well, maybe I can help you on one of your investigations?"

I grinned. "Thanks, Julian. But I'd really prefer to keep you clear of this whole mess. Trust me, it's going to get sticky. You're already on the hook thanks to Durning's drama bomb. Don't want you any closer than you have to be."

"I appreciate that, but I'm not a child. I've traded punches with the worst of the seedy political underbelly Baltimore could throw into the ring. I might not be some kind of wizard, or whatever you call yourself. But it sounds like you're dealing with power brokers and Beltway insiders. I've been spinning that magic for a couple decades, now. Dorian? For once, I think you might actually need me."

I turned to face Julian full-on. His face was drawn. Earnest.

Deadly earnest.

I might have even called it eager.

That was one giant warning bell ringing in my ears. I'd known that thirst for the Game. That need to be dealt into the Secret Knowledge. I'd shared it those twenty years ago, when I was gunning for revenge for my parents' deaths.

Julian was grasping for something, anything, to give his life meaning again. He trusted me. I was his gateway to significance, and that filled me with dread.

Zeal almost always leads to destruction.

"Maybe," I whispered. "Maybe I do. And maybe I will. But not right now. Okay? I'm not even sure what I've gotten myself into."

He nodded with a squint, and shoved his hands into his pockets. "I think Ricky's going to work out. I mean, for now."

"That's good."

"I hope he goes home. But if he doesn't, well, he could have a place here I think."

"You okay?" I asked.

"I'm good."

I didn't believe him. His shoulders were high and tight, and his eyes were downcast. He was hungry for action. Any kind of action. It ripped a tiny hole inside me, but I couldn't bring him inside. It wouldn't be healthy.

I replied, "All right then."

Julian pulled away, and turned a half-circle. "I'll call Ronetta."

Ches stepped up to my side as Julian wandered back to his office.

"What was that about?" she asked.

"He's okay." I turned to her. "Can you stick around, give Ricky a ride back home?"

"Yeah, no problem. I have an idea on these glyphs I want to try out."

"Oh?" I prodded. "Do tell."

"Nope. You're going to have to wait until I'm sure."

"So mysterious."

She smirked.

Malosi boomed from the corner, "You two going to get a room, or what?"

CHAPTER TWENTY

"Ronetta Claye," I said as Malosi and I ascended the steps to City Hall in the crisp morning air. "She was one of Julian's protégés. She's a Deputy Mayor, and Julian's heir-apparent."

"This is your business partner you're talking about?"

"Yeah. He was big mojo in Baltimore until..."

"You?"

I winced. "Yeah."

"No offense, Dorian, but you fuck people up."

"I get that."

Malosi stopped mid-step. I caught up with the fact a few steps higher, at which point we were almost at equal height.

"What?" I muttered.

"That girl? Ches?"

"What about her?"

"You're going to fuck her up, too."

I frowned, and though it conceded a few inches of height advantage, I stepped down into his personal space.

"Let's not talk about Ches, okay?"

"I'm just saying, if you keep her close to you? She's going down."

"I felt I was pretty clear on the Not Talking About Ches issue."

"You in love with her, or what?"

I balled fists, fairly confident that it wasn't impressing Malosi one inch.

"She's my student, Reed. I'm responsible for her education. And by responsible, I mean that a really scary goddamn woman in Portland is going to rain down all kinds of Hell on my head if I don't. If you think that's a good pretext for romance, then maybe you're the one who's fucked up."

"I didn't say you were fucked up."

"Sounded that way to me."

He reached out and gripped my arm before I had a chance to flinch.

"Reed—"

"I'm trying to help you, brother."

I eased my tension as he looked me in the face. His jaw was set, but his eyes weren't drawn in his usual squint. He seemed earnest.

"I'm not trying to hurt anyone, Reed," I muttered. "I'm actually trying to help people, if you can believe that."

He chuckled. It was quick and dry... but I heard it.

Malosi released my arm. "Why do you make everything about you when it isn't? And when it actually is about you, you make it about everyone else. I'm not a psychologist or anything—"

"Don't worry, Reed. I know I'm a special kind of crazy."

We continued up into the stately white building, an anachronism in marble against the steel and glass skyscrapers surrounding it. He was absolutely correct, actually. Every hour I kept Ches close to my drama was another hour she approached certain downfall. It was some kind of inevitable consequence of being part of my Best Case Scenario. Every last person I felt good about ended up either a vicious back-stabbing shit, or horribly dead.

City Hall was abuzz with activity, for no obvious reason. It took longer than usual to navigate through the metal detectors, and by the time we'd reached the fifth floor and Ronetta's office, we had already been queried by city police three times. Security was high, as was the foot traffic. Something was happening.

Claye's office was on the opposite end of the floor from Julian's old office, but that didn't stop me from making the side trip. His door still had his name on it. That was curious. I knew he and Mayor Sullivan were tight. Was it possible Sully was keeping the office open for Julian? And if he made any kind of gesture, how hard a decision would it be for Julian to say "yes"? He was clearly struggling with his sense of direction. This whole retirement debacle may have been a sidebar in what could ultimately be a brilliant political career.

Was Julian part of my Best Case Scenario, too? And if so, would he share in my doom?

Malosi made impatient throat-clearing noises, and I pulled my head out of my own thoughts. We proceeded along the hall to Claye's office, where we were met with two assistants who seemed uninterested in passing along our arrival to Claye. Finally, after she spotted us from her back office sidelite, she waved us in.

Malosi stood near her office door as it closed behind us. Claye reached out to shake my hand with a grin, but as the door finally clicked shut, her smile melted. It melted quick. Oh, crap.

"Have a seat, Dorian," she stated as she wound her way back around her desk.

I took the seat, giving Malosi a warning look.

"Ms. Claye," I began, using as formal a language as I could muster.

"Mister Lake," she responded in kind. Oh this was going lovely. "We need to have a conversation."

"Okay?"

With a testy breath, she stated, "Police cameras spotted the two of you near a crime scene on Charles Street." She lifted a paper from her desk. "A certain Temple of Eastern Solomonic Rites?"

"Yeah. That."

"A particularly gruesome crime scene with occult overtones. That is your field, as I recall?"

"It is."

She squinted and folded her hands in front of her. "Care to assuage my frankly deep concerns, Mister Lake?"

"We weren't involved. The lodge was run by an associate of mine. Perhaps associate is the wrong word. Someone I'd met once or twice is more accurate."

"You're talking about this 'Zeno' character."

"Yeah. Goes by Frater Zeno, though it seems he doesn't care for people outside his lodge calling him Frater. It's like a title... I'm losing you, aren't I?"

"You're not assuaging my concerns, Mister Lake."

"Listen, I'm sure Zeno's a Person of Interest right now, but you should know he wasn't the one who killed those boys."

She gave me half-hearted smirk.

"What did kill those boys? Demons?"

"Yes."

She stared at me.

Malosi shifted uncomfortably by the door.

I held her gaze until her smirk melted.

"Mister Lake, you can't—"

"This was a Goetic temple, Ms. Claye. It's what they do. They summon and bind demons toward several mundane purposes. Money. Power. Girls. I didn't say I approve of it, but it's their business. LLC and everything. Zeno's good at what he does, Ms. Claye. He kept the demons locked down whenever one of his students colored outside the lines. He may be guilty of sink-or-swim magical theory, but he's no killer."

She seemed unimpressed.

"There is a warrant for this Zeno's arrest, Mister Lake. Which means if you know his whereabouts, then you are compelled to share this information."

"It was sabotage. That's why we were there. The park across the street? Someone put a Nordic cursing pole within the public art in the center, and aimed it straight at Zeno's lodge. I came here hoping we could get some information. Names of whatever committee puts those public sculptures up."

She stood up and slapped a folder onto her desk in front of me.

"You are supposed to be assisting Detective Turner in the Enoch Pratt vandalism. Julian said you were the best in this field, and that you could be trusted. Instead, Turner tells me you are uncooperative, antagonistic, and unavailable."

I tapped my finger rapidly on the edge of her desk.

"Yeah, well, Turner's kind of a tool."

So much for mustered formality.

"The more I look into you, Mister Lake, the less I trust you. I don't know what kind of spells you think you're weaving out there, but I'm very sure the only spell you've cast is on Julian. I find you to be grossly insubordinate, self-absorbed, and very likely to be a finely practiced con artist."

"I suppose this is a bad time to discuss my fee, then."

She paused on that one.

With a steady breath a voice brimming with threatening cordiality, she replied, "This is a police investigation, Mister Lake. There will be no fee. Failure to assist Detective Turner, or to otherwise impede either the Enoch Pratt or the Charles Street investigations, and you could be arrested for obstruction. We may even find you to be an accessory."

A heavy silence dropped on the room like a dead whale.

Claye looked up at Malosi. "Same goes for you."

He didn't respond beyond adjusting his cuffs.

"Ms. Claye," I ventured, "I am trying to help you. But there is an entire world of practices and organizations at play in these matters which you have chosen to dismiss. And that's your right to do so. But ignoring it won't make it evaporate into a puff of rationalism."

She sat on the corner of her desk, glaring down at me.

"I couldn't care less about these practices, Mister Lake. The organizations, however, are very keenly interesting to us."

"Outstanding. Then let's talk about this public art committee."

"Mister Lake?"

"Yes, Ms. Claye?"

She leaned down, her violet-polished lips drawn into a tight scowl.

"I am not Julian Bright. I am not some political advisor. My interest is public safety, which means I'm not here in this building to protect the Mayor against political enemies. I'm here to protect the people of Baltimore from themselves."

"I understand."

"Do you? Because you seem to be taking the loss of life with a bit more ease than I find comfortable. This isn't some game."

I straightened in my seat, re-crossed my legs, and inspected my nails before responding, "Ms. Claye, I understand that better than most. The art committee?"

She held her scowl for a while before lifting off her desk. I exhaled when she turned her back, and stole a glance over my shoulder at Malosi. He seemed profusely entertained.

Claye dropped into her chair and reached for a binder from one of her desk drawers. She skimmed several pages, running her finger down until she landed on something of note.

"Here. Committee for Public Enrichment. This isn't proprietary information, so you can access it down on the second floor." She scribbled a name and an office number, and passed it over.

"Thank you. Look, things feel kind of adversarial at the moment, but I really am on your side here."

Her frown softened a bit.

"I'm not at all sure you're on my side, Mister Lake. But I'm used to that. All I care about is whether you come through or not."

"Fair enough."

She stood up, my cue to do the same. When Malosi opened the office door for us, Claye's face blossomed into the same genial, bubbly smile I saw when we first met at the Tavern. She may not have been a political operative, but she sure as shit had her game-face locked tight.

When Malosi and I reached the hallway, he grumbled, "That was enjoyable."

"Sorry about that. She seemed nicer last time."

"I like her."

I gave Malosi a side-eye. "Sure."

"Seriously. She's doing her job. Time we did ours."

"Then let's get that list of names. Odds are, we're going to find some overlap with the esoteric community—"

A voice bellowed from down the hall, and I froze.

"Dorian Lake?"

I turned to find a crowd of similarly-suited individuals winding down the hall with David Sullivan's head looming above the rest.

"Heads up," I whispered as Sullivan's eyes landed directly on us.

The Mayor called out from his entourage. "It's been a while."

As the mob moved in our direction, I spotted Madelyn Sullivan clutching her husband's arm, her face swimming with confusion.

Sullivan's security surrounded Malosi and me, and Sullivan extended his hand to shake. I took it and gave it a quick, brisk grip.

"Your honor."

Sullivan's face wilted slightly. "Listen, I'm glad I ran into you. I wanted to apologize for that business with Durning."

"No need to apologize. Absolutely no one saw that coming."

He nodded with a tight grin. "Tragic, really. He was a good man. And a good friend."

"I'm sure he was."

Sullivan clapped my shoulder. "How is Julian faring in the restaurant business?"

"Hmm? Oh. We're still getting our feet underneath us."

"He's doing okay, though?"

Sullivan lingered on the question, and I picked up on an undercurrent flowing behind the mayor's eyes. Julian was still on Sullivan's radar. It must have been a quiet season for Sullivan, politically speaking. The election was behind him, but if Julian's instincts were correct, Sullivan might be missing his old political advisor sooner than later.

Sullivan's wife chimed in. "Oh, this is Julian's friend?"

I nodded. "I'm happy to be counted among his friends."

She beamed, then turned to her husband. "Did you send Julian an invitation?"

Sullivan's face tightened. "I believe we did. We can double-check."

"Good! We should extend our invitation to Mister Lake, of course."

I smiled at the two of them. "What are we imposing ourselves into, might I ask?"

She reached out and gave my arm a light tap.

"No imposition at all! It's a casual sit-down at North Green with some of our supporters. Short notice, I'm sure, but if you can make it Thursday night, we'll be sure to save a chair for the two of you."

I forced a smile, and replied, "I'll pass along your invitation to Julian."

"We'll be in touch, Mister Lake," she added as she moved on. "We miss Julian terribly, you know."

Sullivan shook my hand again, gave Malosi a nod, then shuffled on.

When the entourage disappeared back into Sullivan's office, I turned to find Claye glaring at me from her office door. I offered an easing gesture with my hand, and moved for the elevators.

After a quick stop at the second floor to collect a single print-out listing the members of the Committee for Public Enrichment, we stepped back out into the light of day onto the steps of City Hall.

"That was a heaping handful of complicated," I grumbled.

Malosi smirked. "I'm missing something, here."

"Hmm?"

"Your business partner. He retired from public service, right?"

"Yeah."

"You sure it took?"

I shrugged. "I don't think he'll ever leave it behind, to be honest. Though I think he's got Claye sized up wrong."

Malosi's phone rang, and he held up a finger and stepped away to answer. I stood alone, looking out over the steps to the sides of the skyscrapers surrounding us. It was like a tiny hole in the center of the city. A black hole sucking Julian back into its clutches. But would that have been so bad? Julian was clearly lost in his own tavern. The whole sex scandal that had ousted Julian from his position was engineered by Sooner, who was now as irrelevant as he was before McHenry tied the puppet strings on his arms. The Durning incident seemed to have dealt a blow to Sullivan on a personal level. He could have used Julian at his side through this.

And perhaps Madelyn Sullivan saw that? Perhaps she was pushing her husband to make the inconvenient but correct decision?

"Yes. Yes, I remember. I'll get it done." Malosi hung up his phone and turned back to me. "I have to tend to some business. You head on back to the house. I'll catch a car back."

I squinted at Malosi. "What kind of business?"

"None of yours."

"I think I kind of need to know, at this point."

He crossed his arms, and seemed somehow taller by at least a foot and a half.

"Dorian? You know I don't actually work for you, right?"

"I... suppose that's not the point."

"You need to get it out of your head."

"What out of my head?"

He unfolded his arms and stepped into me, lowering his volume. "I'm not your thug, Dorian. I'm no one's thug. I may drive the car, I may tend to Mister Clement's security. But I presently have an appointment with an investment banker and a tax attorney, and the subject of conversation... not that it's any of your business... is import duty. You want to step up and take my place, I'd like to see how you do."

I looked down at my shoes.

He continued, "And for what it's worth, you probably had that hex coin sitting in your phone box for the better part of a year. And you never felt it. You never bothered. I know you want to be all alpha-dog, but you're letting shit slip again. Keep this up, and you'll lose every friend you thought you had."

"I'm kind of blind to that sort of thing."

"Best open your eyes, brother."

I looked up to Malosi. He wasn't frowning. He didn't even look inconvenienced. More than anything, he felt like a man giving a friend solid, hard advice.

"I'll catch up with you later."

I nodded, and Malosi stepped down to the street and out of view.

I drove home to find Ches hovering inside the foyer.

"Hey."

She grinned. "I have news."

"Dear God, I hope it's good news. I could use a little good news for a fucking change."

"Well, buckle up, because I cracked the sigils."

CHAPTER TWENTY-ONE

I stood for a moment, staring into her face.

"The Enoch Pratt sigils? You cracked them?"

She nodded.

"That qualifies as good news."

"Thought it would."

I looked around. "Where's Ricky?"

"Upstairs. He hit a wall on the way home, so he's sleeping it off. His coach said these would get less frequent."

"That's good. Show me what you got."

She led me down the stairs into the workspace, where she had several books sprawled out over her desk and my table.

"My problem was I kept looking too far back. I mean, I started with late medieval alchemical alphabets and worked backward all the way to butt-ass Egypt. Turns out, it's not an ancient language after all."

"Do tell."

She pulled a printout from Enoch Pratt and pointed to a peculiar little symbol scrawled across the spines on the Dr. Seuss section. I leaned in to examine it.

"Looks like a hunchback pleasuring himself."

"It's an ampersand, you dork."

"Oh. OH! That's not exactly Sanskrit."

She settled onto her stool. "I looked it up. The italicized *et* ligature didn't show up in this form until the printing press changed the whole text game. That pointed me in the other direction, and from there it wasn't that hard."

"So, quit teasing the lead here. What is it?"

"It's a syncretic glyph set conflating elements of modern scriptum, with some Enochian and Malachim symbology. I found this in an old paperback you had stuffed in one of the storage boxes."

She slid a photocopy of a floridly scripted page across my workbench. "It's a Gnostic treatise from something called *L'Ecole de la Nombre D'or*. They were a short-lived Pythagorean Gnostic cult in Enlightenment-era France."

"France, huh?" I mumbled.

Ches added, "You won't find any of them around, anymore. They burned out right around the turn of the Nineteenth century."

"Define 'burned out.'"

"More like they vanished from records. Kind of disappeared off the face of the Earth. But that wasn't uncommon, turns out. Of the major current cabals in Europe and Western Asia, all were either founded prior to Charlemagne, or part of the spiritualist revival of the eighteen-hundreds. The late Gnostic orders of the Enlightenment were consumed by older cabals or moved into philosophical schools."

I spun the printout around on the table and reviewed the glyphs once again. French Pythagoreans. The Classical Pythagoreans were students of sacred geometry and the orders of reality. But the newer Gnostic schools only used geometric principles as foundations for more complex and frankly self-serving purposes. It was a delicate period of hermetic history after the threat of execution ceased to be the driving force for the alchemical schools, but before the rise of Nationalism put actionable capital in their hands. I was more familiar with the German Enlightenment schools than French. To the best of my knowledge, the French used hermetic principles toward rules of architecture and landscaping.

That meant—

"Fucking geomancy!"

Ches blinked at me furiously. "Huh?"

"I keep running into geomancy. Deirdre wasn't some random test jinx. I'll bet you cash dollars she knows more about this *L'Ecole de la Nombre D'or* than anyone else this side of the country. And I bet someone stuffed a jinx down her throat to keep her from sharing that knowledge."

"You think this cabal is still active?"

I slid the printout back to Ches. "Maybe underground. But it's as good a lead as we've had yet."

Ches re-filed her paperwork, her eyes lifting in satisfaction. "The only hitch, there's no evidence the *L'Ecole de la Nombre D'or* ever practiced Netherwork, much less Chaos magic."

"Well, the world's changed a lot since Napoleon."

She bobbed her chin with a wisp of a grin in the corner of her mouth. Though I noted a cloud hovering in her brow. It had to be Ricky. His detox was progressing, but he was no closer to his family than before. And I wasn't helping like she had hoped.

Malosi's words to me before and after our City Hall field trip echoed in my cranium. Was she dooming herself staying so close to me? Was there any choice?

"You look pissed," she said. "What's up?"

"Nothing. You did good. Real good."

"I know I did, but what's going on in that head?"

I eased away from the table. "Do you think I talk down to Reed?"

"Are you kidding?"

I looked down at the floor, trying to figure some way to un-ask the question.

She dropped her folder onto her desk. "Yes, Dorian. You do. But the thing is, you talk down to everyone. He's not an exception."

"I try not to. I just—"

"I'm very sure you think you try. I don't know, I'm used to it. Why are you worrying about this, suddenly?"

I gave Ches a cautious glance.

She swiveled back and forth on her stool, eyes drawn into a question.

I said, "Just trying to keep my eyes open, is all. Listen, I'm not trying to stick you with busy work here. I appreciate this," I added with a gesture to her dossier, "because it allows me to focus on other things. I'm spread thin, Ches. I'm trying to help Ricky, trying to run down these jinxes, trying to keep the Presidium off everyone's back, and now I have this Parrish spook haunting me for my soul. Now the Mayor's wife is trying to host a dinner party with me and Julian, and I'm worried about you."

She stood up and reached out for my arm.

"Dorian, if it helps, I don't think you're all that clever."

I snickered, and she gripped my arm.

"So stop worrying, already," she added. "You won't run me over in the driveway with your massive ego. I have my eyes open, too." She reached for her desk, lifting a printout of the nonsense letters I'd photographed on Deirdre's wall. "Besides, I'm still getting nowhere on this. Don't know any codebreakers, do you?"

I shook my head and took the printout. "Wouldn't be much good unless they were insane to begin with. Let me take another look at this. I want you to get ready for something else."

"What?" she asked.

"It's time I stopped dicking around with Ricky. We've run out of time. I wanted to workshop this more, but I'm starting to think the only way we're going to break his curse is if we work on him together."

She took a step back, her eyes wide. "You mean you're taking off the handcuffs?"

"What I mean is I think you're closer to this curse than I am. It makes sense to put you on it. You know Ricky better than I do. You share part of his energy signature, genetically speaking. You were in the minds of the Dead Dragons when they fired the curse to begin with. And yes, you're done riding bench."

She laughed once, then pulled her face back into a dismissive grin. "Okay, I suppose that'll work."

"Partners?" I asked, extending my hand.

She reached out and slapped it. "Equals."

"Well, I wouldn't take it that far..."

"Shut up."

I surveyed the room with a squint. "We should give it a shot tonight."

Her smile waned. "That soon?"

"He has to be on a plane in six days. That's five extra days this curse could take to unwind itself, if we manage to lift it."

"Okay."

I urged, "Try to get some rest. Meditate and center."

We returned upstairs, and after touching base with Ricky, Ches took off to get ready for the working.

I needed this to work. More than just helping Ricky, I needed to remove one of the distractions from my list of "I'm Screwed if I Don't Solve This" problems.

Ricky made it downstairs in time for dinner as I had just settled at my desk to review Deirdre's graffiti. He announced he was going to make the best Shepherd's Pie in the state of Maryland. I hoped to all High Hell that he was beta-testing menu items, because the thought of decent food at the Tavern was starting to capture my interest.

As he peeled potatoes, the front door rang. I couldn't stifle the usual gut clench when someone knocked on my door unexpectedly. It was rarely ever good news. I inched the door open on its chain, and stood gape-jawed as Abraham Carter nodded at me from my front stoop.

"Abe?"

"Mistuh Lake?"

I unchained the door quickly and reached out to shake his hand. He was clean-shaven, the first time I'd ever seen him without his white woolen beard. The effect shaved two decades off his appearance. He wore a nice polo shirt and khakis, as if he'd just stepped off a golf course.

"How've you been, Abe?"

"Oh, just fine, suh. Got me a house in Glen Burnie. Doin' fine."

"That's great."

He grinned, then turned to the side to motion for someone lurking near what looked like a brand new Subaru. A young woman stepped out of the car, eyes narrow, lips pulled tight. She paused half-way to the stoop to straighten her simple but appealing dress. Her natural hair was pulled into a plume at the top of her head with a rubber band. Despite her youth, her face seemed worn and haunted, creases bracketing the corners of her eyes and mouth. It wasn't until she stepped up next to Abe that I recognized who she was.

"Minerva?" I gasped.

A grin flickered across her lips.

Abe nodded and laid a gentle hand on her back.

"She wanted to see you, Mistuh Lake."

"Wow. Come in!"

I ushered them into the house. Abe navigated her into the foyer with guiding hands as she took tiny, careful steps.

"How is she doing?" I asked in a low tone, as if she couldn't hear me just a few feet away.

Abe pulled off his ball cap and folded it neatly in his hands. "Oh, she's doin' much better. They givin' her a limited release, with medications. She can stay overnight at home time to time."

"That's incredible news."

Abe turned Minerva away from the darquelle mounted on the wall near the door. Her eyes pulled away and landed on me.

I took a careful step forward.

"Do you remember me, Minerva?"

She nodded once.

Abe prodded her with his elbow. "Go on."

She cleared her throat three times before her voice finally came out.

"I wanna... thank you."

"What did—"

She held out her arms stiff at the shoulders, and took several slow steps forward, eyes nearly to the ground. I braced, and gave Abe a look.

As she stepped into me, she wrapped her arms around me, and rested her head on my chest.

I hugged her back, fighting a frog in my throat.

When she pulled away, I nodded to the kitchen. "Can you stay for dinner? I'm pretty sure we have enough to go around. And if we don't, I'll go to the store."

Abe shook his head as Minerva stepped away to meander around the room. "We're on our way to see Ethyl."

"Ah. I can't tell you how happy I am to see you guys. What's it like being in the old neighborhood again?"

He shrugged. "Nothin' left, really. Just those new buildin's. Can't say it feels like much of anything, to be honest with ya."

"Times change, I suppose."

"They do, at that."

Abe leaned to the side and called behind me, "You put that down, now."

Minerva stood at my desk, holding a page in front of her face, turning it sideways.

Abe rushed forward to remove it from her fingers. "You can't go messin' with people's things."

Minerva shook her head. "But he can't read it."

"What, child?" Abe squawked.

I stepped forward as Abe handed me the paper with another apology.

It was the photo of the letters on Deirdre's wall.

"Well, you're right, Minerva. I can't read it." A notion blossomed inside my skull. "Can... you read it, Minerva?"

She tilted her head to the side and looked over the top of the paper.

"Deirdre," she mumbled.

I shouted, "Yes! But, how did you—"

She tapped six letters in what seemed to be a random order.

I set the paper back down onto the desk and gave Minerva a felt-tip pen.

"Can you translate this for me?" I asked.

She looked up at me, then to her father.

Abe shrugged.

Minerva bent down and began scratching out letters in ones and twos, leaving behind a fresh jumble of fewer letters. Her finger ran lines left, up, right, and down.

"Do you see it now?" she asked.

"Again?"

I followed her finger more carefully this time, as it paused on letters in turn that spelled the word "LENFANT."

I straightened up and repeated the word out loud, "Lenfant."

Minerva smiled up at me. "You can read!"

Abe seemed to sense the intense unease that had settled over my shoulders, as he wound around me to guide Minerva back toward the front door.

"We should get goin' now."

"Wait," I rasped. "Thank you, Minerva."

She smiled, ducked her head, and faced the front door.

I saw the two out, closing the door softly as they took their leave.

Something inside Deirdre's jinx-cooked brain just found a way to reach through the chaos and send me a lifeline. She was the one person I knew who could have possibly known anything about the Nombre D'or. And here she was, reaching through the jinx to send me a single word.

Lenfant.

I tapped my finger on the desktop, staring at the page.

"Who was that?" Ricky's voice called from the doorway to the kitchen.

"Hmm? Oh. Old friends."

"Well, pie's in the oven."

"Yeah. Say, you have a computer?"

"Don't you?"

I stuffed my hands into my pockets. "Well, see, thing is—"

"I have a computer."

"Can we look something up?"

Ricky led me up to his room, which was surprisingly tidy. He pulled a laptop out of his backpack and fired it up.

"What's the word?" he asked.

"I need to look something up."

"Seriously, how do you not own a computer?"

"They kind of freak me out."

Ricky wiggled his head in bafflement, then picked up his laptop and brandished it at me like a torch. "The power of Gates compels you!"

"After what I went through recently, that's not very funny."

"What are we looking up?"

"The word 'Lenfant.' It's French."

Ricky brought up a translator, and typed in the word.

"Child," he said. "L'Enfant."

"Yeah, I know. But what does it mean?"

He brought up the word on his web browser, and cocked his head. "Or, it's a spot in D.C."

"Oh. Holy shit. L'Enfant Plaza." I rubbed the bridge of my nose. "She's talking about L'Enfant Plaza. Does she want to me to go there? Did something happen there?"

Ricky sighed. "Who with the what?"

"Sorry. Talking out loud. I usually mumble like this into a book."

"Bet you were super-popular in high school."

"Shut up."

Ricky pulled up a map of D.C. and hovered his arrow over L'Enfant Plaza, a tiny park nestled against the Potomac across from the Jefferson Memorial.

"Wait!" I grunted. "Zoom out."

He did so, and I urged him to keep going until I could see all of Maryland, and most of Virginia.

I tapped his screen right on top of Gettysburg, then again over Baltimore.

"Planning a trip?" he asked.

"Just playing Monday Morning geomancer."

Ricky snickered. "What's all that about?"

I slapped him on the back. "Ever been to D.C.?"

"No."

"Would you like to?"

CHAPTER TWENTY-TWO

Ricky pulled the Shepherd's Pie out of the oven early, and we hit the road in a hurry. Washington was only an hour south, but I had to get Ricky back before Ches returned.

The drive in was smooth and uneventful. I circled the Smithsonian block a couple times, searching for street parking. Finally, I landed a spot near the USDA building, just a couple blocks away from L'Enfant Plaza.

Ricky and I crossed the street and stood on the edge of an otherwise unremarkable traffic roundabout.

"Looked a lot more interesting from the map," Ricky mumbled.

"Agreed. But there has to be something here."

Ricky turned around. "Think she meant those shops?"

"Doesn't feel right."

"Maybe if you told me what we're looking for?"

"I would if I knew."

He nodded, then strolled around a bit as I stared at the center of the roundabout. What was here? I half-expected to find another piece of public art with a niding pole rammed down the middle, but the scene before appeared less like a cog in a scheme of Netherworking and more like a giant waste of time.

After roughly fifteen minutes of sucking in car exhaust, Ricky finally turned to me and said, "I'm going to get a coke. You want anything?"

I shook my head.

"You still think there's something here?" he nudged.

"Just not willing to give up yet. I don't know. I'm probably being stupid."

He gave me a non-committal lift of his hands and trotted across the nearest crosswalk for the Plaza shops across the way.

I turned back to the center of the roundabout. Circle. Circles are key to geomantic theory, and I surmised doubly so when it came to city planning. I knew the Presidium was about as old as the nation itself, but I wasn't sure exactly how much of the lore regarding the planning of the District of Columbia was in fact due to their machinations, and how much was sterile conspiracy theory spun by those who failed to recognize that some important things in the world were simply incidental.

Why did Deirdre send me here?

A voice called out from behind me, "Sight-seeing, Lake?"

I turned to find a dark town car eased onto the side of the roundabout. A few cars whizzed around it, one laying on the horn. The rear window of the town car had rolled down, and a face leered at me from the space beyond.

Wexler.

I took careful steps toward the car.

"I suppose so," I answered her. "Not doing much for my mood, I have to admit."

"You're a strange man, Mister Lake," she snickered. "I'll assume you've come to speak with us?"

I tightened my jaw, and searched the inside of my skull for the answer least likely to end up with my corpse floating in the Anacostia River.

"Just sight-seeing. Like you said."

She sneered. "You made a special trip into Washington just to glare at a traffic circle? Let's not embarrass either of our intelligences, if you please."

I took a few more steps closer. "What I'm doing in D.C. is my business."

"Which makes it our business," she snapped.

"What, you just happened to drive by and see me standing here with my dick in hand? Metaphorically speaking."

She lifted a brow.

"Right," I grumbled. "Embarrassing intelligences, et cetera. So, how long have you been watching me?"

"Since you left Baltimore. We've had our eye on you since that disaster with Durning."

"Yeah. That wasn't on me. Totally caught me off guard. Like yourselves, I imagine?"

"You don't know the half of it."

I squinted. "I suppose I don't."

Wexler leaned toward the window, a playful lift to her lips easing its way into her high cheekbones.

"Would you like to?"

A chill swept up my stomach.

"Like to what?"

She cleared her throat as another car gave her driver a what-for as it slung around the circle.

"The Ipsissimus has given permission for a face-to-face."

I stepped away out of instinct.

The Ipsissimus? Holy. Fucking. Shit.

I froze, mouth struggling for a response.

Wexler added, "Clearly you're occupied with other concerns, so we understand that we must wait for a more convenient time. But I don't think I should tell you, if the Ipsissimus has dedicated enough consideration to arrange for a meeting with you, Mister Lake... he shouldn't be kept waiting long."

I nodded slowly. "All right."

A smile snapped onto her face as her eyes brightened. She seemed almost gleeful.

"Outstanding news. Can you be made available tomorrow at noontime?"

I nodded again.

Wexler cocked her head. "Are you well?"

"I am not well." The words dribbled from my lips like a drunken slobber.

She grinned. "Bring your mind into focus, then. The Presidium requires your best, Mister Lake. We shouldn't be left wanting."

Her window slid to a close, and with a few seconds of turn signal, the town car slipped into traffic, and rounded the circle back into the heart of the District.

My fingers trembled.

My head throbbed.

I had just been summoned by the Ipsissimus, the head of the Presidium. This individual was by all accounting the most important person on the planet. Apparently, the Ipsissimus was a man. And he wanted me to meet him.

Ricky returned some time later, sucking back a fountain drink.

"Hey," he chirped. "Had enough, yet?"

I pulled in a breath, and checked my watch.

"Better get back," I whispered.

He paused and reached out to touch my arm.

I jerked away out of reflex, and he frowned.

"The Hell's gotten into you, boss?" he grumbled. "Did... did something happen? Did you find what you were looking for?"

"No," I answered with a few coughs to clear the terror from my throat. "It found me."

We returned to Baltimore through some particularly haggard traffic, to find Ches waiting on my stoop.

I waved as we hopped up my front walk.

"Where were you?" she demanded.

I answered, "Out."

Ricky waved his empty cup. "I wanted a Coke, and all he has is Pepsi."

She shook her head. "You two ready, or what?"

Ricky froze next to me. "Ready for what?"

I gripped his arm and dragged him up to the door. "We're clearing your curse."

He squinted. "Um, okay?"

"Yeah."

"Shouldn't I, like, do something to get ready for this?" he asked.

I replied, "Yep. I have a list all the crap you're going to have to do."

Inside, Ricky and Ches hugged briefly before Ricky rounded on me.

"Seriously, though," he grumbled. "Maybe a heads-up next time?"

I shrugged. "Hey. This is what you get for shitting on Pepsi, bub."

"Where's this list?" he asked.

I strolled to my desk, pulled out a sheet of blank paper and a pen, and started jotting down notes. After seven line items, I decided to call it even and handed it over.

Ricky reviewed the notes as his eyebrows slowly lifted. "I have to take a bath? Are you for real with this?"

I shook my head. "You sound so much like your sister."

Ches elbowed me in the side.

"Yes," I explained. "It's a ritual cleansing."

"What's this stuff I have to put in the bath?" he asked.

"Ches will bring them up—" She elbowed me again. "I'll bring them up for you. They're herbs and resins that isolate and strip away coincidental ambient energetic resonance. That's vital if we're going to isolate the curse energy that's anchored you to the caster."

He gave me two slow blinks, and shrugged. "Yeah, I'm just going to assume you know what you're doing then."

He disappeared upstairs, and in a few minutes, I heard the water running.

Ches turned to me. "So, do you?"

"Do I what?"

"Know what you're doing?" she asked.

"In theory."

"Care to share the theory?"

I gestured for the basement stairs. Once we had descended and I switched on the light, I answered, "I'm going to treat this like a hex. It's like I said the other day. Curses are a lot like hexes in their architecture. They impose a consequence on the victim which the victim neither agrees to, nor participates in. Where a hex keeps from turning into

Netherwork, however, is the fact that there are limits. A hex has a time frame. An out clause. And it only ever really takes if the victim deserves the damn thing to begin with."

"Just your hexes," she corrected. "Mister karma police, over here."

I nodded. "That's right."

"But a curse doesn't care about karma," Ches added.

"That's why it takes a stronger power source than a hex. All esoteric workings require a power source. That's basic one-oh-one stuff."

She nodded. "I gotcha."

"Like, Wiccans tie their workings to natural energy. I tie all of my legitimate workings into the subject's karma. It's my safety valve. Netherwork doesn't play with safety valves. Curses are straight perversions of the natural order. They require serious, intelligent governance."

Ches leaned against her desk. "The little bit Quinn taught me was all about powering workings through fragments of our own soul."

"Yeah. That's—barbarism, basically. Crude, painful, but effective. More elaborate curses, like the curses the Dead Dragons would cast, are powered through the Dark Choir."

She scowled. "That's getting a little too, what? Christian for me?"

"Nothing Christian about it."

"You're talking about demons and the Devil."

"Horseshit."

"No," she retorted with a waggle of her finger. "This whole Dark Choir spiel smacks a little too close to Abrahamic religion, Dorian. I mean, I know you're a functioning atheist."

"Who said I was an atheist?"

"But... you're dressing up the power of destructive magic in the robes of the Bogeyman, and it just doesn't come off as genuine. Seriously. Quinn outlined this way simpler cosmology."

"Okay, lay it on me."

She paced a circle around me and my worktable.

"Power is a form of energy, she says. You can't define it as good or evil. You use gunpowder in a nail gun to build a house. You use it in a bullet to commit murder. Same energy. Same source. The combination of intent and result is where someone calls it good or bad. And that's a total bullshit thing to begin with. You kill a guy with a bullet. Okay. Say you're some psycho on a tear. You're evil. Say you're a soldier oversees? You have an entire country calling you a hero. You can hold a gun up to an animal and feed a starving family. You can hold a nail gun up to someone's head and kill his ass, too. Same energy. Same gunpowder. Two weapons. Four outcomes. An infinite number of interpretations. Good and evil, Dorian? It's what people use to make themselves feel better about how bad they screwed up."

I watched as Ches gestured and plead her case. For the first time in weeks, I found that practitioner's flame burning behind her eyes, and wondered if it didn't simply take me treating her like an equal to ignite it once again.

With a smile, I countered, "But we have references to several distinct entities weaving back through written history, which account for various impartations of diabolical power. References that cross cultures, even continents."

"Shared mythology."

"How do the Aztecs share mythology with hills peoples of ancient Thailand?"

She shrugged. "Doesn't matter how they came to the words. It's the human experience. The way our brains are shaped, wired, whatever. We come to the same conclusions."

"And you call me the functional atheist?"

"What I'm saying is that you keep relying on some chorus of ancient evil to color in as your villains. Maybe reality isn't quite so elaborate."

I crossed my arms, and gave her words some thought.

"I'm not going to stop believing in the Dark Choir. I've—met one."

"Come again?"

"Well, an agent of the Dark Choir anyway. I'm sure you can write him off as some shared mythology, Ches. But until you sit across a café table with one of these fuckers, you really don't understand how very specifically screwed we all are."

She peered at me with a sharp, enticing stare. “So what about Ricky?”

“We isolate the energetic hard-wires that link him to whatever the source is. We can assume it’s nothing minor. Nothing innocent. Nothing that won’t decide to jump up and bite our faces off if we let it.”

“Okay.”

“And just like a hex, we sever it.”

She wiggled her head. “Can’t be that simple.”

“No, it isn’t. Break the source of a hex, and you deal with a light slap of energy. Like slapping a rubber band against the wrist. Sever the trunk line for a full-bore curse? It’ll be less like a rubber band, more like a big-ole drooling monster stampeding through your subconscious, devouring your soul bite-by-bite while it fills your mind with nightmares and, perhaps, actually kill you.”

She paled. “I do hope you have a plan for that.”

“I do, as it turns out. Because, every now and then, I actually do my homework.”

I turned to my rack of reagents and started grabbing jars.

With a raspy growl, I added, “We’re going to send the source back to its owner.”

CHAPTER TWENTY-THREE

I set the desired herbs for Ricky's ritual cleansing along my workbench.

"So what do I do?" she whispered.

"You remember the hex coin?"

"Yeah. You salted it. Cleared all of the energy from it. I don't suppose that'll work with Ricky."

"It was an exercise in isolation and severing. We isolate the curse energy in Ricky's mainline, make sure it hasn't tangled itself into any secondary or tertiary chakras. Then we disentangle. What do you think happens when the knots are untied?"

"They snap back to the caster, I'm assuming."

"Nope," I said, hanging the clipboard back on the nail. "It's here, staring back at us with a heaping helping of go-fuck-yourself. It'll be hungry, angry, probably desperate. And most frightening, it'll be without directions."

Her face soured. "Make it sound like some kind of panther."

"Best thing we can do is to re-direct it. It won't go home on its own. We have to sic it on its master once it's off the chain."

I rummaged through one of my bookshelves and found a broad gray-bound spine with dark ink calligraphy. *ON THE PRACTISSE AND RENDRING OF MAGICKS.*

I laid the book on my workbench and thumbed through this primer.

Ches leaned in and read the title out loud, adding, “Robert Argyle. Who’s he?”

“Robert the Heretic. Charming fellow from Scotland. Thrived during the late reign of James the First. You know the King James Bible?”

Ches nodded.

I continued, “Daemonologie?”

Her mouth wilted into a deeper scowl than she was sporting. “The witch-hunting treatise? Yeah. I know that one.”

“Well, old Jimmy was a wee bit obsessed with the occult. Hence Shakespeare writing Macbeth as a love letter to the king. Robert of Argyle came up in the new fervor, a student of an unnamed cabalist who schooled him in near Eastern traditions. Robert took those traditions and melded them with old Pictish fair-magics.” I gave Ches a wink. “He was one crazy son of a bitch.”

“This I see.”

“Argyle’s questionable ethics aside, this is a fairly decent primer book for hex crafting.” I tossed a thumb toward Emil’s Library. “I’ll bet you a bag of doughnuts that Emil has one of Argyle’s next-level Netherwork treatises in that cabinet.”

I paused near a section with odd, hybridized Anglo-Saxon futhorc runes assembled in what could be best described as an Egyptian Gnostic pyramid.

With a snicker, I shook my head. “Jesus. Never thought you’d see Bythos written in Pictish runes, eh?”

“Here’s where I tell you I never really studied runes. Or Bythos. Or whatever else happened before 1960.”

I squinted at her with a smirk. “Gillette’s not a reader, I take it.”

“She’s mostly a hex-from-the-hip type.”

“It’s Egyptian Gnosticism. Valentian, by the looks of it. Yeah, lots of Greek here. I suppose the word ‘syzygy’ didn’t exactly fit in a Pict’s mouth with any kind of comfort.”

“This is all very interesting, but how does it break the curse?”

I slid the book over to her. “Bottom of the page.”

She squinted as her eyes ran over the lines of florid English scrawling hugging the bottom of the parchment.

"A monk wrote this?" she asked. "This is blasphemous as fuck."

"In fairness to the monk," I replied as I gathered up the book, "he was taking dictation from a Netherworker."

I moved for the shelves of reagents. The rush of plumbing overhead had come to a halt minutes ago, and Ricky was likely standing naked in my hall bathroom wondering what the hell he had gotten himself into. After snatching three mason jars of cleansing herbs, I gave Ches a smile.

"Can I talk you into taking these to Ricky?"

"Hey, I'm not your lackey anymore. Remember?"

"Yeah, but I'm not comfortable enough in my masculinity to barge in on a man in a bathtub and sprinkle course-cut agrimony over his bait-and-tackle."

She rolled her eyes and strode up to me, swiping the jars from my hands.

"What," she muttered with a lift of a brow. "You never experimented with your friends when you were in middle school?"

"I didn't have friends in middle school."

Another eye-roll, and she moved for the stairs.

"Wait... did you?" I mumbled.

She cocked her head, gave me a mysterious curl of her lip, then trotted up the steps without an answer.

I returned my focus to the task at hand. Everything I had laid out for Ches was accurate. I had to isolate the strands of curse energy that had wound its way into Ricky's chakra lines. That was the delicate, high-precision part. It would take time and patience. But it had to be done, or irreversible damage could be done to him physically. Then, the sever. Of all of the processes I'd concocted for this ritual, that would be the simplest. One slice of the darquelle, and it'd be over. It was fitting that my darquelle had belonged to Robert of Argyle... a present from Edgar.

Robert the Heretic would give me another boon that night, karma willing. His liner notes on the Pict-cum-Egyptian Gnostic pyramid.

"Horos at agony sum Mixis." It was a bastardized, mangled, horribly inelegant connection between the Gnostic Aeons of separation and comingling, respectively. But the liner notes proceeded to equate the decad of Egyptian Gnosticism with Robert's personal rogue's gallery of "antagonies," which were his polar opposites of the Aeons.

Without really knowing what he was doing, Robert of Argyle was hanging names onto real entities in the Dark Choir.

He gave them charming names. "Insinuous" for his evil version of Mixis. And the one which both Ches and I immediately recognized as key to our task at hand, the polar opposite for Horos.

"Discursus."

I reviewed the following pages, slipping deeper into his book, wishing to hell the concept of the index had been invented prior to the Stuart monarchy. Without one, however, it took me half an hour to unearth Argyle's specifics on how to turn a member of the Dark Choir against another. Such was the purpose Discursus served, it seemed. Even the agents of darkness had their disagreements, and good fences kept good neighbors.

After translating the seventeenth century English into something I could act on, I replaced the book onto my shelf. I spied the dark-wood cabinet across the workspace. A deep curiosity stirred in my chest. If Argyle had a Netherwork tome in that cabinet, could it help us?

No. Whatever the benefit, it wouldn't be worth the risk.

I pulled Ches's stool over to the relatively dark corner by the reagent shelves and huddled up to close my eyes, ground and center.

The racing thoughts were difficult to quell. What was I doing? I had no clue whether this was a good idea. I could be killing Ricky tonight. I could be inviting certain doom onto myself and Ches. All I was going on was instinct, and an annoyingly persistent sense of confidence I couldn't seem to shake.

And where was Malosi? He'd spent all day on his errand for Clement.

The ghosts of my past and present hovered around my head. This was a time to clear my thinking and sharpen my focus. I willed it all away. Every bit of it. So what if I was running on instinct? So what if I felt confident?

It was enough. It had to be, and therefore it would be.

"Magician dictates parameter."

I said that last bit out loud. It sounded like Emil.

Ricky and Ches returned after a space of time that had become meaningless to me. When I opened my eyes and stood up, both of them froze.

I motioned for the workbench. "Ricky, sit."

He did so, without comment.

Ches sidled up next to me, reaching out to touch my arm. She pulled her arm back inches away from my sleeve.

I cleared my throat.

"Ricky?"

He nodded.

"Are you prepared?"

He nodded again.

"Good. You have a curse cast upon you. This is a malevolent thread of energy which is destroying your life. Specifically, your family bonds. This curse was inflicted upon you by others, outside of your consent, and outside of the rule of Nature. As such, we require accounts be settled, and this curse, with its appetites and consequences, returned to the ones who brought its form into fruition." I gave Ches a shrug. "Or, you know... some shit like that."

Ricky exhaled and smiled.

"What do I do?" he asked.

"I need you to relax. Try to keep your mind as clear as you can. Have you ever meditated before?"

He shook his head.

"Okay. The key is not to fight your thoughts, but to let them wash over you, like rain off the hood of a freshly waxed Camaro. Thoughts bead off and fall away. Close your eyes. Think about your breath." He did so. "Good. Now, imagine you're in a dark, featureless room. It's huge. Size of a football stadium. At the other end is a candle."

“What, like on a table or what?”

“Doesn’t matter. Don’t think about the table. Just focus on the flame. You know, just one teardrop flame. Blue at the bottom. Orange in the middle. Bright yellow at the tip. Imagine how it moves and flickers. See the tiny centimeter of smoke as it dances back and forth. Left. Right. Left.”

I gave Ches a look.

She had her chin tucked down, watching as I moved Ricky into a semi-hypnotic state.

I continued, “Left. Right. So far away. Can you see it?”

“Yeah,” he whispered.

“Good. Now, keep your eyes on that flame. It’ll get closer and closer. Slowly. It’ll only get closer if you pay attention. Any thoughts pop into your head, it’ll move back to the end zone. Don’t let that happen. Just relax. All you have to do is watch the yellow part of the flame where it turns into smoke. Where it dances. Left. And right. And left. And right...”

His breathing slipped into a deep, rhythmic pattern, and I knew his energy would be solid.

I whispered, “Ricky, your sister is a walrus.”

Ches cocked her head, but I held up my hand.

He didn’t respond. Didn’t even flinch.

I gave Ches a wink.

“He’s down.”

“I’m a what?”

“Had to check if he was letting outside stimuli interfere. He isn’t.”

“Walrus?”

I shrugged, and walked around to Ricky’s back.

“Okay, step up in front of him.”

She did so, giving me a questioning lift of her hands.

I whispered, “Okay. Time to untangle.”

“Great,” she replied in low volume. “How?”

“We’ve been doing energy palpation for months, now.”

“So?”

"So, this is it. Palpate. Find the energy lines. They're coming from outside of Ricky's mainline. Locate them, then find their branches. Follow the branches."

"You do it," she whispered with a hunch in her shoulders.

"No, you're the better choice. You have resonance."

"You're better at this than I am."

"Not really. You're his sister. You share most of his energy signature by virtue of your DNA. And you're the one the Dead Dragons were trying to hurt with this curse. Ches, you are literally written into the program code of this curse."

She lifted a hand to her forehead. "I don't know if I can—"

"Stop thinking about it. Just palpate."

"Dorian—"

"Really. Turn off your brain. Go on instinct. You can do this. I know your intent is pure. That's huge. This is your brother, Ches. Save him."

Her eyes softened as she glared at me over Ricky's shoulder, and she gave me a quick nod.

Ches lifted her hands in front of Ricky's chest, swaying as she sensed the distinct energies laced within him. She continued up and down, left and right, for what felt like an eternity. I periodically reached out to test Ricky's energy myself. Not to toss in my guidance, but to ensure he wasn't getting the life squeezed out of him by a desperate and vengeful curse thread.

Ches's eyebrows popped up, and she snapped her fingers at me.

"I think I feel it."

I nodded. "Good. Heart chakra?"

"Yeah."

"That's what I thought."

"Family. Connection to children. It's the heart chakra."

"Where do the tendrils lead?"

She clamped her eyes shut, and lunged closer to Ricky's body. I coaxed her along with a quick Lesser Cross visualization to broom away the ambient energy our conversation had dusted up.

"Solar Plexus," she whispered. "Into the spleen. Core. Starting in on his liver."

"That's the addiction."

"I want to kill it."

"Good."

"Seriously, Dorian," she growled with eyes shut and teeth bared. "It's gonna die."

"Just ease it out. Unwind. Start deep, move shallow. It'll start to fight you. Don't let it."

The energy in the room snapped into a sudden chilly caste as Ches plunged directly into the working. Indeed, her energy became so terrifyingly focused I could barely sense her presence in the room. What I could sense, however, was Ricky's mainline snapping in tiny breaks, like fishing line popping under too much tensions. It was at the same time alarming and exhilarating. We were making progress. Hopefully, for Ricky's benefit.

The process was slow. Remarkably slow, as it should have been. Ricky wilted time-to-time as fatigue set in. Each time I tapped Ches on the shoulder to let her know she needed to hold. I felt like the guardian at the watchtower, and the thought was exhilarating. I wasn't playing the part of the grand master know-it-all. I was just giving a capable practitioner a heads-up on a shift in energy, and as an assistant, I coaxed Ricky back into a deep meditative state. Then Ches proceeded with the extraction.

For that precious space of time, she was the alpha dog. It suited her.

By the time the energy had snapped free of each of the secondary chakras, I realized I had forgotten a key piece in this ritual.

My darquelle.

I tapped Ches on the shoulder.

She opened her eyes.

"What?" she rasped. "Bad timing, dude."

"Keep him steady. I have to go upstairs."

Her eyes shot open.

"What? The what? Where?"

"I'll be right back."

Her face drew into a dangerous scowl, but I just shrugged and stepped away gently. The energy bubble around the two siblings spliced together nicely, as I expected it to.

I hopped toward the steps and reached the ground level quicker than I had since I stopped jogging. The darquelle sat mounted on the front wall near the front door, within easy grasp should anything incorporeal come kicking down my door. Or corporeal, for that matter.

I lifted Robert the Heretic's darquelle off its wall mount and gripped it in my hand. This blade had taken a life. Probably some Roundhead, hell-bent on dealing God's justice. It was a dark weapon. With any luck at all, it would serve me against the Dark Choir.

I returned downstairs with a curious smell of wet dog filling my nostrils. I willed it away to return my focus on the task at hand.

Ricky and Ches remained as I left them, a tight bubble of energy clutching them in its shell.

I stepped into this bubble, a snap or two letting my decades-trained senses know it was unhappy, and gave Ches a go-ahead nod.

She reached out with claws as hands, tugging in a pantomime at a thick, savage tentacle of ill intent that had laced itself into Ricky's person. He shuttered briefly, and I resumed my guidance to bed him back into a receptive state. Ches continued to weave and untangle, and the longer she went, the more she gave into the sensory stimuli. Her hands moved with ease, and I felt no urge to speak up and direct her reach.

Ches reached back with her hand, shaking it like a student taking a long essay exam. I moved for my minerals cabinet and pulled out a large hunk of hematite for her to grip. She did so without breaking focus on Ricky. With a few pumps of her fingers over the stone, she dumped the excess energy and continued with her work.

And thus we continued for the next forty minutes. The line was laced deeper than I had imagined. Ches had to backtrack six times to tertiary chakras, making sure she could fully remove every branch and root.

Ricky began to slump, either from fatigue or from having fallen asleep. Either way, he was losing his focus. I wrapped my hands in sage-soaked gauze I'd prepared for clearing ritual instruments, and took the curse line from Ches while the both of them rested. I clutched onto the pulsing tentacle of hatred, throbbing in my grip. It was raw and angry. I captured flashes of its originators. Not visual images, more like the emotional snapshot of the Dragons when they had cast this curse. The flashes were cold, mechanical, mercenary. There was no personal investment in this curse. It was a shot fired in a war, and that was all. The only angry thing was the curse itself.

Ches moved upstairs to bring some water for herself and Ricky.

He opened his eyes and glanced at me.

"Just hold still," I whispered, keeping as much focus on the energy in my hands as possible.

"Is it working?" he asked.

"Yeah."

"Doesn't feel like anything's—"

"I have it right now. We're almost there."

"Can you finish it?"

I shook my head, trying to tune out his suggestion. I couldn't sway my intent at that moment. Doing so could jeopardize everything we had accomplished, and snap the curse back deeper into Ricky's mainline. He continued to ask questions, but I shoved his voice out of my ears. It wasn't helping that the energy seemed to sense my focus had been interrupted, and was doing its best to slither free of my grip.

"Yeah," I replied to nothing in particular.

He muttered something else. I shook my head.

Before I could realize that I had become inadvertently drawn into a near-mesmerized state with my focus fully diverted, Ricky chuckled.

"You're shitting me?"

I sucked in a breath. "What?"

"You are in love with her. She was right. I swore you were just socially stunted, but no. She was right about you."

I gritted my teeth. Crap. He had me in a hypnotic trance, and went right for the jugular.

"Ricky? I have to concentrate here. You read me?"

He nodded. "No sweat, boss."

Ches returned with two glasses of water. She took her time hydrating as Ricky gave her a wicked smirk.

"What? What happened?" she grumbled.

"Nothing," we responded in unison.

"Both of you suck."

I called her over with a nod. "Break's over. Let's finish this."

She reached in and deftly snatched the curse from my control, and resumed her work. I didn't have to work Ricky back down. Seemed he was pretty much opened up already. Nor did it take long until Ches took a step away, the curse energy still gripped in her clutches.

"Okay, I'm down to the core I think."

I grabbed the darquelle.

"Here's the tricky part," I muttered.

Ricky cracked open his eyes, which flew open on sight of the blade in my hand.

"Guys?" he moaned.

"Take it easy. I'm just going to sever the energetic link from your body."

"And not, you know, my body?"

I grinned. "Not unless you twitch."

The blade hummed in my hand as I slid it close to Ricky's sternum, easing its edge up toward his chin.

"This blade has been blooded. It's killed in the service of Netherwork. Now it cuts on both sides of the Veil."

Ches asked, "You're not going to leave any of it inside him, right?"

"Don't worry. This thing won't want to stick around once it's freed."

"When you sever the link, what happens then?"

I gave her a measured look. "Not entirely sure. It might thrash on you like a crocodile. It might sit dormant. We'll send it back to the caster with Argyle's mantra. You got it ready?"

She nodded.

I raised my hand to count down three-to-one so we could chant the thing in unison.

Three.

Two.

One.

The two of us stumbled through the mantra. "Horos at agony sum Mixis. Horos at agony sum Mixis." It took us about six repetitions until we got onto the same cadence, and another twelve before our vocal energies began to meld. That's when the layered resonance took hold. Group workings weren't something I made a habit of, but I had to admit the Wiccans were on to something when they pulled together in tight groups of like-minded practitioners. Wren would have been proud.

The resonance compounded, and my darquelle positively rang with harmonics. The moment felt right. The stars were aligned. The hills were alive with the sound of music, and I was ready to end this fucking curse.

I eased the darquelle up Ricky's shirt, pausing at his chin, then gave the blade a swift twist away.

The basement lights flickered.

The room pulsed warm-to-cold, then back to warm.

Ches froze, keeping her hands still.

Ricky blinked rapidly, eyes still on my blade.

And I inched away from the both of them, eyes on the ceiling.

I could hear the others breathing. Panting, really.

Finally, Ches wiggled her fingers.

"Uh...I think, and I could be wrong here, but I think it's gone."

I gave Ricky a look. "How do you feel?"

He reached up and ran his hands across his chest, then shrugged.

"I don't know," he muttered. "How do you feel?"

"I'm okay. Ches?"

"I'm good," she responded.

She lowered her hands.

I sheathed the darquelle with a slow exhale.

"I'll be here all week, folks. Tip your waitress."

Ricky hopped off the workbench, holding out a flat hand.

"Wait a minute. How... how do we know this worked?"

Ches looked to me.

I answered, "I suppose we'll have to wait for some sign, an indication that—"

A loud electronic chirp filled the room. My heart pulsed hard in my chest before I realized it was Ricky's phone.

He slid the phone out of his pocket as it continued to ring.

"You had a cell phone in your pocket this whole time?" I grumbled.

"Yeah."

Ches lifted a finger. "Wait. Don't you have really awful coverage in this little dungeon?"

"Actually, yes," I replied.

Ricky lifted the phone, and his face blanched.

"What?" Ches whispered. "Who is it?"

He swallowed, and with a lifted brow he replied, "It's Susanna."

CHAPTER TWENTY-FOUR

Ricky held the phone out like a dead rat.

"What should I do?"

Ches released a disbelieving huff. "Answer it, you moron!"

He pulled the phone to his head.

I chided, "Go upstairs. Don't want to lose signal down here."

He nodded as he bustled up the stairs.

Ches and I stood silent for a moment.

"Wow," I said to break the silence.

"That's something."

"It is."

"So, this means it worked?" she asked.

"It has to. There's no way this is a coincidence. The curse was meant to torment his family. His wife suddenly reaching out? That's a good sign, I think."

She smiled. "You did it, magic man!"

"We did it."

Ches took two steps forward and eased her arms around me, pulling me tight into a hug.

"Thank you," she whispered.

I tried to say something distracting and flippant, but words failed me.

She gripped me close for a half-minute, then pulled away.

Before I could ease the tension, she reached up and kissed me.

Time stopped.

All I could think about was the feeling. Her lips on mine, her hands sliding up my back, my hand reaching for the back of her head as we breathed thin breaths between motions.

Then, in a second, she jerked away.

The distance was as jarring as the immediacy.

She held her forehead with the tips of both hands.

"Shit," she muttered. "That wasn't supposed to happen."

"It's okay."

"No, no it isn't. Because I didn't want to do that, and that's not on you. That's on me."

"I really don't mind."

She paced a tight circle. "We're not a thing. We can't be a thing."

I slid my hands into my pockets, trying to present as small a target as possible.

She shook her head, clenched her jaw for a few seconds, then mumbled, "Hell with it."

The distance between us vanished as she rushed back into me, throwing her arms around my neck. This time, her mouth slipped onto mine with considerable abandon. Her tongue parted my lips. The tiny breaths escaping her nose rushed across my cheek as we kissed. Floral perfume. The rising musk of sweat. Everything filled my head except the first thought of what we were doing.

When she pulled away, I kept my eyes closed. It had to be a dream, and I didn't want to wake up to the reality of things. But even as I willed away the thought, it smashed into my head nonetheless. This was going to change things.

I opened my eyes, and found Ches grinning at me.

"What're you thinking about?"

"Trying not to."

"Seriously. I need to know where you're at with this."

I stepped back until I leaned against a wall, and put my hands on my head.

"Words fail me."

"That's a first."

"I suppose I'm worried this will get weird, now."

She shook her head. "That's tomorrow. I mean today, right now. How close are we going to get? How far's too far?"

"I don't think we're going to know until we go too far."

"That might not be good enough."

I smirked. "Suck it up, Magic Woman."

She grinned, stepped slowly to me, then smacked my arm.

"Ow."

"But you're not freaking out?"

"Not expressly."

"Because I'm not freaking out, either. And that's kind of freaking me out."

I pulled my hands off my head. "It's possible we're overthinking this a hair."

She nodded with an air of gloom. "I'm not used to things working out in my favor."

"I know the feeling. But hey, today was a good day. We lifted your brother's curse. Who knows how much of that curse was blowing back on your life? Could be, things are turning around for you, too?"

"Come on," she urged, gripping my shoulders and turning me to the stairs. "Let's see how he's doing. You know, before we do something else we'll regret."

We moved up the stairs to the ground floor. I didn't spot Ricky immediately. After a quick tour of the floor, I cocked my ear upstairs. Still nothing.

Ches shrugged.

I stepped to the front door and pulled the curtain from the door pane. There he was, standing on my stoop, facing the street.

"Here he is," I whispered.

"How's he doing?" she asked, hopping up to the door.

I squinted in the poor light outside, and noticed his phone was in his hand.

I released a "hmm" before reaching for the doorknob.

"What?"

"Don't know."

As I opened the door, Ricky kept his back to us.

"Ricky?" Ches called. "All's good with Susanna?"

He turned, finally, his face drawn, his eyes glazed.

"Ricky?" Ches repeated in a whisper.

He dangled the phone in his fingers. "She found out I'm on the East Coast." With a ragged sigh, he added, "On Monday, she's moving for termination of my parental rights."

Ches groaned, and reached out to him.

He pulled away with a single step.

It didn't work.

I was so sure. Everything seemed correct. The theory was sound. The energy lines were carefully and thoroughly extricated, and the curse form sent back to its creator.

Yet, here he was, worse off than before. Was it the curse, after all? Or would it take more to heal the damage than a hermetic working?

Ches advanced until he couldn't fight her off, wrapping her arms around him.

I stood dumbly on the stoop, hands at my sides. There was nothing I could offer.

I was a fool.

Ultimately, I turned back to my house, retreating from the Bakers' misery. I wound my way to my sideboard, crouching down to pull out my new bottle of Glenrothes. It wasn't the pricey stuff, just something I'd bought a few months ago, then forgot about. Hadn't had a craving for scotch in a while.

I poured three fingers and brought it to my nose. The fumes spread up my nose, wiping away the memory of Ches's floral perfume.

Before long, the old feeling crept into the space between my shoulder blades. The old doom, the certain knowledge that my death was upon me, and I was standing here without a soul.

The door opened behind me.

With another swig, I turned to face Ches. Only, it wasn't Ches.

Malosi stood in my foyer, consuming most of the space, his eyebrows drawn together.

"What's up?" he asked, nodding to the siblings in front of my house.

I set my glass onto the nearest table.

"Your errands finished?" I grumbled.

He nodded.

"Well, there you go."

"Dorian? Something happened, and the longer it takes for you to just tell me, the more irritable I'm going to get. Let's just save us both some agony."

"We tried to lift Ricky's curse."

Malosi blinked, then looked back out the door with a solemn nod. "Fucked it up, huh?"

"Looks that way." I reached for my glass again. "His wife's filing for termination of parental rights. He's going to lose his kids."

Malosi shook his head and eased the door quietly shut.

Before I could take another belt, he rushed forward and snatched the glass from my hand.

"What the—"

He took it to the kitchen. I followed, like trash caught in the wake of a cruise ship. A yelp slipped from my throat as he poured the scotch down the sink.

He rinsed the glass in the sink, set it aside, and cracked his neck.

"So," he announced, "Mister Clement sends his regards, and wishes to offer his assistance with this Presidium bullshit. What should I tell him?"

I glared at Malosi.

He didn't budge. Rock of Gibraltar, that guy.

"You poured my whiskey down the drain."

"What shall I tell Mister Clement?" he pushed.

"How the hell should I know? I'm not sure what I'm doing here, Reed! I have the fucking Ipsissimus summoning me to some meeting

I'm not entirely sure I'll survive. I have Felix Parrish pounding the astral streets, shaking down every shade and demon for the whereabouts of my soul. I have Ricky Goddamn Baker and this stupid curse which apparently I can't lift, and I might have just cost him any meaningful part of his children's lives. Jean wants to throw in? Fine. Just don't know what good it'll do."

If Malosi had a helpful response, he kept it to himself.

The front door opened, and I spotted Ricky brushing past the kitchen doorway toward the stairs.

"Ricky?" I called out.

He paused.

"Need to talk?" It was the best thing I could come up with.

Ricky shook his head.

"If you need anything..."

"I need to turn in. Interviewing staff tomorrow."

My stomach twisted. "Look, you don't have to worry about the tavern. All right? You got stuff to deal with."

He frowned. "Are you firing me?"

"Uh—no."

"Then I should get some sleep. See you in the morning." He added with a wilt, "Mind if I catch a ride in?"

"No problem."

He ascended to his room.

I stepped into the front. Ches leaned against the front door, arms folded across her body. A single tear ran down her cheek as she looked over to me.

"I'm sorry," I whispered.

She nodded, then gave Malosi a weak wave.

Malosi said from behind me, "You two want my help? Then listen up. You put your asses to bed. No drinking, either of you. Get focused. We'll lay things out tomorrow, see what we know and what we don't."

Ches slipped past me and went upstairs without a word.

I turned to Malosi. "You calling the shots, now?"

"I'm the only one left without any skin in the game. I'm not up in your house, giving orders or anything. But you need to pull your head out of this cloud of crap, if you're going to get your soul back."

"You're right. Like always. One of these days, I'm going to start listening to you the first time around."

"Not holding my breath."

I left Malosi with the room-temperature remains of my abandoned Shepherd's Pie and turned in without any scotch or wine or any of my usual remedies for a shit day.

CHAPTER TWENTY-FIVE

The following morning, I found a full spread of eggs and pan-fried ham waiting for us downstairs. Malosi shoved the last grocery bag into the recycling bin and gave me a nod.

"What's this?" I grumbled.

"Protein, fucker."

"Okay then."

It wasn't long until the smell of actual edible food called the Bakers downstairs. Ricky was shaved, dressed, and by all accounts looked like he was ready for a day on the job. However, his eyes hung with a haunted distraction I recognized from so many people I'd seen doomed in my years. His soul had given up; his body just hadn't caught up to the fact.

Ches wasn't much better. I asked her how she felt three times before she heard me. They were a matched set of dreary siblings. I couldn't blame them.

We ate largely in silence, and Ricky excused himself to brush his teeth.

Malosi stood up and gestured for the steel door leading to the basement.

"I got something to show you."

We followed him down into the workspace, which had transformed overnight into a kind of conspiracy command center. A large, ostensibly newly-purchased white board sat over Ches's desk. Words stood in large, neat block letters, connected with lines as Malosi saw fit. Familiar words.

Deirdre.

Durning.

Geomancy.

Gettysburg.

Enoch Pratt.

I stood back to take it all in.

"You missed Lee Harvey Oswald and the Cubans."

Malosi slugged my arm with what he probably thought was a light tap.

Ches stood blank, staring forward. I suspected she wasn't really seeing the whiteboard. Her eyes flickered with rapid thoughts, likely about her brother and sister-in-law.

"It's nice, Reed," I added. "Mind if I make some additions later?"

"That's the idea."

Ricky's voice called from upstairs, "We doing this, or what?"

We all packed into Malosi's car and drove to the tavern. No one was expressly talkative, least of all myself. My brain hummed in several directions, trying to make traction but finding little. The funk remained as we filed through the back door and into the tavern itself. My attention being so wrapped up inside my head, I managed to miss the limousine parked along the front of the building on Light Street. Spotting that limo would have been helpful, too, since it was with a degree of alarm that I found Wexler's driver, Reginald, sitting at the bar chatting it up with Ben.

I froze, reaching up reflexively to keep Ches from advancing. I couldn't play it off, either, as Reginald spotted me almost instantly.

Ben nodded and snickered over some joke Reginald must have told before turning back to pull some bottles from the rail.

I steered the Bakers toward Julian's office, but kept Malosi close.

Reginald pulled himself off his stool and stepped forward.

"You're late," he stated.

"According to whom?"

"I was told you would arrive half an hour ago."

"I'm going to have to go ahead and not give two shits what you were told, friend."

His eyes squinted, but he held his position.

I added, "Not to be uncordial. Please, have a beer on the house."

"I'm here to take you to your meeting."

Ah. Right.

"Wexler sent you to fetch me, huh?"

"We're already late. Time to go."

I had Ricky in the back, and couldn't afford to leave him alone. This was the worst possible time for this.

"Listen," I replied in hushed volume, "I have a thing or six to work out here. Can we do this later? It's really not a good—"

Reginald took a step toward me, reaching for my arm.

"Let's go, Mister Lake."

I didn't hear Malosi move, but when the tower of Polynesian obstinacy slipped between me and Reginald, the impact sent me off my balance. I caught myself on the edge nearest four-top and turned to find Reginald and Malosi chest-to-chest. Two giants in tailored suits glared into each other's face.

Malosi intoned, "Step off."

Reginald didn't step off.

My pulse pounded as the realization of the moment crept into my brain. I was keeping the Ipsissimus waiting. And as much as I loved Malosi for stepping in and finally brooming Reginald off my back, this wasn't a standoff we were going to win.

Before I could work my voice into an audible volume, the front door of the tavern opened.

"Are you sure you're making a sound decision, Mister Malosi?" a voice swept from the daylight spilling into the room.

I hung my head and turned to Wexler.

She held up a hand and sauntered into the tavern with a genial grin.

"Reginald was an Army Ranger," she added. "You could try

something assertive, but I'd recommend against it."

I watched Wexler as she stepped to the bar and gave Big Ben a smile.

"Single scotch. Whatever Dorian drinks will do. It's early."

Ben gave me a look, and I nodded.

He poured her a finger of '83 Balblair, and slid the glass courteously forward.

"Thank you, handsome," she quipped as she took a slow sip.

I eased Malosi back and faced Wexler.

"I'll just be a minute," I muttered.

She nodded and nursed the remainder of the Balblair as I retired to Julian's office.

I found Ricky and Ches sitting across from Julian. He gestured with a handful of applications as Ricky nodded along. Despite last night's setback, Ricky seemed to be on course. Either that, or he was good at tucking it in.

That was a lesson for which I was overdue.

"You guys solid?" I asked when a pause presented itself.

Julian gave me a shrug. "A bit meager. We might have to take what we get."

Ricky kept his eyes down on the desk.

With a quick reach, Ches squeezed my hand, a gesture that didn't escape Julian's notice.

"Good," I deflected as his eyebrows lifted. "Listen, I have to run out."

Ches scowled. "Where?"

"It's a big meet. Last minute, but can't skip this."

"Claye?" Julian asked.

"No. Something else."

"Ah," he prodded. "Your other pursuit?"

"Something like that."

Ches shifted to face me. "Need a hand?"

I squeezed her hand firmly, then released it. "I'm good."

I left the office and turned to find someone I wouldn't be able to brush off quite as easily.

Malosi lifted an eyebrow. "You know this won't be a debate, right?"

"They're not going to let you come, Reed."

He turned and marched back to the front of the tavern. By the time I caught up to him, he had faced off with Reginald again, but was looking past him to Wexler.

"You understand, I'm not letting this man out of my sight," he grumbled.

Wexler cocker her head, finished her scotch, then stood up to straighten her pants.

"I understand your purpose, Mister Malosi. But you must understand that there truly is nothing you can do to stop us."

He stood firm.

With a tiny nod and sniffle, Wexler continued, "This is a friendly meeting. No harm will come to Mister Lake, assuming," she added, "he behaves himself."

I crossed my heart with my finger.

Wexler turned for the door, saying, "He can come, but he stays in the car."

Malosi looked back into Reginald's face. With considerable effort, Reginald turned away to open the door for us.

The ride south to the D.C. beltway was unnervingly quiet. Wexler rode in the front, leaving me to share the back with Malosi. He wasn't feeling particularly talkative. Probably a good idea. The car navigated westward over the beltway, curving south over the Potomac. We exited soon after, winding along a stretch of narrow but well-paved byway alongside the river. We passed lavish properties, gated compounds with guardhouses and gardens manicured on a French monarchy level of precision. Beyond one gate in particular I spotted a tiny birthday party with young children running around an inflatable bounce house in dapper clothing. The sight elicited a laugh from my throat, though I wasn't entirely sure why.

Malosi turned to give me an alarmed side-eye.

"Everyone loves bounce houses."

"I always called them moon walks," he mumbled.

After a space of silence, Wexler announced, "Moon bounce."

"Hmm?"

She swiveled to face us. "My grandchildren call them moon bounces. Seems language is ever-shifting." Turning back to face the front, she added, "As are the prevailing winds of fortune."

"Fortune's a fickle bitch, I'll give you that."

"Best to be the one holding the leash, wouldn't you agree?"

The car pulled into a heavily wooded drive. I wouldn't have noticed it if Reginald hadn't turned in. After a single curve of maples and locust trees, the drive reached a tall wrought iron gate. Beyond the gate and the guardhouse lay a wide expanse of unremarkable lawn. It sloped away from the front of the property so sharply we couldn't see anything beyond the dip. Everything about this property screamed concealment.

No one manned the guardhouse. We sat in front of the gate for several minutes with no sign of activity beyond. Wexler and Reginald seemed content with the situation, so I assumed this was normal.

At last, a golf cart with two suited goons in sunglasses slipped into view at the curve of the lawn. Reginald unlocked the doors, and Wexler stepped out. I followed suit.

Malosi tried to, as well, but his door seemed to have remained locked.

Wexler leaned in through my open door.

"You'll stay in the car, Mister Malosi. That was our agreement."

He crossed his arms and stared forward, his jaw set.

The golf cart hummed up to the gate, which opened on its own.

I asked Wexler, "You sure I'm coming back, right?"

With a chuckle, she replied, "He's invited you here, Mister Lake. That rarely ever happens. I think you'd know by now if the Ipsissimus wanted you neutralized."

"I suppose that's true."

One of the goons stepped up and gestured for me to approach the golf cart.

"You're not coming, then?" I asked Wexler.

"I wasn't invited."

Her face stiffened into some inscrutable mask of patience and quiet resentment. As I turned with a nod to Malosi through the windshield,

I wondered if Wexler had ever set foot inside these gates. My feelings of dread eased as I rolled that thought around my skull. This meeting was a bigger deal than I had previously assumed.

That easy feeling vanished, however, when I stepped through the gates, piercing a particularly prickly and draining property warding. Were I not invited, I doubted I could have stayed conscious.

The golf cart ride down the path was even quieter than our ride down from Baltimore. The thin asphalt cart path led down the curve of the lawn, and soon the front gate was out of sight. Almost immediately, the high gables of a slate-shingled chalet style roof sliced into view above the maples at the far end of the lawn. The house was enormous. Stately. Foreboding. Precisely what I expected from the head of the Presidium.

I released a low whistle.

The goon who wasn't driving swiveled his head and smirked.

The cart path split near the wide cobblestone drive holding three impossibly expensive cars. I almost attempted a remark about the Bugati sitting near the front door, when the cart took the path leading away from the house. I kept my mouth shut.

The Potomac slipped into view behind a copse of trees. It was the charming, rocky part of the Potomac, bubbling as it swept past the crags midstream. The path wound its way to a squat building near a concrete-paved inlet from the river.

Boathouse.

As the cart hummed to a stop, we all stepped out, and the goons assumed flanking positions beside me. With another flat gesture, I was ushered to the side of the boathouse. A pair of barn doors along the far end of the building hung open on their sliding rails. Sunlight only illuminated the space nearest the barn doors, and beyond was darkness. I checked with my escort before stepping inside.

"Uh, hello?" I ventured as I inched into the space.

A cough to my right and the clearing of a throat were my answer. I turned to find a short, emaciated man hunkered over a workbench. A round fluorescent work lamp clamped to the bench hovered near his head. He wound one hand in rapid circles as he loomed over his work. The intense focus was jarring. What working had the Ipsissimus decide to practice at the precise moment I stepped into his boathouse? Surely it would be a message of some kind. Watch your step, boy, or you'll end up at the end of whatever tiny little slice of Hell I'm cooking up. I extended my senses as much as I dared, but detected absolutely no energy. No intent. No will.

Another clearing of the throat, and the frail man muttered, "Just be a minute."

I stepped closer, squinting over his shoulder.

A flat board with nail pegs sat beneath his gloved hands. He gripped a pair of needle nose pliers in his right hand, using it to wind a thread in dizzying patterns over the pegs. I shook my head when I finally deduced what the Hell he was doing.

"Fly fisher?" I ventured.

He made two tiny knots, then reached for a pair of scissors.

"Indeed." He held up his new fly lure with the pliers, admiring it in the sunlight. "You?"

"Can't say I've had the opportunity."

"Shame. Only thing worth doing on this damned river."

He slipped the lure into a divided tray of tiny cubbies, and finally turned to me. His thick glasses made his eyes pop, rendering the rest of his gaunt face in cartoonish relief. He reached out bony fingers, and I shook his hand.

"Joe Adrastos," he declared.

"Dorian Lake."

The Ipsissimus swiveled at the waist to grab two aluminum arm braces I hadn't noticed were leaning against his bench. He slipped his arms into the braces and hobbled forward.

"Follow me," he said.

I obeyed, watching as his feet slid uneasily along the cement floor of the boathouse. He led me to the far end, cloaked in shadow, before reaching up and sliding open another door. My eyes squinted against direct sunlight as the river swept below a deck of chairs and wooden tables.

A woman in a white skirt and navy blouse stepped forward to hold the door open. I noted as Adrastos stepped onto the deck that the gesture was intended for me, not Adrastos.

"Gin and seltzer, Margarite. And whatever Lake's having."

I watched Adrastos as he eased down into a chair, then snapped my attention back to the woman waiting for my drink order.

"Oh, uh... scotch." As she lingered, I realized I needed to be more specific. "Speyside single malt, whatever you got."

She nodded and slipped out of view.

Adrastos set his braces alongside his chair and cracked his knuckles. His eyes drooped as he ran his hands over the arms of his chair.

"Clearly, we've been watching you, Mister Lake."

"I gathered."

"You've shown a remarkable amount of growth in the past year. Those barking for your removal aren't barking quite as loudly, anymore. And for good reason, I suspect."

That was good to hear.

"I've done my best to keep off your shit list." I winced. "Pardon my language. I mean, I don't know. Is it—"

"It will take a lot more than the odd 'shit' to offend me." He sighed. "It seems I've surrounded myself with odd shits intent on offending me, at any rate."

"Bad luck."

"I feel it's best to begin our conversation by clarifying a point or two regarding the late Lillian Hsu."

My stomach knotted.

He continued, "I found her practices and methods to be personally distasteful in the extreme. However, that alone is not sufficient cause to neutralize an individual. Her recent ambitions put our organization at odds with a similar but much older cabal in Beijing. Which presented a threat to national security, a threat our mundane government is ill-equipped to handle. Hence the extreme prejudice."

"The fu dogs?"

"Ancestral enslavement, to be more accurate. Again. Distasteful."

The attendant returned with a tulip glass of effervescent gin cocktail, and a tiny snifter of amber liquid. She handed me the snifter before taking great pains to settle Adrastos's glass onto a tiny end table at his side.

"Thank you, Margarite," he droned without looking at her.

She lingered in front of us until each of us took a sip. I gave her an appreciable nod, and she seemed content to withdraw once again.

The scotch was, in fact, transcendent.

"I want you to understand our rationale," he continued, "regarding Hsu. We are not quick to kill, Mister Lake."

"You seemed quick enough to kill Cecil Rawls."

He lifted his chin, searching the ceiling. "Rawls?"

"Reporter for the Sun. He and his entire family were killed in a car wreck last summer."

"Ah, yes. That was regrettable." Adrastos considered me for a moment. "He had uncovered connections between our organization and Sooner. We had plans for Baltimore, Mister Lake. Plans that had taken years to see into fruition. When confronted, Rawls threatened us. We had little choice." He added with a sip of this gin, "I do wish his family hadn't been involved. We dealt with the one responsible for that unnecessarily brutal oversight in-house."

"An oversight, huh?" I grumbled. "He had children."

"Alas, we are not quite as omniscient as our reputation leads one to believe."

"That so?"

He replied, "We are the silent defense of this nation, Mister Lake. Not some arbitrary gatekeeper of the secret knowledge."

"At this point, I imagine you can keep whichever gate you'd like."

"We couldn't keep Quinn Gillette from entering Baltimore, could we?"

I pursed my lips.

He took a long pull of his drink. "We have to be careful with our assets."

"Assets?" I asked.

"Netherwork is a filthy, destructive practice. Left on its own, it would plunge an entire society into another Dark Age, such as we saw in the histories of Europe and the Levant. The freedoms we cultivate in our society simply may not extend to hermetic practice. However, to extend a metaphor, the best method to prevent a forest fire is to selectively burn away the brush. Maintenance, Mister Lake. We require regular maintenance of our own fold. Too much power in too few hands?" He chuckled. "It's a recipe for tyranny. We realize that. It's one of the reasons the office of the Ipsissimus is elected."

I quickly sipped my scotch. He was the elected leader of the Presidium? My utter ignorance of the matter became painfully clear to me in that moment.

Adrastos gave me a moment to respond, and as I held my tongue, he continued.

"It seems the virtuous few who are tasked with eliminating darker magics are by definition poor executioners. Hence it behooves us to preserve a body of dependable Netherworkers."

I nodded. "Oh. Those kinds of assets. Like Osterhaus?"

"Neil was a simpleton, and as such he was predictable. Which made him reliable."

"I wondered why you let him operate for so long."

With a sigh, he said, "Those cabinets full of soul contracts provided something of a lure for unsavory elements. Those who would buy them, traffic in them. With our guidance, he brought several foreign interests to us, and we allowed him the occasional genuine sale to maintain his business. An arrangement that suited everyone, that is, until Hassam Al-Syriani."

I buried my face into the snifter.

"Alas," he continued, "that same predictability was employed toward his downfall. Many within the organization called for your removal because of that, and again when you managed to derail our plans for the Baltimore mayorship. But better angels prevailed."

"Was Brown one of these better angels?"

Adrastos choked a little on his gin.

"Brown?" he gasped. "His contempt for you borders on alarming. But he is only one voice. There are others, of course."

"And Wexler?"

He turned toward me as far as he was able. "If you wish to gossip about the opinions and proclivities of our members, then this conversation will become very brief."

I tucked my chin. "Sorry. It was just...enlightening."

"I think you know more than you realize. You're looking for confirmation. And confirmation isn't why we're here."

"Why are we here?"

"Assets, Mister Lake. We're here to discuss assets."

I took a moment. "Was Frater Zeno one of your assets?"

"Yes. His dedication to his own ego is so absolute. It requires little effort to prod it toward our ends."

"So, Zeno's a Presidium hit-man?"

Adrastos's face soured. "Not as such. We employ mundanes toward that end. No, his use to the Presidium lies in his contact with the other side."

"Ah. So it wasn't respect or fear that kept him operating so close to D.C.? It was need."

"He has been quite useful to us. And he's done good work."

"Not so much anymore," I grumbled.

"Oh, I'm confident he can be restored. Assuming we can navigate the recent unpleasantness."

"Yeah. That." I took the last sip of scotch and set the glass aside. "Was Carmody one of your assets, too? That's why you let him relocate to the East Coast?"

Adrastos swiveled back to face the river. "He had potential. Again, you ensured that option was no longer available to us. Indeed, our list of assets has been crippled as of late."

"So I've noticed."

"Tell me," he said, gesturing with his glass, "are you not angry at the recent developments? Angry with the Presidium?"

I eased forward in my chair. This question was chock full of trip-wires. He was testing me.

"I'll tell you what I think," I began. "I think someone's decided the

Presidium is weak enough to attack."

He lifted a brow.

I steeled my intestines, and continued.

"That media bombshell with Durning? That was some kind of opening salvo, something to stir the pot and put the Presidium on the defense."

The barest lift of a grin haunted the corner of his mouth.

I continued, "I suspect whoever put Durning up to this, whoever put that list of Presidium names into his hands, had something on Durning dirty and sticky enough to make him commit political suicide. Then they took him out, stopped his heart with a simple curse. And it was all to kick up a Hell of a dust cloud over the Presidium. What's more, I suspect these are the same people who've been firing jinxes across the area. The same people who planted a niding pole inside a piece of public art in order to take out Zeno's lodge. The same people who are taking out the rest of your assets. You've pissed someone off, sir. And these people are taking their time with some very vicious magic."

Adrastos nodded. "I'm impressed. So many are quick to the simple conclusions."

"I have some experience with this sort of thing. Which brings us to the point, doesn't it?"

"What do you perceive the point to be?"

Here it went. "You've run out of assets, and you want me to get in the game."

"If I understand things correctly, Lake, you're already in the game. I'm here to offer incentive."

"Incentive, huh?"

He finished his gin, and Margarite swept back in to gather our glasses. When she disappeared once again, he continued.

"The Presidium is prepared to offer you a mandate to eliminate these renegades."

"Renegades?"

"Chaos magic. Not exactly an orderly business."

"What makes you think I can do it, if you can't?"

"We're hamstrung, Mister Lake. There are interests involved who make the current climate of hostility difficult to navigate without significant internal upheaval."

"What's my incentive? As if I couldn't guess."

"Sorry?"

"My soul. I assume you've had access to my soul for quite some time, now."

Adrastos snickered. "Oh, dear. Oh, Mister Lake. If such a thing were that simple, we'd have secured your soul long ago, and sent you back to your mediocre practices."

"What, then?"

Adrastos labored in his seat to reach for his braces, pulling himself upright with some effort. I fought the urge to assist, recognizing it was neither needed nor likely wanted. He moved for the railing of the deck overlooking the sparse trees separating us from the Potomac.

"Your disciple's brother. It comes to our attention that he has been cursed."

"Yes, that's right."

"A curse isn't something that's easily broken. Not without very specific circumstances aligning for the cursed."

"I noticed that."

Adrastos swiveled to face me. "There are means, however, to mend the damage the curse has rendered. Specifically, Mister Baker's wife and children."

I eased up from my chair, waves of unease sweeping through my chest. "You don't mean..."

"No, no. Nothing harmful. Quite the opposite. We have considerable influence in the Multnomah County District Court. What influence we enjoy on the West Coast, it seems, comes at a price. We'd be willing to expend some of our, shall we say institutional capital, to ensure Mister Baker retains full privileges with his children."

I settled back into my chair.

This was solid. No bullshit that I could tell. No magic bullet, no wave of a wand. I knew they could push a judge when they wanted to.

And he was correct in that the Presidium was considerably weaker in the Northwest. This would've been an expensive move for the Presidium, especially in a time when they were showcasing their weakness to the world.

Which told me how much they needed my help.

"Ricky stays in his kids' lives," I reiterated.

Adrastos nodded.

"What are my conditions for success?"

"Identify and eliminate the parties responsible for the recent attacks on the Presidium."

"That easy, huh?"

He didn't so much as smirk.

I continued, "And I can use Netherwork, if I have to. No repercussions."

"If it serves the interests of the Presidium. This is not a carte blanche to drown our soil in dark magic."

"I get it."

A cardinal in a nearby tree began whistling its guts out. I searched the nearby treetops for the little guy. Adrastos lifted a crooked finger in the direction of a silver maple. Sure enough, there he was.

"Magnificent creatures, aren't they?" he whispered.

"Loud creatures."

"They are proud. Unashamed."

I looked back over to Adrastos. "You have a goddamn deal."

He reached over with his hand. I gripped it gently, and he pulled it away before I could make sense of the cascading personal shielding washing over my wrist.

Margarite ushered me back to the goons with the golf cart, and before long they had deposited me at the front gate.

Reginald stepped out of the car to open Wexler's door.

"Mister Lake," she chimed as she stepped out. "You seem troubled. Was he not what you expected?"

"He was... shorter than I figured."

"Muscular dystrophy, in case you were wondering. So, have the two of you come to an arrangement?" she asked, chin dipping.

She must have known what he was prepared to offer me. I wondered exactly what else she knew.

"We have," I answered.

With a quick celebratory clap, she stepped back into the car. "Let's be on our way, then. This property plays havoc with my sense of calm."

"Know how you feel."

I let myself into the car. Malosi glowered in the back seat. He gave me a stiff nod. I figured he wasn't pleased with the circumstances, but I had expected at least the tiniest of debriefs. His jaw was tight, and his eyes remained set forward.

His fingers tapped the seat between us. He was nervous. Had Wexler threatened him?

To break the silence on our way back toward the beltway, Wexler turned on the local talk radio station. During a loud car commercial between breaks, I leaned over to Malosi.

"You okay?" I whispered.

"We're wasting time."

"It's not so bad," I reassured him. "We have some new options, now."

Malosi shook his head. "You don't get options with these people," he answered with enough volume for those in the front seat to hear. "You lose options."

"Perhaps in the long term," I countered. "Right now, we only have the one."

"So, we're collaborators now?"

"More like independent contractors."

Malosi sneered. "I'm going to have to make a phone call."

"I understand."

Wexler turned her head slightly, her lashes blinking furiously.

I leaned forward. "What's up?"

She held up a hand to shush me, and turned up the radio.

A reporter was describing a multiple alarm fire in Harper's Ferry, WV. Several historical buildings were engulfed in flames. Seemed tragic, but Wexler's prickly energy filling the car led me to believe something deeper was amiss.

I gazed out the right-hand window at the trees that swept past us. Gazing northeast.

Roughly toward Baltimore. And directly ahead would be Gettysburg.

Where was Harper's Ferry from that point? Northwest.

"Hate to ask this, but can we make a stop? Harper's Ferry is just west of here."

Wexler's head swiveled toward the driver seat.

"Reginald?" she muttered.

He nodded.

When we reached the split to either head east over D.C. or north toward the mountains, Reginald steered us north.

Wexler twisted around to face me. "What do you expect to see in Harper's Ferry, Mister Lake?"

"Chaos."

CHAPTER TWENTY-SIX

The fire had been beaten back to the burning remains of a long, wood-sided warehouse on the river. Several colonial-era structures lay in smoldering ruin. The firefighters and local police had the area of immediate danger cordoned off, and a mob of local media trucks and onlookers had choked out most of the walkways nearby.

I surveyed the town surrounding us. Low buildings huddled against the Potomac. It was claustrophobic, especially with the soot-choked air hanging in the valley.

"We need to get higher," I grumbled to Malosi.

He shoved his way through some of the locals to catch a glimpse up and down the street.

Wexler and Reginald stood across our lane, Wexler in deep conversation with someone wearing a fire department shield on his shirtsleeves.

Malosi snapped his fingers and pointed two doors down at a three-story structure with a kind of tiki bar for a balcony. A steel fire escape laced up the side of the building. It wouldn't be stealthy, but it would be direct.

"Right," I barked, winding my way toward Wexler.

She broke from the fire official as he plunged back into the crowd.

"It started here." She gestured toward a hallowed out clutch of walls. "Harper's Ferry Preservation Society. Old Miller's Hall. Served as a kind of museum and set of offices... until now. They're calling it old wiring, at the moment."

I asked, "Does this place have any meaning to you?" After a quick twist of her brow, I added, "To the organization."

"Not to my knowledge."

"How complete is that knowledge?"

Her eyes narrowed, but I stood my ground.

"As complete as the organization needs it to be. What are you getting at?"

"Just a theory."

"Regarding?"

With a sniffle, I replied, "Geomancy."

I turned and trotted after Malosi. We crossed the street and slipped into the alley between buildings with ease. He jumped up and gripped the bottom rung of the ladder. For the barest second, it wrestled against his weight before popping in a haze of rust, rattling down to within a few feet of the street.

"After you," I prodded.

He hoisted himself up the ladder to the first deck with remarkable speed. I took considerably longer. After several minutes, we rounded the top loop-hooks onto the edge of the concrete coping along the roof. The flat roof sat a couple feet below the coping, and our feet crunched on the grit and broken glass spread around the corner. Seemed to be a popular drinking spot.

Malosi scanned the immediate surroundings. Apart from a water tower behind us, we were the highest point on the block, and no one seemed to have taken notice of us.

"Over there," I called out, pointing back to the remains of the museum. "That square bit at the front."

"That's where it started?"

I nodded. "Old museum. Offices for the Preservation Society. Does Old Miller's Hall mean anything to you?"

He shook his head.

"Yeah. Me neither. Nor to Wexler."

The sun took its first shade behind the ridge to our west, and long shadows slipped slowly up the street below us. The embers within the roped-off zone stood out against the black smoke. As the daylight dimmed, and the smoldering wreckage stood out more and more, a chill rushed up my arms.

"You seeing that?" I whispered.

Malosi nodded.

"That's what I was looking for. We have a goddamn pattern, Reed."

Between wafts of smoke, a dark red widdershins spiral flickered in angry waves of heat.

"Another jinx," he grumbled.

"A nasty one, too. Anything strike you as odd about this series of jinxes?"

"What?"

"Colonial-era buildings. The daycare in Gettysburg. Enoch Pratt Library in Baltimore. Now this. For chaos magicians, they're being awful specific, don't you think? They're targeting buildings."

Malosi shook his head as he leaned against the coping. "You're convinced this has something to do with the Presidium. But Wexler doesn't know what this place is."

"Well, on one hand, she could be lying. On the other, the Presidium is a sprawling, multi-layered organization. I honestly think she's in the dark."

"Yeah. She chatted me up like she was nervous as shit. I don't think she's ever set foot inside those gates."

I smirked. "What the hell did you two talk about?"

"Economics, mostly. Eurozone. Some football."

"She's a Redskins fan, isn't she?"

"Figures, right?"

We took even longer to descend the fire escape, due in large part to the gathering dusk. When we reunited with Wexler, Reginald already had the car fired up. She watched us with crossed arms.

"Enjoy your climb?" she muttered.

"It was educational."

"Do tell."

I nodded to the car. "Inside."

By the time we had crossed the Potomac and were back in Maryland, she pressed me again.

"What was this about, Lake?"

"I know what started the fire."

"I'm assuming it's due to the flies in our current ointment," she responded.

I gave Malosi a grin. "Yeah, but do you know how?"

"Arson would be my guess."

"It was a jinx."

Silence fell over the car.

Yep. I had her on that one.

My brain folded over and over with thoughts and suspicions as we returned to Baltimore. Wexler was on the phone when Reginald pulled up to the back of the tavern, so Malosi and I stepped out without ceremony. The car eased around our claustrophobic parking lot and back out onto Light Street.

"So," Malosi grumbled, "you got a plan, or what?"

I froze.

He nudged my shoulder before he followed my eyes to the figure lingering by our back door. An elderly man with a briefcase. A very dangerous man.

Before he could bow up, I whispered, "You need to go inside."

Malosi grunted.

I urged, "I'm serious, Reed."

"How many times you going to send me away when some freak shows up?"

He wilted when I looked up at him. My eyes must have filled with the most convincing kind of panic, because he blanched a hair and trotted across the parking lot without further complaint.

And as the back door closed behind him, I was left alone with Felix

Parrish.

He took neat steps across the broken asphalt, his shoes managing to clop against the surface despite the gravel. Parrish's eyes were narrow, and his mouth pulled tight against his teeth.

"I suppose I know why you're here," I began as he brushed some invisible lint from his sleeve. "You found it, didn't you?"

He drew his lips together in a reply that seemed to take longer to materialize than he had intended.

"Your soul remains itinerate," he finally stated. "But we are closer than ever to securing it."

"That so?"

We stood in silence for a moment, as a garbage truck down the street clattered against a dumpster.

Parrish straightened his shoulders. "I've come to offer you one last opportunity to profit from your situation. Your benefactor remains cooperative, for the moment."

"Still want me to re-sign that contract? Hmm. That's interesting."

His brow lifted.

I continued, "Because the last time we spoke, I was under the impression THAT was my last chance. And if you were as close to securing my soul as you claim you are, then you wouldn't bother with this dog and pony show." I ventured a step closer. "I'm guessing you're getting pressure from this 'benefactor,' and it's starting to worry you."

The corner of his mouth lifted.

"You're not afraid of me anymore. Good. That makes things easier." He cleared his throat and turned to his left. "Your soul has been disembodied until recently, when it was secured by a third party. It is currently ensconced inside a vessel, and is moving across the country."

A chill sliced through my chest.

He swiveled his head toward me. "I tell you this so that you comprehend how much we've learned in how short a time. Once this vessel is delivered to its final location, wherever that may be, we will move."

My voice came out a whisper. "Why bother with me, then?"

"Because we're concerned, frankly. Concerned about your well-being."

"I guess you know something I don't."

He snickered. "Unimaginable volumes, Mister Lake." He reached into his valise and produced a scroll, brandishing it across his elbow. "Sign now, and the consideration from your benefactor may see you through the days to come. It may even save your life." He added with a squint. "And the lives of those close to you."

Something scurried in the shadows by the eve of the building beside the tavern. That familiar sense of doom, of the circling vultures, descended upon me once again.

Parrish sighed. "It's only a matter of time. Your soul remains tethered to this realm while you remain alive. Should that change, your soul will become considerably more portable. No one wants that to happen."

I swallowed, and it caught in my throat.

"I'm... sorry, no."

He glared at me before jerking the scroll back and securing it in his valise. Parrish stared forward, then nodded once.

"Better check your phone, Mister Lake."

He clopped along the parking lot, turning around one of the alleys I never really noticed before.

I pulled my phone from my pocket. It had shut off, at some point. I didn't remember turning it off. Probably some effect of Adrastos's property wardings. When it finally booted up, I found nine missed calls... six from Ches and three from Julian.

Not good.

Before I could reach the back door, it swung open, Malosi consuming the frame.

"You done?"

I nodded.

"Good. We have a problem."

CHAPTER TWENTY-SEVEN

Ben greeted me inside, his face more flushed than usual. "What's going on?" I blurted as he rounded around the edge of the bar.

"Ricky ran off."

I blinked. "What does that mean?"

"It means he's gone looking for something."

"Smack? How do you know?"

"I know, son. I saw his face. He was at the edge."

"Ah, shit."

Malosi added, "Julian took Francesca to look for him."

"Goddamnit. He was so close."

Ben put a meaty hand on my shoulder. "He's not gone yet."

I nodded.

"Reed? You feel like lending a hand?"

He moved for the front door. "He's on foot, right?"

Ben nodded.

"I'll work the block."

He dove out onto Light Street.

Ben crossed his arms.

I turned to him. "Any idea which direction Julian and Ches went?"

"East, I think. He mentioned Pulaski Boulevard."

I nodded. "Well, I doubt he made it that far, to be honest." My stomach knotted. "I'll be back as soon as I can."

Ben gave my arm a firm squeeze and nodded.

I got into the Audi and piloted through the darkening one-way blocks until I found myself at the intersection of the MLK. There was a series of overpasses where an aborted attempt to make a freeway into the heart of the city crossed over the MLK Expressway. Beneath the overpass sat a tiny shanty town of pup tents, mattresses, and the occasional thrown-out sofa that housed a community of homeless. I passed it every morning on my way in from Amity.

More importantly, I knew Ricky had seen it on the way into town the past couple days.

I parked under a streetlight at a gas station near the far corner, and navigated across the expressway to the shadow-choked concrete arches housing the clutch of homeless. The underside of the overpass crawled with hungry shadows, swarming behind the bug-clouded flood lights as I stepped underneath.

There were four distinct groups of men and women. The first were what seemed to be an elderly married couple, huddled together on a brown-and-orange sofa missing most of its cushions. The second were a group of younger men. They stifled their conversation as I approached, and disbanded before I could say anything. The second were a pair of men who asked me for changed. I gave each a twenty note.

And at the far end, nearest the center median, was a sharp-eyed youth in a Rastafarian knit hat. He'd watched me ever since I'd parked, and as I handed out my cash, he nodded for me to approach.

With a clearing of his throat, he asked, "You lookin' for that white boy?"

"Yes. I think I am."

He turned to stare down a lane between a parking garage and the teaching hospital.

"Don't think he's wantin' to live."

In a splash of green illumination from a nearby traffic light, I spotted a huddled mass at the base of the parking garage wall.

"You sold him heroin?" I asked.

"No, mon. But someone else did." He turned to me. "If you're savin' him, you better be quick."

"Not sure I can," I mumbled.

"Ja works, mon."

He reached out to hand me a tiny leaflet. I took it carefully.

It was a pamphlet on addiction with the address of a nearby church.

I waggled the leaflet. "You think God cares, at this point?"

He nodded, his eyes filled with a compelling intensity. "I know it."

"Okay, then."

I'd met true believers before. They scared me.

But this fellow wasn't the sword-edged conversion style of believer. His gravity was immense, but it was a drawing force. Not a pushing force.

I nodded to him and moved to cross the street, noting that the shadows in the corners of the overpass had gone.

Ricky sat hunched over, back against mossy concrete, head hung between his knees. I couldn't tell if he was sober or even if he was conscious. I stood nearby for a moment, just watching him. Perhaps guarding him.

I cleared my throat. "Can't be comfortable there."

He slowly lifted his head. His eyes were red-rimmed, but aware.

I added, "I'll have you know everyone at the Light Street Tavern is combing the streets of Baltimore for you. That's gotta mean something, right?"

"Sorry," he grumbled, hanging his head again.

I paced a slow circle, then shoved my hands in my pockets.

"Are you high?" I asked matter-of-factly.

He unfolded his arms, and held out his hand to reveal a tiny packet of pink-beige powder.

"So, that's a no?" I prodded with a smirk.

"I have nothing left. Suze. The kids."

"Yeah, I can see how it would look that way. I mean, I'm not a user, but my drug of choice is something a bit more insidious."

Ricky dropped his hand and straightened out his legs.

I walked to his side and leaned against the building.

"I'm in the weeds, too. You know? Just found out my soul is basically a day away from getting snatched up by some dark motherfuckers. And aforementioned motherfuckers aren't convinced I'll live long enough to see it happen. Then boom. Every eternal part of my being will become cat food for titanic demons of Creation. So, when you put things into perspective, a cold concrete wall ain't so bad after all."

He coughed to shake his voice loose. "Guess we're both fucked, huh?"

"Well, yeah. We are. I keep trying to find some way out of it, too. Like you. Only, I can't shoot up. That won't work. Only makes it worse if I lose my wits, and I've got people counting on me. Like you."

"No one's counting on me, boss."

"I got a student of mine riding around in a Volvo who'd beg to differ."

He shook his head. "She's better off without me."

"Maybe she should be the judge of that?"

"So, what happens when whatever's gonna kill you kills you? What happens to all these people who are counting on you?"

I lifted my chin and searched for a good answer for that question.

"Hmm. Yeah. Well, I guess I can't let that happen. Can I? There's no way out, Ricky. Only way out is through. Nothing to do but get so pissed off you're willing to make really stupid decisions in order to stay alive. And here's a fun fact... I'm a prodigy at making stupid decisions." I pushed off the wall and stepped around in front of him. "For example, I just made a deal with some powerful people who might just be able to help you out in court."

He lifted an eyebrow.

"I know, you heard this before. But trust me on this... these people are several pay grades above me, and they happen to need me. So, I cut a deal. I do their thing, they pull some shady-ass shit in the Oregon Circuit Court."

"They can do that?"

"It's literally the least they could do, but it's not nothing. Maybe we can't break the curse, but we can do an end run on the Cosmos, here." I crouched down. "It's your kids, man. You can't want to leave them behind."

A store of tears welled up in his eyes. He looked down to the ground, then up to me again, wiped his eyes on his sleeve, then reached for my hand.

I stood up and helped him to his feet. He lingered, considering the packet of opiates in his free hand.

"Got plans for that?" I asked.

"Don't suppose they do refunds out here?"

"Don't figure they do." I winced. "I...I didn't pay you yet. Where did you get the money for that?"

He gave me a miserable look. "Cash drawer."

"Never mind. I'll take it out of your check. Also, remind me to get on Ben's ass for leaving you with the cash drawer."

Chapter Twenty-Eight

I **drove Ricky back to the tavern, where I personally** witnessed him flushing the heroin down the men's room toilet. I then put him to work cleaning the bathroom. Ben had a row of evening customers at the bar, and I left him to keep them happy while I phoned Julian.

"Dorian?"

"Yeah. Hey, head on back. I got Ricky."

After a commotion, Ches's voice railed through the speaker. "Where have you been? I've called like twenty—"

"Sorry, chalk it up to hoojie magic interference."

"—been out here for two hours, and holy shit, this city!"

"Look, hey. Hey."

She finally took a breath. "What?"

"I got him."

"What?"

I leaned back in Julian's chair. "I found Ricky. He's okay. He's back here at the tavern scrubbing grout."

I heard a weird kind of fluttering noise, then a series of sniffles.

"Can you put Julian back on, please?" I asked.

After a space, Julian answered, "Good work, Dorian."

"Thanks. Come on back."

I tried Malosi next, but couldn't get through.

When Ches and Julian arrived, Ches swept directly past the office. I followed her down the hallway to the toilets, where she busted into the men's room, opened every door until she found Ricky, and then kicked a man out of the bathroom so she could give him a reaming. I elected to leave them alone.

Julian stood at the door to his office, arms crossed. "Every day isn't going to be like this, is it?"

I shook my head. "Better not be. I'll need a pacemaker by fifty, at this rate."

I followed Julian back into his office. He reached for a stack of resumes. "Before he went Caspar on us, Ricky hired three kitchen staff and four servers. Really don't think we'll manage them though, without... well, a manager." He lowered his voice. "What's Ricky's situation?"

"Sketch. Very, very sketch. But I'm trying to improve on that."

"As a friend, I understand what you're doing. As a business owner, though, you have to see how this comes across."

I shrugged. "Okay. You want to hire another manager, I'll support that."

"Not necessarily. Let's just see how this plays out, and maybe keep our eyes open. Just in case."

"Just in case. I'd usually say that sounds ominous, but right now you'd have to do way better than that. I mean, you'd need a pipe organ and Castle Thunder or something."

Julian grinned, but his smile faded as he wound around me to his side of the desk.

"You still in trouble?" he muttered.

"You know me."

"I do. Which is why I asked." After I gave him a confused wince, he added, "You love to suffer in silence. Well, maybe not in silence. But you go it alone. All the time. I'm just saying, I'm here. I have experience. If this group you talked about is as Byzantine and political as you say it is, then hell, that's my sandbox, Dorian. I could help."

I inched toward the door. "It's not... not that I don't think you can help."

"What, then?"

With a sigh, I answered, "I just don't want you to get hurt, is all. People get close to this, they end up floating in the Bay."

Julian shrugged. "Offer stands."

I nodded.

Before I could step out, he added, "Cleve called, by the way."

My eyes shot open. "No shit? Is that... are you two?"

"Too soon for anything like that. We talked stuff out, still have things to figure out. I don't think we're necessarily on the same wavelength."

"Well, your wavelength is a little intense."

He laughed. "It's better than drinking wine alone at night."

"I guess so."

"What about you and Francesca?" he needled. "With everything that's happened, is there anything between you two?"

I stared up at the ceiling, then turned toward the open door.

"It's a bad idea," I finally stated. "Always was."

I collected the Bakers, now huddled together on the bathroom floor. Ches mopped Ricky's forehead with a wet paper towel as he clutched her hand. With a bit of effort, we got Ricky put together and into the back of my car. The drive home was unnervingly silent. I tried to start a conversation, but both of them simply stared forward. Ches, in particular, seemed engrossed in thought. I was glad the drive was only ten minutes.

When we reached my house, they both bustled immediately upstairs. I tried Malosi one more time on his phone. Still no answer. After a while, a drum of activity overhead hinted that Ricky was very much active. I stared at the door to my basement, eager to get to work on the Presidium's assignment, but waited for Ches. I'd come to rely on her as a partner in this, and wanted her there to walk me through what she'd already found.

I paced a little in the front room as the footsteps and shuffling overhead continued. For a moment, I considered checking on them, but decided that was precisely the kind of thing that got me into trouble.

At last, steps creaked down the stairs, and I turned to find Ches facing me, arms stiff at her sides.

"Hey, everything settled up there?" I asked.

She nodded once, though her eyes seemed anything but settled.

She mumbled, "Can we talk?"

Uh oh.

I nodded for the sofa. I took a seat, but she remained standing. So, instinctively, I stood back up, stuck my hands in my pockets, then pulled them out again.

"What's up?"

She sucked in a breath, then pulled up her chin. "I'm taking Ricky back to Portland."

"Uh, wrong."

"It's decided."

I chuckled through my nose, then frowned. "You're not going back to Oregon, Ches."

"Yes. Yes, I am."

"You can't be serious."

Her chin dropped, and she lifted a hand. "I knew you were going to fight me on this, and I'm ready to have this out. But I'm really fucking exhausted, right now. Think we can just skip to the part where you tell me Quinn's going to have me killed?"

"Suits me. She's going to kill you. In fact, she was pretty goddamn specific about that."

"I know Quinn. I know how dangerous she can be. I also know her overblown sense of dignity. And it's been almost a year, now. She's probably moved on to other things, and is used to me not being a problem."

I turned for the front window, gesturing at nothing in particular. "Okay, assuming Gillette has mercy, what do you hope to accomplish?"

"The curse is killing him, Dorian. We tried to break it, but we couldn't. The only ones who can are the Dead Dragons."

"So, what? You're just going to talk Gillette into a moment of uncharacteristic charity, then waltz directly back to her enemies and beg them to lift this curse? Do you see the circle of fucked-up decisions you're outlining here?"

"I have to do something, Dorian. Keeping Ricky here? It just isn't working. He needs his family. He's not like you and me. He can't live without them. He doesn't want to."

"Listen. I've already made a deal with the Presidium."

Her eyes narrowed. "What kind of deal?"

"For Ricky. They're going to pull some strings in the court, and make sure Ricky doesn't lose his kids."

She took a step back. "What?"

"Yeah. They have people, even on the West Coast. They can make sure he doesn't get cut out of their lives."

"What's the price?" she spat.

"I have to find these Chaos magicians. And take them out."

Ches shook her head. "You really think you can do that?"

I shrugged. "I have more options available to me, now."

She took another step back. "You mean Netherwork? They're going to let you use Netherwork to solve their problem, aren't they?"

"Turns out, that's kind of what they do. Hypocrisy is, like, the one constant in the history of Mankind."

She closed her eyes, folded her hands together at her mouth, then walked a tiny circle.

"Okay," she said with a slow unfurling of her fingers. "Let me walk you through your circle of fucked-up decisions. One: this is assuming you can both find and defeat users of a destructive, primal magic before they take you out first. Even using your curses, this is something the Presidium can't seem to handle."

"Okay, I'll give you that."

"Two: even if you do succeed, and the Presidium actually, through some miracle, decides they want to honor their agreement with you, Ricky will still have this curse on him. And so, he keeps his parental rights. With this curse, he's going to continue spiraling into self-destruction. What kind of father is he going to be? What happens when he falls off the wagon? When he overdoses?" She stepped forward and whispered, "What if he does it on purpose?"

I hung my head.

"Think you can live with that? Because I'm not sure I can." She took a breath and put her hand on my arm. "Dorian? You did what you could. And holy shit, you did a lot for us. But when it comes down to it, this is my problem to fix. I brought this to your doorstep, and now I'm going to take responsibility for it."

My insides became a slack bag of lead weights.

"I don't like this," I grumbled. "Just feels wrong."

"Hey." She reached for my chin and lifted it, forcing me to look her in the eye. "You taught me more than you probably realize. I mean, I don't want you to know how grateful I actually am, because then you'll get a big head about it and then I'll have to find some fresh new insult to bring you back down to Earth."

My chest lifted in a silent snicker.

She continued, "We had a weird, special thing here. And I hate to admit this, too... but I think this special thing is over." A tear streamed down her cheek. "I have to go work out my own karma, now."

No.

No, I couldn't let her go like this.

But did I have a choice? Those feathery, sun-kissed feelings I had for Ches were always poisoned by our circumstance. The dynamic was wrong, even if the emotions felt right. They filled me with guilt when I thought too long on it.

I felt I'd failed Ches.

I'd failed myself.

She was right, after all. My chest twisted as I admitted to myself that my role in her life had ended.

"Okay," I whispered.

She reached out and pulled me into a hug.

As I wrapped my arms around her, I added, "I never taught you how to make a pendulum."

"Email me, then."

"Still don't own a computer."

"Fuck, Dorian." She pulled away, wiping her cheek with her sleeve. "You really need to join this century at some point."

She withdrew to help Ricky pack up his things. I lingered downstairs in a daze. My eyes locked onto a pothole in the street I always had to steer around before pulling into the drive.

Why hadn't the city fixed that, yet? I'd complained.

I was sure I complained, at some point.

No one seemed to be listening.

Stupid pothole.

The Bakers thundered down the stairs, a pack over each of their shoulders. Ches stood by the door as Ricky held out a hand.

"Thanks for putting up with me, boss. Sorry this didn't work out. The Tavern, I mean. I feel bad about that."

"We'll manage," I replied. "You just get better. Okay?"

He nodded, then stepped out the front door without further comment.

Ches held the door open, and looked me over.

I asked, "You want me to drive you to your car?"

"I already called a cab."

I almost offered to pay for the cab, before I realized how stupid I was sounding.

"So, keep in touch. All right?"

She nodded, eyes reddening as she tucked her chin.

"You too."

Ches stepped out and closed the door quietly behind her.

The silence that flooded my house at that moment was oppressive.

I just stood there, looking out the window. Even after the cab had come and taken them away, I remained at the window, frozen.

At length, my legs got tired, and I walked to the sideboard. As I reached for the cabinet, I spotted the bottle of Grand Reserva that Clement had mailed me.

Emil's favorite sherry.

I cracked open the bottle and sniffed it. Pungent, nutty, with notes of acetone. I poured myself a cordial, then settled in my chair. I drained the cordial quickly, and returned for a bigger glass.

Hours passed.

The silence buried me like loam over a coffin.

At some point a car door slammed out front. Footsteps hammered up the front walk, and the door opened under Malosi's hand.

"Hey," he barked. "What the hell?"

I swiveled my head in his direction. "What the hell what?"

"I went to the bar. Julian said you found him."

I nodded.

Malosi closed the door. "Didn't think to give a damn call to let me know?"

"I tried," I mumbled. "Twice."

He fished his phone out of his jacket, then swore quietly.

"Same thing happened to me," I offered. "I think those wardings at the Ipsissimus property put a whammy on electronic devices." I chuckled. "And she wonders why I don't own a computer."

"Is he okay?"

"He has muscular dystrophy, but he's obviously managing pretty well."

Malosi grunted, "Ricky. I'm talking about Ricky."

With a sigh, I replied, "I caught him before he injured himself."

"Is he upstairs?"

I shook my head. "They're gone."

Malosi stepped around to the front of my chair, his brows high. "Gone? In what manner are they 'gone'?"

"I mean they went back to Oregon."

He looked left, then right, then back to me. "Huh. So, Ches left?"

"Yep."

"Is this a permanent thing, or what?"

"Well, considering her first order of business is to talk Quinn Gillette out of straight murdering her, I'd say the end result will be permanent. One way or another."

Malosi took a seat on the sofa.

I waved my glass at him. "Want some sherry?"

"You know this is a good thing, right?"

"What is?"

"You were taking her down with you, is what I mean." He leaned forward. "And I hate to put it this way, but she was bringing you down, too. This whole Chaos thing? Whoever that creepy-ass gentleman outside the Tavern was? You haven't done anything but think about that girl and her brother."

I looked up at the ceiling.

"Sure you don't want any sherry?"

He stood up. "All right, I'll give you this one. Punish your liver, if you have to. But get this out of your system. Tonight. Because tomorrow, you're back on task." He added after a beat, "I'll, uh... stick around, if you want."

I nodded, and he retired upstairs.

I didn't pour myself anything else to drink. The sherry wasn't particularly palatable, though I doubt anything would have been at that moment.

When the high-rise on my block shut down their lights, and I heard no more noise from upstairs, I finally pulled myself out of my chair, set the glass on the sideboard, and climbed up to my room to bury myself in my sheets.

And I cried.

CHAPTER TWENTY-NINE

I **was up, made coffee, and had sat staring at Malosi's marker** board of conspiracies and doom by the time he joined me in the workspace.

"How're you feeling?" he asked.

"I'm seeing the overarching theme here," I said without actually answering his question. I gestured with my index finger underneath the word *GEOMANCY*.

"But what does it have to do with Chaos magic?" he rejoindered.

I snatched a marker and wrote Deirdre's name underneath the "geomancy," along with Wickham Inn, Enoch Pratt, and Miller's Hall.

Malosi leaned in. "Wickham Inn? What's that?"

"Old building in Gettysburg. First jinx we ran into. Some poor Korean couple ran a daycare out of the joint before these mystery men decided to toss a jinx through its window."

"What's that have to do with Geomancy?"

I squinted. "Not sure. I'm just bothered by the specificity. Three old buildings, all in colonial-era towns or cities. You have a phone on you?"

"Don't you?"

"Yeah, but it doesn't have maps on it. Look up Gettysburg."

Malosi pulled up his map application, and keyed it in.

I muttered, "How do you type with those ball-peen hammers for thumbs?"

"There."

"Zoom out."

He did until I spotted Baltimore and Harper's Ferry on the same screen.

"Damn," I grumbled.

"What?"

"I was hoping they'd be in a straight line. Don't know much about Geomancy, but I figured if we spotted a pattern, they could be on a leyline. Might have given us some clue as to where it's all going."

"Does the order matter?"

"Probably. Without knowing the pattern, it's hard to interpret it." I looked over to the word Chaos on the opposite end of the board. "So, why Chaos? If anyone outside of the Presidium wanted to wage war, there's far more practical modalities they could use. And less destructive. And exactly how the hell are these people getting consistent results with these jinxes? It's the same thing, each time. That's almost mutually exclusive with chaos magic. And what the hell does any of it have to do with geomancy?"

"Well," Malosi offered, "Geomancy is based on physical locations, right? If you're working with physical sites in nature, then you're dealing with a chaotic system."

"But these aren't caves or rivers. These are buildings. Man-made."

Malosi snapped his fingers. "Imposed order onto Chaos. So, you jinx the site, and you return it to a natural state."

"You're suggesting these jinxes are tearing down some kind of magical structure at each of these old colonial locations?"

"It would have to be, or else they'd just use a bazooka."

I nodded. "Then these old buildings have magical significance." I tapped Deirdre's name with my marker. "And I'll bet she would have known what that is, if she saw the pattern. Maybe she did see the pattern, after Enoch Pratt, and that's why they put a jinx on her?"

"Why wouldn't they just kill her?"

"Good question. Maybe they tried, but the jinx didn't cooperate."

Malosi shrugged. "Without concrete knowledge on chaos magic, we're just spitballing here. You got a book on chaos in that cabinet?" He gestured to Emil's Library.

I peered at the cabinet and pursed my lips.

"Maybe. I've only nosed around half of the books Emil left me, most of them on the more 'mainstream' Netherwork, if there is such a thing. I'll take a look later." I swiveled in my chair over to Ches's desk, or what had been. "In the meanwhile, we have a hard-earned list of names to bird-dog."

I grabbed the sheet of Committee for Public Enrichment members we'd secured from Ronetta Claye.

Malosi examined it over my shoulder.

"At least one of these people had to know something about that curse pole," he said. "Any thoughts on how we do this without literally going door-to-door?"

"Not really," I admitted.

"Because, walking up and asking a rich white person if they're aware that a piece of public art is responsible for the deaths of half-a-dozen demon-summoners is exactly the kind of shit that gets the cops called on a motherfucker."

I looked up at Malosi with a grin. "Hey. That... that's actually a good idea."

"On what world is that a good idea?"

I reached for my phone. "Curse poles killing cultists is a hard sell. But public indecency? That's something entirely different."

"Public indecency?"

"What if those glyphs were determined to be profanity in, I don't know... Urdu or something?"

Malosi squinted. "You ever actually seen Urdu?"

"Not the point," I replied as I scrolled through my call list. "We say someone registered a complaint, and it has to be looked into or else they have to tear it down. Then we gauge response. Clement taught you energy palpation, right?"

He nodded.

"Shouldn't take long to beat some practitioners out of the bush."

"If we step around town acting like cops, we're going to get arrested," he countered.

"Very true. Which is why we need the real thing with us."

"There's City Councilmen on that list, Dorian. We'll need a cop who's willing to put his career on the line."

I held up my phone. "I have just the man," I said as I dialed Ronetta Claye's number

Claye seemed happy to hear that we had "boots on the ground," as she put it, looking for a solution to the Enoch Pratt situation. Apparently, they had closed off the children's books section until we could close the hole the jinx punched into the fabric of reality somewhere between R.L. Stein and Dr. Seuss.

She was especially gratified to hear I was interested in working with Detective Turner, whom she sent to meet Malosi and me in front of Light Street Tavern.

When Turner arrived, he seemed far less gratified than Claye.

"So, what's this about?" he growled the second we were within earshot.

"I need you to help me scam some Councilmen."

His eyes lifted a bit, and for an awkward moment he seemed to actually consider it without further context.

Finally, he said, "You're going to need to run that by me again."

"You know about the Charles Street killings?"

"Yeah. That's over to homicide."

"I'm convinced it's the same people who jacked up the library."

His face eased out of its usual dismissive sneer. "I heard they got a suspect already. Some hoodoo bookworm."

"They're after the wrong guy. He was the target. The others were collateral damage."

"You got proof of this, I hope?"

I gave Malosi a smirk, then turned back to the detective. "We have a list of names, members of a public enrichment committee that gave the greenlight to a statue in a public space half a block away from the Charles Street crime scene."

"A statue? What's that got to do with—"

"Inside the statue I found a niding pole, an old Viking curse tool. It was aimed directly at Zeno's house."

The dismissive sneer returned. "Viking curses, huh? You guys are a real freakin' joke, you know that?" His eyes shifted to Malosi. "Who's this guy, your secretary?"

Malosi answered, "I can touch-type and I know ten-key. If you're hiring, I can get my resume from the car."

I quipped over my shoulder, "You are so fired."

"Okay, smartasses," Turner declared. "Let's see this list."

I handed it over, and he squinted at the page like a man who needed glasses but was too afraid of looking old to actually go get his eyes checked. He ran a finger down the list, shaking his head intermittently.

"No good," he mumbled.

"What?"

"Harold Roth. He's a real religious type. Wouldn't be caught dead wigging around with you types."

"You'd be surprise what people do in private, detective."

"Yeah, whatever." He continued. "Tony Janczak's no good."

"Why?"

"Been dead for three months."

"Gotcha." I sighed and looked over the top of the page. "Is there anyone on this list you don't specifically know about? Anyone who isn't all that public? Maybe got appointed and no one knows why?"

He shrugged. "Never heard of these first two names, but I ain't exactly a City Hall insider."

I swiveled for the front of the tavern. "Well, just so happens I have one of those."

I led everyone inside the bar, and Malosi held Turner up at the bar while I maneuvered to Julian's office.

Julian looked up from his computer with a long face.

"Hey," he whispered.

"You all right?" I asked.

"Hungover. Mostly. What's up?"

"Got a couple things. One, we're going to need a new kitchen manager."

He scowled. "Ricky's out?"

"He and Ches went back to Oregon."

Julian pushed away from his desk and stood up. "Wow. I'm sorry, Dorian."

"It's done, I suppose. Anyway, we should get on that."

"A couple of the new hires have experience. I'll talk to them. What's the other thing?"

I handed Julian the list. "Take a look at these names."

"Okay." He gave the page a once-over. "Public Enrichment Committee? What's your interest in them?"

"Anyone on that list stand out as someone who doesn't, well... doesn't stand out? Names you've never heard of?"

He gave it further scrutiny. "You know Janczak's been dead now for a few months."

"I've heard."

"Well, you got the superintendent at the Baltimore Arts College. Makes sense. Two clergy. I guess they don't want Mapplethorpe hung in Mt. Vernon. Former staff, former staff... consolation prizes from the election, I'll bet. One corpse. That leaves four."

"Turner says Roth's the pious type."

Julian smirked. "And how. Why, is religion pertinent here?"

"Could be. I'm just trying to narrow things down."

"Well, if that's the case you're going to have to forget about Hershfeld, too. He's in the Knights of Columbus, and he's at St. Paul's three times a week. That leaves two. Narrow enough for you?"

He circled the first and fourth names on the list. Petra de Haviland and Marcus Pompa.

I took the list from Julian with a nod. "No info on these two?"

"No clue. But then, I wasn't always up to speed on the minor committees. Or the major ones, if it didn't have to do with the political office."

"Thanks."

"No, thank you!"

I looked up at him. "Huh?"

"I've been trying to be useful for a while now."

"Are you kidding me? This place is only running because of you."

"That's not what I meant."

"What are you hung over about?"

He rolled his eyes.

"Ah," I muttered. "Cleve?"

"I'll see you later, Dorian."

I stood for a second, then took my dismissal and returned to Malosi and Turner.

"We good?" Malosi asked.

"Yeah. Got two names we should check out first."

Turner shook his head. "What are you talking about?"

"So, here's the play. We tell these people someone's lodged a complaint about the statue. Say it was something indecent or hate-speechy. We get a sense of whether these people are legit or if they're, as you put it, hoodoo bookworm types."

Turner's eyes glazed a touch, then he shook his head. "I'm out. Good luck."

As he turned to leave, I added, "Deputy Mayor Claye was pleased to hear we were finally cooperating on this."

He paused, then sighed.

I added, "Listen, we really just need you to flash your badge. We can do the rest."

"This is a waste of time."

"Hey, look at it this way. You get to take all the credit if we stumble across a genuine criminal. If all we do is fluff some old hens' feathers, then you have zero exposure."

He faced me. "All right, all right. Let's get this over with. But you're buying my lunch, goddamnit."

I held up my hands and agreed.

Turner insisted on driving, which suited me as I didn't want my car spotted and remembered should we have found a genuine problem. We agreed to start with Marcus Pompa. A quick records search on Malosi's phone showed he was a retired professor of art history who now lived on an inlet of the Back River. His house was smaller than his neighbors', but the water ran right up to his back deck. He had a well-manicured garden for a front lawn. This was a man in considerable control of his environment, and he definitely had an eye for beauty.

Turner took the lead as we stepped through a single-hinged garden gate and took the circular brick-paved path around a fountain to the front door of his white clapboard home. The detective rang the bell, and it wasn't a minute before a voice called from the side of the house.

"Can I help you?"

Pompa waddled around the side of his garden with the gate of a man barely able to walk without a cane. He was extremely elderly, skin covered in brown patches, hands worn down likely from years of gardening.

Turner pulled his badge and held it up for Pompa as he eased slowly toward us.

"Detective Turner, Baltimore Police Special Investigations Unit. Are you Marcus Pompa?"

He nodded.

"These gentlemen want a word with you."

And with that, he turned and waited by the front gate. A real charmer, that Turner.

Pompa looked over to Malosi, then to me.

I stepped forward. "Good morning, Mr. Pompa."

He stepped forward and extended a hand.

I shook it gingerly for fear of snapping his bones, and found no specific energies on his person. Just the normal ebb and flow of a living being.

"Mr. Pompa," I continued, "I understand you sit on the Committee for Public Enrichment?"

He nodded, eyes wary.

"Sir, we've received a complaint regarding a piece of public art that was erected a month ago, just off the twelve-hundred block of Charles Street. A kind of, what do you call it? Modern art? Sailboat and animals."

His face pulled back into the sneer of someone who had just bitten into an apple and discovered that it was, in fact, a dog turd.

"That monstrosity?" he groaned. "It's a scandal."

"So, my taste in art isn't completely sideways?"

"Joel and I were adamant, it didn't belong on public property. But the rest have no concept of composition, nor the eye for aesthetics that God gave a radish."

"Do you know who the artist is?"

His eyes narrowed.

I prodded, "We need to address some concerns."

"What concerns?"

"There was script found on the interior of the statue that, well... it's basically hate speech."

He bobbed his head. "I don't recall any writing."

"It was symbolic."

"Then how was it hate speech?"

This was going well.

"It was runic. Runes. Old Norse runes. Kind of thing," I added, "you find in White Supremacist groups."

He took a step back. "I have nothing whatsoever to do with that!"

I got him.

"That's good to hear, but we do need to speak with the artist."

He lifted his hands in a shrug. "It was a student art project. A small studio in Canton received a modest endowment. I couldn't tell you the name of the studio, if it's still open at all."

I turned to Malosi. He gave me a barely-perceptible shake of his head.

I had to agree. There was nothing going on here but an old man whose only crime was not fighting hard enough to preserve the good taste of our public spaces.

"Mister Pompa," I declared with a smile. "Thank you for your time. We'll look into this studio."

He smiled and released a breath, obviously relieved that he was not, in fact, being accused of anti-Semitism.

Back in the car, Turner gave me a begrudging nod. "You happy with that geezer?"

"He's clean," I replied.

"On to number two," he declared. "Then lunch. I'm thinking crab cakes."

The de Haviland address put us uptown not far from Zeno's lodge. A series of stately row houses lines the boulevard, wrought iron fencing adding elegance if not a sense of security. Massive bay windows loomed over the street, with fine chandeliers glimmering beyond lace curtains. The cars parked on the street were compact, luxurious, and mostly German.

Turner whistled at the house as we stepped out of his car. "Hell of a spread."

"What's the story on these people?" I asked Malosi.

He glanced down to his phone, then up at me with a shrug. "Nothing."

"No records?"

"There's four de Havilands listed in Baltimore City, and none of them are named Petra."

I turned to the house and centered my energy. Time to palpate.

Turner brushed past me, interrupting my focus, and tried the front gate. It was locked.

Malosi marched up and pushed a tiny call button by the latch. A chime sounded, followed by a creaky voice.

"Who is it?"

Turner bent over to speak directly into the speaker. "Detective Grant Turner, Baltimore Special Investigations Unit. I'm looking for Petra de Haviland."

"Goodness!" the woman exclaimed. "What is this about?"

"A statue, ma'am," he replied with a boorish look in my direction. "Public art. We need to ask you a couple questions."

After a considerable pause, during which Turner nearly hit the button again, the front door opened and an older woman with silver hair pulled up into a tight bun emerged from the house. She glided down the short flight of steps and up to the gate with grace. She paused well shy of the gate, however, and gave the three of us a long evaluation.

"Your badge, detective?"

He nodded and produced it, holding it close to the gate.

She took a step forward and squinted through the iron, giving the badge a tremendous amount of scrutiny. I nodded to Malosi, glad that we bothered to bring an actual cop. This woman was careful.

Once she seemed satisfied, she reached out and opened the gate for us. Her face pulled back into a tense yet polite grin.

"Very well. Follow me, please."

She turned and moved back up the walkway. The three of us followed, Malosi hopping forward to hold the door for her.

"Thank you, young man," she chimed as we entered the foyer.

Turner stepped inside without much more than a grunt.

Malosi paused at the door, as did I.

The energy sealing this doorway was, in a word, electric.

Realizing we'd just been invited into the house of an obvious practitioner, I kept my gaze forward and my energy tight to keep from giving away our intentions. It was probably a bad idea, truth be known. Stepping directly into the house of who was probably behind this entire attack on the Presidium... and by the look of the house, a well-funded attack... was a good way to put us at a Hell of a disadvantage.

Malosi, for his part, played it way cooler than I did.

The old woman gestured for the front room bearing one of the bay windows hanging off the front of the house, and reached for a white shawl draped across a divan to gather around her shoulders.

Turner gave me a nod. "Your show, Lake."

At that moment, I regretted volunteering to do the talking. I needed to feel the room, attempt to isolate and identify specific energies and constructs. I couldn't do that and put on a song-and-dance at the same time.

"Yes. You are Petra de Haviland? Is that correct?"

She nodded once.

"Ah. Yes. Good. And, you've been appointed to the Mayor's Public Enrichment Committee?"

"I am happy to serve the city with any means at my disposal."

"Swell," I replied, wincing at my total lack of composure. "There is a statue that was erected in a playground not far from here. Just off the twelve-hundred block of Charles Street. We've received a complaint about some lettering found within the statue itself. Symbols with anti-Semitic connotations."

She held up a finger and pointed to Turner. "Detective Grant Turner," she pronounced before shifting her finger to Malosi, and then to me. "I did not hear your names."

Damn but this old woman was cautious!

I sucked in a breath, trying to arrive at a quick decision whether she'd heard Turner say my name already, and if I should chance lying to a practitioner in her own home. Happily, a pair of footfalls from the plank-floored hallway interrupted our moment.

Petra turned back toward the hallway.

"Clarence? The police are here. They have questions about some art project."

A voice grumbled with precisely zero enthusiasm, and the footsteps approached the archway to the front room.

I turned to greet Clarence, trying to lock down my demeanor unless I end up spraying nervous energy all over this property.

But as I locked eyes with the man who for the past two years I had known simply as Brown, my energetic composure popped like a water balloon.

CHAPTER THIRTY

I**n my defense, Brown seemed as blind-sided as I was. He had** always gone by his pseudonym. A wise choice, being a prominent upper-crustacean as he apparently was. It took a bizarre series of circumstances to drop me directly into his sitting room. The Cosmos, it seemed, wasn't done screwing with my karma just yet.

"Gentlemen," he intoned without breaking eye contact with me.

My brain froze up. What the hell was I going to say?

Petra rounded around Brown... Clarence, whatever... and folded her hands over her arms.

"I was just getting their names. They seem a bit flummoxed."

Malosi stepped forward.

"Reed Malosi." He extended his hand to the two. Neither of them reacted. Malosi nudged me. "And this is..."

I cleared my throat. "Dorian Lake."

"Are you police, as well?" Petra asked.

Clarence continued staring at me, before blinking and turning to his wife. "They work for Sullivan, dear. I've met Mister Lake before. Nothing to fear."

She explained, "They're asking about some sort of racist statue. Swastikas, I believe? I can't honestly believe they'd erect a statue with swastikas in the city. That defies all belief."

"Not swastikas, ma'am," Malosi said. "Runes. Old Norse alphabet. When translated, the content was considered objectionable."

She shook her head. "What kind of content?"

I looked Clarence in the eye, and replied, "Curse words."

The barest squint haunted the corner of his left eye.

Malosi added, "We're responding to an allegation of hate speech. We just want to have a word with the artist that made it—"

I interrupted, still looking at Clarence, "—and how it managed to get erected in a nice, quiet neighborhood over committee objections."

His other eye flickered.

With a sigh, Petra spun around. "I'm sure I have some information in my office. A lot of harangue over profanity. Clearly the permissive society has reached a limit of bowel continence. If you'll follow me?"

Turner shrugged and followed. Malosi moved slower, stepping toward me. I kept my eyes from meeting his.

As we reached the foyer, Clarence called behind me, "Oh, Mister Lake. A moment?"

I finally looked up to Malosi, and gave him a nod. He followed Turner to the rear of the house, and I turned back to face Brown.

His face burned with loathing, but in a voice belying his expression, he chirped, "How have you been?"

"Comfortable," I answered.

He took a step closer. "And how is Mayor Sullivan these days?"

"Doing very well, thank you."

With some unspoken cue that the others had left earshot, he took another step forward and dropped his voice to a growling whisper.

"What the hell are you doing in my house?"

I answered in a matching tone, "Why the hell is there a niding pole in a public park?"

He rushed around my shoulder, gripping my arm as he peered around the archway.

"Quiet, you dolt."

"She has no idea what you are, does she?" I whispered.

"I've taken great pains to ensure that would be the case. And I will inflict great pains upon anyone who informs her otherwise."

I grinned. "I'm not here to out you... Clarence."

"Get out!"

"I find it curious that your wife sits on the committee that gave this niding pole the greenlight. What, did you take it upon yourself to wipe out Zeno's lodge?"

He sneered. "I had nothing to do with that. Zeno was an asset."

"Yeah, well, now he's gone off-grid. And he's one of the lucky ones."

"I told you to get out of my house."

I leaned into his ear. "You're not involved with these foreign cabals attacking the Presidium, are you? I'd find that supremely disappointing."

He gave me a shove in the sternum, and I caught myself on the divan.

With eyes brimming with acid, he whispered, "You forget who I am."

"Hey, I'm working for the Presidium now. I'm one of you people. An asset."

Clarence smirked. "Idiot. You're not working for the Presidium. You're working for Adrastos."

I squinted, and rebuffed, "...who happens to be the head of the Presidium."

"Our organization is a maze of layers, Lake. You've mistaken collaboration for solidarity."

"You're saying the left hand doesn't know what the right hand's doing?"

He shook his head. "I'm saying the left hand doesn't know what its own thumb is doing. And if you have any investment with Adrastos, I'd recommend you surrender this idiotic crusade for foreign cabals."

"What's that supposed to mean?"

He sighed, looked over to his window, and rolled his shoulders.

"Not here. Tonight. Ellicott City. Meyer Livery."

"The what, now?"

"Meet me at 9 p.m. at the Meyer Livery in Ellicott City. Come alone. And that most specifically means leaving your muscle behind."

I peered at the foyer. "I've been ditching him a lot, lately. I'm not all that inclined to trust you at the moment."

He snickered. "Dear God, Lake. I may be the one person in this city you can trust."

I took a step forward, readying a scorching response, but Petra's voice rang into the hallway.

We both turned back to the archway, and composed ourselves.

Clarence added, "Come tonight. Come alone. If you want to survive this." He vaulted his voice into a strong, warm timbre. "Well, be sure to tell Ms. Claye we're with her."

Petra stepped into the room with Malosi and Turner behind.

"We're with whom, dear?" she asked.

"Ms. Claye. Our dear Mister Lake, here, has leant her support." He turned to me. "And I wanted him to know that she is in our thoughts."

I steeled my guts. What did that mean?

Petra waved her hand. "She's a bit out of her depth, don't you think?"

Clarence gave her a smile. "I feel, at some point, we all find ourselves out of our depths. It's a good thing we have people like Mister Lake to depend on."

She tilted her head at me. "Well, I had no idea you were such a valuable person."

I bowed. Just a little.

"Did we find anything?" I asked over her shoulder to Malosi.

He held up a tiny scrap of note paper. "An address of the studio where the thing was made."

"Good enough." I pushed my hands together. "I apologize for this intrusion, Mister and Missus de Haviland. We'll be on our way."

I herded the others to the door.

Petra called from the archway, "Do tell Mrs. Sullivan I said hello."

"I will. I think I'm having dinner with them—" I checked my watch, then swore under my breath. "Tonight."

"Oh, how lovely."

I beat the others to the street. Malosi wasn't far behind, but Turner took his time.

"So, jerkoffs," he bellowed, "what was all of that about?"

"Nothing. Dead end."

"Bull crap." He grinned and thrust his thumb at the row house. "You was on eggshells in there. You found something, right? These people involved with the Charles Street murders?"

They weren't involved. But Clarence might have known who was.

"No chance," I answered. "Just a really weird house."

He glared at me, then turned to take in the house.

"Yeah. Old buildings give me the running shits, too."

He moved around to the driver side of the car.

Malosi stood directly beside me. "Good guy or bad guy?"

"Probably both," I mumbled. "He's certainly not a good person, but he knows something. And he knows that I don't."

To his credit, Turner didn't hold us to buying him lunch. He was happy to be rid of us, and drove us directly back to the tavern. I spent the trip scheming up a means to ditch the Sullivan soiree in order to meet Brown in Ellicott City. The good news was that Malosi wasn't invited to the event, so I wouldn't have to shake him. The bad news?

Julian was.

Malosi and I stepped into the tavern and were struck in the face by the smell of bacon. My stomach growled immediately, reminding me how much I'd been neglecting it as of late. Ben sat at the customer side of the bar housing a plate of potato skins. I sidled up beside him with a hungry eye on his plate.

"This is new," I chirped.

Ben gave me a sour cream-smeared grin, and spoke around a mouthful of potato mash. "Kitchen's up."

"Do we have a menu?"

He reached behind the bar and produced a slip of paper, likely printed in Julian's office and hand-cut with scissors. Typical pub grub.

I handed Malosi the menu and stepped around the bar to Julian's office.

"Any luck?" I heard Julian call out before I even reached his door.

He was leaning over his desk, rifling through a stack of papers.

"Yes and no."

"See the kitchen, yet?"

I shook my head. "Listen, about tonight."

"You're blowing it off."

He said it more as a prediction than a question.

"Something's come up."

Julian turned to face me. "That's all right. I wasn't exactly looking forward to it."

"Well, I mean...you don't have to bail on Sullivan. I just—"

"If I go to this God-awful thing, I'm going to get in a shit mood for a solid week." He lowered his voice. "Cleve's giving me a second chance, besides. He doesn't need any more storm clouds."

I nodded. "Well, sweet. We're both off the hook."

"Not really. Mrs. Sullivan is going have our asses publically flogged for this."

"I'm not worried about her."

Julian smiled. "Neither am I, to be honest." He said it with a bit too much acid to be convincing.

"One thing," I added in a whisper, "don't tell Reed I'm blowing this off."

"More secrets, Dorian?"

I winced. "Yeah. That's my life, right now."

"You should try the nachos," he said, turning back to his paperwork.

I followed Julian's advice, and as I haunted my plate I switched mental gears. I was free of the Sullivan entanglement, but all that did was to kick Malosi back into play. He had taken the charge of my personal security to heart, as much out of professionalism as what I liked to think was a genuine desire to see me not floating in the Inner Harbor. I didn't want to lie to him, but Brown's words rolled over and over in my head.

I was no fan of Brown, and I was reasonably sure he wouldn't bother to spit on my face if my nose was on fire. But in a twisted sense of Netherworker rationale, his naked antagonism was oddly comforting. I knew where I stood with Brown, and in the past couple years I'd learned how far I could push him without getting my eyebrows hexed off.

So, when he told me not to trust anyone, I felt inclined to give him more than a passing consideration. But who was he accusing, here? Adrastos? That made plenty of sense. Any multi-layered secret society housing that much power was bound to breed internal discontent, particularly toward the leadership. Wexler? As much as I found Brown's acrimony to be bankable, I found Wexler's tight-lipped smiles to be spine-chilling. She was a hard woman, deliberate and calculating. I ran back every word that crossed her lips for fear I'd missed a crucial double-meaning. She was exhausting.

It was entirely possible I'd aligned myself with exactly the wrong side in this fight. Had Ches and Ricky distracted me to the point of blindness? Was I, in fact, the fool Brown saw me to be?

"Not bad," Malosi offered, bringing a plate around to the end of the bar.

"So, Reed. I'm short a researcher."

He crossed his arms. "Uh huh?"

"I need you to do a little book diving. Wrangle up everything you can find on Chaos magic. If we find these guys, we still have to deal with them."

His eyes dropped into squints.

I continued, "You specialize in wardings and shields, right? That's exactly the kind of thing we're going to need if we're going to square off against jinx-slingers. Something that will deflect chaos."

Malosi's eyes lifted a touch, and bobbed up to the ceiling. He was thinking.

Perfect.

"I have a notion or two," he muttered. "You plan on giving me access to that cabinet in your basement?"

"Hell no."

"You can't be serious."

"Reed, I don't let my closest friends rummage around in Emil's books."

He smirked. "That's good, since I'm not your close friend."

Malosi had a point, there. In the same way I "trusted" Brown because he had no investment in my well-being, I tended to trust Malosi. We had a very limited history from our affair with Osterhaus. We landed on the same end of that struggle, both with Osterhaus and with Carmen. He had proven himself to be a capable practitioner, at least in the specific arenas I'd seen him work within. And he had yet to let me down, even once.

But I trusted no one with Emil's books. No one. Even those with the best intentions become subverted by their dark allure. And Malosi was already operating in a gray area with Clement, a known Netherworker.

Clement. Shit. He had a straight-up offer on the table for those books. What sense did it make to give his right-hand man access? It wasn't like I could just pop in, find the "Tome of Chaos Magic and How to Stop It" from the cabinet and lock it back up again. Most of the texts I'd inherited from Emil were rambling discourses on various Netherworking principles and traditions, wandering from topic to topic without structure or coherence. The best an anal-retentive control freak like Emil could accomplish toward organization of the cabinet was that pitiful hand-scratched index clipboard hanging on the door.

No, finding useful information in Emil's Library would be a long-term project. And I didn't trust Malosi enough to leave him alone with it while I dicked around with Brown in Ellicott City.

"Sorry, Reed. Not happening."

"If you're that damn worried about it, then you do it. They're your books, and I'm not exactly the researching type."

"Yeah, but I have a thing." Damn it... nouns. "I have a dinner tonight. Me and Julian.

He shrugged. "I'll call Jean. I bet he has contacts."

"Be careful with that. We're not sure who's involved with this coup against the Presidium. If he spreads word around too wide, we might end up tipping off the very people we're trying to nail."

I wished Ches were there.

"I need your help, Reed," I stated. "I'm going a million directions, here."

He slipped his hands into his pockets. "This is going to be over, eventually. You know?"

"That's the plan."

CHAPTER THIRTY-ONE

Night bathed Ellicott City in deep shadows. Its main drag ran along a sliver of land running between the Patapsco River and the sharp rise of hills running parallel. The old clapboard buildings eased in a lazy curve, the streets with cobblestone walkways sliding down to the mill at the bottom of the valley. The area was a kind of Lost World tucked away in the woods just west of Baltimore, weirdly segregated from the urban reality just two miles in any direction.

I stepped along the tiny granite cobbles, squinting in the darkness between buildings. A tour group followed a man in period costume holding an oil lantern. As they passed, I overheard the guide spinning a tale of a haunting nearby. The crisp springtime air hung around the cramped alleyways between the colonial buildings as fog lifted from the river. It was a spectacular night for a ghost tour.

I found the Meyer Livery after passing it several times. The old building, or what remained of it, sat huddled behind the taller buildings along the main street. Three wooden walls clung to the granite rock face of the hills behind, with a modern reproduction of a thatched roof slung overhead. There was very little light to be found. All I had to choose my footsteps by was a buzzing sodium lamp bolted to a building two doors down, spilling an orange light across the top of the thatched roof that managed to add more gloom than illumination.

A voice called from the shadows inside of the three walls.

"You actually came alone. I assumed you'd try to hedge your safety."

Brown stepped out from the interior of the structure, half of his white beard catching the light from behind me.

"Didn't want to dick around," I replied. "I'm running out of time."

"You and the Presidium, both." He gathered his overcoat, buttoning it as he turned back to the wrecked walls. "It'll be in ruins soon, much like this old livery. Unless we choose our steps very carefully."

"Go team," I grumbled.

"Adrastos called you in. This much I'm aware of."

"The Presidium is running out of assets, or whatever you call your passel of sanctioned Netherworkers. He needed someone with dirt under his fingernails, and I was his last best choice."

Brown nodded. "Those whom the Presidium weren't baited into liquidating were disposed of by those who've started this conflict."

"And they are?"

He lifted a finger. "That is the entire question, isn't it? You've been lucky this far, Lake."

"Funny. Doesn't feel that way to me."

"These individuals are dealing in violent, unpredictable forces. I wonder, why would any sane practitioner choose Chaos over something useful?"

My thoughts exactly. "Assuming they're sane. What if we're dealing with lunatics?"

Brown scowled. "Surely you've seen the pattern, by now?"

Aha. So there was a pattern, after all. I had a theory baking in my brain… time to see if Brown could bring me another step.

I asked, "What pattern?"

His scowl lifted into a sneer. "Patterns don't fit into Chaos magic, and only in the most strictly arbitrary sense would they conform to lunacy. No, this is an organized attack against the Presidium. Organized and orchestrated with considerable patience."

"What pattern?" I prodded.

"Gettysburg. Harper's Ferry. Locust Grove."

"Locust Grove?" I blurted. "You mean Enoch Pratt."

He sighed. "You have some catching up to do. No, there have been more attacks. In Virginia."

"Virginia?" My stomach knotted. "It isn't a straight line at all. It's a circle."

"More than a circle, Lake. There is specificity in their methods. A sacred geometry of sorts."

I turned away and shook my head. How blind had I been? This should have been obvious. Painfully obvious.

I whispered, "So, you're saying that they're surrounding the Presidium?"

Brown released a dry chuckle. "Nothing so facile. You've seen these attack sites, I trust?"

I nodded.

"And what do they have in common?"

"Old buildings."

"Specifically?"

I turned back to face him. "Colonial-era buildings."

He snapped his fingers. "And there we have it."

Did we?

"What do we have, exactly?" I asked, my brain buzzing with a notion too bashful to show itself. "Okay, so, these people have a hate-on for the Presidium and decide to start dropping jinxes in a circle around DC. They're choosing specific sites that were all built during the colonial period. At the same time, they've been eroding the Presidium's power base. Kicked up all the dust with Durning. The Presidium goes batshit and drops the hammer on Netherworkers. In the ensuing chaos, they move on to, what? I guess it's Phase Two. Remove the Netherworkers the Presidium keeps on speed-dial, as well as a harmless geomancer whose only threat was her ability to identify this pattern. But all of it was a smoke screen for the jinxes, to keep everyone focused away from these tactical chaos nukes."

Brown crossed his arms, eyes alive with thought.

I continued," You said there were more in Virginia?"

"Locust Grove and Port Royal," he responded.

"That's five jinxes. What the hell are they up to?"

Uncrossing his arms, Brown paced forward lifting fingers as he counted. "First, if you're to appease the Ipsissimus, you must determine who these people are. And I don't mean some vague label to hang over their necks. You'll need names. Two, you will have to deal with the wreckage these chaos attacks have wrought."

"That's about the long and short of it," I said.

He shook his head. "Wrong. There is a third question pertinent to your survival."

"And what is that?"

He replied, "Who can you trust?"

I cocked my head. "A bit obvious."

"Is it, though? You were quick to rush into Adrastos's good graces."

"Didn't have a lot of choice, Clarence," I groused.

"Well," he countered with a knowing grin, "let's consider who would benefit from a complete collapse of the Presidium? Because that's what Adrastos is looking at, right now."

"That's a bit extreme, isn't it? I mean, the Presidium's taking a bloody nose right now, but—"

He shook his head. "You don't understand what it is these people are doing."

"So, enlighten me."

He sighed. "I'm risking enough by meeting you. We have diviners who can spot entangled energies. Your resonance is loud enough, I don't want to mingle my fate with yours any more than I have to. Thus, I won't open the door for you, Lake. But I can save you time by keeping you from picking the wrong lock."

I threw up my hands. "Fine. Keep your diviners in the dark. So, who benefits from the Presidium going tits up?"

"What does the Presidium accomplish?"

"It polices magical practices in America, keeps the Old World cabals from interfering. Makes my life harder than it needs to be. Pick one."

Brown gestured to the livery. "Look to history, Lake. When did that become the Presidium's mandate? Who made that decision, and when? What were the circumstances at the moment? These are the questions that will explain to you both what is happening, and who is doing it." His eyes fell into a sad stare. "These are old enemies."

I grinned. "The Ipsissimus had you figured wrong, I think."

The sadness in his eyes snapped into intense inquiry. "He mentioned me?"

"Well, sort of. I did, and he responded."

He took a step toward me. "What did he say about me?" he asked in breathy gasps.

"Keep your pants on. Nothing big. He made a comment about me having a handler, and I assumed it was you. He implied that you've been trying to have me black-bagged for a while now."

He considered my comment, then nodded slowly. "It seems there's another question you've failed to ask yourself."

I ran a hand over the side of my face, eyes searching out the shadows. "Who… is my handler?"

Brown stepped away. "You shouldn't have mentioned my name to the Ipsissimus. Now our names are joined on an Akashic level."

"Why are you so worried about the Presidium's diviners?"

"We should part company. Now."

He moved to step around me for the front street, but I held up a hand.

"This isn't an attack from outside the Presidium at all, is it?"

Brown smiled. "You are at the brink, now. The door is before you. If I say anything else, we're both dead."

He hopped away, easing down the alley.

I called out, "You said to look to history. How? You people don't exactly publish textbooks."

Without turning, he waved an arm over his head. "It's all around you, Lake. Literally all around you."

Brown increased his speed, and slipped onto the street and out of sight. If I didn't know better, I'd say he was spooked.

Who was I kidding? I didn't know better.

I stood in the darkness behind the front buildings, lingering by the inkier shadows within the ruins of the Meyer Livery.

So, this was some kind of civil war within the Presidium, a coup d'état at the hands of some subgroup, some junta within the Presidium itself. It made sense to me, as I thought about it. Adrastos needed outsiders to solve this problem, likely because even the Ipsissimus himself wasn't sure who was on his side and who wasn't. He didn't even let Wexler onto his property.

Was she part of this? It was as likely as anyone.

Old enemies, Brown had called them.

As I made the short drive back home, it became clear to me that I'd have to hunt down some Presidium history. Could Emil have collected anything with that kind of information? It would be my first stop.

CHAPTER THIRTY-TWO

F**or the first time in what felt like months, I came home** to an empty house. Malosi was somewhere, ostensibly researching chaos magic or otherwise tapping his pipeline of contacts for the information we needed.

Ches and Ricky were probably in Oregon by now. I wondered how long it would be before she reached out to Gillette. Or the Dead Dragons. I felt like saying a prayer for her, but I wasn't sure who the hell would listen.

And so, without distraction for well or ill, I descended into my basement workspace and stood stiff-armed as I stared across the room at the cabinet. It loomed, massive, its dark-stained wood absorbing light like a fly trap. The cedar planks lining the interior of the cabinet did what it could to contain the malevolent energies resident in those tombs, but I knew what was inside. And because I knew, it had a hook in my brain. Brown had spoken of undesired resonance. I had truckloads of resonance with these books, and none of it was desirable.

I fished out my keys and unlocked the doors. They swung open on ancient hinges, oddly silent for their age. The aromas of cedar and musky parchment washed over my face. I snatched the clipboard from its nail on the inside of the door and gave the makeshift index a good once-over. I found nothing that screamed "Presidium History and How to Deal with It." There were several promising candidates for the chaos study. Early industrial age Golden Dawn-era booklets. They seemed innocuous enough, but there had to be a reason Emil had sequestered these from the shelves upon shelves of legitimate hermetic theory he didn't bequeath to me.

I pulled one of these booklets from between two hand-stitched leather-bound texts, and held it up to the light. *A DISCOURSE ON HIDDEN MAGICKS.* Lame title. Perhaps from a Victorian sensibility, this would have been a scandalous piece of publishing.

What the hell... I opened it up and skimmed the first couple pages. Florid prose made a case for hermetic practice, stitched heavily with spiritualism and a fawning eye toward Deist thought. It was utterly forgettable, though before I put it back, one phrase caught my eye.

"The darker aspects of human thought owe their patrilineage to a host, a choir parallel of and sinister to the angels of Creation. Such ancient and forgotten beings dwell not in eternal flame but in shadow, watching and at times guiding the wickedness of Man toward their own amusement and nourishments."

A wave of nostalgia poured over me. My brain injected the memory of tarry cigarette smoke and Emil's awful sherry into the scents wafting from the cabinet. Was this passage the inspiration for Emil coining the term "Dark Choir"? I continued skimming over the booklet, but found little else of use. Some further discourse over the justifications in dealing with the Dark Choir, but nothing on the Presidium or chaos magic.

I took some time to grab books almost at random and rifling through their pages. As was generally the case on the rare instances I dove into the Library, time became somewhat fluid. I indulged in some academic free-fall, pausing to swallow up sections of interest, and running a thread into another text from another century. By the time I came up for air, three hours had passed.

I gathered the alarming number of books I'd pulled out and set them back inside the cabinet, locking it up before giving my neck a good stretch. My eyes shifted to Ches's desk. Her study materials sat in neat stacks with tiny multi-colored stick-on tabs spraying from the sides. I walked over and rummaged over the top of the stack. Basic energy theory. Palpation. Divination. Dowsing. My Hermetic Theory 101. I noted that most of the language texts sat at the bottom. She truly hated studying dead languages. And lively ones, for that matter.

A separate stack of papers remained tucked underneath her desk topper. I snagged the top sheet to find a series of logograms and the name Matilda Garcia written across the top. Ches's private addiction consultancy work. At the time, I thought she was lashing out against my prohibition against practicing the art. In truth, she was finding a way to help Ricky. In general, it was a good idea. Charms for addiction recovery. It was something I'd dabbled with in the past, but never really committed to. They weren't real money-makers. But it did feel good to help people, I had to admit.

That used to be my thing. Helping people. Karma manipulation was my tool, a check-valve against the consequences of Netherwork. But there were moments when I managed to do the right thing despite myself, and those were the memories from ten years' worth of practice that I tended to dwell upon when I was alone in my basement, wondering what the hell I was doing with my life.

As I slid her personal notes back under her desk topper, a slip of notepad paper curled up and fell to the side. I reached for it and placed it neatly on top, and as I did so, the messy pencil scratching on the paper caught my attention.

LENFANT.

Minerva's scribblings, her decoded message from Deirdre.

I turned to the marker board and wrote the word "L'Enfant" near the center. I took a step back, then reached up to add the accent... L'Enfant.

"Mais oui," I said out loud with a self-amused grin.

That grin faded slowly as I considered the word.

The French word.

I returned to Ches's desk and reached for her research stack once again. I rifled through her papers until I found print outs of the Enoch Pratt sigils.

Ches had written "*L'Ecole de la Nombre D'or*" in large block letters across the bottom of the last photo. Behind that, I found a few pages she'd printed from some website outlining the basics of the old French Pythagorean school. Short-lived, fading in and out of existence between the 1730's and 1790's.

Right about the time the colonists decided they'd had enough of England and formed a new nation.

"Look to your history, huh?" I whispered as I scanned the page with eager eyes.

Did the *L'Ecole de la Nombre D'or* actually disappear? Or did it transform into something else? Something on a new continent.

Something like the Presidium.

I pulled my keys back out and opened up the cabinet. In my academic free-fall, I stumbled across at least three French texts, all of them pressed in movable type. I pulled book after book out, restacking them on my workbench, until I finally found all three. For a change, I wasn't interested in mechanics or hermetic theory. I was looking for history. My French wasn't terrible, but I was used to poring over recipes and ritual prescriptions. The prose in this book was a bit thick, but I managed. Good thing French hadn't changed much in the past couple hundred years.

The first book was too recent to be any use, a catalog of basic disease curses from the early nineteenth century. The second, however, was a bit more my speed. Nearly half the book was dedicated to chronicling several secret societies on the Continent from the late Crusades to the Industrial Age. It was a veritable Who's Who of the cabals that had survived the Burning Times. The Nombre D'or wasn't hard to find, though its entry was short. Everything I expected to find was there. The school was dedicated to the observance of sacred geometries and an Enlightenment Period take on Pythagorean practice, but with most of the Gnosticism stripped away.

My eyes shot wide when I spotted the name of the school's one and only adherent whom the author had deemed worthy of mention.

Pierre Charles L'Enfant.

Holy shit. Deirdre did have it figured out!

Continuing on, I learned that L'Enfant had studied under the Nombre D'or during his terms at the Royal Academy, where most of the practitioners had established their base. They had experimented with a method for platting a modern village according to strict geomantic principles. However, a deep rift had developed between those still clinging to Egyptian ideals for spatial confluence, and those who felt no desire to re-create a Necropolis in rural France. Despite this rift, the village of Nouveau Marché was granted a charter by King Louis XV. A crude lithograph of the plat filled an entire page. Largely unremarkable, excepting for five city gates leading to roads that were clearly redirected in order to accommodate a scheme that didn't conform to the points of the compass.

Five points surrounding the town.

Unfortunately, the economic pressures on the throne suspended the completion of the village, and soon after most able-bodied members of the Nombre D'or enlisted to fight abroad for the Colonies.

And there, the entry ended without further comment.

I set the book down and massaged my face.

L'Enfant was a practitioner of geomancy. What's more, he was on the side of the new planners, those insisting on creating something based on pure hermetic symmetries rather than leaning on tired old doctrine. That would have made him a bit of a maverick.

But someone felt he was important enough to name a Metro station in DC after him, so I figured his story didn't end in the Revolutionary War.

I looked over to the marker board. Five jinx sites.

Five sites, nearly surrounding D.C.

Could someone have been attempting to use the Nombre D'or's geomantic principles as an attack on the Presidium? Something about the pattern didn't seem right. I needed a map. Unfortunately, I had to concede ground to Ches and Malosi at this point. It would have been super-handy to have a computer or a smartphone at that moment. I knew I had a road atlas in the trunk of the Audi. I could probably piece together Maryland, Pennsylvania, and Virginia from the pages, and go full-conspiracy on this marker board.

I locked up the cabinet once again and hustled upstairs, snatching my keys from the bowl on the foyer table. The night air outside was heavy with springtime humidity. Probably would be fog tonight. My headlights flashed as I unlocked the car trunk, sending quick beams into the mist.

One of these beams illuminated a face, sneering at me. If my brain wasn't swimming with thoughts of French geomancy, I might have reacted to it quicker than I did.

Instead, I froze in my tracks, just long enough for the goon I didn't spot lurking behind my car to grab me around the chest and lock my arms in a full Nelson as I dropped my keys.

The leering thug in front of me swaggered forward. He seemed vaguely familiar, but I couldn't place him.

The thug grunted, "Hey, you smartass. Nicky Polo sends his regards."

Before I could gasp a response, he lunged forward and slammed a fist into my gut, knocking the air out of me. I groaned, and gasped for breath as he wound up again and hammered another one home, this time against my ribs.

The goon holding me unwound his arms and shoved me forward.

I fell, landing on hands-and-knees in front of Polo's thug, who swept my hands with his foot. My chin slapped against the driveway. I didn't see his shoe heading for my ribs, but the pain of the kick was dulled by my struggling breath.

He leaned down with a smile.

"I'll tell him you apologized." He reached over and grabbed my keys from the pavement. "You owe him back payments on your shitty little bar. I'm thinking your car will bring you up to date."

I rolled to my side, finally catching my breath. It must have taken longer than I'd figured, because as I tried to protest, I craned my head to find my Audi pulling out onto Amity, and out of sight.

CHAPTER THIRTY-THREE

Shit, my ribs hurt. Not so much that I'd actually go to the emergency room, as the policewoman crouched in front of me kept insisting. I waved off her urgings as I shifted on my sofa. Her partner stood just outside my front door, which he'd left standing wide open. I found myself oddly nervous about the amount of flies he was letting in. He concluded his conversation with his walkie-talkie, rounding the doorway with a long face.

"They found your car."

I straightened as much as I could. "That's good news, at least."

"Not really," he said. "It was found totaled on the side of Pulaski out by the airstrip."

"Totaled?"

"And on fire."

I leaned my head back against the sofa.

The policewoman stood up and pulled off the latex gloves she'd snapped on to inspect my head. "If your head hit the concrete, you should have it checked out, sir."

"Get my head checked? I suppose that's a long time coming." I smiled and sighed. "I'm fine."

Her partner approached with a tablet. "Here's your case number. You'll want to phone that into your insurance company as soon as possible."

"Is there anything worth salvaging?" I asked.

"Not really, but you'll have to pay for towing to impound. Again, insurance company should take care of that."

She asked, "I highly recommend you reconsider—"

"—my head's fine."

"I was going to say reconsider giving a description."

I scowled. "No need."

"Sir, I—"

"I'm fine."

She looked at her partner and shrugged. "Is there anything else, sir?"

A figure rushed through the door, and the police turned with hands on their hips.

Julian held up his hands and stepped back.

I called out, "It's okay."

Julian paced around them and reached for my head. "Jesus, Dorian. What've you done now?"

"Who called you?"

"Turner."

I shook my head as much as my aching brain would let me. "The hell's he got to do with this?"

"Said he heard your name on the wire. He's on his way."

"Crap."

The officers wrapped up and left me a handwritten note with my case number and a business card. When they'd left, I sat forward, wincing as my side splintered into several bright suns of piercing pain.

"It was Polo," I grunted.

"Who's Polo?"

"Remember that chowder-head that tried to roll us a couple weeks back? The one I dropped into Bettis's lap? Yeah. Him."

"Retaliation?" he asked.

"Basically. I recognized one of his goons. Guess Bettis didn't pick that goon up at the tavern when they arrested Polo."

Julian straightened up and looked around. "So, this has nothing to do with the 'Life'?"

"Nope. Just my usual mouth-check ass-cashing situation. Still, he might not be leaving us alone."

"I'll call Ronetta."

"Don't. She's not going to want to get involved."

He smirked. "Dorian, I think I know Ronetta better than you do."

I glared up at Julian. "I really don't. She's scary serious about her job. And she's basically eleventy-hundred percent done with my personal drama."

"That's called professionalism," he jibed. "Don't confuse it with antagonism."

"I don't think she's sold on my value as an outside consultant."

Julian chuckled. "Neither am I, but the good news is this mugging, car theft, whatever the hell just happened, has nothing to do with your magic business."

"Isn't Polo behind bars?"

"Not really sure, but if I had to guess, I'd doubt it. Probably posted bond the same day he was arrested. If you want to go in against this meathead, we can do it. He's a small timer, just has some reliable muscle. If we go hard against Polo, we can take him down."

I stared at the darquelle hanging on the wall beside my front door, its silver blade gleaming in the lamp light.

"Oh, I'm going hard alright. Son of a bitch killed my car."

Julian crouched down in front of me, his eyes alive with interest. "I thought you weren't into those... aggressive practices."

"Well, no. I suppose I'm not."

Which was true, since Adrastos was pretty clear on the point that Netherwork was permitted only in the pursuit of these chaos tricksters. Chaos tricksters with a French geomantic pedigree.

Julian slapped my knee. "You look like you need a drink."

"Yes, please," I moaned.

Julian moved to the sideboard, holding up a couple bottles until I nodded at the Talisker. He began pouring two glasses, then froze mid-pour as the front door swung open and the enormous frame of Reed Malosi swept into the foyer.

Malosi glanced around the room, checking corners and windows before finally stepping up to my sofa.

"The hell's been happening over here?"

I gestured to my face. "Had a bad night."

He turned to Julian, then back to me. "You get attacked?"

I nodded.

Julian stepped around Malosi to hand me the whiskey, brandishing his own in front of Reed.

"Care for a scotch?"

"Hey, easy there handing out my whiskey," I jibed. As Malosi waved him off, an irritable curl twisting his brow, I asked him, "Who called you?"

"What?"

"You knew something was up."

He nodded. "My wardings were pinging like a motherfucker."

I supposed they were. I'd forgotten he'd bolstered the wardings on my house, and with the comings and goings of the police and Polo's men, Malosi's skin was probably crawling... wherever he was.

"Sorry about that."

He lifted expectant hands. "So, should we call the police or what?"

"Come and gone," I answered.

"And?" Malosi pressed.

"Nick Polo sent some thugs to work me over. Just tit for tat, revenge for baking his brie the other week."

Julian sipped his whiskey, then added, "Don't feel bad. I had to get a call from Detective Turner. Came over as quickly as I could and the cops were basically out the door." He turned to me. "And he should be here any minute, now. So if you have anything you don't want him rummaging over—"

Malosi interrupted, "What do you mean, you came over?"

Julian looked up at Reed, his face blanched. "Um, drove here. In my car."

Malosi turned to me with a squint. "I thought the two of you were at some dinner party with the Mayor."

"Oh, yeah," I mumbled.

Julian winced, and stepped alongside Malosi, holding a finger up from the hand holding his glass. "Sorry about that. Slipped my mind. I, uh, had to cancel."

Malosi gave him a heavy stare.

"Look, Reed," I began, trying to stand up unsuccessfully. "You got me. I had a thing. Couldn't take anyone along."

Malosi spun away, running his hands alongside his head. "Fuck's sake, Dorian."

"Listen, Reed. I couldn't make the meet with you tagging along. Or behind. Or watching from fucking space. He'd have known."

He turned back to face me. "It was that de Haviland person, wasn't it?"

"Yeah, I'm still calling him Brown."

Julian's eyes widened. "Brown? From the Druid Hill Club?"

"That's the one."

He snickered. "His name is de Haviland?"

"It gets better," I added. "First name is Clarence."

Malosi lifted a palm. "This isn't a joke, people. Dorian? I'm here to help you. I can't do that if you're ditching me at every opportunity."

"You couldn't help me tonight, Reed."

He circled his finger over my face. "All evidence to the fucking contrary."

"Also, let's not get too pious. You're here because Clement wants my books."

"Oh, very nice," he hissed.

"Hey, I jerked you around. I admit that. But it was worth it," I stated. "Absolutely worth it. I'm making breakthroughs, here."

"Care to share?" Malosi demanded as he loomed over me.

Julian looked on with interest, swirling his scotch.

I took them both in, and clamped my mouth shut.

Was Malosi here because he wanted to be here? Or was I correct? He was sent here as a deal-sweetening gesture by Clement. I'd been as final as I could be with Clement, but he wouldn't let go of this mission to acquire Emil's Library.

Clement.

The man was very… French.

I peered up at Malosi. "If I called Clement right now and told him, absolutely, without any possibility that I'd ever change my mind, that I will not sell him Emil's books… what are the odds he'd recall you to New York?"

Malosi put his hands on his hips. "The hell are you talking about?"

"I saying, if you're here for Clement, then he must have some reason for you to be here that has nothing to do with that Library downstairs."

Malosi looked over to Julian for clarity.

Julian shrugged. "Maybe he should go to the emergency room?"

"Yeah," Malosi grumbled. "Because he's starting to sound like his head and his ass got rearranged."

I pushed off the sofa, and this time managed to make it to my feet, despite the searing pain in my side.

"What's Clement been doing these past few years? He said he's semi-retired, that he's more or less a full-time Collector at this point. But where's the money in that?"

Malosi blinked.

I pressed, "Imports and exports. That was his business. And I'm not talking about pottery or European luxury cars. He dealt with the old cabals. He traded in soul trafficking, didn't he?"

Malosi muttered, "If he did, that was the past."

"The past, huh? Then why does he have you running side trips to law firms to discuss import duties? Or is he actually importing pottery, and I have him completely wrong."

"I never said he's a legitimate practitioner," Malosi stated. "Neither was Osterhaus, if you remember."

"You're hitching your wagon to some shady shit, Reed," I grumbled.

"Because there aren't as many options for me. You know who paid for my college? I did. Know who stumbled into the Life all by himself, without anyone to hold his hand? Yo. I didn't start off with a trust fund or some world-league practitioner ready to move my ass to England to study full-time. I've been working and paying bills the whole time I've been studying hermetic practice. So I take what I can get, you know. And Clement is as close to a best-case scenario as I can find. So, yeah. I'm not going to get all up in his face about anything, because it ain't my damn business, Dorian!"

I turned away. "No, but he's making it my business."

Julian tried to step between us, but Malosi swept him back.

"What are you saying, here?" he muttered at my shoulder. "Clement's the one dropping jinx bombs against the Presidium? That I'm some kind of spy, or pawn in his grand scheme?"

I spun around to face Malosi. "Are you? Maybe not knowingly. Maybe you fell into this mess by accident."

Julian tried once again to separate us, saying, "Dorian, do you have some evidence that Clement is involved with whatever this jinx thing is?"

"There's no evidence. I'm just pursuing a line of thinking, here."

"Well," Julian sighed, "perhaps we should outline this thinking instead of throwing around recriminations?"

I took a breath, then tried to deal out my words carefully. "I just got the shit kicked out of me. Someone just stole then torched my car. Forgive me if I come off a bit brusque."

Silence hung over our heads for a moment as I searched for a decent response. But my blood was up. Anger and paranoia flooded my brain. I didn't know who to trust, anymore. Malosi looked wounded by this, but wouldn't a good liar do exactly that? And even if Malosi was simply being used, it was too dangerous keeping him around, stitching his energy into the wardings of my own home. Clement was older than me. More experienced. Arguably smarter. I had no clue how deep his intrigue ran, but I had to find some way to get out in front of it.

I looked up to Julian. "The Presidium is an organization as old as this country, itself. It's an elite body of hermetic practitioners that polices this continent. Protects it from outside influences, and keeps the peace. I'm not saying they're good, bad or sorry. But I am saying that someone has gone through tremendous lengths to plan a long-term assault on the Presidium. They've undermined their power structure, their credibility, and they're using some insane magic to do it. If someone was capable of that, and if that someone was Jean Clement, then I'd have to be extremely stupid to let him throw me into the fire like this." I looked to Malosi. "I have to be very, very careful whom I trust."

Malosi nodded with a stiff lip. "That's how it is, huh?"

I didn't respond.

He sniffled, looked at the ground, and nodded one more time before saying, "All right. I'm out of here."

Julian held up a hand. "Gentlemen, let's take a breath. Dorian's been through a lot tonight. There's a lot of emotion spilling out right now."

Malosi shook his head. "No, this isn't emotion. This is paranoia. And the worst part is that he isn't completely nuts."

"Thanks," I grumbled.

"What pisses me off, however," he added, his voice adopting an aggressive volume, "is that this should have been about you and me." He waved his finger between me and him. "You should've known I had your back."

At that point, I didn't know anything. So I said nothing.

And he stormed up the steps, adding, "I'll pack up."

I didn't have to see Julian's face; I could feel his glare. He didn't say anything, though, leaving me to stew in my own sauce as Malosi thumped around upstairs. Finally, he returned, completely changed, with a duffle bag over his shoulder. He stopped by Julian, who shook his hand with a nod.

Then he turned to me.

"You should get yourself looked at," he offered.

"I'll be okay."

Malosi adjusted his duffle, then stepped out the front door, leaving it ajar as he took his exit. His car cranked, and as it pulled onto the street and down Amity, the energy of the wardings snapped a few times before draining entirely. The house suddenly felt thin, weak, and cold.

Julian finished his scotch.

"Well," he sighed, "that was quite the spectacle."

"Julian, please. My ribs are killing me. Head's not much better."

"That would explain the complete lack of judgment I just witnessed."

I reached for my glass, but my midsection decided I needed to stay put.

Julian continued, "I'm going to talk out loud, and you're going to indulge me."

I nodded.

"So, here's what I know. A well-respected Congressman stands in front of our tavern and calls out a list of deep government occultists who supposedly control everything that happens in this country, effectively ending his public career. Same Congressman dies that night of a heart attack. Then you get evasive on me, while at the same time scurrying around like some damn insect trying not to get stepped on."

I sucked in a breath to respond to that "insect" comment, but decided it wasn't worth the pain.

He continued, "Then Ricky enters the picture, and you latch onto this pure quest to help him. Maybe for Ches, maybe for yourself, either way it had ignited that glimmer of decency I've always respected in you. Then it all went to Hell. Ches is gone, and this pure quest is now replaced with your bug stepping again. And you've driven someone else away."

He stood with arms out, searching for a conclusion.

I said, "If it matters, this bug stepping is all about keeping everyone safe. It's not just another conspiracy."

"Well, if that's true, then you're whittling away at your base. You can't do this alone, Dorian. You need help."

"These… these are dangerous people, Julian. We can't out-think them."

He smirked. "Well, maybe *you* can't."

"Vast shadow-government cabals don't scare you off, huh?"

"I've been in the secrets trade for a long time, now. I don't understand the magic at play here, but I know politics. And I know when a man's been leveraged."

I made a stronger effort to reach my glass, this time with success.

After a belt, I asked, "You think I'm being leveraged?"

"Did they offer you something?"

I nodded.

"Is it something you can't get on your own?"

"It's for Ricky and Ches."

Julian paced, his eyes rolling in thought.

"You need to deal me in, Dorian. I can help. At this point, I don't see how you have any choice."

At that moment, I couldn't disagree.

He reached over to shake my hand. I took advantage of the offer and pulled myself up, with a little help from Julian.

"All right, you want on the inside?" I took a cleansing breath. "Come on. I'll show you what I have." I added with a slight lean around Julian's shoulder, "You too, Detective."

Turner squinted at me from the front door which Malosi had left ajar.

"You got something tangible," Turner grumbled.

I shrugged. "All pretext and supposition, but there's maybe just one or two pieces missing. I feel like it'll fall together if I can just catch a break."

He pulled a slip of paper from his coat pocket. "Maybe I got a piece here."

I hobbled forward, reaching for the paper.

"What's this?" I asked.

"After you jokers ditched me yesterday, I followed up on this address we got from that old bat up by Charles Street. Turns out, it was an art studio. Kind of. For maybe two months."

I peered at the paper. The words *TREE OF LIFE STUDIO* were written in Turner's weirdly immaculate handwriting.

He continued, "It was leased week-by-week by a Brandon Carruthers."

"Brandon Carruthers," I repeated. "Never heard of him."

"I'm giving his chain a tug tomorrow," Turner said with an air of smug self-satisfaction. "I'll catch you up when I'm done."

Julian interjected, "What is this about, again?"

I took a slow turn, gripped my side, and moved for the steel door in the hallway.

"I'll show you."

CHAPTER THIRTY-FOUR

The lights were still on from when I went jogging upstairs to fetch my road atlas, which was probably still smoldering in the remains of my car.

Turner stepped around my workbench, occupying more room than his frame ought to have. He scanned the workspace and all of its trappings... the reagents, the books, the octagonal workbench with a golden spiral worked into the surface... without betraying the first hint of discomfort or even interest.

He released a slow whistle, then said, "You people are freaks."

"Don't suppose I disagree on that particular point," I mumbled, easing my way to the marker board. "Julian?"

He stepped up, face filled with substantially more awe. He bordered on reverence.

I pointed to the marker board with its lists of names and arrows and question marks. "We've had a series of attacks on colonial-era buildings lately. They're using a kind of magic that uses chaos to create random, usually destructive effects. Only, they end up being not so random."

Turner made a guttural huffing sound at the word "magic."

I continued, "I've come to believe that these sites were specifically chosen, and that they hold special interest for the Presidium."

Julian leaned in. "Where are these? I recognize Enoch Pratt."

"Locations in Gettysburg, Harper's Ferry, and this newest one in Locust Grove, Virginia."

"You got a problem already, hot shot," Turner chided.

"What's my problem?"

"Well, for one, you're kind of a prick. Two, though… your colonial times mumbo jumbo don't wash with the Enoch Pratt. It wasn't built until, like, the late 1800s."

"That a fact?" I asked in genuine interest.

"Yeah. Where you from?"

"New York."

He snickered. "Yeah. Work this city long enough, you pick up the deep history, y'know?"

"Well, that's a good point. Everything else dated back to the founding of the nation, which was hand-in-glove with my theory that this was some kind of attack on the Presidium."

Julian suggested, "May still be. The Library building itself isn't as old as Washington, but it was built over a site after all. Some of the original bricks were used in its construction."

I looked over to Turner, who nodded.

"Like the man said," Turner declared.

"Okay, so let's assume there was an original site at that location. Some site, like the others, that the Presidium needed intact. Now," I said, pointing at Turner, "remember those sigils in the library?"

I snatched the photos from Ches's desk, and he nodded.

"Sure," Turner replied.

I said, "Turns out they aren't any kind of ancient language. They're a kind of parlor script devised by a short-lived cult of geomancers in France."

Turner scowled. "The fuck's a geomancer?"

"They use physical locations, distances and situational awareness to channel Cosmic energies for their own purposes."

Turner snapped his fingers. "Like feng shui, right?"

I blinked. "Uh. Yeah. It's exactly like feng shui."

He smiled and gave Julian a satisfied nod.

"So," I continued, "these geomancers suddenly disappeared, right about the time the French came to assist the colonies in the Revolutionary War. The one name from the cabal that made it to memory was Pierre L'Enfant." I grabbed Deirdre's page of incoherent scribblings that Minerva decoded for me. "The one good dowser I know was hit by one of these chaos spells. It drove her mad. I think she was targeted by these same people because she would have known what they were up to." I held up the scribblings. "And she sent me this message."

Julian squinted at the page, then nodded. "L'Enfant, again."

"She knows who this guy was."

Turner coughed. "Well, no shit."

Julian tucked his chin with a grin.

I lifted a hand at Turner. "What now?"

"You go to school up in New York, or what?"

"Of course."

"Bet it was one of those private schools that cost my entire year's wages to attend."

I squinted at him.

"Ain't that a kick in the ass?" he snickered. "All that money and he don't know who L'Enfant was." He pronounced it "Lin-fint," but that didn't steal any of the sting from his words.

With a breath, and a reminder that I needed this info, I asked, "I'd love to learn."

Turner's grin melted a touch, and he looked at me with a brief, but intense, understanding. He must have realized he was jerking me around a little too hard.

With a cough, and a shift of his weight from one foot to the other, he answered, "Well, he's the guy who built D.C., isn't he?" He looked to Julian. "I'm thinking about the same guy, right?"

Julian nodded, and added, "He was hired by Washington himself to lay out the street plan for the federal district, when the States got around to making one."

"So, that's why they named a Metro station after him," I surmised.

Turner said, "Yeah, you hear a bunch of shit about him being a Satanist or something."

I snapped my head in Turner's direction, instantly regretting it as my brain throbbed. "Satanist?"

"Yeah. Like, he hid the Number of the Beast in the shape of the streets. Y'know, 666?"

I stepped toward Turner, and for the first time ever, he stepped back.

"Tell me about that!"

"Hell, I don't know. My sister's husband's this conspiracy nut. Reads these books about the Illuminati and shit. Says they made Washington to be the capital of the New World Order, and L'Enfant was their architect."

Julian lifted a hand to his head. "Christ God, Dorian. Please don't let the next words out of your mouth be 'The Illuminati actually created D.C. to be the capital of the New World Order.' Because if that's what you're about to say, I'm going to need more scotch."

"It all follows," I admitted, muttering to myself. "L'Enfant was disenchanted with the Nombre D'or and enlisted to move to the Americas. He must have found the hermetic practitioners already situated in power. Jefferson, Franklin, Blake, Marshall... He finally had real estate to try his grand scheme." I looked to Turner. "I'd really love to meet your brother-in-law."

He snarled. "No, you really don't. He hits the sauce, like, at lunch time. Smells like piss and whiskey."

"Stop it," I jibed. "You're starting to turn me on."

He shuddered. "Freaks."

"Seriously, though. Can you arrange a meet? I need to wax eloquent with an up-to-his-wrist conspiracy nut."

"Sure," he said. "After I'm done with Carruthers. Got Claye up my ass about this."

Julian cocked his head. "Why's she so obsessed with the library vandalism?"

"Well, for one," he replied, "they can't re-open the children's wing until we fix it. And for two, I think she's gunning for Lake, here."

"Gunning for me?" I squawked.

"Either that, or him," he added pointing to Julian.

Julian shook his head. "I've never given her the first reason to feel antagonistic against me, so I'm going to rightly assume you're the problem."

He wasn't wrong.

"Remind me to send her a fruit basket or something."

Turner shuffled on his feet. "Look, guys. I'm running on four hours sleep, here. I'm happy to play your game tomorrow, but I'm calling it a night."

I reached out my hand.

"Hey, Detective? Thank you. Seriously." I looked him in the eye. "You're really helping me out here, and I'm grateful."

He stared at my hand, then looked up to my face.

And he gripped my hand like a hydraulic press.

"I have my moments," he said. "You still got my card?"

I pulled my hand back, examined the patch of floor near my feet, and admitted, "No."

He reached into his pocket and produced a dog-eared card, and handed it over.

"No offense taken," he said. "Call me in the a.m. when you're done with whatever the fuck it is you do in the morning, and we'll run Carruthers down, and my brother-in-law."

I took the card. "Thanks, Detective."

"Call me Grant."

Turner gave Julian a quick two finger salute, keeping plenty of distance. He was helpful... he was even a human being. But he still wasn't okay with Julian. I'd have to work around that.

When he had bounded up the stairs and left my home, Julian set his glass onto my workbench. I relocated it to Ches's desk as he said, "I'm guessing I need a little more material to work off of than he does."

"You probably do. But I don't think I can manage that just tonight." My side was killing me, and I really needed some manner of pharmaceutical to keep me from crying.

"You're staying here tonight?" he asked.

I thought about that. Shit. With Malosi's wards gone, I was down to an admittedly pathetic level of protection. I wouldn't have worried so much about it before that night, but the fact of the matter was... I was screwed.

"You know," Julian added, "I have detected a pattern here."

"The what now?"

He pointed at the marker board. "L'Enfant. Golden Ratio. Sorry... Nombre D'or."

"Yeah?"

His finger fell onto the first name in the last column. "And Clement. Seems you're drawing some broad strokes here, Dorian."

"It's not just his heritage, Julian. He shows up out of fucking nowhere right before this all goes down. He sends Malosi here, ostensibly to 'help' me, but what he's really doing is watching every move I make."

Julian squared his shoulders against me, and for the first time in, basically forever, he yelled at me.

"Dorian Lake, you need to pull your head out of your ass!"

I stiffened.

He continued, "Sorry, but you need to hear this. You are a terrible, actually appalling judge of character. What's more, you seem to wallow in such depths of self-loathing that you possess this instinct to drive away anyone who sees you as a human being, and accepts you. That must really terrify you, for you to treat us with such naked aggression."

I shook my head, a sob forming in my throat. "I don't."

He lifted a finger. "You're hurting yourself, and you're hurting anyone who actually gives a damn about you and your peculiar little dramas. So, if you're going to find your soul, whatever that means, you're going to have to listen to Julian. Okay?"

I nodded.

He urged, "Say it. Say, 'I'll trust Julian.'"

A spark of amusement flickered in my chest.

I repeated, "I trust Julian."

"Good. So, am I putting you up tonight?"

"I, uh… indelicate question, here."

"Hmm?"

I squirmed as I searched for the best way to ask the question. "Is Cleve, like, at your place?"

His eyes lowered. Shit. Julian overreached again. He'd invited me to his home without thinking about Cleve. I imagined Julian had cultivated a bad habit of unilateral action in his own household… one which his boyfriend likely didn't appreciate.

I quickly added, "Because that's a super-bad idea."

Julian sucked in a breath, and nodded.

"So, anyway, I need a place to lay low, that has established wardings. No offense, but your place isn't exactly Fort Knox."

"How do you know?"

I smirked. "Because your energy is fucking everywhere, Julian. Seriously. I need to teach you how to center one of these days. No, I have a place in mind. No one's going to bug me there."

"Okay," he grumbled. "I guess you'll need a ride?"

Crap. I did. My poor car.

"Well, I mean, if you don't mind."

Seriously. Nicky Polo was going to rue the fucking day.

CHAPTER THIRTY-FIVE

"You sure you're allowed to be here?" Julian asked as I unlocked the Swain's back door.

"Yeah. They gave me a key."

"Just making sure they don't have an alarm system or something. I've heard stories about Frederick police."

I paused after turning on the light switch. "What stories?"

"Nothing."

"I'm not joking, Julian. What stories?"

"I'm sure you're fine."

I convinced myself Julian was fucking with me, and shuffled into the back of the antique shop. Julian lingered by the door.

"You coming in?" I asked.

"I should get back to Baltimore."

I nodded. "Tell Cleve I said hi."

"I absolutely will not do that," he said with a half-grin.

As he turned, I called out, "Julian?"

"Yes?"

"Thank you."

He bowed his head, then stepped back out into the night.

There wasn't much night left, but I needed rest. And painkillers. I wound my way to the wrought-iron spiral stairs leading to the

Swains' living area on the second floor, and sighed. This was going to suck.

About ten minutes later, I'd hauled my aching body up the stairs and arrived in the land of brown shag carpeting and pagan décor. The tiny living room was a patch of the aforementioned carpet with a television and a couch that sat between the kitchen and the stairs. The clock over the range in the kitchen showed it was past two in the morning. Cute clock. Lunar phases and everything. That would have been Wren's choice.

I moved into the kitchen and reached for the cabinet I recalled they kept the drugs in. Three Ibuprofens later, I sat on the couch, feeling the Swain wardings envelope around me and settle. I was a welcome presence in this building. Maybe more so than my own, at this point. Before I settled horizontally, I fished my darquelle out of my jacket and laid it gently on the floor. I didn't have Malosi to watch my back, anymore. I was on my own.

Once the drugs kicked in, I fell asleep fast. Maybe it was Ibuprofen. Maybe it was that weird security of feeling off-the-grid. If the Presidium wanted to locate me, they could. But this felt safe. My ribs woke me up only once, as I shifted my weight and fell back asleep.

I was aware of sunlight at some point, and willfully ignored it. My body needed to catch up on sleep. I reached for a ragged throw pillow behind my head and pulled it over my face. Perhaps it was a good thing the light had awakened me, because if I hadn't taken that moment to move the pillow, I might not have heard the shuffling downstairs.

My heart hammered as adrenaline rushed into my system.

Whispers.

Someone was in the building.

I reached down and grabbed the darquelle. Easing my feet off the couch wasn't easy, but I bit down on my lip and swallowed the pain, treading light against the carpet as I crept around to the back of the couch.

The wrought-iron spiral stairs creaked slightly as someone began to ascend. They were moving slowly and quietly.

I crouched low, keeping an eye on the platform above the stairs.

Something eased into view. Thin, shiny. It looked like chrome, or stainless steel. It slipped higher into view, and I recognized it was the tip of an actual sword.

This was about to get interesting.

I doubled my grip on my darquelle. The "blooded" working blade was meant to sever energetic constructs, but it would work against flesh and bone in a pinch.

The sword lifted further into view as the one wielding it poked his head into view.

I released a breath, and slowly lifted my body into view.

"Careful with that sword, Edgar," I called out.

Edgar froze, blinked several times, then nearly dropped the sword as his shoulders relaxed.

"Holy crap, man," he coughed. "You about gave me a heart attack."

"Sorry about that."

Edgar turned and called down the stairs, "It's okay. It's just Dorian."

A series of noises erupted downstairs, including at least one grumbled pejorative from Wren and a whoop of excitement from the kids.

I set the darquelle back down on the pillow.

Edgar stepped into the room, still shaking his head. He lifted the sword and propped it against his shoulder.

"Where did you get that thing?" I asked, leaning gingerly against the couch.

"Not really sure. Picked it up at an estate sale in New Jersey a few years ago. I think it's a prop from a movie or something." He reached out to chuck my shoulder, then froze when he noticed the state of my face. "Holy shit, man. What happened to you?"

"Got in a fight."

He hissed and inspected the cut above my eye. "Nasty."

"You should see the other guy."

"Mess him up?"

I smirked. "Not really, but he's going to need to polish his shoes. So there's that."

Tiny footsteps stormed up the stairs. I braced as Eddie and Elle rushed around Edgar. They clamped onto my midsection in bear hugs, both of them weirdly strong for their size. This family didn't play when it came to hugs, and I sucked in a breath as they squeezed a fresh shot of pain into my ribs.

"Ah, Jesus..." I wheezed.

Edgar pulled Eddie off my side as Elle took a quick step back, wincing up at me.

"Hear that, kids?" Edgar chuckled. "That's the sound of a man with a broken rib. A man who I'm guessing hasn't been to the damn emergency room yet?"

"I'm fine."

Wren rounded the top of the stairs with two enormous suitcases. She power-armed the first up onto the landing before lugging the second one behind her. She glared at us all.

Edgar shook his head. "I, you know, could have helped."

"You were busy," she panted, "saving us from an intruder."

"Sorry about that," I offered. "I needed a place to crash."

Wren cocked her brow. "You left the back door unlocked."

"Oh. Uh, yeah. Sorry about that, too."

Edgar asked, "Where's your car?"

Wren interrupted, "Never mind that, why do you need a place to crash?"

"It's been a hell of a couple weeks," I answered.

Wren sighed. "It always is." She turned to the kids. "Who wants some bacon and other stuff but mostly bacon?"

The kids nodded furiously, as did Edgar.

She turned to Edgar with a finger lifted. "Sorry, buckaroo. You're going to bed."

"Damn, man."

"Uh-uh," she chided. "You drove the night shift. Hit the sack, dude."

He shuffled past her, stopping to kiss her cheek. "Save me some of that bacon."

"No promises."

Edgar paused by me. “You seriously okay?”

“In a roundabout manner of speaking, yeah.”

He shrugged, then smiled. “All right. I’ll take it.”

Once he had plodded down the hallway and shut the bedroom door, Wren broomed the kids away. “You two need a shower. You smell like feet.”

Eddie groused, but Elle said nothing. She lingered at Wren’s elbow staring at me.

I muttered, “I’ll get out of your hair.”

Wren reached for my head, jerked it to the side and peered at my eye. With a whistle, she said, “Nope. Gonna dress this first. I get not going to the emergency room, by the way. Nothing but doctors and people with qualifications and medical credentials up in those joints.”

“And MRSA.”

She smacked my arms. “Up.”

Wren shoved me down the hallway. The kids followed, and she gave Eddie a jerk on the ear. “You’re in the shower, buddy boy.”

Eddie glanced up at me, then at his mother. “You’re all in the bathroom.”

“Nothing Dorian can’t handle. Come on. Let’s get that butt moving.”

Wren manhandled me onto the lavatory and pushed my head back to get a better view. Elle hovered by the door, watching.

I gave her a wink, and she grinned.

Wren grabbed a dark brown bottle of what I hoped wasn’t hydrogen peroxide and a handful of toilet paper. Eddie turned on the shower and scurried out of his clothes and behind the shower curtain quicker than human sight could register.

“So, you start this fight?” Wren asked.

“Yes.”

“Figures.”

“So, drove all night?” I asked, changing the subject.

“We were going to stop at a motel, but we decided we wanted to come home.”

Elle huffed, and Wren rolled her eyes.

I asked, "Did I miss something?"

Wren smirked. "You missed having a dramatic teenage daughter."

I hissed as she pressed the peroxide against my eyebrow.

"Well," Wren mumbled, "looks like you were right, kiddo."

Elle straightened, and explained, "I knew something was wrong with you."

"Something's always wrong with me," I said.

"No. Something really wrong," Elle protested. "Like you were hurt."

I glanced to Wren, who was fishing a bandage from the drawer under my knee. "You training her up in divination or something?"

"Not yet," Wren answered, "but I'm starting to think it'll happen sooner than later."

"Awesome," I said, holding out a fist to Elle. "I need a diviner in my corner."

Elle bumped my fist with a blushing grin.

The shower turned off, and Wren spun on her heel. "Oh, uh-uh. You're going full soap, dude."

Eddie groaned and turned the shower back on.

I hopped off the lavatory after Wren applied the bandage, and stole out of the bathroom to let Eddie shower in peace.

"Hey you," Wren called to Elle, "you're on deck."

Elle crossed her arms, and Wren closed in with her.

"Give Dorian some space, okay," she whispered at a volume I figure she thought I couldn't hear.

Elle nodded, then gave me a deep glance.

I made a shooing gesture with my fingers, and she disappeared to her room.

Wren turned to me and swept past me for the kitchen.

I followed, saying, "The least I can do is make the coffee."

"Nope. You make it wrong."

"It's just water and coffee grounds, right?"

"Yeah, but you skimp on the grounds. That doesn't make coffee. That makes liquid sadness." She bustled around the kitchen assembling the coffee maker.

"So, Elle's going better?"

Wren nodded.

"How's the nightmares?"

"Hasn't had one for a few weeks. Knock on all available wood."

I knocked on the casing to the kitchen.

"She's good," Wren continued. "She's eating again. She's sleeping."

"These premonitions are new."

Wren paused and looked out the window. "Yeah." She swiveled her head to me. "And she never stops talking about you."

"That's not new."

Wren laughed. "Oh, sit down. You're making me nervous."

I did as ordered, looking up at the pentacle she had hung over the doorway to the kitchen. "Hey, quick question for you. Magic related."

"Shoot."

"Chaos magic. Ever deal with anything like that?"

Wren nodded matter-of-factly. "Time to time."

"No shit?"

"Why?"

"I might have a thing."

"Well, I've studied Himes and Neuwaller. Basic stuff."

A flutter in my stomach overtook the pain in my side. "Tell me."

She hoisted a skillet from the cabinet and settled it on the stove top. "What's to tell? It's intuitive. Mostly it's a wrangling act... lassoing chaos where you find it. Like, from Nature or the subconscious."

"Subconscious?"

"Lots of chaos practice involves voluntarily breaking the mental connection."

I blinked. "Making yourself insane?"

"Doesn't have to be quite that dramatic, but insanity sure doesn't hurt if you're trying to play with Chaos. If you rather not actually break your brain, you can accomplish the same goals with a strict mental discipline of subconscious... why are we talking about this?"

"No specific reason."

She turned to face me full-on.

"Maybe a couple specific reasons."

Wren turned off the stove and stepped over to the table.

In a low but firm voice, she asked, "I know I'm going to regret this, but what trouble are you in now?"

"You really want to know?"

"I asked, didn't I?"

I gave this a moment's thought. I'd already corralled Julian into this fight. Wouldn't I rather keep the Swains out of the crossfire?

"Let's just say this. I'd really rather all of you were still in Orlando."

"You need any help?"

I closed my eyes. "You're a Wiccan, so you know more about Nature magic than I do. Tell me about chaos and physical locations. Like, say someone jinxed a piece of land. What would that do, exactly?"

Wren leaned back and crossed her arms. "Well, it's not like cursed land. That's way simpler. A land curse creates an area effect for a spell, like disease or bad luck that plagues anyone who lives on it. A curse stays with the property, but doesn't really do anything to it. That's why land curses are relatively easy to cleanse. It doesn't go deep."

"So what about a jinx?"

Her eyes narrowed. "That's totally different. A jinx actually punches a hole through the substance of Nature, Herself. It's an open wound called a 'nihil.' Not just some stain of evil, it's a hole into a realm of pure destruction. You can't just clear a jinx; you'd have to repair the damage. But at this point, we're not dealing with Wicca anymore. We're dealing with the old craft."

"You mean Stregheria?"

She unfolded her arms and stretched. "Yeah, so, if you know any Streghas who aren't interested in cursing the living dogshit out of you, I'd ask them." She added after groaning through her stretch, "Though I can't imagine why a Stregha would give you the time of day."

"One might," I answered, "if they were an old customer."

CHAPTER THIRTY-SIX

I housed several pieces of bacon, then wrapped my darquelle in some silver cloth Wren loaned me. Elle gave me a hug goodbye, squeezing tight again. I sensed she understood it was painful, but couldn't stop. I honestly didn't mind. She had fought a long, hard fight back to whatever "normal" means to a fourteen-year-old. She was lucky to be alive, and with such a vibrant soul. I honestly envied that girl.

Wren asked as I turned to the stairs, "How much of this do you want me to tell Edgar?"

I gave it some thought. "Really, I trust your instinct. He's going to want to get into it, if you tell him. It's your call."

She nodded, then reached around my shoulders and gripped me tighter than Elle had.

"Be safe, asshole."

"I will."

I reached the bottom of the stairs, and spotted the door to Edgar's collection. "Oh, I might have bought something."

"What?"

"You'll see."

I hurried out the door before she could bust my balls over liberating a cursed object from Edgar's collection.

Curses. I was already deeper into Netherwork than I had ever planned to be… than Emil had ever wanted. Every time I used the Gregori pendulum, I was risking my disembodied soul, banking on the fact that I couldn't damn the thing while it was outside of my body. Hell, the curse I cast against Osterhaus could be free-and-clear, if that were the case.

As would any curse I might use in defense of the Presidium.

My soul was in someone's possession, according to Parrish. Someone owned it. That notion filled me with dread. How had they found it? Did it fall into their laps? Were they fishing out in the Nether and just snagged it on their line?

Or was this someone who knew exactly what they were looking for?

None of these possibilities made me feel like singing *Oh What a Beautiful Morning* as I limped my way along Carroll Street to meet Julian. He'd offered to pick me up when I called him shortly before breakfast. My existential dread notwithstanding, I had a lot to feel good about. I had three solid leads. That was three more than I'd had all week. My whole notion that the Nombre D'or was almost entirely behind this conspiracy was materializing day by day. But something still wasn't lining up in my thinking. If Pierre L'Enfant managed to swing his mulligan in the New World, then what went wrong? What were these people trying to accomplish by nuking his node sites, turning them into nihils?

And what was Clement's role in all of this?

Julian pulled up the street with his typical punctuality.

He rolled down his window and called, "Hey, stranger. Need a lift?"

I slid into his Volvo and braced as I clicked the seatbelt over my midsection.

He peered at my face. "Got patched up, there?"

"Yeah," I wheezed. "The Swains came back this morning."

"Oh. Awkward."

"Tell me about it."

"To the tavern?"

I caught my breath and forced a smile. "Actually, how would you feel about a drive to the Eastern Shore?"

Julian snickered, then scowled when he realized I wasn't kidding.

"Eastern Shore?"

"Yeah."

"Any particular reason?" he asked.

"I learned a little more about the land jinxes these mystery men are throwing around. I need to talk to someone who, well... moves in this arena."

"Someone I'll want to meet?" he ventured as he pulled back onto the street.

"Probably not. In fact, you should probably wait in the car."

"I think you know, at this point, we're way beyond that."

Julian's dark interest was piqued again. But I remembered Annarose Rodolfi. She was a dangerous witch, and not particularly forbearing. This wasn't an encounter I could indulge Julian, or we'd both end up with diseases, or worse.

I turned to him without too much pain from my ribs. "I need to see a Stregha, Julian."

"Okay."

"You have no idea what a Stregha is, do you?"

He shook his head with a bemused smirk.

"Okay. So, picture my life. I'm a book-learning, ancient languages, specific metals and reagents in specific orders on specific strokes of will kind of practitioner."

He shrugged. "I suppose I follow that."

"Well, you know my kind of practice has a dark side. Right? They're the ones who twist the will of men, subvert karma itself, conjure demons and generally wreak havoc with the order of things."

Julian scowled. "Charming."

I flipped my palms up. "Right? So, scary shit. Now, let's talk about the other side of this Life of mine. The people who worship Nature. That's Nature with a capital N. You know, the same Nature with sharks who savage basically everything, flesh-eating bacteria, wasps that turn ants into zombies, city-leveling earthquakes, floods, volcanoes,

Hurricane Katrinas, and motherfucking Ebola. Now. Those are the 'good guys.' Imagine if they have a dark side, too. That's the person I'm about to meet. Still want to put your thing down, or would you rather just sit in the car and give this a miss?"

After a block or two of consideration, he responded, "I think I'll take the car option."

"Then you're a smarter man than I."

By the time we reached the Chesapeake Bay Bridge, I still hadn't come up with a good way to approach Annarose Rodolfi. She was the genuine article, an Old World Stregha who had set up shop just outside of Easton, Maryland. Not a year after I'd moved back to the States after Emil's unfortunate demise, she had contracted my services against a clutch of Jesus Freaks who felt nostalgic over the Burning Times. It was a messy little caper... highly educational, all things considered. But the end result was a Stregha who had precious little love for me in her heart, but owed me at least the benefit of an audience.

Which wasn't saying much. Streghas are as close to the Hans Christian Anderson style of haggard witch as one actually finds in the Life. And holy ball-sweat, this woman was terrifying.

I kind of liked her, to be honest.

The trip was easy to navigate. Nearly nothing ever changed in Delmarva, least of all the highways and byways. I guided Julian through the flat lands of corn fields, soy beans, and commercial chicken operations to the tiny patch of land that housed Annarose and her makeshift animal rescue.

At least, that was what I had expected.

What I hadn't expected, and what was in fact what greeted my eyes as we pulled up to the front of the property, was a renovated brick-veneered structure with a tiny parking lot at the front.

Julian lingered on the street before turning to me. "Should I park here, or what?"

"I honestly have no idea."

"You called this person, right? I mean, they know you're coming?"

"She didn't have a phone last time I dealt with her."

Julian sighed. "So, this may be someone completely unrelated, and we just drove an hour and a half for nothing?"

"You're judging me, aren't you?"

Julian pulled into the parking lot alongside a Subaru crossover.

"Okay," I muttered, "hang out here. I'll see if this is, like, a yoga studio now or something."

I pulled my aching body out of the Volvo and stepped up the freshly-paved parking lot to the front of what was once a ramshackle clapboard farm house with a creepy-ass goat that used to glare at me from around the corner of the porch.

That was, regrettably, before it was beheaded and used as a curse against my client. But that had largely been an enormous misunderstanding.

I knocked on the door, and the first face I saw was very familiar, and that alone was an enormous relief.

"Mister Lake!" Sarah Camp screeched as she reached out and gave me the fourth painful hug of the day.

"Hey there, Sarah. Okay. Okay!" I eased away, trying without any appreciable amount of success to conceal my physical pain. "How's tricks?"

She stood with hands on her hips. "Well, I mean. Wow! Dorian effing Lake!"

She actually said "effing."

"Yep. In the flesh."

"What's going on?" she chirped, a blithe smile painting her face.

"Well, actually, funny you should ask."

"Oh, what am I doing? Come on in!"

I lingered by the door jamb. The last time I'd crossed this threshold, I was jackhammered by a Stregha witch's inhospitable wardings. It wasn't an experience I was eager to experience again.

Sarah peered over my shoulder. "Wait, who's that with you?"

"Oh, him? Nah, don't worry about him."

"Oh, come on. Can't leave him sitting in the car."

Before I could protest, she whistled with an ear-shattering two-fingered cow call that Julian could have heard if he were still at the tavern in downtown Baltimore. He killed the engine and stepped out.

"Sarah, really," I groaned. "I'm here to see Annarose."

Her face fell into a mix of rebuke and disappointment. Looked like I had really stepped into it this time.

"Oh," she whispered.

"Not that I'm not completely, thoroughly astonished at what you've done here," I attempted. "I mean, what's going on?"

Her face perked right back up, and she grabbed my arm and jerked me inside. There was no energy wall to speak of, only the baseline threshold of people who actually call a house "home." Definitely not Annarose's work, and that bothered me on a profound level.

Julian stepped inside after us, beaming and extending his hand.

"Hello there," he chimed in a tone I hadn't heard since the first day I met him at the Club. "Julian Bright."

"Hi. I'm Sarah."

I took a quick inventory of the place. It had been completely renovated. Instead of warped floorboards and dusty herbs hung around the kitchen to dry, the space had sheetrock and oriental rugs and fresh coats of paint.

"You've done a lot with this place," I said.

Sarah smiled and took a quick walk around what appeared to be a common-use area with a large television and a game console.

"It's our home."

"And by 'our,' you mean...?"

Another girl rushed down the new staircase from what was now a second story, halting as she spotted us.

"Oh," she blurted.

Sarah gestured to her. "Our coven."

Julian extended a hand to the newcomer as well, but she demurred and slipped around us for the kitchen.

I inspected a bookshelf built into the underside of the stairs. Several books on witchcraft and basic nature worship. Mostly primers, but I recognized more than a couple of the authors.

"You've built yourselves an honest-to-Goddess covenstead? Good for you!"

She sighed and nodded. "It's been work, but we're making it so far. Lets us share expenses while we study."

"Nice."

Julian ran a hand over the leather sofa in front of the television. "You should try this, Dorian. Sharing expenses? Their furniture is much nicer than yours."

"Not really a group-think kind of guy, Julian." I turned to Sarah. "But that's a good point. How did you afford all of this?"

She turned her head and walked toward the back door. "The lawsuit."

"Lawsuit?"

"Yeah. We used the money to build."

She opened the back door and led me out to a new multi-level deck with vine-draped arbors and stands for candles. Beyond the deck, nestled in a series of box hedges arranged in a maze, stood a stone-paved circle. It was meticulous and impressive, but my stomach soured as I ruminated over what was missing.

"Sarah? Where are all the animals?"

A voice slithered from the side of the deck, husky, laced in an Old World inflection. "They took them all."

I turned to find Annarose Rodolfi lounging in a white wicker papasan chair. She wore a thin, dark dress that hung off a shoulder. Most of her hair was pulled up into a chaotic bun with a few strands of jet black ringlets falling alongside her temples. Her eyes were sharp, dark points of vicious will boring a hole through me.

I gave her a smile and actually bowed a little.

Her eyes shifted to Julian. "Who is this?"

"Oh, this is Julian Bright. He's my business partner."

"Is he a side-speaking Lodge weasel, like yourself?" she asked with a sharp smirk.

I couldn't clamp down the laugh that shot out of my throat.

Julian cleared his throat and approached her. "Alas, not yet."

"So, a student?" she prodded.

"Not as such," Julian answered. "At the moment, I'm really more of a chauffeur."

He held out his hand.

She considered it for a moment, then bent her hand into the air. He took it and kissed her knuckles. It was a little slice of baroque theater, but Annarose seemed to appreciate it.

She unfolded her legs and stood up before releasing his hand. Her eyes shifted to the back yard circle as she stepped closer to me.

"They were my babies. But they were suffering."

I whispered to Julian, "She ran a kind of animal rescue. Got heat from the county for it."

Annarose stepped beside me, her eyes still gazing into the past, to a time when fences and pens extended down her back acreage to the tree line beyond. Thin, wounded, neglected animals, either healing under her care or enjoying a moment of peaceful dignity before they passed.

"The county sent more letters. Then they came with trucks," Annarose lamented. "And in a day, they were all gone."

Sarah chimed in, "So we sued their butts!"

I looked over to Sarah. "You sued the county?"

Sarah clarified, "Well, not the county. The people they hired to transport the horses and sheep. Annarose had me follow them a while. Turned out they sold them to a kill-buyer, which was against their contract with the county. I took photos and brought them to a lawyer." She held up her phone.

Annarose smiled at Sarah.

"She was my angel."

Warmth spread through my chest as I observed the thin smile on Annarose's face. She had been so angry before. So aloof. Apparently, Sarah had an impact. Hell, Annarose even looked younger, somehow... which probably wasn't due to magic. Probably.

Annarose waved her hand up at the renovated house. "And so we had money, and she asks if we should adopt more animals. I was tempted, but... this had been my task for so long. I felt my time was finished." She squeezed Sarah's shoulder. "It was time for new blood."

I asked, "How many do you have living here?"

Sarah answered, “Almost nine. Most of the rest are at work or school right now. You should see us at night time. Especially at an esbat!”

“Sounds nice, but just at the moment I need to have a word with Annarose.”

Annarose nodded, before shooing Sarah into Julian.

“I believe this man needs a reading,” Annarose declared.

Julian lifted a brow. “I do?”

Annarose waved a stern hand. “We all do, you silly man.”

Sarah grabbed Julian by the arm and tugged him toward the back door. He followed without much complaint. I chose never to attempt a divination on someone I knew personally. It was never my strength, and I couldn’t tell for sure if I was inserting my personal commentary, or if the cards really were coming up Towers.

Annarose moved for the short flight of steps leading to the garden labyrinth and held out her hand. I assumed she was expecting another baroque gesture, so I took her hand.

She sucked in a breath and pulled it away, eyes wide.

“What’s up?” I murmured.

She leaned into me, eyes searching out my face, the space around it and over my head.

“What have you done to yourself?” she whispered.

“I got into a fight. Looks worse than it feels.”

“No,” she chided as she ran a hand along the side of my face and down to my chest. “Here. Something has happened.”

“Oh, yeah. That.”

“You’re hollow.”

“It’s a very long story.”

She shook her head and stepped down to the garden unassisted. “You’re in danger, now. I have seen this before. It’s too easy for an empty shell to become a home to something unwelcome.”

“I know. I’m working on it.” After she shot me a confounded glance, I explained, “My soul isn’t gone. It’s just detached at the moment.”

“Then it’s not lost?”

"Lost... but not, like, lost-lost. Apparently it's moving across the country inside some kind of vessel."

"How do you know that?"

I weighed the benefits of full disclosure, and decided against it. "A reliable source."

She led me into the labyrinth, stepping neatly through the maze. "The girls use this for meditation before ritual. Focuses the mind, clears distraction."

"Your design?"

"No. The girls researched it."

"So, it seems retirement agrees with you."

She squawked. "I am not that old!"

"Well, maybe it's not the years, but the miles?"

"Not so much older than you, I think."

I smirked. "Then it's definitely the miles!"

We reached the center of the circle, and she stepped out onto the flat flagstone pavers running in concentric circles toward the central fire pit settled beneath a dolmen arch.

Annarose turned back to the house. "I'm not as angry, anymore. It's healthy."

"I'm glad," I chimed. "I mean, I'm glad for you."

She looked over to me with sad eyes. "It was hard-earned."

I nodded.

"What do you wish to speak of?" she asked with a quick shake of her head.

"Chaos magic. Nihils. How to repair them."

She cackled. "So, you have lost your soul and now wish to practice Stregheria?"

"It's a job. I'm trying to help some powerful people, who are up against even more powerful people."

"I hope you collected a deposit, because your customers may not survive this."

I shoved my hands into my pockets. "That might not be the worst thing in the world, either."

"Who are these people?" she asked.

"Really shouldn't say. I mean, I'm not acting like a Priest or a lawyer or anything. But it could be dangerous for you to know."

Annarose crossed her arms and kicked out her hip, glaring holes through me again. I could feel it palpably in my chest.

"All right, it's the Presidium."

Her mouth fell open just a little.

I mumbled, "Right? I'm an idiot."

"You work for those monsters?" she huffed.

"In a roundabout way. Someone is attacking them, trying to tear them down."

She scowled. "Good. They should be torn down."

"I don't argue that point, but I have people who matter to me, and they need their help."

"Then you help them, and let the Presidium die."

I took a breath. "I tried, Annarose. Look, I'm not a friend of the Presidium. But these outsiders are even bigger assholes, and they really have it coming."

"Tell me about these nihils."

"They're casting jinxes at specific locations around D.C., punching nihils into the fabric of Nature. And people. I suspect these locations are important to the Presidium."

"They must be nodes," she stated. "Convergences of ley lines. Sources of power."

"So, say the Presidium set up these nodes to draw their power from the land? That would explain how they source their magic without the use of major deities."

"A nihil is the reversal of a node. A place not where power erupts, but where it drains. It is effective against all magics, even gods."

"Sounds dark as shit," I grumbled. "And clever. First they distract the Presidium with a public spectacle, they remove anyone to whom they could outsource their dirty work, then they pull the plug on their power source. All that's left is to go for the throat."

Annarose put a hand on my arm. "If it is so far gone, there may be nothing you can do."

"I think the Presidium realizes that. They got pantsed, and hard. I think what they're looking for is retribution."

"Then stop worrying about healing the Presidium's ley nodes, and focus on finding and destroying their enemies."

Here was that Stregha logic. Vengeance at all costs.

And she had reason to want revenge on the Presidium. They'd nearly destroyed her. I wasn't quite ready to go Corleone on the Presidium just yet.

I lifted a finger. "But, in theory, if one were to repair all of these nihils, the Presidium could get their power back?"

"As distasteful as it is to say it, yes." She gripped my arm tight. "But you must not do this. They are watching you. And now, they will be watching me."

"Still have that handler in town? That bartender?"

She shook her head. "She has gone."

"Your doing?"

Annarose released my arm, and turned away without response, though I caught an air of satisfaction alongside her lips.

"If you restore their power," she stated, "they will destroy you."

"They gave me a blank check, Annarose. I can use whatever—"

"Their word means nothing. They are liars, and the second they are done with you, they will eliminate you."

I shook my head. "They use Netherworkers all the time. It's not in their interest to take me out."

"It is not in their interest... until it is. And then what?" She pulled my shoulder around to face her. "You see them as benevolent dictators. But they are still dictators. They reserve the right to end your life at any moment, and that is a liberty I would not surrender to anyone."

I pursed my lips. She wasn't wrong. I had grown so accustomed to accepting the Presidium as a given. The thought of a world without them to keep the peace? It was terrifying, yet exhilarating.

"Why are you so nice to me all of a sudden?" I muttered. "I was convinced you hated my guts."

She lifted a hand. "I can count on five fingers the people who have shown me kindness in my darker days. My days of hate and shadows. He who accepts me at my worst, deserves my best." She offered her arm, and as I took it, she guided me back to the maze. "If you choose to heal these nihils, I can help you. But you should make that choice with eyes open."

"I'm trying my best to keep them open."

"Then be mindful of the eyes that are upon you. They are watching you. They are manipulating you, pushing you to decisions that benefit only them."

I shrugged. "They have diviners that I can't dodge. Not much I can do about that."

Annarose grumbled. "No divination is needed, when they have someone close to you. Bending your ear. Strumming your heart-strings."

I released her arm. "What are you talking about?"

She cocked a brow at me.

"You're talking about a handler," I deduced. "The Ipsissimus owned up to that."

"And would he do so if he did not think you would embrace it?"

"I haven't embraced anything, Annarose. I'm just keeping my head low and trying to finish the job."

She turned me back to the house and stood at my side.

"As I said," she replied with a nod to the house. "Keep your eyes open."

It finally dawned on me that she was trying to tell me something. I spied Sarah and Julian through the glass door. He seemed engrossed in Sarah's tarot reading, and she seemed oddly flustered.

"You don't mean..." I shook my head. "That's not even remotely feasible."

"Are you so sure?" she countered.

I scowled at Annarose. "Julian is not a Presidium spy. I'm absolutely sure of that."

She continued winding her way through the maze, adding as she proceeded, "I feel people, Lake. I feel their intentions."

"Handy."

"This is why I knew you can be trusted." She added with a sly smile over her shoulder, "And why I know that I... interest you."

Well, then.

"Let's not stray from the subject, huh?"

"If you wish."

I sighed. "Julian's not my handler. I've known him for too long." Even as I said it, the shadow of doubt curled into my brain. When had I met Julian? And where? It was at the club, shortly before I'd shrugged off the memory charm Carmen had used to deep-six my entire charm-crafting career. I knew nothing about him before then.

I met another man not long after that day. Clarence de Haviland, a.k.a. Mr. Brown. Had I known that the Druid Hill Club was a hotbed of Presidium members, I might have been more reserved in my acquaintanceship.

Or would I? Julian was so clearly uninvolved in the Life. He was open, eager to learn... and I had turned him away at every opportunity. He was always there for me, even sacrificing his entire career to save a good man. No, he wasn't my handler. Couldn't have been.

Still, though, if a man is always there for you, doesn't it necessarily mean that he's always... there?

"What are you picking up from Julian?" I whispered.

She cleared the maze and turned to wait for me. "He is concerned for you."

"Not exactly a smoking gun, Annarose."

"And he's curious about this place," she added with a wave of her hand to the house.

I countered, "He's interested in the craft."

She took a step forward and whispered into my ear. "He is shielded."

I blinked the words away. "I didn't feel any—"

"This warding is masterfully wrought. Tread carefully. He is no novice."

She reached around my head and pulled it down to her face. Her lips slid across mine, waves of floral-laced energy washing over me, with just a hint of tar. Her dark ringlets slid across my nose as she slowly pulled away. She wiped her thumb across my mouth with a predatory smile.

"What was that about?" I mumbled.

"Perhaps you interest me, too?"

"No offense, Annarose, but you still scare the shit out of me."

A razor smile lifted across her lips. "Good."

My head reeled for a moment, overloaded by the recriminations and titillations of the last minute. I gathered my composure as Annarose reached the top of the deck. I trotted after her, wondering why she was always taking the lead.

We stepped inside, where Sarah was clearing her throat in rapid successions. Julian leaned back in his chair, a satisfied grin on his face.

"Well, this is all terribly interesting," he chuckled. "I mean, I picked up a couple books before, trying to study the Tarot. Never really took, though. Probably because I never had time." His eyes found me. "Oh, Dorian. You'll be happy to hear that she's drawn the Death card on my very first spread."

I shrugged. "That card gets a bad rep, you know. Just means you're due for a transformative period. Something will end, but something else will begin. Basic life journey stuff."

Sarah looked up to me. I prepared to apologize for overstepping her table, but something in her eyes put a hook in my gut.

"Or, maybe you should get your colon 'scoped," I added.

He chuckled, then reached out to shake Sarah's hand. "I enjoyed myself. Though, it seems you're unhappy with the cards?"

Sarah shuffled her deck and sighed. "No, I'm sorry. I'm just really scattered right now."

Annarose held out a hand, and Sarah calmed. As did Julian.

She reached for the deck, and slid her fingers alongside the cards. She lifted the deck ever so slightly, allowing the cards to fall into a neat stack beneath her hand until at some unknown cue she halted the flow.

When she held up the cards, she nodded.

"Mister Julian, you are right to wonder how it will end."

He stared at the card, his face easing into a loose mask of confusion and alarm.

"What is it?" I asked as she held the card away from me.

She arched a brow. "It is not for you. Unless you would like your own."

I lifted my hands. "Sure."

She allowed more to slither from her fingers, and halted again.

With an easy cock of her elbow, she inspected the card, then nodded to herself.

"And?" I urged.

She angled the bottom card so that I could see it while muttering, "My offer stands, Lake."

I gazed down at the revealed card.

The World.

The card of endless possibilities.

"I'm going to need your phone number," I whispered.

I had to make do with the covenstead land line number and Sarah's cell number. Seemed Annarose was of my philosophy when it came to modern electronics.

We said our goodbyes, Annarose holding my arm fast for just a longer moment than I had expected. It was a message. She was concerned, that much was certain.

And, as Julian drove us back to Baltimore, so was I.

CHAPTER THIRTY-SEVEN

When we reached Light Street Tavern, Julian seemed positively filled with electricity.

"What's next?" he asked as we stepped through the back door and approached his office.

"I'm cooking on that."

"What about Turner? You said something about his brother-in-law. The one with the tinfoil hat?"

I agreed with Julian, if only in my own head. I found myself reluctant to volunteer a specific course of action.

Damn, but Annarose put a thorn in my noodle! Julian couldn't have been a Presidium lackey. I would have known.

Surely, I would have known.

"I might go grab some coffee," I grumbled.

He cocked his head. "Uh, okay. Are you feeling well?"

"Tired. Slept on the Swain's couch last night for, like, maybe three hours. Plus, my side's still killing me, so..."

He nodded. "I can take you wherever—"

"I'll walk."

He clamped his mouth shut.

I added, "There's a deli a couple blocks down. Might get a bagel." We stood awkwardly for a moment, so I added, "Shmear."

Julian rubbed his neck. "All right, then."

"Hey," I blurted. "I'm not pushing you out."

"Sure."

"I'm totally not."

I totally was. Even if he was completely innocent, too many people were receiving collateral boot-squash thanks to my insane life. I needed Julian to be that guy that was always there for me, not the One Who Was Always There.

Julian reached over and tapped my shoulder. "Go get your caffeine. I'll be here. When you're ready for the next move, let me know."

I turned away and stepped out of the front door, and directly into the mass that was Big Ben Setleigh.

I coughed as I bounced off him, and chuckled. "Sorry, Ben."

"Where you running to in such a damn hurry, son?"

"Coffee. What else?"

"Figured it weren't the whiskey. Got plenty of that inside."

"Yeah. Honest truth, I think it's time I woke up more than I checked out."

Ben hammered a flat palm onto my shoulder. "Son? I've been waiting for you to say that for years now."

I smiled, then added, "Hey. I'm coming right back, and Julian's my ride at the moment. Make sure he doesn't leave. Okay?"

Ben winked at me. "No problem."

I trotted up the street, fishing my phone from my pocket to dial Turner.

He answered, "What?"

"It's Lake."

"No shit."

"I need a ride."

After a pause, he answered, "Ever heard of car rentals?"

"I want to have a word with your brother-in-law."

He made a noise I couldn't quite identify. Possibly a cough, a sneeze, or a combination vomit-sigh.

"Still with that?"

"It's important."

"Can't your boyfriend drive you?" he groused.

I rolled my eyes. "Trust me. He's way out of my league."

"Whatever. Where are you?"

"Half a block from City Hall," I responded as I spotted the white façade of the old building between skyscrapers as I turned onto Fayette.

"You're a pain in my ass, Lake."

"Likewise. Now come get me. We're burning daylight."

Turner arrived in remarkable time. He unlocked his door of what proved to be an alarmingly malodorous Crown Victoria. I crinkled my nose as I fastened my seatbelt.

"Christ. The hell are you keeping in this car, Turner?"

"Head cheese. Also, go fuck yourself."

He turned us up one of the main avenues leading to the Baltimore Beltway, and we rounded the city to the northeast.

"Where's he live?" I ventured after about twenty minutes of silence.

"Edgewood."

"Oh, God."

He snickered. "Hey, this was your idea."

"Is he, you know, of sound mind?"

"I've asked my sister that many times. Know what she tells me?"

"What?" I asked.

"To mind my own business and maybe consider getting an electric car. She's all about electric cars and wind power. Kind of a fruit loop, but what can you do?"

Edgewood arrived as a patchwork of early 60's bungalow style houses strung together like Christmas lights, most of which had gone out. Bushy lawns punctuated those that were maintained. The occasional front porch sat adorned with mismatched furniture intended for interior use, and more dogs on and off leash than was probably necessary and legal.

Turner drove into a cul-de-sac and parked his car well off the lawn on the street.

"George gets pissy when people rut up his grass," Turner grumbled as he killed the engine. "And by pissy I mean he keys the shit out of people's doors. Almost shot him once when I caught him with one of those garden claw things circling my Vic."

"Sounds like a justifiable shooting to me."

"I know. It's like he wanted a trip to the emergency room."

"Still, lot of paperwork. Right?"

Turner snapped his fingers. "Exactly what I was thinking."

He trotted ahead up the front walk and knocked on the door.

"It's Grant, George. Don't shoot."

I noticed the Don't Tread On Me flag hanging from the corner post and braced myself.

The door eased open, and a surprisingly young man with wire rim glasses and a mop of red hair exploding in every conceivable direction peered from inside.

"Oh, hey Grant," he rasped.

Turner stood for a moment, shifting weight foot-to-foot. "So, uh, you gonna to let us in, or what?"

"Who's he?" George asked, his eyes still held directly on Turner.

"Oh, this here's Dorian Lake. He's a consultant for the precinct."

"I don't know him," George mumbled.

"I barely know him, but he's harmless. Seriously." Turner gestured for the door.

George finally looked over to me, examining me head to ankle, before some unspoken line of reasoning cleared me in his head and he held the door open.

We stepped inside. The odor of cat urine hit me full in the face, and I choked back a cough. I spotted the first cat immediately, sitting on a multi-level carpeted perch in the corner. The second cat trotted from a hallway and immediately began making love to Turner's ankles.

George closed the door behind us and latched no fewer than three deadbolts, a chain, and something electronic screwed to the side of his front casing. I wasn't sure what it was, but I imagined he'd assembled it on his own from instructions he found on the Internet. All he was missing was a length of Edgar's magic yarn.

Turner stepped around the cat and moved for a laminate counter pass-through connecting the tiny kitchen with the wall-paneled living room.

"Lake, here... he's a kind of expert in bizarre phenomenons. Secret groups. The occult."

With each statement, George's eyes widened, until he finally turned to face me square-on with a lifting smile.

"Oh, yeah?" he wheezed.

I nodded. "Specifically hermetic practice. Hexes and charms. Nothing with aliens," I added, just in case.

"That's fascinating," George offered, gesturing me forward into the living room. "Let me show you something. I picked this up at a convention in Pittsburgh. It's supposed to be a talisman worn by a Nazi lieutenant during the Third Reich." He fished a tiny brass medallion on a gold chain from a cedar box and held it up to the light. "As you know, Hitler believed in ancient occult practices, and believed he could yoke mystical powers in order to establish his thousand-year reign."

I leaned in and examined the medallion, finding a laurel wreath imprint surrounding the edge of the Nordic rune Thurisaz.

"Well, there does exist a kind of modern mythology over the Reich." I ventured, "Most of which was spun out of whole cloth to sell books."

He eyes narrowed. "Are you familiar with the Völkisch Movement?"

"I am."

"Then you'll know that the late 18th Century push against modern industrialism found roots in ancient Germanic mysticism?"

I shrugged. "More like folklore. And yes, the movement did exist. But no, it was not occult in nature. It was more socio-political than anything."

George put a hand on his hip. "What about Lanz von Liebenfels?"

I rolled my eyes. "Here we go with the mad monk."

"What?" George sputtered.

"Look, Hitler didn't meet von Liebenfels when he was a child. Old Lanz didn't put the idea into young Adolph's brain to summon a master race to restore order against the Jews."

"He had published works!"

I nodded. "True, and he was an outspoken proponent of Ariosophy, and it's possible his writings helped inspire the climate in which the Nazis blossomed. But he wasn't in contact with the Devil, and he didn't imbue Hitler with a Holy Mandate for genocide. Liebenfels was a son of a bitch of the highest magnitude, but his peculiar brand of bastardy was entirely human in nature."

George scowled, scooped up the medallion into his palm and replaced it into his cedar box. I'd lost my audience already. Time to hook him back.

"Now, if you want to talk about the actual cabals operating in Germany at the time of the rise of Hitler, you're going to want to start with the Thule Society."

George spun around, his face rising in excitement. "They... they're real. Right?"

"Oh yes. Very real, and very active. It was said they were seeking the lost Aryan race of Hyperborea, first by physical crypto-archaeological exploration, and later by isolating the blood of the Aryans by eugenics."

George snapped his fingers. "Bilderberg!"

"Huh?"

"You know, the annual Bilderberg Conference? They gathered western European leaders together to discuss anti-Americanism and the formation of an Atlantic society. No one knows who arranges these conferences, but they are super-secret, heavily guarded, and it's quite obvious to anyone who puts thought into it that the Bilderberg leadership is run by successful Hyperborean scions from Hitler's eugenics program!"

I sucked in a breath, then held it.

I wasn't sure if the crazy was catching, but I suddenly had an urge to make a few phone calls and figure out how the Presidium felt about these Bilderberg people.

Turner shook his head at the counter. "You people are loopier than a bat on acid."

George snarled at Turner as he slipped around him to the kitchen. "What did you want to, uh, what do you want, Mister Lake?"

"I wanted to talk to you about secret organizations within the United States government."

His head nodded violently. "Skull and Bones? Council of Foreign Relations? FEMA?"

"FEMA?" I blurted.

"Oh yeah! They wield absolute power within a time of crisis. The entire agency is utterly unconstitutional, and yet they're the first ones called in whenever people's property is up for grabs. They can relocate you, your family, appropriate your belongings. They set up and operate entire refugee camps in which they control who comes and goes, who gets medical treatment and who dies. You really think they answer to the President?" He snickered and shook his head.

"Actually, George, I wanted to discuss something a bit more historical. Occult influences in the forming of our nation."

"Oh," he shouted as he pulled a bottle of bottom-shelf vodka from his sink cabinet. "Then that's all about the Freemasons."

It really wasn't, but I was going to let him roll with this.

"Have you ever heard of a group called The Presidium?" I asked.

George wrinkled his nose and poured himself, and only himself, a glass of gut-rot.

"Is that what this is about? Durning's thing? Please. He was an amateur. Made up names and some fabricated society. Orgies? In the Capitol? You've seen those people, right? I think old Durning was a little..."

He made a winding motion with his finger near the side of his head, just before taking a belt of vodka and doubling over in a coughing fit.

I gave Turner a look, and he waved me off.

George continued, "Washington. Jefferson. Madison. Franklin. All Freemasons of high orders. And is there any question as to why these were the men who were chosen to lead our fledgling nation?"

"Do tell."

He held up a finger. "Washington. Horrible leader. The worst. Know how many battles Washington actually won in the Revolution?"

"More than a couple, I think?"

"One!"

I scratched my head. I was fairly certain Washington had done marginally better than that, but I needed his crackpot theories so I let it slide.

"Saratoga! And that's it!"

"What about Yorktown?"

He took another swig as his eyes filled with condescending pity.

"Please," he gasped after pounding the vodka. "That hardly counts. The French were in the war, by that point. He can't be given credit for walking in and mopping up."

Turner smiled at me, and I tried my best not to notice.

I said, "What do you know about Pierre L'Enfant?"

He actually bounced up and down. "Oh, yeah! That's exactly what I've been writing about on my blog!"

"You have a blog?" I didn't have to actually be here?

"Come on!"

He grabbed his glass and led me to the first door off the kitchen, and down a short flight of stairs to his basement. I noted that Turner elected to remain behind. It was probably better that way.

George snatched a drop cord and clicked on a fluorescent light. I blinked at the harsh blue-white fixture and took in a scene of Lovecraftian insanity. Yarn ran over my head, connecting multiple corkboards of newspaper clippings, slate chalkboards and white marker boards, magazine cutouts of recognizable political leaders, and large birthday party-style letter cutouts spelling familiar words such as Illuminati and Israel.

"Huh?" he prodded, as he approached his computer. After entering a password, which was by my count over twenty characters long, George called up his own blog. A lithograph of a dapper little fop greeted my eyes. "Voila. Pierre Charles L'Enfant."

To George's credit, he pronounced the name in a very serviceable accent.

"That's the man who laid out Washington D.C., huh?" I asked.

He tilted his hand with a dubious grunt. "He started the job. But he wasn't on board with the Freemason Plan, know what I'm saying?"

"Not really, but I want to."

"Okay, so not many people know this, but Pierre L'Enfant was actually a practicing hermeticist."

I snickered. "That, I knew."

"Then you also know that he planned the street grid of D.C. specifically to channel otherworldy energies to power the Freemasons' rituals?"

I crossed my arms and let the crazy wash over me. George was closer to the truth than anyone might have given him credit for. He had the Masons wrong, clearly. But all he had to do was swap "Freemasons" with "Presidium" and he'd have a blog post that would get his ass black-bagged and floating in the Chesapeake for sure.

"Go on," I urged.

"Take a look." He stood up and gestured at a laminated map of the Baltimore-Washington area he had stapled to the wall, replete with thumbtacks and dry-erase commentary. "Right there. The Washington Monument. Phallic symbol. The reflecting pool. Vulvic symbol."

"These came well after L'Enfant," I suggested.

"Yeah, but the organization took the plan and ran with it. Besides, they canned his ass before they even broke ground."

"They what?"

George bobbed his head in self-amusement as he turned and reached through stacks of paper to produce another lithograph, a meticulous hand-sketch of a very early District of Columbia with the Potomac and its Eastern Branch curling beneath.

"This is the official plat for D.C. It's what everyone thinks L'Enfant submitted to Washington for the city grid."

I took it in, then eyed George. "I'm guessing this isn't the actual grid, then?"

"Nope." He flipped the page over. "Here... is his actual plat."

He handed me the page, and I held it to my face, scanning every detail. George had taken a colored pencil to the paper, illustrating what I figured was not only his point, but the very design I was hoping to find.

“A pentacle.”

George grimaced. “Actually, it’s called a pentagram.”

“So sorry.”

“And not just one. Sure, you got the White House Devil Siphon.” He traced the first of the pentacles with the tip of his finger. “Dupont, to Mount Vernon, to Washington Circle, to Logan Circle, and finally to the White House.”

I nodded, then looked to the right, at a second five-pointed star drawn in blue. “And this one?”

“The Legislative Glyph,” he announced. “I’m thinking about trademarking those, by the way. Siphon. Glyph. I’ve read up. No one’s called them that, yet.”

The apex of the blue pentacle began at a space of land that I assumed was somewhere around the current Lincoln Park, swept to Union Station, then jogged up into two points L’Enfant didn’t bother to mark, and finally dropped back into Seward Square.

“What are these two points,” I asked.

“Old Masonic lodges,” George whispered. “They’ve since moved, but at the time, there were plans for a kind of exodus of Freemasons to the New World. You know, a flight from religion. A New World Order? It’s on our money!”

He went to fish his wallet from his pocket, but I held out a hand.

“I get that. Novus Ordo Seclorum.” I inspected the blue pentacle closer. “This misses the Capitol Building, entirely.”

“The Capitol is at the base of the pentacle. It’s the receptacle. Notice how it’s facing East? It draws its power from the rising sun, or the old European Ways, and grants it to the Congress. The red pentacle, however… well, it draws power from the North, and deposits it into the hands of the President.”

“What’s so special about the North?”

He smirked. “Ultima thule?”

“Huh?”

"The Most North? Hyperborea! See? It's all connected!"

I handed him the paper and took a step away to keep his excitement from spraying onto me. But the evidence was there. L'Enfant had indeed attempted to re-create Nouveau Marche in the Americas. This time, he created two separate power sources for two separate branches of government. He might have worked on the Judicial Branch, but was removed from the project before it was ready.

"So, wait. You said L'Enfant was fired. This was never built?"

"Nope. Washington fired him for being a burr under his wig. He began demanding more money. Made bizarre requests of the Masons. He was fringe even for the Satanists!"

"They weren't... never mind. So, what happened to the plat?"

George sat in his computer chair and laced his hands behind his head. "They gave it to one of their own. A man by the name of Andrew Ellicott."

I sucked in a breath.

"You don't say."

"Yeah. L'Enfant ended up designing the state house for New York, one of the most haunted buildings in North America, before he died bankrupt and in disgrace."

I stepped over to his laminated map, fingering the location of Gettysburg. I traced a line to Baltimore, then to Harper's Ferry, and then down to Locust Grove, Virginia. No, it wasn't working.

"This isn't a pentacle," I mumbled.

"Huh?"

"Oh. There have been a series of vandalisms, lately. All colonial-era buildings, or sites that were important at the founding of D.C. Each one was hit with a kind of occult bomb, let's call it. I figured these were L'Enfant's chosen sites, but if he lost his job under Washington then it couldn't have been."

In fact, the four points I had to date were too spread out to form a pentacle. If I squinted, I could make them into a hexagram, a six-pointed star. But even that was a stretch.

Fucking geomancy.

I turned to George. "Ellicott City. Was that named for Andrew Ellicott?"

He shrugged, then swiveled to his computer to type something in. After a short moment, he shook his head. "Not exactly. Close, though. It was a group holding from the three brothers. Joseph Ellicott, John, and Andrew. It was Joseph's mill that operated there, so technically it was named after him."

I wandered off a few steps.

"It's close enough."

My thoughts returned to the previous evening, where I had met Brown. At the Meyer Livery.

In Ellicott City.

He had told me just as we parted, that the truth was literally all around me. He clearly knew more about the identity of these chaos magicians than I had figured. Why would he keep the truth from me, if he wanted me to succeed?

The only answer that presented itself was that Brown needed me to learn the truth, but needed the Presidium to think he wasn't involved. Of course not. These attacks had come from within the Presidium, itself.

I thanked George profusely as Turner and I took our leave.

Turner gave me several looks as we drove back into the city.

"So?" he finally asked. "Did that do anything for us?"

"More than you realize," I mumbled.

"And?"

"The problem here, Detective, is that the value of what I learned is utterly lost on anyone who doesn't believe in the existence of the key players. So thus, I'll have to satisfy you by saying that Santa's sleigh does, in fact, run on the blood of reindeer."

"Why don't you try me, anyway?"

"We're up against a civil war," I stated.

"Hmm."

He turned into the parking lot of a utility company, turned the car around, and put it into park as he checked something on his phone. I watched with interest, holding my tongue, as he typed a text, checked his email, and pocketed his phone.

After a swift moment of contemplation, he pulled back out onto the road, taking the on-ramp for the Jones Falls Expressway.

"What's up?" I asked.

"You and your boyfriend are always pissing on me because you think I can't follow your conversations. But you know what? I know exactly what you believe in. Here's a news flash... I have to connect all kinds of batshit dots in my line of work. I have to get into the heads of criminals on a daily basis. You think criminals have their heads screwed straight? They don't. But I have to get in their heads if I'm supposed to stay a step in front of them. So, you say there's a civil war going on, I'm assuming it's this Presidium cult Durning dimed out two weeks ago. They're in-fighting, and all of us are caught in the middle."

I sucked in a breath, and ran a finger over my nose.

"Detective, I owe you several apologies."

"And I don't need you to like me," he continued. "In fact, I'd rather you didn't. So tuck it in, deal with it, and let's go talk to this Brandon Carruthers fellow."

CHAPTER THIRTY-EIGHT

Turner said as he pulled off onto Cold Spring Lane, "I got the address of the old Tree of Life Studio, but I figured that wouldn't help much since it shut down a month ago. Carruthers did, however, enter an address on his lease agreement, so that's my first stop."

I held up a hand. "Wait. What... what did you say?"

"I said he put his address—"

"Tree of Life?"

"Yeah. The art studio where that fucked-up statue was made. What's going on?"

My head spun, and I gripped the inside door handle as several dozen facts finally clicked into place.

"I need a map. Of Maryland and D.C. I need it now."

Turner buttoned his lip and moved for the nearest gas station. I jumped out and ran inside, searching for roadmaps. After securing one from behind the counter, I paid and hopped back out into the sunlight where Turner was leaning against his car with crossed arms.

"Is this going to make sense in a minute?" he asked.

"It'll make sense to us both. Got a pen?"

He reached into his shirt pocket, pulled his Arrow pen, and tossed it to me.

I spread the roadmap across the hood of his car. The District of Columbia sat in the center. Just barely visible above the Mason-Dixon line were the outskirts of Gettysburg. I called it close enough and put a star on it. I then starred the approximate location of the Enoch Pratt library, Harper's Ferry, and Locust Grove on the map. I then drew a triangle between the first three, then dragged a straight line down from Harper's Ferry to Locust Grove.

Turner sniffled. "I hope you didn't drink from George's cup, because whatever he has may be catching."

I held up a hand to shush him, then used my forearm as a crude straight edge to locate points south of Baltimore and east of both Harper's Ferry and Locust Grove.

I plotted further points south of each. Marshall, VA. Port Tobacco, MD. Port Royal, VA. I drew lines connecting them in what was a familiar pattern to me, then I slapped my hand against the hood after circling Alexandria, VA.

"Hey, easy," Turner grunted.

"That's it. Egypt! L'Enfant wasn't nuts. He just lost the internal divide."

Turner rolled his eyes, sighed, then asked, "What internal divide?"

"The Nombre D'or. In the late 1700's, they tried to use geomancy to create the center of a New World Order. But it never got off the ground, because of a schism in their philosophy between Egyptian Gnosticism, and the new wave of Enlightenment thinking that was all about developing new scientific methods."

"Science and magic?"

"Yes. Exactly! That was what L'Enfant and his compatriots were trying to do in France. But the war with England pulled them abroad. L'Enfant thought he had a blank slate to work with. Washington and the other seed members of the Presidium had invited him specifically to hammer out the same pentacle node system they tried in France. Then something happened, and I think I know what."

I pointed at the map.

"Know what that shape is?"

Turner shook his head.

"It's the sephiroth."

"What's that mean?"

I explained, "It's the Tree of Life, a geometric representation of Qabalistic cosmology. Each of these circles represents points of divine energy that bring energy into existence from a Higher Source. Boom, boom, boom," I spat as I tapped circles with my pen. "It's Qabala."

"You're going to have to rewind the tape for me."

"Qabala is an ancient school of Hebrew mysticism. It's one of the cornerstones of modern hermeticism."

Turner shook his head. "But you said this Number Door cult—"

"Nombre D'or. French for Golden Ratio."

"Whatever. These Number Door people were about science versus Egypt. Where's this Qabala come into it?"

I handed Turner his pen before I dented it or his hood further. "It's widely accepted that the Hebrews first developed the precursors to Qabala during the Egyptian captivity, drawing influence from the ancient polytheistic rites. They spun it into their own school of thinking, but the secret knowledge they uncovered most likely shares its DNA with Egyptian Gnosticism."

"So," Turner lowed as he pocketed his pen, "your modern day Presidium, these jag-offs that are supposed to run the country, are actually the Qabala people, and L'Enfant got the reach-around?"

I nodded. "L'Enfant lost the fight. He was angling to make D.C. in his image. But the other half of the Nombre D'or won. And I'll bet you a bucket of wings that Andrew Ellicott was one of them."

"What does that mean to me?" he asked.

"To you? Well, I'm working on that. But it means something to the Presidium. It means that the loyalists to L'Enfant and the New World Order have probably been hiding inside their ranks, biding their time until the Presidium was weak enough to attack. It means there's no outside cabal trying to tear them down to make in-roads to North America." I scowled. "And it means I probably owe Reed Malosi a gigantic apology."

"He's in good company."

I folded up the map. "These sites were selected not by L'Enfant, but by Ellicott. The Presidium set up this geomantic energy siphon to power their hermetic dominance for the last two centuries and change. And now someone's punching holes in them as a part of a multi-layered plan to overthrow the whole organization. If this is a L'Enfantine sect of the Presidium, then they can't want the power source to collapse entirely."

Turner snapped his fingers. "So they're setting up their own hooziwatzits in the original design?"

I snickered. "I'll make a practitioner out of you yet, Detective."

He consulted his watch. "Ready for the Carruthers Experience yet, or are we going to grab some chicken while we're here?"

"No, I really want to meet this guy."

We hit the road again, and it wasn't long until Turner got us lost in the middle of Hampden. After a few U-turns, we ended up nestled between an organic food store and an abandoned bottling plant. A line of row houses ran down the hill from the plant, and down a side alley, I spotted a concrete masonry unit with a coat of beige paint tucked just behind the food store.

"I think that's it," he said. "No numbers. That's against code, by the way."

"Don't think they were going for noticeable." I quipped. "So, should you ring the bell, or should I?"

"Well, let's give it a minute."

"Why?"

He didn't answer.

After only about fifteen seconds of me starting to work on a new ulcer, wondering why Turner was trying to stall us, a car pulled up behind us and killed the engine.

I gripped the door handle, and twisted in my seat.

Turner held up a hand. "Now, don't go crazy. He just asked me to keep him in the loop. And I didn't—"

"Who asked you?"

"Who do you think?"

I spotted the car as the driver side door opened.

It was a Volvo.

"Oh, for fuck's sake."

I stepped out of the car in time for Julian to reach the back of the Crown Vic.

He crossed his arms, and I just stood there like a man caught with his mistress.

"Hi, Julian."

"That's a hell of a coffee break, Dorian."

"Look," I offered with outstretched hands.

"No. I'm not going to let you push me away. Not like the others."

I reached deep for a response, but ended up stuffing my hands into my pocket and dropping my chin.

"How long have you known me, Julian? Is this really that surprising to you?"

"Oh," he spat with more attitude than I've seen from him before. "That's an excuse? Sorry, but you brought me in, Dorian. I'm on the inside. You don't just pull me in and shove me aside like I was some lackey. You need my help? I can't help you if you—"

"I need to check you."

He blinked rapidly, then took a step back.

My gut twisted. I was committing to this. Wasn't it just paranoia? Did I really think Julian was capable of this level of deceit?

No, I truly didn't. Part of me wanted to get this over with simply to ease my mind. But it was still a dick move, nonetheless.

"What?" he whispered.

"I'm sorry, but I need to do a scan on you."

He shook his head. "I'm not carrying a gun or anything. Dorian..."

I pulled my hands back out of my pockets, the chain of the Gregori pendulum tight between the fingers of my right hand.

"Again, I'm sorry about this," I muttered. "Based on my recent judgment calls, this will probably end my relationship with you, but I have to check you for wardings."

"What does that even mean?" Julian asked, eyes twisted in confusion.

"It means I have reason to believe you're on the Presidium's payroll. I know, it sounds like lunacy, and it probably is."

Turner chirped, "It definitely is."

"Shut up," Julian and I barked in unison.

I watched Julian as he looked down at my pendulum, then up to my face. His eyes were soft, defeated. He shook his head and lifted his hands.

"I'm sorry you have to do this," he muttered. "But I meant it. I'm not going to let you push me away. You need to satisfy this paranoia, go ahead. But you know me, Dorian. You're as close to a brother as I've ever had. That's a sentiment I've held onto for a while now."

My eyes stung as I stepped forward. This felt like a friendship-ending bullet that I was about to fire directly into Julian's brain. I held my hand up, then pulled it back.

"No," I whispered. "This is totally stupid."

Julian urged, "Just do it. You're going to cook on this until you do, so just do your magic, and then we can move on. Okay?"

He was right. I was going to obsess on this until I knew for sure. Hell with it.

I sniffled, then nodded. "Okay."

"Do I have to do anything?" Julian asked.

"No, just hold still."

I held up the pendulum, lifting it toward Julian's face. I didn't get far.

The pendulum snapped directly to his chest as if there were a magnet in his pocket and the pendulum was a car-sized hunk of iron.

Turner made a grunting noise.

As did Julian.

I looked up into Julian's eyes, which were wild with alarm.

I held a breath, then asked, "What's—what's in your shirt, Julian?"

He lowered his arms, then sighed.

"Damn it." He reached into his shirt and pulled out a chain. "This is what you're looking for."

A tiny coin dangled from the chain around his neck. A gold coin.

"What is it?" I prodded.

Julian whispered, "They said you wouldn't be able to find it. They said it was safe."

I took a step away. "Who? Who said?"

Julian answered, "The Presidium. They said it tied some kind of energy line to their diviners. Something about added resonance, helping to keep an eye on you. They said you wouldn't be able to detect it, though."

I held up my pendulum with tight fingers. "They didn't plan on Gregori the Bastard."

"Oh," Julian mumbled.

I clamped my eyes shut and turned away. Fuck me, Annarose was right. She was absolutely right, and I was a complete moron.

I growled, "God. Damn it. Julian!"

"If it helps, it's not what you think," he offered.

I spun around and thrust a finger into his face. "You shut up. You shut your damn mouth."

Julian moaned, "Dorian?"

I trotted away, putting distance between him and me.

Julian called out, "I'm not one of them!"

I stood in silence.

Julian continued, "They came during the election. After Sooner outed me."

I brushed a sleeve over the tears that had formed in my eyes, and cleared my throat. When I turned around, I found his face was flushed.

"What?" I wheezed.

"It wasn't Sooner who leaked that story. It was them."

"That thing with the college student?"

"It was them, the whole time. Someone visited me, told me who they were, and what they wanted. I knew enough of your world to understand that this was real. They were pissed at you, Dorian. Pissed that you were pushing Sullivan back into City Hall, when they wanted Sooner. They could control Sooner. They would've had a lackey in Baltimore. But you screwed that plan, and they were ready to take you out. I was their sacrificial lamb, I suppose."

I ran toward him and shoved him in the shoulders. "No! I never asked you to do that!"

He caught his balance on the edge of the Crown Vic.

Turner shifted to intervene, but we both gave him a stern glare.

Julian said, "I know that. This isn't about you asking for anything. This is me trying to keep a good man in the game. Just so you know, this wasn't me trying to leverage anything."

I shook my head. "What did you tell them? What was your purpose?"

"I just had to keep them apprised. They needed to know where you were, what you were investigating. Lately, they've been calling me a lot."

"So, all this wanting to be involved… it was just for the Presidium?"

Julian dropped his head and took deep breaths. "It was for you, and it was for Sullivan. Don't turn this into a martyr situation."

I turned away again.

Julian said, "You should know, they actually do need you."

"Who?" I asked. "The Presidium?"

"The Ipsissimus," Julian replied. "He's been blindsided by all of this."

I sneered. "You don't say."

"I've been in political life ever since undergrad, Dorian. I know when a man has lost his grip on his own organization."

I rubbed my face, took a cleansing breath, and walked a wide arc around the front of Turner's car. I calmed my thoughts enough to latch onto Julian's words.

"He's going to lose more than his organization," I said. "There's an entire sect within the Presidium that's been planning this move for a long, long time. It goes deep, Julian. And I'm not entirely sure these people are the ones who should lose."

"I understand that," Julian muttered. "But the Ipsissimus is the one who's holding the keys right now. So, we have to decide if he's the one who should remain standing, or if this wiper sect should win. Either way," he added, "I'm okay with the one you choose."

"Why is that?" I asked.

With a ragged breath, he answered, "Because you've never led me wrong."

I shook my head with the faintest of smirks. "You're such a kiss ass."

"That was a touch schmaltzy, wasn't it?" Julian said.

I pocketed the pendulum and stared at my feet for a moment. "Did they threaten you?"

"They threatened everyone I knew. Including Sullivan."

I bit my lip. Annarose may have been right about the Presidium, too.

Julian took another step forward. "I wouldn't do anything to screw you over. Nothing they wanted from me would have hurt you. It was just... surveillance."

Perhaps he was right. Nothing about this was inherently evil. The Presidium kept tabs on everyone. That shouldn't have surprised me. My anger settled more on Adrastos than Julian, and a pang of grief lanced through my gut.

I sniffled. "This isn't my first rodeo with these people. The more they know, the more dangerous they become." I looked up at Julian. "But for what it's worth, I believe you."

He blurted, "If I had any options—"

"I get it," I said with lifted hands. "I really do. Hell, I'm as much under their thumb as you are, at this point. We're all just doing their dirty work."

Julian nodded thoughtfully.

I swiveled toward Turner. "You got any last-minute confessions, Detective?"

He looked up to the sky for a second, then replied, "I own all of Manilow's albums on vinyl."

"You're clearly an agent of evil," I said. "Come on. Let's talk to this Brandon Carruthers."

Chapter Thirty-Nine

The address proved to be a one-story office jutting from the side of a warehouse like a swollen tick. Ancient blinds shuttered the tall windows framing the aluminum siding, and the lights were off. The building looked empty, and there was no signage on or above the door.

"Any doorbells?" I mused.

Turner reached out and grabbed the door, pulling it open.

"Ah," I muttered.

"After you, hot shot," Turner announced.

Julian asked, "Don't we, like, need a warrant?"

Turner answered, "It's a commercial building, and it's unlocked. We can enter, but we can't search."

With a shrug, I stepped inside.

The crackle of warding energies snapped across my face, and I held up a hand before the others stepped inside.

"Hold it."

Julian whispered, "What is it?"

"Oddly strong wardings on this threshold, especially for a commercial building. Definitely a practitioner here," I said.

"We kind of figured that, hadn't we?" Julian replied.

"I suppose so. But we're at a disadvantage if we step inside."

"We're not here to start a fight, though," Julian posited. "Are we?"

I replied, "I suppose that depends on Carruthers."

I proceeded into the office, mostly dark with only a little sunlight filtering in from between the cock-eyed blinds.

Turner reached for a light switch and pawed it on. One single fluorescent fixture buzzed to life, spilling a notably insufficient amount of light into the room. Two old laminate desks stood side-by-side, ratty fabric-covered office chairs loitering behind. One file cabinet stood in the corner, covered in dust.

"Hello?" I called.

No response.

"Looks abandoned," Julian whispered. "Maybe they left the door unlocked a long time ago."

Turner grunted his agreement.

I responded, "If this place was abandoned, the shieldings on that door wouldn't be so strong."

"I couldn't feel anything," Julian said.

"Energy palpation. It's a basic skill, but you do have to train in it. I'll get you up to speed one of these days."

Julian replied, "Seriously?"

I grinned. "Hey, I lost my only student. Kind of got used to this whole teacher scene."

As I spoke, I recalled leading Ches through the daycare center in Gettysburg. Energy palpation. I really should have been feeling my way through this office instead of flapping my mouth. I extended my open palms as I calmed my thoughts.

Waves upon waves of rolling energy swirled around my fingers, shifting to the left, and then to the right.

Continually shifting, without pattern.

"Shit," I whispered.

"What?" Julian asked.

"I think we're standing on a jinx, fellows."

Turner harrumphed, "I've been thinking that since I met the two of you."

I shot Turner a hard glance. "This isn't a joke. I'm not talking about some bad luck or minor inconvenience. This is a fresh pocket of chaos." I added as I reached further, "May even be forming as we speak."

Julian asked, "Should we leave? Is it dangerous?"

"Yes and yes."

Turner sniffed. "Are either of you two smelling this, or is it just me?"

"Smell what?"

"I don't know," he answered. "Something hippie."

I shook my hands off and inhaled. Sure enough, the spicy tang of burning resin lingered over the stagnant air of the office.

"Incense. There's a working going on right now."

Julian gestured for the door. "Then, I'm back to the leaving?"

Turner asked, "What's that?"

I followed his finger to the short hallway leading to a couple doors to back offices. The space beneath one of the doors flickered with movement.

"Hello?" I called again. "Is someone in here?"

Turner muttered, "If they ain't answering, then they're up to no good."

"Maybe. Or maybe they're refusing to break focus."

"Should we go and break their focus for them?" Turner asked with a grin.

I nodded. "If it keeps a jinx from breaking a piece of our asses off, I'm all for it." I turned to Julian. "You can wait outside, if you like. Might get a little... weird."

He shook his head. "Hey, you want to be the teacher, then I'll be your student. Not backing out now!"

I stepped into the shadowed hallway. The smell of incense grew stronger. The lack of air conditioning kept the aroma stagnant in the back half of the building. The energy continued to swirl forward and backward, up and down.

Turner reached for the doorknob with one hand as he unbuttoned his blazer with the other. The blazer fell open around his ample midsection, revealing a holstered gun strapped against his side.

I gave Turner a nod, and he opened the door.

It creaked against its hinge, the obnoxious sound winding down as the door finally reached the side wall.

Julian whispered, "Really?"

I peered inside the room, which was thick with palpable malevolence. I reached inside for the switch, but nothing happened when I flipped it.

At the far end of the room, a lone candle sat on the floor. Just one candle. It seemed to be a simple white taper, hardly enough to fill the office with incense.

"What's that writing?" Julian asked, pointing over my shoulder.

I squinted into the darkness and spotted some white script on the floor beside the candle. I gave the light switch another jiggle, with the same result as before.

Turner pulled a penlight from his blazer pocket, and twisted it on before handing it to me.

"Thanks," I whispered.

I swept the light into the room. It was utterly empty. Four bare walls. The beam of light sliced through wafts of smoke.

The energy in the air pulsed as I took a step inside, aiming the light for the walls. I expected to find the "house script" of the Nombre D'or sketched onto the walls, but found no such thing. It was a clean room... absolutely empty.

Except for the candle at the far wall.

And the summoning circle in white chalk the beam of my penlight illuminated as I swiped it across the floor.

I shot my arms out, catching both Julian and Turner as they leaned in to look into the room.

"Watch it!"

Turner looked down at the circle ringed in the glyphs of the Clavicula Solomona. "Oh, great. More Satan shit."

Julian asked, "Do you recognize that?"

"Vaguely. I know what it is, at least. It's a Goetic summoning circle."

"What does that mean?" Julian urged.

"It means Carruthers is no dabbler. Stay here, and don't touch anything."

I slipped sideways into the room, keeping my toes well away from the chalk on the floor. If this had been one of Zeno's circles, I wouldn't have been as delicate. But my limited experience with Goetia had taught me two important facts about the summoning of Solomonic devils. The first was that you had to lay every millimeter of your summoning construct in an exacting, precise manner, if you didn't want the Dark Choir to reach through the void and rip your face off. The second thing my experience had taught me was to stay the hell away from Goetia.

I panned the penlight over the scribing on the floor. It was large, nearly consuming the entire room. I found five more candles on the perimeter, extinguished, marking the points of a hexagram. Someone had extinguished these candles recently, judging by the smoky air. Yet they left the one burning. Had we surprised them? Did they rush to end the circle?

By the thrumming, hungry pulse of the energy lashing out at my hand, I recognized that this circle was anything but dismissed.

"There's something by the candle," Julian called in a throaty whisper.

I aimed the penlight for the candle, and found an envelope set against the side. I stepped gingerly around the perimeter of the chalk work, pausing where the hexagram reached the wall. Holding my breath, I took a long step over the first corner of the hexagram and one of the extinguished candles, then again on the next. Only when my feet landed on clear ground beyond the chalk, did I exhale.

I crouched down and inspected the envelope. Ink calligraphy swirled across the front, and as the electric beam of my light steadied the wavering illumination of the candle, I realized this wasn't a rushed circle. We hadn't barged in and halted this summoning. No, we'd been expected.

"It's addressed to me," I called.

"What?" Julian gasped.

"Carruthers knew I was coming."

I squinted at the envelope, wrestling with the decision whether to take it or leave it be. With a good, solid reinforcement of my personal shielding, I reached out and took the envelope, making sure not to disturb the chalk just beyond.

I held the penlight in my mouth and slid my finger inside the envelope, pulling it open. A tiny card inside bore similar calligraphy. I slid it out.

The lettering, in strokes so graceful they seemed to mock me, spelled, *Good luck...*

"Oh, fuck," I muffled against the penlight.

A rushing noise and a clattering sound erupted from across the room. Two smacks of fist against flesh, and both Turner and Julian stumbled forward into the room.

I dropped the penlight into my hand and shone it at the door. I caught a glimpse, the barest peek at a figure looming in the hallway just outside the room. He was thin, wearing a hooded sweatshirt with the hood pulled up over his head.

And that was all my eyes could register before the figure slammed shut the door to the room.

Turner coughed and released a string of profanities as he moved to rush the door.

"Don't move!" I shouted, holding up both hands.

Turner halted, his toes just outside the chalk circle.

"Ease back, Detective!"

He gave me a look, then slid his foot away from the perimeter of the chalk.

I released a breath.

"Dorian?" Julian moaned.

I slid the light to Julian to find him on his knees, frozen halfway through pushing himself up from the floor.

A wide swath of disturbed chalk traced a path from his legs to the doorway.

My stomach lurched, and I took a quick stock of the room.

"Stay put," I said, forcing the tremble from my voice. "Don't break any more of the circle."

"What do I do?"

"I said stay put."

"But what do I do?"

I searched the room. Useless. Completely empty.

The energy in the room stopped circulating, and for a fleeting moment, I considered whether the circle was, in fact, a bust.

An enormous thump of basal energy pounded my midsection, and I nearly gagged. I caught myself from falling into the circle, myself. The energy in the room began to rise. It geysered up from the circle. The air moved, I could tell by the smoke washing up to the ceiling.

"Ease out of the circle, exactly the way you came," I shouted as the wind began to pick up volume.

Turner shouted, "What's happening?"

"Something horrible," I answered.

Julian fought his way to his feet, wobbled a bit, then took a step backward.

The flame of the candle at my feet flickered out. The smoke circled me before tracing a line to the ceiling.

The penlight blinked a few times, then went dead.

As did the movement of the air.

The entire room fell into utter silence and complete darkness.

I could hear Julian's breathing. Or was it my own?

"Dorian?" he whispered.

"Are you at the door?" I asked.

Before he could answer, another sound filled the room. Low. Deep. Predatory.

It was like a panther growl, calling from the depths of a vicious chasm.

Julian's breathing increased, and I heard Turner's feet scuffling backward.

I reached underneath my jacket and unsnapped the sheath of my darquelle. As I slid it out, something brushed against my leg.

"Dorian?" Julian wheezed in a panicked pitch. "Something's in here!"

"Try to stay calm."

"I... I just felt it!"

I clapped the penlight against my leg, trying to coax its light back. Whatever was choking the battery relented for a split-second.

In the miniscule beam of light, I spotted something long, massively thick, and covered in scales.

The growl rumbled the room again, and as the penlight died once more, the sight of two slitted red eyes blinked at me from the center of the room seared itself into my brain.

I shouted and swung wildly at the air, but my darquelle found no purchase.

A second later, I heard a gasping. Then a gurgling.

Followed by several loud *thumps*.

I reached with my hand, swatting for something to stab. I found nothing but floor.

Circle be damned.

I crouched to my feet and leapt into the center of the room. My knees landed into something soft, and clothed.

A hand gripped my arm.

The gasping reached a feverish timbre, and the hand dug hard into my arm.

Another loud *thump*, and light spilled into the room as Turner jerked the door open. I blinked at the intensity of light, and a horrific sight met my gaze below me.

Julian lay on his back, his eyes wide, mouth gaping open. His throat seized, throbbing to catch some air.

"Julian!" I shouted, dropping my darquelle.

Turner swept out of the room, his gun in hand.

"Turner!" I shrieked. "Call an ambulance!"

Julian gripped my hand as his entire frame began to spasm, his chest lurching as he tried to breathe.

I examined his throat. No marks. Nothing. He was simply suffocating.

He released me and clawed at his chest.

My thoughts ran in several directions at once, slamming into one another as panic set in. I had to do something. But what? Julian was dying!

Lesser banishing cross? It was worth a shot, but did I have time to ground and center? No way in hell I was going to meditate now.

Warding? I focused my hands over his heart chakra, trying to envelop it with a protective shell of my own energy. However, the searing absence of life energy at his mainline sent waves of panic up my arms and into my chest.

I was running out of time. I had to solve this mechanically.

I fished on the ground for the darquelle, and knelt over him, pinning his arms to the floor.

"No, no... you just hang on." I felt his throat for the soft spot beneath his voice box. "I'm going to open your airway."

I ran the tip of the darquelle onto his throat, and steadied it, placing the palm of my free hand over the hilt. I'd never done this before. Shit, I could kill him myself! But his lips were turning blue. I couldn't wait any longer. Had to act.

Before I could push the tip of my darquelle into his trachea, Julian's eyes rolled back and he sucked in a tremendous, violent breath.

His eyes opened slowly, focused on something impossibly distant.

Then his eyes found me.

Julian's mouth lifted into a peaceful grin. He reached up for me as a tear slid down the side of his face.

His lips moved. I crouched down to hear him.

"Don't... trust..."

I straightened back up. "Don't trust who?"

His eyes lifted, staring up to the ceiling.

And he released a long, slow breath.

I watched and waited, but he did not take another.

"No," I moaned.

I checked his neck for a pulse. Nothing.

I checked his mainline.

Cold.

Vacant.

With a desperate tingle shooting through my chest, I tossed aside my darquelle and knelt by his side. I laced my fingers and pumped at his chest.

One.

Two.

Three.

I reached down to pinch his nose, covering his mouth with mine to blow into his lungs.

His chest rose.

I returned compressions, and shouted, "Turner, goddamnit!"

Turner rushed back into the room, and paused as I continued CPR.

"What's happening?"

"Call a fucking ambulance!"

He stumbled backward until he hit the far wall, then rushed off.

I could hear him speaking from the parking lot, calling something in to someone. It was far away, but my ears had to hear it. I had to know something was being done.

Because even as I continued the CPR, the entire energy of the room dissipated into the stillness of death.

I stopped the compressions at a point, as I found myself weeping uncontrollably. All of the strength had left my arms. I rolled away from Julian, gripping my knees. He just lay there, staring up at some other place.

I sat there, my chest heaving through sobs, even as the paramedics arrived. Someone gripped me under my arms and dragged me backward from Julian's body as the paramedics picked up where I had left off.

They brought in a spine board, then carried him out into the hallway.

And I was alone.

The chalk art on the floor had been completely wrecked by the comings and goings, but even as I cleared my eyes and the numbness of the moment set in, I recognized a familiar pattern forming in the dust as it settled.

The widdershins spiral.

Turner loomed in the doorway, his face pale.

I looked up to him, and the sight of me must have been more than he could handle. He turned away, and composed himself.

"That," he wheezed. "That wasn't real."

I couldn't speak. The cranial part of my being wanted to validate this moment for him, to ease him into the one-way door through which all of the people in the Life had passed. That moment when you could no longer disbelieve.

But my cranial self was shut deep below several oceans of anger and grief. It stained my entire being. A cry of pain echoed through the hollow of my being, where my soul had once resided. It cried out for retribution. Vengeance.

It cried out for blood.

It was all I could feel.

Turner added, "You people are real. Aren't you?"

I managed a nod, which brought forth a new stream of tears. I scowled as they flowed. Nothing would stop these tears.

I grabbed my darquelle and sheathed it behind the small of my back. Nothing would stop me.

Ever again.

CHAPTER FORTY

A crime scene investigation unit arrived, and Turner deflected them as much as he could, allowing me a moment to collect myself. I pushed off the floor to stand, and my fingers brushed against the envelope. I peered over to the doorway, and as one of the investigators turned her back, I curled the envelope and card into my hand, slipping it into my pocket.

I stepped directly across the ruined chalk circle, and as the investigators noticed my approach, made a path for me to take my exit.

Turner had one of his colleagues cornered, shouting at him to the point of spraying spittle. His posture was intense and aggressive. This must have been Turner's fear response... rage.

I understood that.

He spotted me as I moved for the front door.

"Whoa," he called out, rushing to bar the door.

I glared at him.

He muttered, "Give me a minute, and I'll drive you to Shock Trauma."

I simply nodded, then stepped outside into the fresh air. There was little comfort in the warming spring afternoon. The sunlight was pale. The air filled with ozone and the smell of tar from a roof nearby. The jagged parking lot, scattered with weeds at the cracks, had filled with official vehicles. It was like navigating a labyrinth, weaving my way back around until I reached the front street and Turner's car.

I sat on the trunk, staring down the street.

Julian deserved much better than this.

But he was just another casualty of having known me. He should have been a rising star in politics. Deputy Mayor. Congressional aide. Perhaps more.

But he had a taste for the Life. It was how we met. He hired people like me to gain his edge. Perhaps in a karmic sense, that was his undoing? He used the secret knowledge without having studied it. He had, to a degree, cheated the system.

Who was I kidding? Everyone cheated the system. The fact was there were no rules to cheat. Money, connections, magic... they were all shortcuts. And we were all stupid not to use them.

Julian's dark interest in the hermetic arts wasn't his undoing.

Brandon Carruthers had been his undoing.

At length, Turner arrived and gestured for me to get into the car. The drive to Baltimore Shock Trauma was short and silent. Nothing needed to be said, and Turner had a lot to sort out inside his head, I was sure.

As did I.

When we arrived, Turner waved us through a pair of uniformed police and on through a pair of double doors off the side of the emergency room. A doctor stepped in front of us, her face tight with the portent of bad news.

Turner asked, "Bright?"

She shook her head. "He was unresponsive. We called him shortly upon arrival."

"What was it?" he prodded. "What happened?"

"Sudden cardiac arrest," she explained. "Could be several causes. Embolism, infarction. We're gathering Mister Bright's medical history now, and locating his family."

Family. I had no idea if he even had family. He'd never mentioned them, if he did.

The doctor added, "I'll want to speak with you both, regarding the incident. Any details will help."

Details? The details we'd provide would only get us admitted for psychological evaluation. I had no intention of cooperating with anyone, and Turner's blubbering for the doctor indicated that he was fully aware of the threat the truth posed to his career.

And so, after an hour's delay, we were released from the interrogations of doctors and police, and I shuffled my way toward the exit.

Turner caught up with me, gripping my arm.

"Hey," he whispered. "We need to talk about what happened, you and me."

I looked down at his hand on my arm, then up into his face.

"You'll want to let go of me," I said.

He let go.

"So, yeah?" he urged. "I need to know what I saw."

"You saw what you saw." I turned back toward the exit, adding, "Don't let anyone, not even yourself, try to rationalize it away."

"But this changes everything."

I kept walking.

Before I reached the door, I paused. A wave of sobs threatened to quake through my ribcage. This wasn't the place to melt down. I held myself up at a nearby column to fight against the spasms in my throat. Fight the tears. Fight the dawning realization that I had so utterly, completely failed Julian Bright.

As the wave subsided, I felt a tug. Not physical. Energetic.

I swiveled on my heel, following the pull, until I spotted Wexler standing near a vending machine, tapping away at a phone. She looked up to me, her face drawn and pale. She gestured with her head for me to follow, then stepped around the machine and into a side room.

I checked on Turner, who had given up on me and had retired back behind the double-doors to join his co-workers. Free at last, I followed Wexler.

She stood alone in an examination room, lingering by a drawn curtain, still typing on her phone.

I cleared my throat, and she turned to face me.

"I'm sorry about Bright," she said. "Truly."

"So am I."

She slipped her phone into her purse, which she hoisted onto her shoulder. "Bright was on our watch list. When the ambulance logged his name, we were notified."

I snarled. "A watch list?"

"We find it useful." She shook her head. "Again, you have my condolences."

I took a step forward, my shoulders braced, hands clutching in and out of fists. "Your little spy talisman wasn't enough?"

She held her ground, eyes narrowed. "I understand you're upset. You have every reason to be."

"Tell me something, Wexler."

She blinked at my use of her name. If it was, in fact, her name.

I continued, "When you people threatened his career, and the livelihood of everyone he knew, was that before or after you put him on your watch list?"

Wexler's brow curled into a scowl. She said nothing, instead turning toward the curtain, eyes moving rapidly. "Do you have any information?"

I took a breath, checking my anger. "I do. But I'll only give it to the Ipsissimus."

She checked the curtain, and a voice called from behind it.

"It's all right, Deborah."

The curtain pulled back to reveal Adrastos leaning against a bed, drawing the curtain with the end of one of his braces. His eyes blinked at me through his wire frames, his face stony.

I crossed my arms. "I'm stunned the Ipsissimus, himself, deigns to visit Baltimore on account of Julian Bright."

His blinking paused, and he sniffled.

"Not that it is any of your concern, but understanding your love of full disclosure it bears commenting… we were here on other business." He nodded to Wexler. "One of our own has fallen, as well."

Wexler took a deep breath. She seemed rattled. And as I noted that she had summoned me herself to this otherwise unguarded meeting, I realized who had fallen.

"Reginald?" I asked.

She nodded once.

I snarled at Adrastos. "Feel good about yourself? Completely ruining a man's life so you could spy on a renegade hex-maker?"

Wexler held out a hand, but Adrastos shook his head at her.

I added, leaning into him, "You are a genuine piece of shit, Joe. How's that for full disclosure?"

He grinned.

"Mister Lake, I recognize the emotion of the moment, and your justifiable sense of outrage. And with as much aplomb as I can muster at the moment, allow me to convey to you how very little I care about Mister Bright's demise."

"Excuse me?" I hissed.

He cocked his head. "His life is one of several dozen lost this week, all at the hands of these opponents. I tend not to make friends, a policy you should consider in your future dealings. Thus, I'm left unmoved by emotion, governed instead by reason. Circumspection. I fail to rush in against my better judgment, as you were likely to do if I hadn't sent Deborah to gather you."

I waved the back of my hand at the two of them.

"Fuck you all. Best of luck."

"You won't leave," Adrastos stated.

I countered, "You think?"

I moved for the door.

Adrastos added, "Because it was academic, until now. The danger."

I paused with my hand on the door latch.

He continued, "But now you understand these people. You know they've been watching you, too. And if I'm right, and if you've shed some light on their identity, then you know you don't stand a chance against them alone."

I released the latch.

Adrastos clinked forward a couple steps, clearing the curtain. "You need us, Mister Lake. Hate us, despise us, plan your ultimate revenge. That's all fine and well. But for the moment, you are one of us, at least in the eyes of the enemy. So why not allow reason to prevail? Share with us what you've learned. Then perhaps we can settle accounts on behalf of Mister Bright?"

I dropped my chin. Nothing he said was wrong.

I muttered, "It's not chaos magic."

Wexler stepped to my side and whispered, "Nonsense."

"No, I've seen it now." I turned to face them both. "I was wondering how these people managed to control their jinxes. Keep them contained, focused, without accidentally giving you more power by some random turn of fate. It's because it's not a jinx at all. It's Goetia."

Adrastos looked up to the ceiling, then nodded briefly.

Wexler nudged, "How could it be simple Goetia?"

"Not so simple. I mean, it's a completely different arena of magic, but the end result is the same. A jinx punches a hole in the fabric of Nature to create a nihil. A Goetic circle, if poorly executed, punches a hole through the Veil, allowing denizens of the Dark Choir to interact with our plane of existence. I'll bet it's why they took out Frater Zeno's lodge. Zeno was uniquely qualified to stop them. He would have known that if a circle is intentionally miscast, the result is a permanent scar on this plane. And that's what's been torpedoing your geomantic Tree of Life."

Adrastos snapped his head toward me.

I smirked. "Yep. Figured that out, too. You want the real kicker? This isn't some foreign cabal. The people setting fire to the Presidium come from inside your own organization."

Wexler released a disbelieving cackle. "That's ridiculous."

Adrastos squinted at me. "The L'Enfantines?"

I nodded.

Wexler shot Adrastos a quizzical stare.

He explained, "It's been a source of puerile speculation for decades, whether the L'Enfantines had survived the purge of 1812. Our first purge, in fact. Cheeky irony that they should disguise their first attacks on our assets as another purge."

Wexler's lips tightened. "The L'Enfantines, Joe?"

"Jefferson decided they couldn't be trusted to behave themselves." He turned to me. "He was the first Ipsissimus, you know. And the last to attempt to hold the office alongside the office of the President. He was the one who had removed Pierre L'Enfant from the plan."

"Replaced him with Ellicott," I said. "Someone more keeping with the Qabala, and by virtue, the ancient Egyptian tradition."

"It was, in fact, tradition that forced L'Enfant from our number," Adrastos corrected with a lifted finger. "The double pentacle? Preposterous. One to siphon power from the mythical North, and another to draw from his homeland. He was a progressive in name only. You must understand, at the time, leaning on the European seats of power was utterly anathema to the Founders, Jefferson in particular."

Wexler interrupted, "You're not suggesting the Jeffersonians are involved with this?"

Adrastos gave a curt shake of his head. "They've long since faded into history."

"As had the L'Enfantines, or so we thought," she countered.

Adrastos chuckled. "Übermenschen from Hyperborea, Deborah? Please. You see, Mister Lake? Even among our number, mad rumors steal away our reason."

Wexler stiffened, then folded her arms and leaned against the wall, seemingly resolved to exit the conversation.

I asked, "How many nodes have they corrupted?"

"All but one."

I sucked in a breath. "They're that close? How could you let things get this far?"

"They have access to our internal conversations," he suggested. "They've enjoyed a long space of anonymity. We are, as it seems, only human."

"Well, cat's out of the proverbial bag now," I said. "They know I'm on your payroll."

"Indeed, but that was always a likelihood."

"But now you have a name."

He lifted a brow over his wire frames.

I continued, "Brandon Carruthers. He's the one who left the half-cast summoning circle that killed Julian. He's the one who made the niding pole that took out Frater Zeno's lodge. If the L'Enfantines have an active specialist, he's your man."

"I have never heard of this Brandon Carruthers," Adrastos muttered before looking to Wexler.

Wexler simply shrugged.

"Well, he's clearly a student of Goetia," I offered. "If you don't have a list of known Goetics, then perhaps there are people I can talk to."

"Do so. In the meantime, they have eliminated all but one of the nodes. There are layers to the privilege of information within our group, as you may well be aware. The last known Ellicott Node is not general knowledge. This is very much intentional, for precisely this sort of reason."

"You're betting they won't find it?"

"I'm wagering they will, specifically due to the fact that I'm having Deborah leak the information discretely. Should they attack, we will be ready for them, and we will know where the loyalties of key Presidium members truly lie."

I followed his train of thought, and didn't care for where it led. "So, you're basically done with me, is what you're saying?"

"To the contrary. I expect you to be there, waiting for them. We intend to drop the ax directly onto their necks. You're the ax."

I stared at Adrastos, whose unflappable demeanor won the moment's tug-of-war.

"Fine," I grumbled. "Where's the last node?"

"Marshall, Virginia. Old schoolhouse, now home to the Fauqier County Living History Museum. It's an old school house built just prior to the war for independence, when the town was known as Salem."

"Cute. I'll need a way to contact you. A manner more immediate than getting checked into Intensive Care."

"Deborah?"

Wexler sighed, then reached into her purse to produce a tiny silver case. She snapped it open to produce a business card. Before handing it over, she brandished it in the air.

"I'll have you know, only members of the Fifth Order and higher have ever received one of these cards."

She held it out.

As I took it, I responded, "Am I supposed to find that flattering?"

Her eyes hardened.

I addressed the two of them as I returned to the door. "This is on you. You know that, right? The entire mess. All the lives lost. You people let shit slip, and we're the ones paying for it. I'm not going to forget this."

"I'm sure you won't," Adrastos replied.

"Yeah. I guess this détente is a fragile thing."

"It doesn't have to be," he said. "It could be enduring."

I ran a hand alongside my face. I was exhausted. This entire day had punched me in the chest and pulled my will to continue out through the gaping wound.

I left them behind, skirting out of the emergency room doors and into the fading light of sunset to call a cab.

When I got home, I closed the door neatly behind me, settled my keys into the bowl on the front table with the tips of my fingers so they wouldn't make too much racket, then turned to my sideboard. If ever there was cause for a drink, this was it. Julian deserved that much.

I reached inside and dug deep for the last bit of my Glenrothes '87. I'd saved it for some good news, but at that moment I realized a spot of whiskey this choice was better spent in honor of the passing of a good friend.

A brother, really.

I poured the last bit into one of my leaded crystal lowballs, and held it up to my lamp, gazing at the deep amber rays of reflected light.

A knot filled my stomach, and my fingers clamped hard against the glass. I lifted it to my lips, but they wouldn't part. The smell of the scotch, usually such a soothing swirl of vapor, felt acrid in my nostrils.

The callous that had numbed my grief faded in an instant, and with a primal growl, I twisted and hurled my glass against the far wall. The crystal shattered, spraying the foyer with the last of the Glenrothes.

I dropped to a crouch and jerked out more bottles. Scotch, bourbon, gin. One by one, I hoisted the bottles over my head and smashed them down against my floor. The bottom of my pants soaked up the spirits as the glass pelted my arms, and even the bottom of my chin.

I screamed. I sucked in heavy breaths, and continued screaming.

I moved on to the wine. Reds. Whites. Sake. Everything in the sideboard, everything that had brought me comfort… it all had to die. I threw the bottles almost randomly, covering wall after wall. The sofa. The chair. My writing desk. The room filled with a putrid bouquet of alcohols, and my stomach lurched.

Finally, as I doubled over panting, I gripped the last bottle. The very last one.

I picked it up with a trembling hand, willing strength into my arm.

But I stopped.

The feel of the thin netting covering the bottom of the bottle caught my attention. It was the Gideon Reserva.

Emil's sherry.

I took a moment to catch my breath, easing the bottle back down onto the sideboard.

This wasn't a bottle that comforted me. It was a painful memory. It was the reminder of how far I had fallen from Emil's dream, his plan for me. I was to be his salvation, and I couldn't even save Julian.

Or Ches.

Or anyone.

Well, if Emil's magnum opus was to become his ultimate failure, then it seemed time to make that failure as complete as I could.

I straightened my spine and ran my hands along the front of my shirt. Tiny droplets of blood had erupted along my forearms where glass had nicked it.

I turned toward the hallway, my shoes sloshing through spilled wine, and trod with wet footsteps toward the basement door. I pulled it open, and took the first steps down to the basement. The bulb snapped to life with an odd eagerness. Perhaps that was my imagination.

The shadows writhing in the corner of my eye were certainly not my imagination. They were hungry. And agitated.

I spun around, and stared at the spot I thought I saw them, and lifted fists.

The entire room hummed with energy. Something new, something vicious.

And it was coming entirely from me...

...and leading to the cabinet.

I pulled my keys from my pocket, found the tiny brass bastard belonging to the Library, and unlocked the cabinet doors.

They swung open, pouring the intoxicating scent of ancient parchments, pressed leather and cedar over my face.

CHAPTER FORTY-ONE

T**he fall into the inhuman ferocity within Emil's** Netherwork tomes was brain-spinning. I had slipped into an unprecedented resonance with the malicious intent held within the books. I felt welcomed by it. Within minutes, I was drawn into texts I had always avoided when attempting to catalog the contents of the cabinet. Dark tomes of killing magic. I was astounded at the relative ease of the Netherwork. No need to contrive elaborate fail safes and checks. No need to squeeze blood from a stone in order to power the curses.

They had their own power source.

I didn't sleep, nor was I aware of when the sun rose. Exhaustion never took me, or rather it had long since taken me and I'd learned to ignore it. I discovered new curse vehicles, objects to be wielded in battle. Tiny needle-spangled packets of pre-prepared conjuration and mortification. They weren't quite as sweeping or elegant as the slow-burn curse that took months of preparation, but they seemed useful in a scrap against, say, chaos magicians.

I even ran across the old text I had used to craft the curse doll that had killed Osterhaus. An odd nostalgia filled the same pit that had once brimmed with bile when considering these books. It felt like home.

My phone rang upstairs, pulling me out of a book of late Macedonian blood rites. I climbed the stairs, my legs remarkably weak, as I mused on the nature of the Netherwork I had been studying. Even for the quantum jump of power and relative ease of assembly, these workings exacted specific material requirements, and a high price for casting.

The requirements were almost always some horrific laundry list of reagents, often involving human corporea. Not to mention the vitae from the victim. It was a limiting factor for Netherworkers of hermetic traditions. One must acquire a piece of the target in order to align the energy to that target. Other traditions allowed for longer range castings… traditions such as Stregheria. But these fell in the arena of Nature magic, and were impossible to adequately focus. Easier to curse an entire field of crops than to curse the farmer, himself.

And the high casting price? That was simple enough. Casting a Netherwork curse was a damnable offense. One paid for Netherwork by putting a lien on one's soul. This lien was held by the Dark Choir, and as Felix Parrish attested, their bookkeeping was staggeringly thorough.

But I had no soul. At least, it wasn't resident in my body. I knew I could execute a curse with my soul disembodied… I'd done it to Osterhaus. But as Father Mark put it, that was an act of defense, not only of myself but of the other souls he was prepared to sell overseas.

My present mission, however, wasn't so noble. I wanted Carruthers and all of the L'Enfantines to pay for Julian. Perhaps "wanted" wasn't the most accurate term. It was a fundamental consequence of what they had done, the equal but opposite reaction the Cosmos demanded of them.

And I would be the force of nature that rained it down upon them.

I didn't catch the call before it rolled to voice mail, but I could see by the caller ID that it was Ben. Seemed he had been calling me most of the morning. And morning had long since passed. It was almost noon.

Ben.

Shit. I had to break the news to him and the rest of the staff. There was an entire business at the tavern that hinged on Julian's direction. I wasn't prepared to step into his shoes. I had no idea how to run a bar.

I moved upstairs to shower and change, wondering if I wouldn't have to close down Light Street Tavern.

When I arrived at the tavern, Ben rushed me, face flushed.

"Where the hell ya been, son?" he blustered. "Cops been coming in all morning."

I took a quick look around. The tavern was empty save for one day-drinker at the bar, hunkered over his glass of whatever.

"Ben? A word."

He crossed his arms, but finally relented and followed me into Julian's office.

I broke the news to Ben as plainly as I could, leaving out any details about the esoteric circumstances of his death. I left it as a sudden heart attack.

He nodded profusely, as if forcing his chin to accept the situation would convince his brain to follow suit. He took a seat in front of Julian's desk and reached for a stack of papers.

"There's... we have more people starting today."

I put a hand on Ben's shoulder. "We have to discuss the future of this place."

He shrugged off my hand. "The future is we have new kitchen staff, and I have to get them trained by dinner service. Where's the goddamn resumes? We got manager applications online, and he files them somewhere."

Ben stood up so quick the chair slapped the wall behind him. He swept around the back of the desk, pulling open the desk drawers.

"Maybe he didn't print them out, yet," Ben grumbled. "He usually does. Said he hates reading anything on a computer."

"Ben?"

He held up a hand. "Not now."

"We have to have this conversation."

Ben exhaled and dropped into Julian's chair. "We're not shutting down."

"I can't suddenly be here. I have a lot of shit to deal with."

"Then go deal with it, son. It won't change anything here."

“I don’t know if I can ever be here. I’m... in a different place.”

He squinted. “Look. I’m going to focus on today. I’m going to get us a kitchen manager, and we’re going to get the new menu served, and we’re going to move on to tomorrow. That’s what I’m going to do.” He sighed. “Then, when I’m not fighting to keep this joint running, I’ll get a loan and buy you out.”

“Ben...”

“I got nothing socked back, Dorian. This ain’t some hobby. Ain’t some retirement job. This is all I got, and I need this to live.”

He turned back to the computer and wiggled the mouse until the screen flickered to life.

I nodded as he began clicking through Julian’s files, swearing under his breath.

Leaving Ben to his work, I moved back into the tavern, stepping behind the bar to shoot myself some water from the bar gun.

“Don’t react,” the day-drinker said, his head still hung low. “Act as if you don’t know me.”

I leaned down to view his face. I didn’t recognize him at first, by virtue of a haircut and the fact that he wasn’t wearing his glasses.

“Zeno?” I whispered.

He held out a hand, gripping his glass of what also appeared to be water.

“Quietly. They’re watching this place.”

I nodded and moved aside a couple steps, pulling a newspaper from behind the bar and setting it down to pretend to read it.

“Where have you been?” I whispered.

“Hiding from absolutely everyone.”

“Taking a risk showing up here, then.”

He swiveled away from me slightly, head tilting to check the hallway leading to Julian’s office. “I heard about Bright.”

“From whom?”

“Brown. He called me last night.”

I turned the page of the newspaper, and shifted a little closer. “You sure he can be trusted?”

"He's equally as unpleasant as I am. It's the ones who smile and promise a brighter future whom I'm sure are ready to shoot me in the back of the head."

"Fair enough."

"Brown kept me close in case he needed my services. Seems the Ipsissimus has done the same with you."

I sneered. "We're all just assets to them."

"Do you know what's happening?" Zeno asked, briefly looking up at me. "To the Presidium."

"Yes, and I think Brown does, too."

"If he does, he hasn't told me." He looked away again, taking a sip of water. "I visited Brandon's workspace this morning. Where Bright died?"

I balled a fist. "I take it you know Brandon Carruthers?"

He continued, "I know all the Goetics in America. But him, in particular. He was a founding member of our Lodge. An erratic practitioner. He left after six months, and I lost track of him. Until recently, when I was forced to seek out any friendly faces. So I found his workspace." He took a sip of water. "Seems 'erratic' is being charitable."

"Learn anything useful?"

"There wasn't much left to read, but I saw enough to recognize the rank and choir of demon he summoned. None of that is particularly helpful to you, since it's not the same circle Brandon cast to attack the Presidium nodes."

I straightened up, abandoning the pretense of reading the newspaper.

"Now, how do you know about that?"

"I may have lost my students," he replied, "but I still have eyes and ears on the other side. I can tell you the following. The sigils on the walls at each of the node sites were not Goetic. They were instructions left for the enslaved to dismantle the nodes."

A car pulled up near the front of the tavern, and I returned my notice to the newspaper. I stole a glance out the window, finding a man in a heated conversation on his cell phone. Once he had finished, he put his car in drive and continued up the street.

"Why are you here, Zeno?" I asked. "What's your play?"

"This isn't going away on its own. Brown doesn't trust the Presidium to take care of its own business, and he can't involve himself. So it's up to us."

"I owe that man neither jack nor shit."

Zeno smirked. "I understand the sentiment, but understand that the two of us are essentially all that's left of the independent practitioners. Can I be frank with you?"

I nodded without looking at him.

"I just want my lodge back. I have long-term projects across the Veil which, if left untended, will create a considerable amount of trouble for some very unforgiving people. The sooner we put the Presidium back on its pedestal, the sooner life returns to normal."

I swiveled my head in his direction. "I'm way beyond normal at this point, Frater."

"I can try this on my own. I'm inclined to prefer it that way. But my chances of success are greater if I involve you." He finished his water. "It was simple math, Lake. But I'll go."

I folded the newspaper closed. "Next target is Marshall, Virginia."

He paused by the front door. "Are you certain?"

"It's the only one left. The Ipsissimus filled me in. The Presidium will be guarding it, as they can't know who's an insider and who isn't. As soon as I grab a hold of some reliable transportation, I'm heading there to stake it out."

Zeno turned back to the bar. "Brandon isn't going to let them see him. His glammers are too strong. If they wait... if you wait... you'll miss him."

"Why do you think I'm bringing you on, Frater? Simple math."

He nodded. "I have to gather some materials. Shall I meet you there?"

"It's the Living History Museum. Old schoolhouse. I suggest we meet somewhere at a distance, or the Presidium might just throw a bullet through your head."

He pulled his phone and brought up one of those map apps which I was slowly becoming convinced was a necessity for this business.

"There's a gas station a half-mile up the county highway. Meet me there in three hours, if you can."

"I'll find a way. Let's just hope we beat Carruthers there."

Zeno gestured to his face, probably a tic to adjust glasses that weren't there.

"And if we don't?" he asked. "What then?"

"Then we watch the free world burn."

Zeno took his leave, and when he had passed the front windows, I pulled Carruthers's envelope from my pocket.

Along with the Gregori pendulum.

I pulled out the charming little note Carruthers had left me, and settled the tip of the pendulum on the ink. It wasn't his vitae, but it was his handwriting. Script holds its own kind of power, and I banked that the pendulum with its centuries of ill intent had experience ferreting out all manner of energies.

I lifted the pendulum just a little, and calmed myself, watching for the tell-tale swing of the instrument, and the flashes of intuition it sent up my arm and into my limbic regions.

It told me exactly what I had expected to hear.

I pulled my phone and dialed the number on Wexler's card.

"Is this Lake?" she answered.

"Carruthers is on the move."

"Is he moving for the Node?" she asked.

"Yes. Looks like Adrastos's plan worked."

"We'll be ready."

"No," I replied.

"Excuse me?"

"I want your people to back away. I'll be en route shortly."

"Lake, you've done enough. There's nothing you can do, now."

I snarled. "There's plenty I can do. Plenty I must do. Besides, I'm bringing reinforcements. A specialist in this matter, as it turns out."

"I'm sorry, but we can't leave this entirely in your hands. If Carruthers succeeds—"

"I'm not asking your people to leave entirely. Just let Carruthers in.

Then me. If I fail, then you can finish it. But I get the first shot at Carruthers. You people owe me that. You owe it to Julian."

After a considerable silence, Wexler answered, "We won't wait long."

"Shouldn't take long."

"Then you'll have your first shot at Carruthers."

She hung up.

I just had one more call to make, and then it would be time to drop Adrastos's ax directly on Carruthers's neck.

CHAPTER FORTY-TWO

I took advantage of the mile-long walk to the gas station to clear my mind. Repetitive motions were excellent tools of meditation. Left foot. Right foot. Left arm. Right arm. Breathe in. Breathe out. My entire mainline was tight as a funeral drum, and burning with intent. The mile disappeared in what felt like a minute, and as I stepped into its parking lot I spotted, Zeno lurking by the front doors.

He approached with a lifted brow. "Where's your car?"

"Totaled. Long story."

"How..."

"Have you ever actually hitch-hiked? It's a bit of a gamble. You take what you can get."

Zeno took in my words, then nodded once. "Are you prepared?"

"Are you?"

He hoisted a backpack onto his shoulder. "I have the means to summon a third-choir arch-devil inside this bag. That would take time, however. The good news being, I won't have to. Brandon should be attempting the circle prep now. All we have to do is interrupt the containment, and the enslaved should seize on him like a bear on a salmon." He added, leaning in slightly, "He should die the same way Bright died."

I gave Zeno a meaningful glance. "That's exactly the plan." I cleared my throat and started toward the schoolhouse. "Live by the demon, die by the demon. I've always said that."

The short half-mile of county road was mostly devoid of traffic. I counted more roadkill than moving vehicles. We reached a narrow clearing in the trees and spotted a yellow-painted building with a sign easily twice as expensive as what the property was worth.

Fauqier County Living History Museum.

"Some museum," Zeno grumbled.

"I think the Presidium sets up these puppet societies to act as caretakers of the node sites. In Harper's Ferry it was a Preservation Society. Enoch Pratt, well, that's pretty much always under their guard."

"Not well enough," Zeno said.

"Apparently."

"Did you bring any weapons?"

I unsheathed my darquelle and held it a little in front of me.

He nodded. "It's blooded?"

"By a very bad man."

"We might need it. I know Brandon. I trained him myself, at least partially. He's careful. Deliberate. There's a reason, I suspect, these splitter Presidium members picked him for this task."

I sighed. "Well, it sure as shit wasn't the health plan. Speaking of plans, are we just going to stroll right in, or what?"

"I'd recommend some care. He may be absorbed in his work, but there's a limit to one's focus."

"Fine. I'll take the back, assuming it's unlocked. You take the front door, same assumption."

Zeno nodded and dropped across the driveway, cutting across a patch of tall grass stretching in front of the old schoolhouse. I hugged the tree line, stepping behind trunks as I got within sight of the windows. Entering this building at precisely the right moment would be key. I held my position to give Zeno time to take his. I spotted him crouching across the front of the porch, lingering behind the large cape cod-style posts holding up the massive overhang.

I upped my pace, slipping through brush, the odd blackberry bramble stabbing me through my jeans. I pulled out my sachet of salt, opened a corner and spilled enough into my palm to rub into the tiny droplet of blood soaking into my jeans. I wasn't going to give any son of a bitch my vitae if I could afford it!

My blood neutralized, I pocketed the salt and continued on up onto the gravel path, easing on gentle feet as I approached the building.

I took a second to check the street. Wexler's people must have been around, but they had done a fine job of staying out of sight. I wondered if I wouldn't regret that in a moment.

The back of the building appeared to be the original, as the front was a bit more modern... in a relative sense. The rear of the building was a tiny, twenty-foot-by-twenty-foot cube of stone walls, mortared together without care or concern. It seemed a miracle the building was still standing, but here it was. A relic from another time, housing the last gathered node of Andrew Ellicott's geomantic sephiroth. The source of all power for the Presidium.

And I'd allowed a renegade Goetic to infiltrate it. Indeed, that was the plan.

I took a moment to ground and center, as my mainline had gone all sloppy on my walk up the drive.

I focused on Julian. The way his face gasped in terrified suffocation. That last breath he was allowed before his heart had the life squeezed out of it.

His final words.

Don't trust.

That did it. I was focused again. Ready to do battle.

I crept up to the back door and gave the knob a shot. It twisted easily in my hand, and as I eased it in, the door moved without complaint.

Inside, I found a quaint patch of multi-colored carpeting lying in the center of several book stacks. I wound my way to what appeared to be a doorway leading to the dead center of the entire structure. No windows. Roughly square. Perfect place for a circle.

I spotted the flickering light before I even reached the door. Candles had been lit already. The corner of a summoning circle met my eye. What's more, across the casing I spotted red-painted glyphs. The Nombre D'or language. Instructions to whatever hellish beast was intended to appear.

Or so it would seem.

But, I knew better.

Carruthers wouldn't be casting a circle for this node, not just yet. He knew I was coming, and that I was already here. I'd seen to that personally.

I stepped into the room, admiring the chalk art on the floor. Like the last one, it was slip-shod and easily sabotaged.

A noise sounded from behind me. I looked over my shoulder to find Zeno peering from the front rooms.

I gestured for him to join me.

"Is he here?" he whispered.

"Oh yes," I answered at full volume.

Zeno blinked, then straightened up. "Where?"

I gestured for the summoning circle. "It's a nice touch, really. The chalk? Easy to sweep up after the ritual is completed. Just leaves these old glyphs," I added pointing at the walls. "Which no one without a brilliant goddamn researching student would have ever latched onto."

"Where's Brandon?" Zeno prodded.

"You know, it's an old notion in our circles. The working name?"

"What?"

"Pseudonyms, Frater. It's said if someone knows your true name, they hold power over you. So many take working names, to keep that from happening. Like Frater Zeno, for example. Hell of a moniker you chose."

Zeno curled his brow and shook his head.

I turned back to the ritual room. "So, Goetic theory. If I just sweep a foot across the chalk, either it'll dismiss the circle, or it'll sic whatever creepy-crawly it was meant to summon on me. Right? It kind of depends on what the circle was cast for. Either punching a hole through the Veil to render the Presidium's node into a nihil. Or, another trap set just like the one that killed Julian."

A hand brushed along my side, and my darquelle slipped from its sheath.

I exhaled. “Part of me really wanted to be wrong about this, Brandon.”

I turned to face Frater Zeno, the working name for Brandon Carruthers.

He brandished my darquelle with awkward menace.

“I have a bad habit of underestimating you, Lake,” Zeno stated.

“We all have our flaws,” I replied.

“How did you put it all together?” he asked.

“Honestly? It was when you said Brown was the one that sent you.”

He smirked. “You’ve never trusted him.”

“In point of fact, I actually did. And that’s when everything started going wrong. Brown’s one of them, the L’Enfantines, isn’t he? Hell, he might be the only one, for all I know. He knew the whole conspiracy. And I rattled his cage when I busted up into his house. Took him a moment to spin the situation, but he did. He managed to turn me around, get me to distrust Clement, and Malosi.” I winced. The memory was a bit fresh. “And it dawns on me that good ole Clarence de Haviland lives literally ten blocks away from your lodge. You must have been working as his asset for the better part of a decade.”

Zeno shrugged, then nodded.

“I also found it convenient that a Goetic devil trap killed Julian, and you show up almost immediately, trying to enlist my help. I had to double-check with my trusty pendulum, but sure enough. Your energy matched the handwriting on the note. Thank you, by the way, for leaving saliva on one of my water glasses.”

He swore under his breath.

“But it was you, wasn’t it? In the hoodie. You’re the one that shoved Julian into the jaws of Hell.”

“It wasn’t personal.”

“Funny,” I growled. “It feels pretty fucking personal to me.”

“It was supposed to be you, to be honest. Brown was getting worried about you. So, he left this fictional art studio for his wife to hand over. It was just a matter of time until you found it.”

"How were you so ready for us yesterday?"

"Oh, I've enjoyed the dubious honor of tailing you ever since I had to wipe out my own lodge. You've been an utter pain in the ass, you know that?"

I sneered. "I knew you were a bit of a heavy hand with your students, but slaughtering them on behalf of Brown? Can I ask you why? Why are you helping him accomplish this?"

"I told you. I have several interests on the other side. I require peace and quiet. Adrastos and his high-minded polished-badge arbitrators are doing little more than wasting the time of those who are getting on with real workings. Change was inevitable. But, your suspicions may be confirmed in that I truly don't care about L'Enfantines or Presidium, or even Dorian Lake. I just want it all to go away."

He stepped forward, the point of my own darquelle aimed at my solar plexus.

"So, what?" I asked. "You're just going to shiv me?"

"I have too many enslaved on the other side whom I owe consideration. Why waste blood when it can serve two purposes?"

"Is that what Julian did? Paid a debt to one of your demons?"

Zeno rolled his eyes. "You keep muddling the issue with sentiment. I don't care whose blood I have to use. We're all going to die, eventually. Might as well make use of the resource while I have the opportunity."

I glared at Zeno as he tightened his jaw. It was an odd gesture. Almost boyish. Poor child, trying to look brave.

I held out my hands. "So, here we are. You're going to just toss me to your wolves, then you'll sweep the floor, recast a new circle, and deep-six the Presidium's power supply. I suppose that'll bring Brown into his end game?"

"I'm not a part of that."

"No. You aren't."

He lunged forward, and I took a careful step backward into the doorway.

Zeno said, "You could make this easier, you know. I understand they feed quicker on willing participants."

"That's very Neolithic of you."

"It's an old art."

"But not the oldest."

He cocked his head.

I looked over his shoulder, and smiled. "No, there are older crafts. Older, and angrier."

Zeno shook his head, before he realized that my gaze was held on someone just behind him.

He spun around, blade held at arm's length, to find Annarose Rodolfi consuming the space behind him. She wore a dark-laced blouse tucked into a pair of western-style blue jeans. Her hair was pulled back into a tight bun, her face hard, eyes burning with the dark flames of hatred-fueled power.

Zeno made a confused noise in his throat, then asked, "Who is this?"

I answered, "For the longest time, I've considered your peculiar practice to be one of the most frightening. It's like playing chicken with a freight train. You're just really good at ducking out of the way and letting others take the hit. And now that I have a wider perspective on things, I realize that you are basically just a giant coward."

He shook my darquelle at Annarose, whose energy washed forward onto his face. She was charming him, in that classically non-targeted manner that Nature magic followed. Were I not filled with absolute focus, I might have felt the tugs of her glammer, as well. But as it was, hatred kept me immune from her working.

Sentiment, it seemed, was my strength.

"A witch?" Zeno sputtered, shaking off a good portion of Annarose's glammer. "You can't be serious."

"Not just a witch," I answered. "A Stregha."

His eyes darted to the side for a second, and his grip tightened on my blade.

"I brought reinforcements, as it turns out," I said.

He squared his shoulders toward Annarose.

She pulled her hands up onto her hips and raised an eyebrow. "You poor, pathetic boy."

Zeno pulled in a breath to respond with what I was sure would have been a condescending and fruitless rejoinder.

Instead, I jumped him from behind, bowling him down onto the floor. My cracked ribs sent electric waves of pain through my midsection. I hissed and willed away the distraction.

He thrashed with his free hand, his other crowded by the nearby bookcase.

I reached to grip the back of his hair, and jerked it up.

He grunted as his head pulled back.

I hammered the front of his face down against the carpet.

And I did it again.

And again.

A kind of war cry roared from my throat as I bashed his face against the carpet.

Annarose knelt down and lifted a finger. The gesture, and perhaps a good portion of enchantment pouring from her aura, snapped me out of my rage.

She drew a half-circle in the air with her finger, running it down Zeno's chin and swiping it up the bloodied space underneath his nose.

She held out her left hand, cupping it as she painted her palm with Zeno's blood. She then spat into her hand and mixed her sputum with his blood.

I dug my knee into his back as he reached up with my darquelle. His angle was too awkward, and as I applied sufficient pressure, he dropped my blade.

Annarose closed her eyes, lifting just as her eyelids sealed solid white orbs, and began to chant.

"Portami ai vostri fianchi, O Satana, e mi riempiono di tuo odio."

I knew enough Italian to recognize this was an adequately dark working.

She dipped her finger back into her palm, and reached for Zeno.

He stiffened, renewed in his fight to avoid Annarose and her magic, but I gave him no room to retreat.

Annarose painted a simple glyph onto his forehead as he snarled against her.

She looked up to me, and nodded.

And I released Zeno.

His entire frame trembled as he kicked the floor.

I reached down to reclaim my darquelle, sheathing it as Zeno twisted supine, his mouth gaping. His chest convulsed, fingers ripping away at his shirt to gain air that would never come.

I crouched down over him as his lips began to turn cyanotic.

I intoned, "And thus Carruthers will die the same way Julian died."

Zeno's eyes were wide, searching the ceiling for salvation. They paused on me briefly, but I found nothing but inevitability in my heart for this sad sack of shit.

His entire body lunged up, then crashed against the floor.

And again.

The third time, his hands reached his throat before going limp. His spine relaxed, dropping his frame slowly to the carpet. One final breath released before his eyelids went slack. His head dropped to the side, casually inspecting the air between Zeno's lifeless body and the bookshelf beside us.

I gripped my fist, rammed it into his chin, then relaxed.

It was done.

Julian was avenged.

I took several deep breaths before pulling myself to my feet.

Annarose wiped her hand against his sweater vest.

"Are you sated?" she asked.

I held my aching ribs, and stared at Zeno's corpse.

Was I?

No.

I was not sated.

"Nearly," I whispered.

"Is it not over?" she asked with narrowing eyes.

"There is one more."

"And our agreement?" she demanded, taking a step forward.

I looked up into her face. It shone with alluring wrath.

"I'll hold up to my end. Don't worry."

She nodded. "Then, who is your next victim?"

I curled my fists, unfolded my hands, and replied, "Brown."

CHAPTER FORTY-THREE

Wexler trod into the building with four men in suits and dark glasses in tow. She held out a left hand, three fingers extended, sweeping the energy in the room in an artful manner.

When she spotted Zeno's body on the floor, she lifted a brow at me. "What happened to him?"

I responded, "He tripped and fell on a Stregha."

Wexler eyed Annarose in the corner, then nodded curtly.

"How did you figure it out, out of curiosity?"

"Technically, it was Adrastos's plan," I admitted. "I baited the hook with the location of the final node. They may have expected the ruse from you, but not from me."

"Was he alone?"

"Today, he was. He was only an 'asset,' as you people like to call us. Not the mastermind."

Wexler folded her arms. "I'm going to venture a guess, here. Our friend at Druid Hill?"

"Had your eye on him, have you?"

"I had sent Reginald to Baltimore the day he died specifically to follow Clarence. We found Reginald's car in the Patapsco River. All four tires had blown out."

I winced. "Exactly the subtle kind of curse that keeps you under wraps if you're a closeted Netherworker."

"Rather like dropping a half-ton steel window frame on the competition?"

I pursed my lips to stave off a grin. "Something like that."

Wexler turned and barked orders to the men, two of whom gathered Zeno's body, spraying the blood on the floor with a potent bleach solution. The other two advanced to the summoning circle.

"I'd watch your ass in there," I grumbled. "It's active."

One of the men reached inside his suit and produced a long, machete-length blade inscribed with ornate runes.

Wexler said, "I think they can handle it."

"You people get the best toys," I muttered.

"Doesn't have to be 'you people,' Lake. Adrastos is serious about you joining."

Annarose shifted in the corner, before exiting the room.

I waited for her to step out of earshot, then whispered to Wexler, "The question you'll need to ask yourself, Deborah? Is it too late for you to leave?"

She blinked, then laughed. "We've stopped the attacks on the nodes."

"But is it already too late?"

"What do you mean?"

"Listen," I said, stepping to her side to avoid the men dragging Zeno's bagged corpse out of the room. "They've already taken out all but one of your nodes. You haven't lost your entire power base, but the Presidium is weaker than ever before. It may be enough to attack."

"Not all."

I peered at her.

"Besides Marshall, there is one more node."

"I checked the map," I blurted, wishing I had the map now. "All of the nodes of the sephiroth were accounted for."

She grinned. "One of us has actually studied Qabala, Mister Lake. I suspect I'd trust her opinion on the matter."

"Okay, what's the other node?"

"Tiferet," she said. "The Balance. It's one of the internal vertices of the Tree of Life."

I nodded with a frown. I had forgotten the center, itself.

"Tiferet is the headquarters, isn't it? The home base for the Presidium."

"We are not as weak as you may think we are."

"Aren't you?" I countered. "You're down from ten to two nodes, and they are oblique nodes. No direct paths of power."

"If the L'Enfantines want to take us on in our own seat of power, then let them. They'll be crushed."

"You keep thinking the L'Enfantines are outsiders. They're not. They are Presidium. They've been there. They know the wardings, the traps, the loyal members, the splitters. They know more than you do, and they've been planning this for a long time."

Wexler looked away with ambivalence.

"Brown may have accounted on Zeno failing, here. It was a gamble, and I wager it was personal against me. Nothing about this assault on the Presidium was haphazard. What's more, if his people have set up their own geomancy over the original L'Enfantine nodes, they may have you out-gunned already."

"I should call Joe."

"You'll need help," I declared as she lifted her phone.

"Only the first five circles of the Presidium are allowed inside the Sedem Regni. You can't help us."

I sighed, then shook my head. "The Presidium can't save itself. That's my point. Even the L'Enfantines had to hire outside help. We 'assets' aren't the pawns in this game. We're the goddamn Queens." I winced. "Okay, so I tortured that metaphor, but you know what I mean."

Wexler dialed the phone.

"It's me. Yes. It's done." She looked over to me. "Still alive. I did. Joe? He's convinced it's de Haviland." She lowered the phone. "Did you get confirmation?"

I nodded.

"Yes, it's certain. I told him, but he's insisting. Oh."

She lowered the phone again.

"The Ipsissimus is requesting your aid one more time."

"Well, he didn't get to be Ipsissimus for making stupid decisions, I suppose."

She spoke into the phone, "He graciously accepts."

After she had hung up, I asked, "Okay, so, where is this Sedem Regni, exactly?"

"Washington's Masonic Tomb," she said.

"Isn't that a public building?"

"We have a hidden complex beneath. Besides, hiding in plain sight is our *modus operandi*."

I turned as an electric whine buzzed from the ritual room. One of the suited lackeys had a hand-held vacuum and was sucking up the chalk art.

"You'll keep me on speed dial?" I asked. "We won't have the element of surprise anymore. Not with what happened here. Brown's going to have lost contact with Zeno, and he'll know I'm still alive."

Wexler pocketed her phone. "First sign of trouble, you'll be my first call."

I nodded, and turned to rejoin Annarose before she decided this entire intrigue wasn't worth her involvement.

Wexler called out as I reached the front door. "I note that you had someone else perform the curse."

I turned to Wexler, whose face was filled with thoughtful mirth.

"Your point?"

"You have your mandate. You could have killed him yourself. I was just wondering if you weren't holding out hope."

"If you think I'm not fully complicit in this man's murder," I responded, "then your understanding of karma is in dire need of readjustment."

I stepped out the front door and onto the shade of the long overhang of the front porch. Sure, those words were for Wexler, but they hammered my brain as I sucked in several breaths. This may have been self-defense, but it sure as shit felt like murder.

And... I didn't feel the least bit bad about it. What would Father Mark say?

"You have a storm inside you," Annarose said from the end of the porch.

I turned to find her leaning against one of the porch posts, arms crossed.

"I'm trying to feel guilty, is all."

She scowled and paced toward me. "What is this talk about you joining the Presidium?"

I looked over my shoulder, then reached around Annarose to corral her away from the door. "They're pushing hard for that, but I'm not biting." I looked up into her eyes. "You have to believe me. That's the last thing I want."

She turned toward me as my arm gripped her side. Her eyelids drooped as she lifted a hand to my chest.

"I know how tempting it can be."

"What, power?"

"Safety."

A length of her coal-black hair that had escaped her hair tie brushed against my cheek.

"I stopped believing in safety a while ago," I said. "We have a job to do, but I'm not sure we can do it."

"We can," she urged.

"How can you be so sure?" I asked, discretely pulling away from her.

"You have ability," she declared. "You're afraid of it, but you possess it. Perhaps it is time to embrace your power."

She looked at me, eyes aflame.

"Maybe."

I phoned Sarah and had her drive up to the property, where Annarose and I met her on the street. As we climbed into her car, I said, "Thanks for doing this."

Sarah smiled at me through the rearview as we pulled away. "No problem. I'm thinking about putting you up as an honorary member of the coven."

"I thought that was a girls-only thing."

"Oh, God. That's so last century."

Sarah drove us back to Baltimore, and I loomed in the back seat, thoughts swimming through my head. Brown would have insiders already at the Presidium HQ. They'd probably already be waiting for some kind of order. The moment Adrastos and Wexler became aware of the attack, it would already be too late.

Would that be such a bad thing, I wondered? Were it not for the fact that Brown had already indicated a complete willingness, if not an outright desire, to have my ass liquidated, I would have considered the L'Enfantine perspective.

Oh, hell with them. They put me on the wrong side of their ledger, and they were going to pay for that error.

When Sarah pulled up Amity, I reached out and touched her shoulder.

"Hold up," I said as I spotted two different vehicles parked in front of my house.

Sarah pulled up to the curb, alas too close to avoid notice.

"What's going on?" she asked.

"Looks like a fucking convention," I grumbled as I stepped out of the car.

The first vehicle was a very familiar Jeep, empty by virtue that the entire Swain clan was hovering on my front stoop. Edgar lifted a hand at me, and Elle bolted from the steps. I rushed across the street to make sure she didn't fly into traffic, and braced as she hammered into me with a tackle-hug.

"Hey," I wheezed through the pain in my torso. "What's up with you?"

She gripped my waist tight.

I pulled myself away, and lifted her chin. She'd been crying. "Holy crap, what's this about?"

Edgar closed the distance between us and the porch, and answered, "She had a freaky-deek feeling, man. Got hysterical, said we had to check on Dorian."

Wren added from behind him, "Her exact words were that you had just fallen into darkness."

I clenched my jaw, and looked down at Elle.

"I'm okay, kiddo," I whispered.

She shook her head. "You aren't."

Wren reached around her and hugged her. "We're going to get you some training on this. Divination and empathy can be a hell of a combination."

Edgar shrugged. "I'm sorry about this, but knowing you, it was a possibility."

I glanced over my shoulder to the second vehicle. "Well, do me a favor. Okay? Head on inside the house. Get the kids whatever they can drink and not get us all arrested, and wait for me."

Wren set her jaw. "What's going on?"

I nodded at the silver town car looming in front of my property. "I think I'm about to have a very interesting conversation. I don't need help."

The dark-laced accent of Annarose's voice drifted over my shoulder. "That was a lie."

The Swains looked behind me to find Sarah and Annarose approaching.

Wren lowered her brow. "Who's this?"

"Oh..." I turned and selected the more diplomatic of the two to introduce first. "Wren, this is Sarah Camp. She's just opened up a covenstead on the Eastern Shore."

Wren's face broadened into a bright smile, and she reached out a hand to Sarah.

Sarah shook it with a polite, "Blessed be."

"Blessed be, to you!" Wren chimed. "Dorian, you're finally opening up to Wicca?"

Annarose snickered, and the warmth in Wren's face cooled several degrees.

I answered, "It's a remarkably long story, but I really need all of you to go inside just right now."

Wren eyed Annarose, then asked, "Have you heard from Ches?"

I blinked away the question. "Uh, no. Please, guys?"

I nearly shoved them all toward my front walk before they took the hint. Annarose, as it turned out, took the lead, strutting up to my front door. She waited as Edgar produced the spare key to my house from his pocket. The last one inside was Elle, who watched me with dread before Wren pulled her inside.

When they were all safe inside my wardings, I turned to the town car.

The driver's side door opened, and I released a long-held breath as Malosi stepped out.

"Reed. Jesus shit, you had me ready for a fight, here."

Without answering, he stepped around to the passenger side rear door, and opened it.

I squared my shoulders as Jean Clement stepped out, his face stony.

"Or, then again..." I mumbled.

Clement stepped delicately over the crumbling curb and onto my sidewalk.

"Lake," he stated.

"Jean?" I answered. "Your friends in the Free Market cut you a hall pass?"

Clement replied without mirth, "We have business."

I looked over at Malosi, who remained by the car, arms stiff, eyes moving up and down the street. Yeah, he was on the clock, and probably wouldn't be much more genial if he wasn't.

"Okay. Let's talk business." I asked.

"Reed told me what you said about me. About him. About everything."

I nodded. Here it came.

Clement continued, "And I feel particularly disappointed."

"Yeah, well," I mumbled, "you're just going to have to get over that."

He stiffened. "I'm not accustomed to sterile accusation, Mister Lake."

I gave him a squint. "Oh, please. Don't act like this happened in a vacuum. You know who I'm up against. On some level, you recognize I'm throwing fists with some elegant and dangerous people. They've out-maneuvered the entire Presidium so far, and all of the signs pointed to you being involved."

He looked down to his suit, brushed off a couple specks that weren't there, and took a deep breath. "I find it regrettable that we've reached this level of paranoia."

"Paranoia?" I squawked. "You don't know paranoia until you have Felix Parrish visiting you every other week to dangle your soul over your head."

Clement's face blanched, and he took a step away. "Did you say Felix Parrish?"

"Oh. Shit. I keep forgetting who knows what." I shook my head. "You people are killing me."

"I know Parrish," Clement stated.

"What? Like, personally?"

"No. But I have met him before. He attempted to purchase one of my most valued items. I refused, as much because I trusted neither him nor those he represented, but also because an item of such power would have been dangerous in any hands."

I considered Clement's expression. "I keep forgetting you were a Collector."

Clement continued, "Parrish swore retribution."

"What happened?" I asked.

"It remains to be seen," he replied. "But by his reputation I understood him to be in earnest."

I sighed. "So, we're both on the hook with Parrish. Joy."

Clement turned to Malosi and beckoned him forward.

Malosi stepped up to his side without making eye contact.

Clement declared, "I think an apology is called for."

I nodded, and drew in a breath to speak the long overdue apology I had locked and loaded for Malosi, when Malosi spoke instead

"I'm sorry I abandoned my post," he grumbled. "I left you with weakened wardings when you needed more protection, and not less. I reflected poorly on Mister Clement, and as such I offer my—"

I held up my hand. "Oh, barf. Please. I'm the one who should be apologizing."

Malosi finally looked me in the eye.

I continued, "Reed? I was wrong. Dead wrong. Brown had me turned around in my head, but you know, that's on me. It's a twisted life, this Life. We all know that. So, it's even more important to know who your friends are. I lost sight of that, and it's already cost me. I can't guarantee I won't fuck up again sometime, but I can promise that, when I do, I'll feel wretched about it."

Malosi lifted a brow, then turned to Clement. "You were right."

"See?" Clement jibed. "I told you if you apologized first, he'd be effusive."

I sneered, "Oh, both of you can go to Hell."

Clement snickered. "Very likely. One might say inevitable."

Malosi grunted, "Speak for yourself."

"Anyone want some wine, or something? I mean, I'd offer if I hadn't..." I winced, remembering the state I'd left my house in. "Oh, shit. The kids."

I trotted up the steps and into my house. I found Edgar sweeping glass in the center of my front room. Both he and Wren gave me powerfully judgmental looks as I thundered through the front door.

Eddie took careful steps toward the kitchen. "It's sticky everywhere!"

I rubbed my face. "So, this deserves an explanation."

Sarah rushed in with a dustpan, declaring, "Found one!"

Edgar nodded and began shoveling the broken glass into the pan as Sarah crouched down.

Wren stepped forward, put a hand on my shoulder, and said, "Not really."

I cocked my head as a hard knot formed in my throat.

I managed to choke back a sudden sob as she gripped me in one of her freakishly strong bear hugs.

She let me go and smiled. "Just stop doing this solo. Okay?"

I nodded, blinking tears away.

Something tugged on my shirt, and I turned to find Elle.

"Hey, kiddo."

She asked, "Do you need another hug?"

"Only always," I answered, as I grabbed her neck and pulled her in for a hug.

Clement stepped into the front door with a grunt. "What's happened?"

"Oh, I just went to the zoo. You know. It's a thing." I circled my finger at my own temple.

He squinted around the front room, surveying those gathered. Sarah and Edgar, cleaning up a mess. Wren overseeing, hands on her hips, eyes sharp for missing shards of glass. Elle and Eddie looking for a clear place to sit. And Annarose, draping herself on my chair, the one I always sit in, giving me a long, cool look.

Clement cleared his throat, and reached toward Malosi, who dropped a tiny box into his hand.

He turned and held it out to me. "I bring a gift."

I surveyed the tiny box in his hand, then looked up to Clement. "I'm not interested in marriage, but thanks for the offer."

"Just open it, you snipe."

I did. The tiny red-stained wood box snapped open to reveal a black velvet cushioned interior cradling a large golden ring.

"Again, with the marriage..."

"It belonged to Cesare Borgia."

My eyes snapped open.

As did Edgar's.

"You can't be serious," I whispered. "This belongs in a damn museum."

"No, it is a tool for Netherwork."

Edgar trotted up, surveying the ring, and swore under his breath.

Clement grinned. "A fellow Collector, I presume?"

Edgar took in a lusty breath. "Dorian, man, this is next-level. That's the cursed ring of Cesare Borgia. He used it to extract blood from his targets. It, like, had a little lever."

Clement pulled the ring from the box, and held it up for examination. With a twist of a tiny mechanism along the ridge of the ring's crown, a tiny needle ejected from the palm side.

"It's a hollow needle," Clement explained. "Wicks the blood up from the victim and saves it in a reservoir." He tapped the crown. "This ring was used to curse entire families during the early Renaissance. As well as his brother, Giovanni."

"I thought poison was their game?" I asked.

"As you can imagine, the more direct of curses can appear to be diseases or toxins in nature." He turned and looked at Annarose. "Particularly those practiced in the old ways of Italy."

She returned a gracious nod.

Clement held out the ring.

I lifted my hand, and he dropped it into my open palm.

The ring coursed with malignant electricity. It was thoroughly steeped in murderous intent. Less brash than the Gregori pendulum, but more confident. This was not a heretic's blade, or a mad monk's divination tool. This was the close, palm-charged tool of one of the most notorious Netherworkers in human history.

And it was mine.

"I don't know what to say," I whispered, truly unable to interpret my own emotions.

Malosi offered, "'Thank you' is customary in these situations."

I practiced triggering the ring a couple times, then slipped it onto my hand.

And I took in the room.

The Swains, looking gratified at the change in my demeanor.

Sarah, probably wondering who the hell Cesare Borgia was.

And Annarose, searing me with a look as sinister and enticing as a glass of poisoned wine.

"Jean," I said, "I'm not selling you the Library. That's the last time I'm going to say this. Are you comfortable with that?"

He nodded. "I withdraw my offer. It's clear they will not go unused."

I scowled.

But he was right.

It was time I stopped outsourcing my own curses.

And as I felt the eldritch, triangular collision of energies from my darquelle, my pendulum, and the new ring on my finger, my phone rang.

CHAPTER FORTY-FOUR

I answered, "Hello?"

"Lake?" It was Wexler.

"That was fast."

"Joe has the play. He's called a conclave tomorrow. All local members with active status must attend."

"That's kind of brilliant," I admitted. "If dangerous. How do I fit in?"

"He wants you there."

"Now it's not so brilliant. Brown will see me. He'll recognize me. He'll throw a curse up my ass."

Wexler sighed. "You wouldn't get in to begin with, not with the security we're posting."

"So I'm back to my original question."

"I can sneak you in tonight. You'll be in one of the side chambers under glammers and wardings."

"Ambush, huh? Okay. But there's a wrinkle."

"You want to bring your witch," she stated as if observing a fact.

"More than just her."

Wexler sighed again. "There are limits to Joe's magnanimity, Lake. This isn't a tea social."

"No," I snapped into the phone. "It's war. Listen, you have your people." I looked around the room at the expectant faces. "I have mine.

It's a package deal."

"I'll have to make more calls."

"You do that. I have some cats to wrangle. Call me when you get the clearance."

I hung up and addressed the faces staring at me from all angles.

"So, it's going down tomorrow. The Ipsissimus is calling a conclave."

Wren lifted a hand, and I waved her down. "There's a kind of coup d'etat transpiring inside the Presidium. I've been working directly for the Ipsissimus, trying to shut the splitters down."

Sarah raised her hand. I pointed to her.

"The Presidium is an over-arching cabal of hermetic practitioners that have guided the American power structure since the Founding Fathers, and the Ipsissimus is their head officer."

Edgar began to lift his hand, and I turned to him. "There was an early schism within the Presidium that followed a French school of Enlightenment-inspired geomancy. Pierre L'Enfant was their central figure, who laid out the original plat for Washington D.C., before Thomas Jefferson, the first Ipsissimus of the Presidium, booted him in favor of someone more Old School. Fast forward to today, and the philosophical descendants of L'Enfant are taking revenge."

Edgar nodded and lowered his hand.

I continued, addressing everyone, "One way or another, the Presidium will never be the same after tomorrow. I'm trying to help someone in the process." I looked over to Annarose. "A couple someones. There's no upside here for me, to be honest."

I turned to Clement. "If the Presidium ends up on the losing side of the equation tomorrow, you might end up coming out of retirement. There will be open season on foreign trafficking."

I turned to the Swains. "It'll also mean the chaos on the West Coast will go nation-wide, and people like us who are used to sitting on the fence will end up having to choose sides. Because the whole continent will end up in a turf-war between upstart lodges and Old World cabals."

Elle sat on a bar stool near the kitchen, gripping her legs tight to her chest.

I gave her a wink. "But even then, if we stick together, I think we'll end up being the scariest, best-funded independent cabal on the East Coast." I turned back to Clement. "I'm leaning on you here, guy. Because all my money is basically tied up in my tavern."

He considered his suit for a second, straightened his tie, and continued to ignore my comment.

Sarah asked, "What do you want us to do?"

"That's basically why I'm doing the whole pre-game pep talk thing, here. I can't ask any of you to participate in this. It's scary dangerous. Might even be fatal. I'm not joking about that. These guys killed Julian."

Edgar and Wren exchanged glances, then stepped forward.

"Oh, fuck me," I whispered. "You people are killing me."

"Dorian?" Wren whispered.

"Yeah. Sorry, it's been a hell of a couple days."

Wren shouted, "Julian died, and you're just now telling us?"

I looked into her face, bearing that expression which for years had brooked absolutely no back-talk.

And I stared it down.

"I've had to deal with more this week," I stated in a collected tone, "than you realize. I didn't tell you because I had to lose my mind over it before I could deal with it."

I gestured to the dustpan of glass shards.

Wren looked around, lifted her chin, and nodded with narrow eyes.

I continued, "But you know what I'm not going to do? I'm not going to take responsibility for his death. No, that was entirely on someone else. I have decided, however, to take responsibility for his justice. And that's what I'm doing now. I'm trying to help Ches's brother. I'm trying to see right by Julian. I'm trying to keep everyone alive, and find my soul at the same time. I'm doing everything I possibly can..."

My voice failed. My throat clenched.

Clement reached out and gripped my arm in support.

Edgar trotted up, as did Elle.

I forced as much resolve into my face as I could to keep the tears back, but failed.

"Hey, man," Edgar whispered. "No one's judging you. We're all just figuring it out, you know?"

The hands left me, and I ran my sleeve over my face to clear my eyes. As I looked up, I found Annarose had stood up, and the others had given her space.

She took several steps toward me, stopping in the dead center of the room.

"No," she stated. "Your moment is over."

"Huh?" I blurted.

"Fine. You had your moment of weakness. Now you have to push it aside."

Wren turned on her.

"Excuse me? Who the hell are you?"

Annarose turned to face Wren, and for an electric second, the two glared holes through one another.

"A realist," Annarose finally responded. "You are his friend, no?"

Wren cocked a hip and nodded.

"Then you know he wants to be a good man." Annarose turned to look me in the eye as she said, "But he is not a good man. He is also a realist."

Wren tossed her hands in the air and stepped away, presumably to keep herself from starting a fight she knew she couldn't win.

Annarose took another step toward me. "He is weak. We all know this. Yet he does not allow weakness to bring him low. He finds his way to the right and proper course because he is, at his core, both a bastard and a fool."

I blinked at her.

She smiled. "A bastard for thinking he deserves to win when others clearly deserve to. A fool for thinking the Universe owes him anything at all." One more step, and an outstretched hand. "And a true magician, because he makes it happen nonetheless."

I took her hand.

"I'll own that," I said. "So, who's in and who's out?"

Edgar raised his hand immediately, as did Malosi.

Clement nodded at me.

Annarose sighed, and I knew better than to assume she would be anywhere else.

I turned to Wren. “You’ll keep the kids safe?”

She leered at me. “You have to ask?”

Sarah shuffled on her feet. “Um…”

“Can you give Wren a hand? Talk some shop, maybe get her to stop slugging me in the arm?”

Sarah grinned. “You can borrow my car, if you want.”

“Thanks, but I might need you mobile.” I turned to Edgar. “So?”

“Yeah.”

“I’m going to need some supplies.”

He rolled his eyes. “Not again.”

“You still have your contact with the godawful creepy shit?”

With a sigh, he nodded.

“Guess what I need.”

Edgar muttered, “Godawful creepy shit?”

I grinned. “It’s like you know me.”

Edgar rubbed his neck. “Give me a list. I’ll make a call.”

I looked over to Clement. “Sorry, I buy local.”

Clement offered a shallow bow.

I nodded and moved for my workspace.

“Dorian?” Wren called.

“You should take the kids home, Wren. I have some evil to craft.”

CHAPTER FORTY-FIVE

T**he sun had set an hour before our two cars reached** Alexandria, and our entourage ended up finding street parking across Duke Street from the Washington Masonic Memorial. I stepped out the back of Clement's town car, slinging my backpack of materials over my shoulder as Malosi joined the two of us. I turned to spot Edgar and Annarose trotting up Dulany.

"Is that it?" Edgar asked, pointing to the Memorial.

"Underneath, apparently. We're supposed to be escorted through some super-secret entrance."

"And who made these arrangements?" Clement asked.

"Woman by the name of Wexler. At least, that's what they call her officially. I'm finding the Presidium has a fetish for *nommes de plume*."

Malosi sneered. "Magical names. Basic defense. There's power in a true name."

"Can you believe I actually had that figured out?" I quipped. "Which reminds me, for those of you in the darker practices. Our primary adversary's actual name is Clarence de Haviland. He goes by 'Brown' in the local circles and is your basic son of a bitch."

Malosi cleared his throat, and reached into his pocket to produce several gold chains draped with tiny medallions.

"I made these for each of you," he said. "A little extra sumpin-

sumpin in case these people can't hold up their end of the bargain."

He passed them out. As I took mine, Malosi's familiar energy washed over my hand... the same energy that had warded my house the days he lodged with me. I clasped the talisman around my neck, and after a brief second of focus, melded its energy into my aura. I felt stronger, more distant. Like I was sitting inside a tank.

The others followed suit, except for Annarose, who walked up to me with her talisman in an outstretched hand.

"Would you, dear?" she announced, turning and pulling her hair clear of her neck.

I reached around her throat and clasped her talisman behind her neck, saying, "Not at all."

She turned on her heel, arranged her hair, and dropped the talisman beneath her blouse.

After enduring a lecherous wag of Edgar's eyebrows, I stepped up the street toward the towering edifice across the highway. Massive spotlights bathed the bottom portion of the obelisk-styled structure in green light. The actual "tower" of the building lifted high above Alexandria in a venerable shaft of masonry.

We advanced up the main drive, nearly reaching the front when a pair of goons in suits waved us down.

"Are you our welcoming committee?" I asked.

They didn't respond, but simply gestured for us to continue with them in front and behind.

Annarose took nervous steps closer to me.

"It's going to be fine," I said. "Assuming we survive."

"Naturally," she replied.

They led us up into one of the doorways leading inside the building. As our feet clapped against the marble flooring, we took in the sight of the main chamber of the memorial. They say the cathedral builders of the Middle Ages designed the old churches to elicit a sense of awe and compel a sense of both the existence of and obedience to a higher power. That old art had not been lost on modern-day Masons. The building was majestic! Towering arches led a colonnade toward a statue of Washington, eliciting a Zeus-like sense of reverence.

The goons in suits ushered us deeper into the central chamber, the glistening and polished surfaces of marble and granite reflecting as much light as the sound of our footsteps. Before we reached the halfway point, they halted and motioned for the side. An elevator with brass doors lingered in the shadows behind a column. They opened as if waiting for us, and we filed in. Only one of our escorts joined us, pulling a key from his pocket and inserting it into the controls. The doors slid closed, and we began a descent beneath the monument.

Either the elevator was remarkably slow, or we had plunged well beneath the surface of Alexandria. When the doors finally opened, we were greeted by the Ipsissimus, himself.

"Welcome to the Sedem Regni," he announced.

Before I could introduce anyone, or really respond at all, he turned and clacked down the hallway on his braces.

"I have prepared some ritual garments for you, myself."

We followed Adrastos down a terrazzo-clad hallway and into a vestibule. An array of white robes with gold-threaded embroidery hung on hooks along one wall. I could feel the charms on them from across the room.

"What are they carrying?" I asked.

"Obfuscation charms, primarily. There will be upward of a hundred members gathering here tomorrow morning. A sea of faces, but one can't be too careful."

Annarose loomed behind me, her energy hot and prickly.

I turned to her and gave her a reassuring nod.

Clement stepped forward, and with a graceful gesture bowed to Adrastos.

"Ipsissimus, allow me to introduce myself. My name is—"

"Jean Clement, lately of New York City, originally of Lyons, France. A purveyor of illicit items restricted for use and sale by this organization." Adrastos peered over his glasses. "There's no one inside this building I haven't studied."

Clement stiffened, and stepped back to regain his dignity.

I said, "And yet, the L'Enfantines have prospered underneath your nose."

Adrastos swished his mouth left, then right, and smiled. "True enough. In a way, I prefer the company of those who despise me." He navigated around me, standing fully before Annarose. "I trust their motivations above those of my own allies. Even if they are murderous."

Annarose didn't respond.

"I know you intend my destruction, Miss Rodolfi. And I do not begrudge you this desire. But you should know, I'll never allow it to happen."

"We shall see," she stated.

"I suppose we shall." Adrastos moved on to Malosi, gave him a once-over, then nodded in satisfaction. "You have a natural ability with wardings, Mister Malosi. Your loyalties to Clement notwithstanding, you could prove to be a useful member of our organization."

Malosi stood rigid, but the corner of his mouth lifted ever so slightly.

Finally, Adrastos stepped up to Edgar. His face eased as he looked Edgar over, and he hung his right brace onto his left arm and extended his hand.

Edgar looked over to me for direction.

I simply shrugged.

Edgar shook Adrastos's hand.

"I knew your father, Mister Swain," Adrastos said. "I was proud to count him among my friends."

Edgar's eyes went wide. "Huh?"

"He wouldn't have spoken of me. There was a time during the Reagan administration when our organization had developed something of a combative relationship with the White House. It was a unique moment in time, and under the Ipsissimus at the time, I found myself in the company of several independents."

"Right on," Edgar replied.

Adrastos continued his progress for the robes. "These should prevent anyone not specifically attempting to identify you from doing so. I'll ask that you remain in the wings as the congregants arrive. I can't foresee what the L'Enfantines intend to do tomorrow. I expect there will be violence."

"We're ready," I replied, with a pat on my backpack.

Adrastos squinted over his glasses. "I can see that. Take care with your devilish little workings, Lake. We've given you latitudes, but I'd hate to see any collateral damage in my Sedem."

"I don't think you'll have to worry about that."

He nodded, then clacked off through a door hidden in the paneling on the far end of the vestibule. I suspected there were countless such doors in this building.

Edgar walked up and took one of the robes off the hook. "Where are the 'wings,' do you think?"

"I guess we'll know when we see it," I answered.

Edgar slipped the robe on, wrapping it around his body, searching the front until he found the eye hooks. When he had fastened it, he held out his arms, the gold embroidery glistening in the light from fixtures tucked in coves near the ceiling.

"How do I look? Presidium-worthy?"

I looked into his face. It was... Edgar's face.

Malosi grunted, "Some glammer."

Clement shook his head. "We know who he is, and we know what we're looking for. It may be the best charm he could craft with the power base so eroded."

"If that's the case," I said, "then we're going to have to do the heavy lifting, I think."

I shuffled the bag off my shoulders and inspected the contents as the others grabbed their robes. The bag wasn't heavy, but it was filled with all kinds of Hell. Tiny leathery balls with dark script on their surface etched in my own blood. Sharp needles protruded from the seams of the sachets, each containing the finger bone of an unearthed corpse. I wasn't sure where Edgar had sourced these materials, but it was someone he wasn't a fan of.

As will all curses, the real power of these vicious little bastards came from a combination of my own hatred, and the invocation of an ancient, Cosmic evil. Its name was inscribed in Persian along the insides of the needle balls. I lifted one of the balls into the light, inspecting my handiwork.

Annarose knelt down beside me. "A lot of effort for a tiny curse."

"It's contained. Focused. Targeted."

"Are you saying my magic is untidy?"

I smirked at Annarose. "You could say that."

She leaned closer and whispered, "How are we going to touch Adrastos? He knows we intend him harm."

"Knowing a thing and stopping a thing are very different. He's weak. The whole Presidium is weak. We'll find a way. When the shit hits the hermetic fan, we'll find our moment."

Clement watched us from across the room, his eyes narrow.

Annarose offered a hand and helped me to my feet, as Edgar brought me my robe.

"Time to get official," he quipped.

I dropped the curse ball into my bag and zipped it up, hanging it backward across my chest. Malosi secured the latches across my back, and I stood with my papoose from Hell.

I took the robe and slid my arms into the sleeves. It fell loose over the bag as I had hoped it would. As I hooked the eyelets over the bag, I tested Adrastos's charms. I couldn't see the glammer on my compatriots' faces, but I could certainly feel the charm as it laced a cocoon around me. I reached out to palpate the energy in the room, but found it muffled, like I was underwater.

"This will make it more difficult to sense," I muttered.

Malosi nodded. "You noticed that, too?"

"We'll just have to use our eyes and ears."

I led the way back into the terrazzo hall, and continued away from the elevator. The side wall opened into a trefoil Gothic arch. Light spilled from the arch as if reflected off water. I took a breath, then stepped through the arch.

What greeted my eyes knocked the breath back out of my chest.

It wasn't water that was reflecting the candlelight. It was gold.

Everywhere, gold.

A cavernous, hexagonal space opened up above us, lined with the trefoil arches along the perimeter, gilded masonry lining the walls as they gathered into graceful seams along the ceiling. Enormous chandeliers flickered with candlelight, washing up and around the ceiling, sending the entire room into a dizzying radiance.

Varying alloys of gold punctuated the masonry, creating wide lines along the walls and ceiling, connecting in the vertices of an enormous glyph.

I sucked in a breath and reached out for anything or anyone to help hold me up. Lacking that, I simply marveled at the ceiling.

"Am I seeing this?" I whispered.

"The Zauberstein Key," Clement answered.

I craned my neck high, mouth agape. "I'm guessing it's not just a myth, then?"

Annarose shook her head. "What is this key?"

I explained, "One of the alchemical keys of creation. Said to create substance from light. Matter from energy, in a nutshell. Real next-level quantum physics magic."

Malosi grumbled, "Sounds like a lot of horseshit to me."

"I'm inclined to agree with you," I answered. "But the Presidium certainly seems to think it was worth investing a lot of gold into." I looked into the eyes of those gathered around me. "Watch your energy, folks. I don't know what this key actually does. Could amplify, could transmute. Things may get... weird."

Annarose folded the side of her mouth into an unimpressed smirk and moved on.

We explored the space. An enormous series of inlaid granite and marble stones outlined a hexagram inscribed and circumscribed, providing what I concluded was the ritual space for the Presidium. At the center, an enormous gilded pyramid rose to point to one of the cardinal directions, with the Eye of Providence staring up to the center of the vaulted ceiling. It was highly stylized, far more elegant than the dollar bill. Indeed, there was an Egyptian quality to it. A Sun God Ra effect, poised atop a pyramid, centered in the classic hexagram of the Star of David. The Qabalistic elements laced together in a tremendous "fuck you" to the Nombre D'or. I imagined for the L'Enfantines, circling in this space every month would stoke a slow burn for revolution.

I stepped onto the ritual circle, reading some of the languages carved along the surface of the stones. Aramaic, Greek, Latin, Hieratic... a panoply of magical scripts and dead languages. I took in the entire space, light wavering around me, the vault of the ceiling soaring above my head. Reality felt thin, here. I could understand the allure of such a powerful space. And I figured, as smart as Adrastos was, having me here was another opportunity to lure me into his fold.

He wasn't malicious, per se. Indeed, he believed in his mission, perhaps to a fault. Certainly to the exclusion of empathy. But I couldn't feel antipathy against him.

But that really didn't matter. I'd made a deal with Annarose. Her assistance in taking out Zeno and Brown, in exchange for my assistance in taking out Adrastos. It was my payment to Annarose, an unholy oath. I couldn't violate it, especially now that she had already made good on Zeno's life.

And she was correct... Adrastos saw right through us both. He had to have divined somehow that we intended to take him out before the end of this confrontation. So, too, had Clement by the look he had given the two of us in the vestibule.

That was just one more variable, and admittedly a minor one in comparison with taking out the L'Enfantines.

I realized as I pulled myself out of the reverie in that ritual space that I hadn't planned to survive this. I had no sense of making good on my deal with Annarose. Some instinct deep inside me recognized that the events of the next morning would render that agreement void. Which meant one or both of us would be dead.

I smirked as I thought of Felix Parrish. He'd be sorely disappointed if I died now. With my soul in someone else's possession, my death would dissociate my body from that soul. It would become the property of whoever had their hands on it. I could only hope they were, to some degree, less wicked than Parrish.

A series of cushioned benches lined intermittent spaces between the trefoil arches, creating a kind of gallery around the space.

Malosi pointed them out, and said, "I'm thinking those are the wings."

"All the Presidium's a stage," I said. "And we poor bastards are merely players."

Clement suggested, "Perhaps we should separate, and not present a single group to arouse suspicion?"

"Sounds good to me," I said.

Clement held out an arm to Annarose. "Miss Rodolfi?"

She looked to me, gave me a slight tip of her chin, then strode off arm-in-arm with Clement.

He'd separated us. Clever.

Malosi turned without saying a word and crossed the space to sit alone in a separate gallery.

Which left Edgar and myself. We took the closest alcove, sitting near the back.

Edgar reached down and felt the red velvet cushion. "Nice."

"So, what do you think? The hermetic life for you?"

"I gotta admit, man. This is a hell of a Lodge!"

"Eh, not bad. Bet it's a bitch to heat in the winter."

Edgar smiled.

"You got everything set with Wren?"

"Hmm?"

"Your affairs."

He turned to me. "What, you mean like my will and stuff?"

"Edgar, you know we might not survive this." I shifted to face him fully. "You know that, right?"

He waved me off. "Eh. We'll be okay."

"How the hell can you be so relaxed? I'm only asking because this whole thing was my problem, and I'm freaking out."

"Do you believe in God?" he asked.

My face pinched. "What?"

"God. You know, big combat boot in the sky?"

"You're not seriously asking me that question."

"Why not?" he pushed. "I'm asking you if you believe in God. It can't be a hard question to answer."

"Well, I mean, no. Not like you mean."

"How do you know what I mean? What's God mean to you?"

I shook my head. "A missing variable in the Cosmic Equation. I mean, I believe in the Dark Choir. I've seen evidence. But there's no evidence that the equal, balancing force for the Dark Choir actually exists. It's like, if there is a force of good out there, then it's really phoning this in."

Edgar nodded, and looked back at the center of the Sedem.

"What about you?" I asked.

"Nah. Pretty much an atheist."

I chuckled. "You fucker. You brought it up, and you didn't have a point to it?"

"What?"

"You're supposed to give me the pep talk, here. Tell me there's some reason you believe there's a God. Tell me it's in control of things, and that I'm not a completely lost cause."

He swiveled his head, and reached up to rub his chin.

"Are you dead yet?"

"Clearly not."

"Well, there you go."

"Thanks."

He snickered. "Hey, for you, that's saying a lot."

I nodded.

After a space of silence, I said, "I'm worried about Elle."

He replied, "Me, too."

"This empathic divination gift coming out of nowhere? Looks like she can't control it."

"Wren's talking to some people online, getting a plan."

"Think it came from what happened last year? Maybe she picked up something from the servitor? Or perhaps it left some kind of wound in her own soul, and this new sensing ability is some kind of psychic scar tissue?"

Edgar made a dubious sneer. "Maybe."

"If we make it out of this alive, I'll look into it."

We sat together in silence. An odd calm fell over me as I sat next to Edgar. I felt as if we would be fine. And even if we wouldn't, we had said our last words.

Chapter Forty-Six

Time passed in a strange fashion inside the Sedem. What felt like minutes could have been hours, and vice versa. I was certain it was a combination of nerves, the complete lack of windows, and the energy pouring up from the geomantic node beneath us. After a while, footsteps echoed from the side passage, and the first of the congregants arrived. They wore the same robes as we, and moved directly for the gallery Malosi had occupied. These new arrivals weren't impressed by the vaulted space of gold. It was just another day for them.

More arrived, and then more, filing in by ones and twos. After another hour, a low murmur began to echo through the space as hushed conversations folded onto one another. I stood up to stretch my legs, and Edgar sucked in a breath, snapping awake from a quiet nap.

"What's up?" he mumbled.

"Just getting numb," I answered.

I looked across the way to find Clement had moved away from Annarose and had engaged someone in conversation. My stomach knotted for a moment. We weren't supposed to engage. It could jeopardize the glammer. Still, if anyone among our party were to chat up casual Presidium members, it might as well have been Clement.

I checked on Malosi. He remained in his seat, stiff and stony. I was going to have to find a way to break through to him again, should we walk out of here.

Edgar whispered, "Got a lot of people now."

"Less than a quarter of what they're expecting," I replied.

A group of four newcomers arrived, and moved for our gallery. I suddenly worried that these were like season ticket seats, and wondered what would happen if we ran into the people who usually sat here.

The white-robed congregants stepped up into our gallery. Two of them looked up at Edgar and me briefly, nodded, then took seats. I didn't recognize them. More to the point, they didn't recognize us. I had no way of telling whether Adrastos's glammer was functioning correctly, but for the moment, I was satisfied.

As more and more arrivals increased the volume of the echoing murmurs, Edgar and I straightened in our benches and kept our eyes open. Brown would be arriving at some point. I felt my odds of survival hinged on spotting him early and keeping him in my sight. But the robes made everyone appear homogenous, as if we were all affected by some kind of glammer. It was the basic charm of crowds.

A bell sounded at a point, and a new flood of congregants arrived. These wore red robes with the same gold embroidery. The gold stitching stood out in sharper contrast against the crimson, and I identified the Eye of Providence in the design. The red-robed congregants did not approach the galleries. Instead, they took their position along the outside ring of the floor's hexagram. Conversations hushed as they filed in one-by-one, and I realized the conclave was about to start.

And I hadn't spotted Brown yet.

I leaned in to Edgar and whispered, "This must be the Third Circle. The Second Circle will be next on the inner ring."

Soon, a line of black-robed members arrived, slipping between each of the outer ring members to take positions upon the inner ring.

I grimaced as it occurred to me that Brown was likely a member of the first two circles. I wouldn't be close enough to reach him before he made his move.

As the last of the black robes took their positions, the entire space fell silent, save for the occasional cough and sniffle echoing against the gilded bricks.

A door opened somewhere, its latch sounding like a rifle shot, the hinges groaning in histrionic cacophony.

I clenched my fist, trying to scan the faces along the inner circles as Adrastos hobbled out onto the granite floor.

A hand tapped my arm, and I nearly jumped out of my skin.

I turned to the congregant sitting beside me on the bench, and found a woman discretely passing me a folded slip of paper.

I took the paper cautiously, unfolding it to find the words: *OUTER CIRCLE, NNW.*

My eyes lifted to the crimson robes. I took the pyramid to be my compass rose pointing to north and ticked through three Presidium members until I spotted him.

Brown.

Clarence de Haviland, standing in a red robe, his face no longer obscured by the charm which had been concealing him.

I turned to the woman beside me, and sucked in a sharp breath.

She held up a finger to her lips, urging quiet.

And as Madelyn Sullivan returned her attention to the ceremony before us, I regretted not making that dinner party after all.

I passed the paper to Edgar, who seemed to follow it as easily as I had.

Adrastos reached his position on the Eye of Providence, not precisely centered in the circle. Indeed, he was closer to Brown than I would have liked.

"Haire, Abraxas!" Adrastos bellowed.

The entire gathering chanted, "Haire."

Adrastos continued, "We are, and have been, and shall have been the ascetic and liberated brethren of the Presidium. Guardians of the Nova Regna Potentum. The Keepers of the Basilean Flame. To the West, from the East, as the North and the South bear witness, we call the Ancient Rite. So it shall be."

"Haire," the gathering answered.

One each of the red and black robes withdrew to gather censers. A finger full of incense fell into the swinging braziers, and white smoke began to lift. The red robed censer walked deosil around the perimeter of the Outer Circle while the black robe walked widdershins within the Inner Circle. Clockwork hermeticism.

When they had completed their circles, they returned the braziers and took their positions once again.

Adrastos lifted a free hand and declared, "We exist in a place beyond all places, in a time beyond all time, in the company of the Theurge and Demiurge, in the eyes of Sophia and the Aeons of Creation."

His posture fell, and he collected his brace and stepped to the center of the circle.

"We have business, brothers and sisters. As is likely no revelation to any of you, thanks to a regrettable sense of indiscretion among our gathering, we are under attack from an opposing philosophy. The ultimate conclusion to which I have arrived, is that this opposition comes not from without our organization, but from within."

A few gasps rippled through the crowd, likely from those out of the loop.

"As you may have noticed, our numbers today are thin. Our power, diminished. This is due to the loss of our situational nodes surrounding us. They have been despoiled, punctured, reversed by these splitters who would have us abdicate two centuries of continuous tradition. All in the name of a bygone school of thinking."

I watched the faces of the gallery surrounding me. There were many brows lifted in alarm, a few faces set and angry, and even one or two pulled back in disbelieving confusion.

Adrastos clacked in a circle, eyeballing the Inner Circle. "It is to our shame that we have allowed this poison to infiltrate our brotherhood. And as such, we shall see the end of the Presidium as we know it. Yes, brothers and sisters, the Presidium will die today."

The gasps that had rippled the chamber now positively flooded it.

He shouted over the din, "And it should die! For it has always held a canker, a mislead sentiment, a reliance on the Old World. The *Ancien Régime*," he added in a passable French accent, "has fallen to our New Kingdom."

A voice shouted from one of the galleries. I couldn't make it out, but the words sounded profane. A clutch of white robes stood to their feet around him, and an altercation proceeded.

The white robes surrounding us rose to their feet to catch a glimpse of the fists being thrown.

Adrastos's voice called out, "Our first Ipsissimus saw to the end of the Monarchy. He carried our first doctrine of democracy to the shores of Europe, and we saw it take hold. Our power was truth. Our truth, power!"

I spotted a congregant sitting in front of Edgar balling a fist. His lips pulled back into a snarl.

I nudged Edgar and nodded to the snarling man in front of him.

Edgar glanced down and gave me a wink.

Adrastos shouted above the increasing commotion, "The misguided blasphemies of that madman, Pierre L'Enfant, perished with his diseased mind. And good riddance!"

At that final provocation, the snarling man reached into his robe and pulled out a silver blade.

Before he could jump forward, I reached for his right arm, gripping it tight.

Edgar slipped one arm beneath his, and another around his neck, pushing against his chair with his legs. The man flailed with his only free hand, but found no purchase. I beat his hand against the chair in front of me, knocking his blade loose.

The man's eyes fluttered, and he collapsed into his chair.

Edgar released his neck and exhaled.

"Where did you learn to do that?" I asked.

"I wrestled in high school, man. It's like you don't even know me!"

I reached down to collect the blade, but Madelyn Sullivan snatched it from the floor before I could reach it.

"Better keep this safe," she said, dulling it against the wall behind us before snapping the blade in half in the space between her bench and the side masonry.

I nodded to her, confident she was on our side.

A scream filled the circle space, and between the swaying heads in front of me, I watched one of the red robed congregants fall to the ground, clutching her chest. The air adopted a sizzling energy of death.

A curse!

I'd never felt a curse literally whiff through space like that. The energy was palpable, almost visible.

The galleries began to empty into the ritual space as shouting and swearing roared into my ears.

Adrastos had done an efficient job of goading the L'Enfantines into violence.

I took a step down, and Mrs. Sullivan stopped me.

"For Julian," she said, eyes hard.

I nodded. "For Julian."

Edgar and I slipped into the crowd, dodging fists as rage-faced congregants began to lash out one against another.

Energy crackled around me, and the medallion slung beneath my neck warmed. Someone had thrown an offensive energy against me, but Malosi's warding seemed to have shrugged it off. It was probably a glancing curse, aimed either for someone else or not aimed at all.

I turned to find a sneering white robe turning away from me. I balled a fist and followed, urged by the increasing violence and rage in the crowd. When I caught up with him, I grabbed his shoulder and spun him around.

A blade slashed in the air just below my nose, and I staggered backward, tripping on my own robe. I fell against the hard floor, my injured ribs slicing pain through my chest.

He stood over me, blade flipping in his hand. He held it up to his face, and prepared to bring it down.

I reached into my robe and pulled out one of my curse balls.

"Don't!" I shouted.

He flinched, then dropped his weight to plunge the knife into my neck.

With a flick of my wrist, I tossed the ball into his chest.

The needles penetrated his robe with ease, digging into the vitae beneath. The engine of the curse.

I had to roll to avoid the blade, and as I did, my attacker sputtered. He staggered to his knees, the flopped onto his belly. A menacing crackle of energy shot across my arms as my curse fired. He convulsed, back arching as the effect of the curse proved to be both immediate and violent.

A shadow passed over my eyes.

My second curse, ever. It shouldn't have been that thorough. I didn't craft these to be death curses. They were meant to defeat, vanquish... whatever. But the corpse at my feet paid testimony to the unexpected nature of Netherwork.

Or, there was another explanation. My eyes lifted to the Zauberstein Key above us. Amplification and manifestation. Intent became reality.

A foot slammed into my side, directly into my cracked ribs, and another white-robe fell over me. I yelped, then pulled up my hands to defend myself. The woman who had tripped over me watched in alarm, hands raised in apology.

I nodded her away.

The lunacy in the Sedem approached a dizzying timbre. I had to find Brown quickly, before he killed Adrastos.

I spotted Edgar bowling into someone in a red robe. They dropped a curved ritual blade, sending it sliding underneath too many people to re-collect it. Edgar rammed his shoulder into his victim a few more times, and I left him to his scuffle.

Reaching into my robe, I readied another curse ball, then made my way toward the ritual circles.

Two faces turned to me, and I felt the glammer on my robe flicker as they stared me down. One of the two barked, "It's him!"

They lunged toward me, blades drawn.

I hurled one of the curse balls. It barely nicked my attacker's collarbone, but it was enough. Hateful energy erupted between us, and he fell in a gurgling heap, back arched.

The second paused, gauged our distance, then rushed me anew.

I braced for impact, keeping an eye on his blade.

A meaty fist slammed into his face, knocking him unconscious.

I spied Malosi as he looked me over.

"Still warded?" he asked.

"Yeah. It's locked in tight."

He nodded. "Follow me."

Malosi leaned his shoulder down and rushed through the onlookers. A slice of angry energy flew across Malosi's shielding, bouncing to those nearby. They held their heads and shrieked. Probably a fear charm, or worse.

We finally burst through a line of onlookers, and directly into what they were watching.

Three blade-wielding L'Enfantines had torn off their robes and were cutting their own arms, spilling blood over the seal on the floor. Two more held the others off with tiny, leathery spheres swinging from chains. I winced as I realized they were, in fact, shrunken heads, imbued with a powerful counter-magic.

Malosi moved to step forward, but the first of the counter-magic guards aimed the shrunken head at Malosi. He grunted, reaching up for his neck.

My own medallion blazed with absorbed energy. These fetishes were hammering the wardings Malosi had crafted. Much more of this, and we'd end up without protections, and probably a nice scorch mark on our chests.

The onlookers nearby moaned in unison, many grabbing their stomachs, others passing out entirely.

The fetish counter-magic abated, and I watched as the first of the guards vomited all over the front of his robe.

Onlookers rushed away, not from the vomit, but from the figure plodding forward behind the back guard.

Annarose had removed her robe. She chanted with her palms held up, throwing a wide swath of unfocused energy in front of her. More people got sick, including all of the arm-cutters. Vomit mixed with blood across the floor, and in a moment, their working was ruined.

Annarose curled her fingers and shouted something in Italian, summoning dark Stregheria into being through the power of the Zauberstein Key above us. She strode with intent, hair alive with energy, like one of the Furies dragging Hell in her wake.

All of the L'Enfantines over the ritual circle dropped to their knees.

Malosi's warding managed to brook the majority of Annarose's indiscriminant curse, though enough leeched through for me to feel fingers of disease slip into my chest.

White robes scattered as Annarose reached the circle. Her face pulled back into a visage of rage, fingers outstretched, curling for the first of the fetish guards.

A black-robed man crept behind her, blade raised.

I reached into my robe for a curse ball, but fumbled as needles pricked my fingers. This wasn't the moment to work out the hermetic details of mingling my own blood with the target of the curse.

The man lifted his blade over his head, and sputtered as a foot landed in his ribs.

Clement swung another foot, hooking it up against his arm. The blade dropped with a clatter.

Before the man could react, Clement slammed a flat hand against the side of his head, and swept his feet from underneath him.

I stood staring as Clement dusted off his hands.

"You gotta be shitting me!" I shouted.

Clement straightened his robe. "Six years in the *Escouade de contre-terrorisme*," he declared. "One learns a thing or two."

Annarose spun around, claws outstretched.

Clement held up his hands, and fortunately Annarose caught herself before she laid into him with her magic.

She caught her breath, and nodded him past.

Malosi, Clement, and I joined her in the center of the circle. Most of the surrounding congregants had fled Annarose, and the only ones remaining were tending to those writhing on the ground, puking up their own guts, or paralyzed with fear.

I turned a slow circle, scanning the space for Edgar. Many of the white-robes were flooding for the exits, but among them I couldn't spot Edgar.

"What were they doing?" Malosi asked as he glanced down at the remains of the L'Enfantine bloodletting.

"Probably trying to unseat the node," I suggested. "Anyone seen Edgar?"

Everyone shook their heads.

As sound and commotion waned, and more people fled into the side halls, a knot formed in my stomach.

Where was Adrastos?

Or for that matter, where was Brown?

A whistle rang from the northern-most end of the Sedem.

We all turned to find Edgar waving us forward.

"That guy with the glasses went through here!" he shouted.

CHAPTER FORTY-SEVEN

W**e rushed for the end of the Sedem. A partition** wall slipped into view, its masonry set against the far wall in such a masterful way that it faded away from view from any appreciable distance. Behind the partition stood a towering oak door, inscribed with the Eye of Providence.

"Through here?" I repeated.

Edgar nodded.

I stepped up to the door, and reached out to sense its energy. It felt completely dull.

But when I reached for the latch, a sharp snap arced into my hand, and Malosi's medallion burned my skin.

"Shit," I coughed, tugging at the eyes and hooks along the front of my robe. I shrugged it off, and immediately a tempest of energy pile-drove my brain. I staggered for a second, reaching for the wall to support myself. Adrastos's charms did more than just obscure us. They shielded us from the immense energy pouring through the Sedem.

Annarose snickered. "You are a fragile man."

I pushed myself upright, and considered the door. It was positively glowing with a spiny shielding energy.

"Any suggestions?" I wheezed.

Edgar stepped up, squinting at the door. "Yeah."

"Okay?"

He reached into his pocket, and pulled out a pocket knife. With several quick stabs into the wood, he began to chisel a glyph into the oak. As it took shape, I cocked my head.

As did the rest.

When he finished, Edgar stepped back and snapped his pocket knife closed.

"That should do it."

"The hell?" I muttered.

Edgar reached for the door, flipped the latch with his thumb, and pulled it open unmolested.

"There's no way that actually works," Clement whispered in my ear.

I shook my head at the smiley face Edgar had carved into the door.

"Remind me to tell you about his yarn," I responded as I moved for the door.

Edgar said, "Have a nice day," as we passed him into the back rooms of the Sedem Regni.

The back halls were nowhere near as labyrinthine as I had imagined them. To the contrary, a single hall clad in cedar panels led to a series of offices. I noted a separate elevator at the end of this hall. The Ipsissimus Express Elevator, I concluded.

I took point as we stepped past doors, pausing to check for ambush. We met with no resistance.

Malosi tapped my shoulder and pointed to the second-to-last door on the left, where shadows of moving people slipped beneath the undercut of the door.

I reached into my bag to produce the last two Persian curse balls.

Clement cracked his knuckles, and nodded to Malosi.

I stood aside as Malosi inched toward the door. He held up a fist, then extended three fingers as we formed a line along the wall.

Two fingers.

One finger.

Then Malosi turned the knob and threw his shoulder into the door.

A deafening clap hammered the air, and Malosi grunted, staggering backward until he hit the wall opposite the door.

His eyes widened, and his hand reached for his stomach. A pool of red seeped into his shirt.

"Reed?" I shouted.

"You should collect him," a voice called from inside the room.

I pulled my hands behind my back, concealing my weapons, and stepped into the doorway.

Brown stood with a pistol in his hand, lifting it as I made my appearance.

His face was cold, emotionless.

"Oh, there you are," he said. "I was wondering if you'd lost your nerve."

I looked past Brown to find Adrastos leaning in the corner, rubbing his ear.

"Clarence," I growled. "A gun? Really?"

He waved his weapon at the door. "Your companions have this one opportunity to save his life. They may withdraw uninjured and make it to the emergency room up the highway. If there isn't too much of a gridlock of panicked idiots congesting the elevator, that is."

"Jean? Edgar? Get Reed topside."

Brown squinted. "The witch, too."

I swiveled the needle balls in my hands.

"You too, Annarose."

I kept my eyes on Brown and his weapon as a series of grunts and scuffling filled the hallway behind me.

"Dorian?" Edgar muttered.

"Get home to your kids, Edgar."

Brown nodded. "You do that, Swain."

I clenched my jaw, but held my tongue.

"Come," Clement ordered.

Malosi sucked in breaths, and the panting and shuffling in the hallway quickly faded into the distance.

Brown lowered his gun. "There. Was that so difficult?"

"You can't win, Clarence," I stated. "You failed to destroy the Marshall node. You failed to dismantle the Sedem circle. Even if you kill Adrastos, the entire Presidium knows about the L'Enfantines now."

Brown turned to Adrastos with a snicker. "Yes, thanks to Joe's convincingly melodramatic performance."

I gave Adrastos a careful glance.

He lingered just behind Brown, removing his glasses to wipe them with a handkerchief.

Adrastos said, "It was a bit of sensationalist theater, I'm afraid. But it served its purpose."

"What purpose?" I hissed.

"Why," Adrastos replied, "outing the L'Enfantines, of course. Turning popular opinion against them, exposing the conspiracy that ran so deep the Presidium could never trust its own members again."

I nodded. "Seems the conspiracy ran all the way to the top."

Adrastos shrugged. "If the seat of power conspires against the destructive elements against its own organization, can it be called a conspiracy at all? Or a ruse to root out the weakness?"

I looked to Brown. "The two of you just hamstrung the Presidium. You must realize that?"

Brown crossed his arms at his waist, gun still in hand. "What we've done is to bury a weak and festering corpse. The Presidium had grown fatuous and self-indulgent, content with its personal fantasies of power and political puppeteering. Meanwhile, the rest of the world laughs at us. Even the cabals on the West Coast openly defy us. It was time for change."

I asked, "Are you two even L'Enfantines?"

Adrastos scowled. "Oh, Good Lord no. They do exist, mind you. But they were never more than a ridiculous seed of loyalists, easily swayed, easily provoked. A necessary scapegoat." Adrastos replaced his glasses. "I'll be happy to continue discussing our vision for the future, if you'll drop that curse you have clutched behind your back?"

I took in a long breath, then pulled my hands to my sides, cupping the sphere in my left hand while tossing the one in my right onto the ground.

"I thank you," Adrastos cooed. "Polite discourse is so difficult with a proverbial gun held at one's face."

I nodded to Brown. "I know the feeling."

"You'll note Mister de Haviland is not aiming his weapon at you. You may also note your continued survival, despite being thoroughly outmaneuvered and strategized. And that fact is owing to our observation of your character, Mister Lake."

"That so? Then, please..." I waved with my right hand. "Enlighten me."

Brown chuckled. "I told you he'd be resistant."

Adrastos lifted a hand to Brown. "Steady on, Clarence. His sarcastic bluster is a veneer he's constructed to avoid betraying his own doubt. And you do doubt, don't you? You're ready to execute me, on behalf of the Stregha. But only after I've saved your student's family. And therein lies my evaluation of your character, Mister Lake. You aren't swayed by tradition. Certainly not by reason. You are slow to grant loyalty, but require it of those with whom you surround yourself. Do you know what that makes you, Mister Lake?"

I pursed my lips.

Brown answered, "A leader."

"Correct. You have the capacity for greatness, Mister Lake. I've tried again and again to tempt you into the fold, but you've resisted. Because deep in your brain you believe that you are a more capable leader than I am. And I respect that. I've counted on that. And I intend to rely on this quality, such as it is, in the coming years as we rebuild the Presidium into something the Founders would have admired."

"A junta?" I spat.

Brown shook his head. "The last hope we have against... oh, what the hell do you call them? The Dark Choir?"

"How messianic of you," I snarled.

"Oh, don't rant," Brown chided. "You know there are portentous wheels in motion."

Adrastos continued Brown's line of thinking, "Ever since 9/11, a growing strength has emerged in the Middle East. Ancient Persia and Babylon. The old systems of Central Asian mysticism have grown turbulent, and potent. Those that dwelled before time are preparing a shift in the human race, Mister Lake. A shift that may lead to our erasure."

"Extinction," Brown added.

Adrastos prodded as he took a halting step forward. "You can decide to indulge in your wounded pride. Your anger. Or, you can live up to your potential, harness these capable practitioners who appear to pledge themselves to your service, and allow reason to govern your next few words. Because I'm going to ask you to choose these words carefully. What say you? Would you join us?"

I glared at the two of them.

"Well, gentlemen," I stated, straightening my posture. "This was one doozy of a presentation. And you know what? I would have been way more receptive to this pitch three weeks ago. You know, before someone had a Congressman unzip his fly in front of my tavern. Before my student was made into a pawn to manipulate me. Before one of my best friends had his heart squeezed to death by a demon. So, yeah. I would have loved to help you in this quest to save the human race, but right now... I have to choose my words carefully. Hmm. Okay. I think I'm ready. Only need two words, too."

Brown sighed. "Don't do this, Lake."

"Fuck. You."

I flipped my left hand up to my chest and hurled my second curse ball at Brown's torso.

He lifted his right arm, and the ball connected. Its needles slipped effortlessly through the folds of his sleeve.

Brown lowered his arm slowly, eyes twisted in confusion.

He sucked in a breath, then released it.

The dark energy slid up and down my arms, and just as it snapped into visions of death and hatred across my eyes, Brown shook his sleeve and allowed the ball to drop onto the floor.

The energy dissipated.

Brown gave me a cold look.

"What was that?" he grumbled.

I looked down onto the floor. Both of the curse balls sat side-by-side. With one more look, I poised to reach down and grab one again.

The sound of Brown's gun cocking held my action.

Brown crouched down, gun aimed at my chest, and snatched one of the balls.

"Take him," he called out.

The walls surrounding me slid back, forming pockets of darkness. Men in suits rushed into the room from the hidden doorways. Seemed I was correct in the assumption that this entire complex was littered with those damned things.

Two goons slammed into my sides, pushing air from my chest as they gripped my arms.

Brown spun the leather ball in his hand, squinting at the script.

"Leviaton? In Persian? Interesting choice."

Adrastos hopped up next to Brown, and rested one of his braces on his right hand as he took the sphere in his left. "Naturally. Immediate effect. Made it a suitable weapon in a brush fight such as this."

Brown shrugged. "A bit clumsy, invoking Leviaton for a faction skirmish, don't you think?"

"Well, he was concerned for the well-being of his friends."

"Hmm, yes."

I caught my breath and looked up at the two of them. "You're a pair of bastards!"

They ignored me entirely. Brown tossed the ball back onto the ground and shook the remaining curse energy off his hands.

"Take him to the back entrance after you shoot him," Brown ordered. "Have the cleaners dump him in the Bay. I'm sure he'd find that poetic, somehow."

The goons lifted me off the ground and spun me around.

Then they dropped me. Wholly dropped me. My body hit the floor, followed quickly by theirs.

Malosi's medallion hummed and burned against my skin once again, and that familiar sickness twisted into my guts. The room filled with moaning, and one of the suited thugs began to retch.

And I smiled. I knew this curse.

Annarose stepped into the room, hands held out at her sides, lips pulled back into a feral snarl.

She didn't leave me, after all.

I clawed my way along the floor until I had escaped the cone of her will. I caught my breath, and rolled onto my feet.

Brown and Adrastos stood stiff, eyes hard, jaws set.

Annarose growled, "You men shall die for this!"

Brown lifted his gun at Annarose.

The moments when time seemed to stand still were, in my understanding, simply artifacts of the illusion of consciousness. Many have argued that Time itself was only a biochemical means for our organic brains to interpret a greater reality than our gray matter can fully comprehend. And in such times, when our bodies and minds meld with the speed of thought, and we take action that proves, ultimately, to be a deciding factor in our own mortality, we humans experience the phenomenon of our lives "flashing before our eyes." Well, such is the cliché, at any rate.

I didn't experience this as I jumped into the space between Brown and Annarose. Even as his gun roared, the barrel flashed, and a bullet chirped into my flesh, I didn't see so much as a single slide from my childhood. Not one birthday party. Not one late night cram session on Aramaic with Emil in our flat in London.

No, all I felt was pain.

And anger.

Happily, these moments allow us a brief flash of clarity. And as what felt like the weight of an NFL linebacker slammed into my shoulder, spinning me in the air, I managed to trigger the Cesare ring on my finger and slap it against Brown's gun hand. It was, as it turned out, a decent slap, as the gun shot down onto the floor.

I landed against the near wall, electric pain slashing through my arm and shoulder.

And the moment ended. I drew in breath, hissing against the pain.

Annarose shrieked, a banshee call that made my guts quiver.

She rushed Brown, claws outstretched. She managed to dig a nail or two into his neck before he hammered her arms with his, dropping her to her knees before him.

She began to chant, and the energy in the room took an apocalyptic caste... but Brown halted her working by reaching down and gripping a handful of her coal-black ringlets and jerking her head up.

Annarose gagged and coughed, then snarled. She lost all sense of humanity, writhing like an animal taken in a bloodlust.

Adrastos shouted, "Enough!"

He shoved Brown with his left arm as he steadied himself with his right arm brace.

"I tire of this drama. The two of them. Now."

Brown reached for the ground and retrieved his gun.

When he stood up and cocked his gun, he aimed it first at me.

And that was his mistake.

In those three seconds it took for him to fetch his gun from the floor, I produced something else from my backpack. Something I had prepared the night before in my workspace, with the macabre materials Edgar had secured for me. It was a familiar object to me... human skin folded around a shot glass, scribed in Linear B for the uneven calling of accounts for my victim.

I held the Cesare ring to the curse doll, the same kind of doll I used to end Osterhaus, and plunged the needle into the skin carapace.

Brown held a breath.

"Know what this is?" I rasped. "It's karma, asshole!"

I slammed the doll down onto the ground.

And for a second...

...nothing happened.

I blinked.

Then I looked up at Brown.

He smiled at me.

"Well," he chuckled, "seems karma is overrated."

I took several breaths, wondering if I had finally lost the fight.

Adrastos gestured behind Brown.

The hidden door behind Adrastos was filled with a figure in a black robe, with silver hair cut to her shoulders.

Her hair matched the darquelle which she held to Adrastos's throat.

"Put the gun down, Clarence," Wexler ordered.

He released Annarose's hair. She lurched forward, catching herself on the floor.

Brown swiveled at his waist, swinging his gun toward Wexler and Adrastos.

And he fired.

The loud thunderclap rang in my ears as I flinched.

When my eyes opened, I found two images of blood.

Brown stumbled backward, his neck painting the near wall with crimson arterial spray. He spun around, dropping his gun, and fell to his knees. The skin of his face blanched as he bled out, his carotid artery perforated from a remarkably unfortunate ricochet of his bullet against the one column of gilded brick in the room.

He reached for me, fingers trembling, before karma zeroed its ledger on Clarence de Haviland.

I glanced up at Wexler, who loomed over Adrastos. He slunk against the wall, hand to his throat barely containing the rush of blood from the wound Wexler had opened. His mouth opened and closed, sucking in air, or trying to speak. After a second, he stopped trying, and just sat back to die.

Wexler clutched the bloody blade in her hand. Her eyes were wide as she panted in shuddering breaths.

"I... I didn't..."

She swallowed hard, then took a moment to gather her composure. With a slow, deliberate swipe of her blade against Adrastos's sleeve, she nodded and sheathed her blade inside her robe.

Annarose turned onto her knees, taking in the scene.

Brown was dead. Adrastos as well, lying in a heap at Wexler's feet, throat slit.

Wexler looked over to me, her face hard, but not emotionless.

"Are you hurt?" she whispered.

I nodded, clamping my hand onto my shoulder.

Annarose pulled herself to her feet, with a little help from Wexler. The two women sized up one another.

"And you?" Wexler asked.

Annarose ran her hands along the sides of her head, gathering her hair, then abandoning it.

"I am well," she whispered.

The goons not yet unconscious from Annarose's curse writhed along the ground. Wexler stepped over them to guide me into the hallway.

"That's an ugly wound, Lake."

I sputtered, trying to find something clever to say.

But nothing came.

Annarose slipped under my wounded shoulder, helping to carry my weight as the two women aided me into the Ipsissimus Express Elevator.

"Wexler," I gasped.

"Yes?" she replied.

"Ricky."

She cast a quizzical glance at me, and asked, "What are you saying?"

"Ricky Baker."

She looked up to the ceiling, then nodded. "You've fulfilled your duties to the Presidium, Lake. We will honor our word."

I nodded, then passed the hell out.

CHAPTER FORTY-EIGHT

"So, it's over," I muttered to Deirdre, who sat on her cot, staring into space.

I shifted in my folding chair, easing my right arm in its sling as my cracked rib complained. The green-gray paint in Deirdre's room cast a dull, uninspiring pall from the rest of the psychiatric ward into her tiny space of refuge.

I continued, "The Presidium is still there, but only barely. It's about to get crazy in this country. Every cabal and splitter sect is going to jockey for significance."

Her eyes swiveled toward me, and her lips quivered.

"But I do have good news. What I thought was a jinx on you, was in fact only a demon. Well, a Goetic enslavement. The so-called jinx at Enoch Pratt has already begun to subside. I think the same will happen with you. Maybe another week, and you'll be free of the effects."

A smile crept onto her lips, but she still lacked the capacity for speech.

I looked across the room to Father Mark, who stood with hands folded over his belt.

"This is Father Mark, Deirdre. He's been a great help to me these past few months. He's a soul-finder, I guess you could say. He's offered to come and walk you back to reality, now that we know this isn't a permanent thing."

Father Mark stepped forward and took a careful seat on the edge of her bed. He extended a hand, and held it out to Deirdre.

Her fingers twitched, then her arm, and then finally she managed to reach out and place a trembling hand onto Mark's.

He nodded with a warm smile.

I excused myself and walked down the hallway to the bleary sunlight filtering through the low clouds overhead. My taxi was still waiting for me, counting down more minutes I'd owe the driver.

Deirdre was going to be okay. And when her wits had returned, I'd extend an invitation to relocate to Baltimore. There would have to be safety in numbers in these coming months. Anyone of worth whom I trusted would need to stay close.

The cab drove me from St. Agnes to the tavern. I paid my driver and stepped inside. The smell of warm food flooded my nostrils. An appreciable Monday business lunch crowd had gathered. Someone I didn't recognize stood behind the bar. He gave me a nod as I approached.

"Get you a beer, sir?"

I shook my head. "What's your name?"

"John."

An unexpected chuckle rose from my aching midsection.

"What?" the bartender asked.

"That's my father's name," I replied, and moved toward the back office.

Ben sat in Julian's office. No, it was Ben's office, now. He looked up at me with a wink and a grin, and continued typing up the evening menu on the computer. I left him alone to his work, and moved for the back door.

I stepped outside into the back parking lot. Julian's funeral would be the following day, and I had plenty of emotions left to deal with.

So many deaths.

And me, directly in the center.

Yet somehow, I'd survived it all yet again. Annarose called me a true magician, because I managed to make it all happen. Maybe I was just lucky.

Maybe I was damned, after all, and the Cosmos was holding its judgment just in case I had something worthwhile yet to contribute.

I turned a slow circle, and paused as I spotted something beautiful.

Something shiny.

A freshly-waxed, seemingly brand new Audi A5 Cabriolet.

I looked around for its owner, assuming that neither Ben nor John the Bartender could have afforded the cherry vehicle.

I took a couple steps toward the car before spotting a slip of paper tucked underneath the windshield wiper. I pulled out the paper, and held it up.

A single word was printed on the underside. *COMPLIMENTS.*

It was followed by the Eye of Providence, the seal of the Presidium.

Ah, a peace gesture.

Something moved inside the car, and I took a cautious step backward. As I crouched down to peer inside, I spotted a figure hunched in the back seat.

I moved for the passenger side door and pulled it open, sliding the seat forward to find a bound and gagged Nick Polo watching me with trepidation.

Compliments, indeed.

"Hello, Nicky," I muttered.

He tried to say something around his gag, but was unsuccessful.

I held a finger to my mouth to shush him.

"Oh, let's not ruin this moment with chit-chat."

I reached for the Cesare ring and triggered the needle.

CHAPTER FORTY-NINE

A sea of dark suits and dresses spread along the paths and lanes of the Brookhaven Cemetery as six pallbearers carried Julian's coffin to his final resting place. I looked on through dark glasses, finding them unnecessary to hide my eyes which remained untouched by tears. They were tired, perhaps, but my grief for Julian had long since poured out of me.

Madelyn Sullivan stood to my right, looking on as her husband joined the other pallbearers in settling the coffin onto its dais. I would have joined them as well, had my shoulder not been perforated by a bullet. And so I looked on, my arm in a sling.

The Swains stood to my left. Elle gripped my hand, and seemed unwilling to let it go. Wren kept an eye on me, likely making sure I didn't need a shoulder to weep on. I knew hers would be available, but I wouldn't be needing it. As a young woman sang *Amazing Grace*, I searched my chest for the proper emotion for the moment. It alarmed me how empty I felt. If there was ever a time to feel grief, it was this. Instead, all I could think about was the future.

I had dodged the Presidium for so long, considering my workings, weighing them against whether it would finally tip the scales against me in their eyes. But things wouldn't be the same, even if Wexler was elected to the office of Ipsissimus and began restoring the organization. There was a power vacuum, now, and the interests waiting for the proper moment were likely already in motion.

Sullivan returned to his wife's side. I could tell by the complexion of his cheeks that he was positively racked with grief. He wouldn't be addressing anyone today. Indeed, Ronetta Claye had delivered the eulogy earlier, leaving Sullivan out of the spotlight.

At length, the ceremony drew to a close, leaving the casket on its stand for the attendants to inter later in the day. The crowd slowly unraveled, some of the strictly political interests rushing off to make their meetings, others ganging up on Sullivan and Claye. The media gave the funeral a pass, as Julian had ceased to be a going concern for the city. A reporter for AM radio took comments, but was quick about it.

The Swains kept a halo around me, Edgar trying to make jokes to lighten the mood, Wren making sure no one tried to hug my bad arm, and Elle and Eddie looking lost as to what to do. I turned to find Madelyn Sullivan weaving past Wren.

"I'm so sorry for your loss, Mister Lake," she announced with a soft tone.

"He was a good man," I answered.

She turned to the Swains with a polite cock of her chin.

"Would you mind if I had a private word?"

Wren and Edgar smiled, and withdrew.

Mrs. Sullivan took my hand and leaned in. "Pray with me."

I bowed my head toward hers, and as we clasped hands, she whispered, "The vote is tomorrow. Wexler will be the new Ipsissimus."

"I figured as much."

"There have been too many deaths," she continued, head still bowed in mock prayer. "There is very little trust within the inner circles, now."

"Well, here's the thing," I said, lifting my head and opening my eyes. "They weren't wrong about the Presidium. It had become fatuous and self-indulgent. There will be some rebuilding to do, but I'm sure Wexler's up to the challenge."

Madelyn looked up at me with a wrinkle in her brow. "But will it happen in time, is the question?"

"No way to tell. If there is some major campaign happening, if the Dark Choir is about to leverage the entire human race, then we're going to have to come together as a species. Can't be America vs. the World, anymore." I added with a clearing of my throat, "Any word on the Bakers?"

She sighed, and shook her head.

"You will keep me posted?" I stated.

She patted my hand. "Rest assured, we will."

She stepped away to rejoin her husband. Mayor Sullivan turned to me and gave me a sheepish nod.

I returned the gesture.

"He was one of a kind," a voice called from my left.

I turned to find Ronetta Claye approaching, glasses lifted to the top of her head, a tablet tucked under her arm.

"No argument here," I answered.

Claye stared at me for a moment, then pulled the tablet from under her arm to open her schedule.

"I spoke with Turner this morning. I don't know what you said to him, but he's made a complete one-eighty regarding your value as an independent consultant. So, it seems Julian made the right call about you."

"Meaning?"

"Meaning... Special Investigations has several open cases they'll want to discuss with you. You'll be compensated, off the books. As long as you continue to produce results, and as long as you behave yourself."

I smirked at her. "No promises."

She smirked back.

Claye turned away and added, "Turner will be calling on you Thursday."

"I'll be around."

I gave the scene a good, long glance. How quickly the crowd had disappeared! I looked for the Swains, who had returned to their Jeep. I noted Elle had stayed behind, still staring at the cemetery. I turned back and approached Elle.

"Hey," I muttered.

"She's going to be mayor."

I lifted my brow. "Who?"

Elle pointed to her left, where Claye was climbing into the back of a black town car.

"When?"

"Before the end of the year," Elle whispered.

I frowned. "How... how do you know this?"

She shrugged.

"Well," I asked, "what about the current mayor?"

Elle shrugged again.

I ran a hand along the side of my face. "We should talk to your mother about these visions you're getting."

Elle looked over the gravestones. "They're so quiet."

"That's the idea, I suppose."

She looked up at me. "Those people you killed... did it make you sad?"

I crouched down in front of her with a frown. "What have your parents told you?"

"Nothing."

"Who do you think I killed, Elle?"

Her bottom lip quivered.

"Elle? Did you see something?"

"You can't do these things, Dorian."

My eyes stung. Tears gathered in the corners, one managing to break free and trace a line down my cheek.

"Yeah. I'm trying." I stood up, wiped my face on my sleeve, and reached for her hand. "Come on. Let's go do something fun for a change."

"Like what?"

"I don't know. Skydiving? Cliff jumping? Tiger shaving?"

She laughed.

As it turned out, we didn't go skydiving. Instead, we drove to the Inner Harbor for lunch. The sky had cleared up nicely. Deep, solid blue with plenty of sunshine reflecting off the water. Elle and Eddie destroyed a dozen crabs between them. I watched as the kids tried to smear crab fat over each other as they chuckled.

Life felt weirdly normal. Maybe it was stranger than normal should have felt weird, at all. But it didn't matter. For a good hour, nothing weighed on me. No worries about the Presidium, Julian, or even Ches.

I was in the moment.

We all took the long way back to the car, and the kids spotted a street cart selling snowballs. They immediately launched into hysterics, and Wren reached for Edgar's back pocket to fish out his wallet. They dragged her up the street while I lingered behind with Edgar.

"So," he said with a huge grin on his face.

"So."

"Clement called."

"Yeah?"

"He wants to show me something in his collection. Said I should bring you along."

I shrugged. "Always game for a trip back home."

"Are we going to be safe?" he asked in a hushed tone.

I watched the kids as they nearly collided with the cart, and Wren giving them hell.

"No." I turned to Edgar. "But, what else is new?"

The hairs on my arms rippled with uneasy energy. A wave of something sinister washed over me, and I sucked in a breath.

Edgar squinted. "What is that?"

"You feel it, too?"

My eyes lifted past Edgar, to an obscure figure standing across the street. The obscurity lifted, and I clenched my jaw as Felix Parrish lifted his glammer.

"Edgar," I whispered. "Go to Wren. I'll catch up with you."

He turned to look across the street, then back to me. "What's up?"

"Please."

He nodded slowly, and trotted up the block.

I waited for the light to change, then crossed the street. Parrish stood near the corner of a high-rise hotel, a briefcase in one hand and a cardboard tube under his arm.

"Lake," he greeted me.

"Parrish?"

"You've made some interesting decisions lately. I won't go so far as to say that I'm impressed. But I am surprised."

"Thanks." I checked the Swains across the street. Edgar was watching me, but the others seemed unaware that I'd even crossed the street. "I'm guessing you have news."

"I do, as a matter of fact."

"Am I going to like it?"

Parrish sighed. "I've come to inform you that the offer for your consideration has been rescinded."

"Wasn't it already?"

"You misunderstand. Your soul has been located."

My head spun, and I paced a quick circle before leaning against the side of the hotel.

"So, it's all over?" I whispered.

"For the time being, you have nothing to worry about. Your soul has been... secured. As much as it pains me to admit it, we are presently unable to affect its release."

"Wait a minute. What does that mean, you can't affect its release?"

"Your soul is safe, Mister Lake. For now."

I shook my head. "You said it was secured. Who secured it? I don't understand."

Parrish smiled. "Surely you realize it is not in your benefactor's interests to share such information. He simply wanted me to inform you that your consideration is no longer on the table. It is now a waiting game for us, until your soul becomes available once again. And we are very, very patient."

My mouth tripped over too many questions at once, sending me into a fit of halted sentences.

Parrish lifted his hand, and looked across the street. He nodded to the Swains.

"If I had to guess, I'd say you have another four years. Possibly less. I'd suggest you make the most of it."

He nodded to me and stepped away.

"Wait!" I called.

But in a flurry of passing foot traffic, his glammer snapped back to life and I lost him in the crowd.

I stood still, staring up the street.

Four years?

Then my soul would fall into the hands of the Dark Choir.

Better get to work!

ABOUT THE AUTHOR

J.P. Sloan is a speculative fiction author ... primarily of urban fantasy, horror and several shades between. His writing explores the strangeness in that which is familiar, at times stretching the limits of the human experience, or only hinting at the monsters lurking under your bed.

A Louisiana native, Sloan relocated to the vineyards and cow pastures of Central Maryland after Hurricane Katrina, where he lives with his wife and son. During the day he commutes to the city of Baltimore, a setting which inspires much of his writing.

In his spare time, Sloan enjoys wine-making and homebrewing, and is a certified beer judge.

THANK YOU FOR READING

http://jp-sloan.com

Please visit http://curiosityquills.com/reader-survey to share your reading experience with the author of this book!

Yea Though I Walk, by J.P. Sloan

Linthicum Odell, a Union Army deserter, seeks atonement by hunting monsters in the untamed West. His road to redemption leads to Gold Vein, a mining town with two afflictions: a corrupt justice named Lars Richterman, and a horde of cannibal wendigo in the surrounding hills. Odell joins forces with Denton Folger, a newspaper man intent on exposing Richterman's schemes. Odell soon realizes that Folger's darkly mysterious wife, Katherina, may hold the secrets to saving this valley from a war between devils...and the true reason Odell was called to this valley.

The Dead Detective, by Rod Kierkegaard, Jr. and J.R. Rain

When hard boiled police detective Richelle Dadd wakes up to find herself lying dead inside a chalk outline, her only mission is to find out who killed her--and laid a Gypsy curse on her that keeps her alive, sort of, as a zombie assassin. Now she must stop them before she is forced to kill again and again.

Chest of Bone, by Vicki Stiefel

As magical and mundane worlds retwine, empath and unawakened Mage Clea Reese must team up with the secretive James Larrimer to hunt her mentor's killer and stop the forces of corruption from obtaining the Chest of Bone, the ultimate source of otherworldly power. A woman whose true nature is hidden. A man whose reality is anathema. Together, they create something extraordinary. A Mage... A Monster... A Mission... And a Melody That Binds.

Dust Bath Revival, by Marianne Kirby

16-year-old Henrietta Goodness - Hank to all that know her – has heard all the stories about how the Dust made the dead rise. But that was a long time ago, and Hank is ready for another normal Florida summer. That's the plan until an itinerant tent revival rolls in with a Reborn - one of the risen dead - and Hank has to solve a mystery the government doesn't want unraveled. There's nowhere to go when the night isn't safe and there's no one to trust when everyone is part of a conspiracy to keep the Reborn walking.

CPSIA information can be obtained
at www.ICGtesting.com
Printed in the USA
LVOW03s1023040318
568589LV00003B/691/P

9 781620 072059